Elizabeth Lavender's

DECEPTION'S HOLD

BOOK 2 OF THE SUNSPEAR SERIES

Publisher's Note: This is a work of fiction. Names, characters, places and incidents are a product of the author's imagination. Locales and public names are sometimes used for atmospheric purposes. Any resemblance to actual people, living or dead, or to businesses, companies, events, institutions, or locales is completely coincidental.

Deception's Hold/Elizabeth Lavender

EBook ISBN: 987-1-951741-03-7

Paperback Print ISBN: 978-1-951741-04-4

Hardcover Print ISBN: 978-1-951741-05-1

ACKNOWLEDGEMENTS

Special thanks to Rebecca and Rachel Latimer, who read the manuscript and gave valuable feedback. Also, thanks to those at Arcane Book Covers for once again taking what I saw in my head and creating an incredible image that captured my book. Many thanks go to family and friends, whose constant enthusiasm about the book series encourages me daily to write the story. Special thanks to my husband and my two kiddos for their patience and encouragement as I continue to write the story. Added gratitude to my husband and my older son for reading through the manuscript and making editing suggestions, most of which I accepted.

And thanks goes to you, the reader, for traveling with me. You started this journey already with me, and I'm so glad you have chosen to continue. I said it at the beginning, and I mean it when I say the story is written for you. As you can see, the spear-bearers and their friends have quite the challenge ahead of them. The battlefield is overwhelming before them. Not unlike other battles, though faced by others, maybe still faced at times. Continue in this journey all the way through. The journey is hard sometimes, but I still believe you will always find it worth continuing forward.

Wandering at times, but never lost...
A relentless pursuit one is forever grateful still happens.

CHAPTER ONE

The Dark Lord sat in his chambers, still unhappy over the recent event at the facility. His lady companion visited him the previous evening but reported no headway locating his stolen prisoner. She also had no information on the identity or whereabouts of those who took the prisoner. She had found no substitute to satisfy him or one who could easily be obtained.

The Dark Lord briefly turned his thoughts from it. He was sure the larger operation proceeded better, and some time had passed since he received an update from his Black Dragon Commander. There was no concern. His Commander never failed him. He felt an eagerness to see the operation at work sooner since Abigail's operation got off track. He knew the Black Dragon Commander planned another attack in a couple of days. The Dark Lord certainly did not want to interrupt progress.

"Yes, Black Dragon Commander, I need to speak with you today. No, when you finish. In my chamber, please. Yes, I'll expect you within the next couple of hours."

The Black Dragon Commander continued to watch the present proceedings and wondered what the Dark Lord needed. The Dark Lord did not sound unhappy at all during the transmission, and they had not talked for some time about the operations. That was probably all. The Black Dragon Commander hurried to wrap up the current task with his soldiers.

"Always pleasant to see you, my Black Dragon Commander." The Dark Lord greeted. "You look tired, Commander. I'm working you too hard. I told Duvessa to assist as you needed. Should I speak with her further?"

"No, Dark Lord. There is just much to do for the operation."

"Please sit, Commander. I assume everything progresses as you like, but I have not spoken with you recently. You are more than capable of handling everything I place in your hands, so I sometimes take for granted it goes well."

"I'm glad you continue to possess such confidence in me. Yes, the attacks move forward as planned. We keep them on their heels every few days. They get only enough time to recover from the previous attack before facing another. We accumulate what we need for the operation, and the building of it is coming along well."

"How close are we?"

The Black Dragon Commander thought for a moment. "The one you know, so I suppose you are asking about the..." The Black Dragon Commander glanced at the Dark Lord and saw confirmation.

"Yes. What is the timetable you foresee with it?"

"For it to do everything we wanted, three months."

"Your estimate is for everything. To test it on a smaller scale, do you think in two months or even a month?"

The Black Dragon Commander appeared puzzled, but he nodded. "Yes, Dark Lord, if you wished, we could test it, and the damage would still be substantial." He hesitated, "Although I do admit surprise by your desire to move up the operation, it's not unwelcome. I'm eager as well to test it. My Dark Lord, I will do as you wish as I await your orders."

"I'm considering it, and I knew you would not object to it. Go ahead and make sure your men work on the key components, so if we decide to move the timetable up greatly, we retain the option. The anticipation becomes too much for me." The Dark Lord laughed. "We will be moving up the timetable, but I can't decide by how much yet. I will let you know further, Commander, but now I must allow you to return to supervising the operations."

The Black Dragon Commander nodded and walked away, pleased with the development. It would begin the dagger in the Elders' heart. There remained a long way to go, but he would relish each step. Then there was Dante. Once they began the unmasking of the Elders, Dante would see their treachery, and the Commander vowed to have his son back.

The Dark Lord sat back and felt better. Maybe he would move it up only one month. The loss of his prisoner angered him more than he realized. The power which would have flowed through his body when he finally took her life would have been priceless, so satisfying. His master had assured him. It was supposed to be her. He controlled the husband already, and taking her life was the second half of it. It had been nothing short of perfect. Yet, his Master said one like her, who followed his enemy with such passion could work now. None of those were easier to capture at the moment, though. He smiled. Perhaps with all the blood that would flow when this operation began, his master would be appeased. Or he could take each prisoner and spill them out until he found one whose blood proved worthy. He laughed.

CHAPTER TWO

Dante and Seth came back in and joined the others.

"Are you truly all right?" Seth asked Dante.

Dante smiled. "I am. It has been a long day and a half, but it's time to ready for an attack. In between the attacks, you'll prepare me to get my father back. We all know we're running out of time, so let us get to work."

Seth patted Dante on the shoulder and turned to Lana. "You heard your cousin. Let's get the rest of the commanders here and back to work."

Lana turned to Caleb and Ryan.

"They're on their way down as we speak," Caleb said.

The other commanders sat, unsure what to say to Dante. He spoke for them, "I know you heard the news about our friends who came yesterday and the information they brought concerning my family and what it means to me. You don't need to tiptoe around me. I'm not going to break into pieces." Dante smiled, and a collective silent sigh of relief passed through the commanders. "Yesterday there were ugly moments, but today is much better. My mother is here safe, but we don't know how to awaken her. We know the Dark Lord and his lady agent are responsible for everything that happened concerning my family. At some point, I will make it known to my father and try to get him back. I know it makes no sense to you. You see him as the Black Dragon Commander, who causes nothing but heartache and pain. He massacres whole planets in the Dark Lord's name. He killed members of your own family. I see all that too, and it pains me, though I didn't do it. That is not the person I seek to get back. I go to return my father to me, the one I knew as a child, and Ethan, the husband of Abigail. I was shown it can be done, and I will do it at the proper time."

"Dante, we will help you in any way possible. Unfortunately, we know this is a battle that the traditional military strategies will not assist you," said Commander Gabe.

"I know as well. Seth will prepare me for the challenge ahead, and I'll be ready when the time comes. We need to get started, though. This situation put us behind, and the next attack will come on the same timetable as always. We also have an extra item added to the mix during the box swap, and it must get done." Dante turned to Lana and Seth.

Lana addressed the group. "Yes, our friends ask for our assistance. Considering all the help they gave us, it's a small favor. If it yields the results they hope, it will provide them a starting place to discover the location of the Dark Lord's operation and what he is planning. Of course, if they learn new information, we'll receive it as well." Lana glanced at Seth.

"They know as we do, time is not on our side. Here is what they want us to do." Seth proceeded to tell them about the tracking devices and the task of placing them on the supplies.

Commander Gabe nodded. "It will get done, Seth, whatever it takes."

⸺ℓℓℓ⸺

The girl, Alena, and Alika returned home. Everything was as they left it. The girl had been quiet on the way back. They sat at the table, still silent.

Alena reached over to the girl. "Are you all right?"

Her blue eyes reflected calm. "I am. It's time to follow the advice I gave Dante, to focus on the task at hand. Our time is running out."

Alika watched her carefully for a moment but was reassured. "Why don't you lead us today?"

"I can do so if you prefer. We can assume the attack will come soon as in the past. Hopefully, everything goes as we intended, including planting our tracking devices. As far as that part, we're on hold until we see where the supplies go. With that being said, we may be able to start planning how to pull this off without knowing the where. We need to head off other issues to successfully complete the operation. Those I believe we can begin preparing for before we obtain the information from the tracking devices."

"It sounds like a lot turned around in your head," said Alena.

"I needed it to change directions for a bit. I know one of these things we will definitely need help with or to think about outsourcing because of the time factor. I'm not sure."

Alika was puzzled. "What is it?"

"Let me tell you both the idea forming in my head once we get a location. If we use it, our product must pass inspection. It can't be like at the warehouse where Dante knew he held a fake from the first moment or the person at the lab who, within a minute, realized he didn't have anything close to the chemical which should be in the container."

Alena probed. "Let's hear it."

The girl told them her idea. They agreed it was good but dangerous. However, any plan would be full of that unwelcome but unavoidable element going forward.

"At this point, they have not figured out they are leaving with their own fake shipments," said Alika.

"We could be doing unnecessary work," Alena said, but her voice sounded doubtful.

"I don't think any of us believes that. Once Dante and the others get this box swap done, frankly, I'm sure that's the end of it. I think the next time they exchange fire with the Black Dragon soldiers at the warehouse and the lab, it will be discovered, or at least there will be suspicion that something isn't right. I'm certain it'll end up being about the time we do this operation. Anything we bring in will be examined."

"At least a few boxes," said Alena.

"And if they don't pass, you'll both be signing your death certificates."

"Yes." sighed the girl. "There are always numerous possibilities to sneak in. We don't yet know where we are getting into, so there is probably a better plan."

"I'm not sure of that conclusion," said Alika.

The girl waited on Alika to see what he wanted to do.

"Do you think he has someone to do it?"

"I would prefer him to do this one, Alika. I have no doubts he can do it for us based on his past work. I don't think the items from the warehouse will be difficult. It's the items from the lab. I don't see the soldier being a master chemist examining it, but it's crucial they're better fakes than what the Black Dragon switched, or we're sunk. Unfortunately, I haven't brushed up on my chemistry lately." She sighed. "Where is the lab tech when you need him?"

Alena peered at Alika. "What do you think?"

"We prepare as if this is the plan. Alena, why don't you start with the items from the warehouse? Try to see which you think would be easiest to create the most authentic fakes. That does sound strange to say."

"I know, but I understand. I'll get to it."

Alika turned to the girl. "I can help with the chemicals. The medical knowledge comes in handy now." He teased her, "Finally, I found a gap in your training."

The girl grinned. "Great. One day when everything is calm, I created my next training session."

"Calm doesn't appear anywhere in sight, so there is no cause to worry. I believe, together, we can come up with chemicals to easily mimic another without the nasty effect of the original. You're right, though. It will be slow going. Maybe something will surface as we work."

Alika and the girl worked together as Alena labored on the other part of the task.

"I can't believe how late it got," Alena said, glancing up at a display.

The girl and Alika both looked up in surprise.

"You're right. It's almost dinner," said Alika.

"How are you coming, Alena?" asked the girl.

"Sick of poring over this list and the data pad, but I've about got a handpicked list from the warehouse. What about you two?"

"It's coming, but I think Alika would agree we're stuck a bit."

"Yes, you summed it up, dear."

"How about you finish helping me with the warehouse list, and Alika can work on dinner? After dinner, we can all work together on the chemical list. Working together, surely it will come to us. Perhaps the two of you need to bounce it off me."

"Sounds like a plan," the girl agreed. Alena and the girl finished the list from the warehouse, and Alika took care of dinner. They ate and talked about the dilemma with the chemical list.

Alena listened. "That does present a problem."

"Yes, it was one of the things with the lab person. He smelled it and instantly identified it as fake. Smelling is the simplest of tests, so it has to get through that first test. As soon as you inhale most of these chemicals, there is a reaction with your eyes or something. We know the Black Dragon soldiers are mostly machine inside, but they do have the basic senses built into their programming. They will sense it. They aren't as harmed by it as us," said the girl.

"Yes, it must pass that test, but most chemicals are ones we don't want to place in their hands," added Alika.

Alena pondered a solution as she ate another bite of food. She smiled at Alika. "It's amazing how you spoil us with your cooking, Alika. Only a couple of days of being gone ..." Her grin widened.

Alika and the girl stared at Alena, both wondering what she was thinking.

"Inspiration comes from all places," said Alena shaking her head. "What if it's not a chemical added? What about a spice or seasoning?"

The girl and Alika looked at each other and Alena and smiled as well. The girl got up and hugged Alena. "You're brilliant."

They hurried to finish dinner. The three reviewed the chemical list and found the ones causing the trouble before the dinner inspiration. They quickly became unstuck. They knew precisely which seasoning and spices could make a person feel like their eyes or nostrils were set fire temporarily but would not leave any damage. There was also the agent they were inserting to make their additions undetectable, whether seasonings or other less dangerous chemicals. The chemical list was finished. Thankfully, it only took their chemistry knowledge, Alika's medical knowledge, and Alena's love of spices and seasonings. It proved a strange combination, but it worked.

"What's left?" asked Alika.

"Nothing further tonight," answered the girl. "Tomorrow, we get this in motion."

⁓ℓℓ⁓

"What are you still doing?" Alena came over to the girl.

"This sample. I remain puzzled by it."

"Can I see?"

"Be my guest."

"How long have you worked with it tonight?"

"About thirty minutes?" The girl rubbed her neck.

Alena analyzed the sample under the scope, and she stiffened. "How strange. It moved, but that can't be."

"Okay, I don't know if I feel better or worse. I thought I saw it do that a number of times, but I figured I was tired."

"You didn't imagine it, and I feel the Darkness from it too."

"It's as if it has a life of its own. It's unnatural. It makes me ..."

"Yeah, exactly. Why don't you put it up, like now?"

The girl nodded. "You're right. I'm done with it for the night." She sealed it back in the cylinder and placed it in the locked compartment.

CHAPTER THREE

The next morning arrived, and the two headed out.

"I will see both of you back soon."

"Of course, this should be a piece of cake compared to lately. We'll be careful as always, Alika," said the girl as Alena nodded her agreement.

"I'll see what he says," said the girl to Alena once they landed. Alena turned to the ship's monitoring system, and the girl exited the craft.

The girl walked into one of the many bars common to the area and searched momentarily until her eyes rested on a familiar face. She slid into the other side of the booth.

"How are you today?" asked the man.

"Well, but busy."

"Good. There isn't anything I need your assistance with now, and I don't possess any intel to help you at the moment. You sense both of those things somehow. This must be one of those few times you need my expertise. It doesn't often happen with you, so I'm curious to see if I can help."

"I believe you can. Normally, I wouldn't mind discussing it here, but I'm hesitant."

"Understood," said Christopher. "With others, I would insist on staying here, but I have always had a good feeling about you, and I have long learned to trust that feeling with you. Besides, you have been to my ship several times now. Come, we can speak further there. Shall we?" He got up and motioned with his arm to her.

The girl nodded and followed him out the door.

Christopher and the girl sat in his ship.

"Chris, can I get you something to drink?"

"No, I'm fine, Christopher. Thanks for the offer, though."

"What brings you to me today?"

"I know you're busy, but what I need to have done I needed doing yesterday. I will pay your price and double to see it completed. I don't want it outsourced to someone else. We have no complaints at all about the work done by anyone else. Please understand. However, this job must remain very ..."

"Confidential. I wouldn't hike up the price on you just to do so, Chris. Surely you know that by now. The higher cost would come because of the rush you need it in. I can move things to do this job for you. I know you wouldn't come and ask with this urgency unless you felt it necessary. Tell me what the job is."

"Thank you. I have two lists of items. The first is various things, such as possible building and weaponry materials. The second is a list of chemicals. We need fakes made of the items. They must be able to pass inspection."

Christopher stared at her, visibly perplexed. "This is beyond frowned on in this line of business. It's a strange request."

"I understand. It's not going to anyone we know, I promise."

"I assume you'll present these."

"Yes, and my friend who works with me."

"I also assume this isn't going to a small shipping agent somewhere. This is going to someone who, if they possessed the real supplies, it would be ugly for everyone." Christopher leaned back in his chair, his face concerned.

"Yes, you assume correctly. We could do it ourselves, but ..."

Christopher searched her face and could read the anxiety in her eyes. "You're running out of time."

The girl locked eyes with him as she spoke. "Yes. The fakes must be good, extremely good, Christopher. We saw some fakes done, and they were uncovered in moments for what they were. Not by those we attempt to fool but by others. The first was discovered as soon as the person handled the item. They could tell the material was not what it appeared to be. A simple scan of a data pad confirmed the suspicions. With the chemical, it didn't react as it should. Even without that, it failed a basic smell test. The agents our materials must pass through will not forgive if it fails."

"For one so young, you choose to travel in dangerous circles. These fakes passing inspection may decide whether you and your friend live or die?"

"It will, Christopher."

Somehow her eyes reflected the usual calmness despite what she had told him. "May I see the list?"

"It's right here." She handed him her data pad for the moment.

"These supplies are everywhere. What are they doing with them?" He peered back up at her. "It's understood this conversation never happened."

"We don't know."

Unfortunately, he could tell she told the truth when he saw her face. "These chemicals could be terrible in the wrong hands."

"Yes, they could."

"I understand why you only wanted me involved with this job for you." The girl regarded him with the obvious question. "There is a couple of these chemicals which could give me problems obtaining the substitutions with the time factor before us. The rest, I'm not concerned about. I said that, but you told me I hold two people's lives in the balance." His face read only concern. "Are you sure about this? You haven't told me where you and your friend are going, but my guesses of the territory you could be headed only increases my worry."

"Yes, I'm sure. I know you can do it, and that's why I came to you. Tell me which substance. I'm sure I know which one it could be."

"This one. I can get the substitution, but not easily," he said, while handing the data pad back to her.

She pulled something out of her bag and handed it to him. "We anticipated as much. We had it. Here is enough to do the samples and a little more to play with if the first attempts don't go well. We can give you more for the rest later." She took her data pad back and sent the encrypted list to his.

"You have it covered as always. So, when? After all, I know what you said."

"First, we need a sample of each one. I want to check them before you make the rest. It's not that I don't trust you."

"I completely understand. If my life and a friend's life hung in the balance of an item, I'd be sure too. There's no offense taken. I'll finish it, and you can make sure you're satisfied before I go further." He thought for a minute. "As for the when, rest of today and tomorrow, so maybe we shoot for lunchtime the next day."

"Sounds great, but incredibly soon. Are you certain that is enough time?"

"I can pull late nights, all-nighters if necessary. Don't worry. They will be first quality fakes." He said to her softly. "I understand what is at stake. I'll do it for you and your friend."

"Thank you so much, Christopher. Please, this must stay with us only."

"I get it. I don't want to jeopardize anything you do or get you or your friend hurt." He moved over to his ship's control.

"Your ship's cameras. None of this happened."

"That's what I came to do. There will be no record of this or of you on the ship. Be safe, Chris."

"I will, and we'll see each other soon. Be safe as well."

Christopher watched the girl walk to her ship. He had been in this business for many years, and few continued to surprise him as this young girl did. His concern mounted for her as his mind already whirled with the critical work ahead of him.

"Let's head back to Alika," said the girl as she entered the ship and the door closed behind her. "I have the most wonderful feeling."

"Because?" said Alena, puzzled by the girl.

"Do you realize for the first time in what feels like forever, we went somewhere, and it went exactly as planned?" The girl laughed.

Alena laughed. "I understand now."

"We're back, Alika," said the girl as she and Alena came out of the ship.

"It went ..." said Alika.

"Perfectly, finally," said the girl, laughing again.

"Let's eat lunch, and we'll see if we can continue this trend," said Alena.

CHAPTER FOUR

Dante and Ryan finished the last bit of the plans for the attack. They checked in with Seth and Commander Gabe.

"What do you think about the swap?"

"I don't know. We'll make sure it goes well enough one more time, so whatever boxes they leave with, get the tracking devices on them. I promise, Dante," said Commander Gabe.

"Yes, we always knew it would only work a couple of times," said Seth.

"I don't usually wish for an attack, but I'd like to see this one done. I want the tracking devices on so our friends can go ahead and get the location," said Ryan.

"It's going to be dangerous, so I'm not eager to see them racing into this operation. On the other hand, being in a holding pattern is probably frustrating."

"I don't get the impression Alika's students are sitting around, especially now. I'm sure they found ways to start preparing a plan though they don't know the location yet, Dante."

"You're probably right, Seth."

"It appears your cousin is satisfied with the progress for the evening. It's time for everyone to get some sleep."

"I'm going to check on my mother before I go to my quarters."

"I'll go with you tonight unless you prefer to go alone," said Ryan.

"No, the company would be good."

Dante and Ryan said goodnight to the others and went toward Abigail's room. Lana and Caleb came over to Seth and Commander Gabe.

"Is Dante okay?"

"Yes, your cousin wanted to go check on his mother before bed. Ryan went with him tonight," said Seth.

"I feel this will become a nightly routine for Dante. He appeared fine, though. I wasn't with him yesterday, but I imagine he is remarkably better compared to when he first received everything," said Commander Gabe.

"He is, so this is an encouraging sign," said Caleb.

Dante and Ryan went to Abigail's room. They sat by her bedside for about twenty minutes and talked easily while there.

Dante walked over to her bedside at the end of the time and kissed her on the forehead. "Goodnight, Mother. I'll see you tomorrow." Dante turned to Ryan and shook his head.

"She'll find a way to wake up, Dante. We must keep hoping."

"You're right. Come on. We need to get sleep, so we're of help to Lana tomorrow."

Both camps awoke and started another day. Another day and evening passed for Seth's and Alika's camps, and it was quiet. Both groups got substantial work done. They both knew the lull could not last much longer.

CHAPTER FIVE

Another day began.

"Are we ready?" asked the girl.

"We are, and it's almost lunchtime," said Alena.

"I will see you two when you return," said Alika.

⁓ele⁓

The girl walked into the diner and found her lunch companion. He glanced up immediately and smiled as she slid into the booth opposite of him.

"Perfect timing as always," Christopher said pleasantly.

She smiled sympathetically at him. "I'm sorry, you're tired, and I'm the cause."

"Don't give it a second thought. I'm fine. Are you ready?" He got up and waited for her.

"Of course," she said as she stood back up and followed him.

Once she sat down inside his ship, he asked, "Would you like something to drink? Before you give your usual response, going through these items could take considerable time."

"You're right. Water is fine, Christopher."

"Easiest request you've made of me." He chuckled as he brought her a glass of water. "What do you want to go through first?"

"Probably the building and weaponry. I'm not eager to go through the chemicals. They're not the real thing, but they're supposed to mimic it. I have confidence in your work, so I'm not sure how I'm to feel for a minute after getting a whiff of those."

"I promise nothing is strong enough for you to pass out on the ship, but I made them how you and your friend wanted."

They got their data pads out and started down the list. Christopher got the first item out and handed it to her. She took it from him, examined it, and scanned it. She took her time for at least five minutes analyzing and handling it. This was the item that did not fool Dante from the moment he touched it. She smiled.

Christopher studied her. "You're smiling. Is that good, bad, or are you not sure yet?"

"Extremely good. This is the item that didn't fool the other individual as soon as he touched it. I believe it would now, or it would take much examination to not pass. If everything is like this, my friend and I may live another day."

"That's fairly optimistic, I suppose," said Christopher, sounding concerned.

"You'll have done your part for us. My friend and I must accomplish the rest and return. You're not responsible for anything else." she said softly. "Let's move on to the next item."

"All right." Christopher handed her the next item. She took the item from his hand, but he saw her pause for a moment. A strange expression overshadowed her face. "Is it not right?"

"No, it's not the item. Give me a second, Christopher," answered the girl. He heard her speaking with someone else. She received a message through her earpiece. The girl's ordinarily calm expression was troubled. He could only hear her part of the conversation.

"Yes, I understand. Just now. They're right on schedule since the last time." she sighed. "There is nothing we can do for them. We let them know they would probably be on their own for a while. Hopefully, they stay safe. We'll know soon enough."

She turned back to Christopher. "I'm sorry for the interruption. I needed to take the call." She returned her attention back to the item.

He could see the girl forcing herself to focus back on the task at hand. The call clearly bothered her. "Do you need to go back to your ship to tend to something? I can hang out here and wait for a bit."

"No, this is what I need to do now. If this whole thing is successful, it will decrease my anxiety about the call I received."

"Is there anything I can do to help, Chris?"

"No, I'm afraid not, but so far, the items are good though I'm only on the second one." She closed her eyes, opened them again, and breathed. She reminded herself of the advice she gave Dante a couple of days ago. In her head, she said, "Focus on the task at hand." And she did.

CHAPTER SIX

Dante and the others sat down to lunch when an advisor came into the room. Everyone grew used to this, yet a collective groan filled the room.

"Doesn't the Black Dragon Commander's soldiers ever break for lunch?"

The others laughed, including Ryan, who said, "Dante, all his soldiers are mostly machine at their core, so no."

"Be safe, everyone, especially you, Dante. Try not to think about your missed lunch too much. I'll warm it up for you when you come back, promise." Lana laughed and hugged him.

"Funny, but I'm going to hold you to that, cuz." He hugged her back, laughed, and ran out with Ryan.

"All right, commanders, another round begins," said Caleb to those in the air with him.

"The usual number it appears," said Ryan.

"Let's get to it. We know something uglier is coming around the corner." Dante got his sunspear out, and it swung into action with lightning speed. The Black Dragon men tried, but Dante was too fast. Something caught Dante's eye, and he rushed to Ryan. His friend found himself dangerously outnumbered for a moment.

"No, you don't!" Dante responded as he ran to Ryan's side. Some of the squadron realized Ryan's terrible situation at the same time, and within seconds, the Black Dragon soldiers found the tables turned on them.

"Thanks, Dante. I'm not sure how I got in that predicament so quickly."

"Believe me, it happens. I know from experience, remember?" chuckled Dante.

"Yeah, we're a fine pair." Ryan rolled his eyes at Dante, and he groaned as a familiar sound was heard. "Is that what I think it is?"

"Yeah, Ryan, it's the uglier around the corner. They have arrived." Dante signaled for the small group of soldiers to follow him in the direction of the sound, and Ryan and the rest followed close behind to support them.

Seth and Commander Gabe watched as the Black Dragon group walked up to today's warehouse of choice. Seth worried about both distractions working, and Commander Gabe shared his fears. They must get the two tracking devices on those supplies. The Black Dragon group walked into the warehouse and began their standard practice of the loading and unloading of the boxes to make the switch. Seth signaled to Commander Gabe that it was time. The Black Dragon soldier reached the point where the switch would take place. Suddenly, the Black Dragon men heard blasters going off outside.

"Come on, and let's take care of this. I'm growing tired of these colonists. We will teach them to challenge us," said the Black Dragon soldier in charge. All the Black Dragon soldiers cleared out. Seth and Commander Gabe quickly switched the carts. Next, they went over to the boxes the Black Dragon soldiers would take back with them and slipped one of the devices in one of the boxes. The device would appear as a part of the packing material. They got back into place to watch and wait. The Black Dragon soldiers came back moments later.

The Black Dragon soldier in charge spoke, obviously irritated. "They are gnats, and I would squash the life from them if they would but stay long enough. Get the boxes unloaded and the other cart transported away. I am ready to complete this and return to the ship."

Seth and the Commander began to head over to the lab as soon as the Black Dragon soldiers had finished the last box. One down and one left to go.

—ℓℓ—

"We'll start with an explosion today," said Dante.

"It was nice last time, Dante." Ryan shook his head. "Would you just do it, please?"

Dante ran toward the first tank, and in no time, it was a giant fireball.

Dante stood by Ryan. "Two trees and the next tank will be passing between it in a couple of minutes. I might need help."

"Love to, Dante. Tank hooking. Now I've heard it all," said Ryan sarcastically as he and Dante ran toward the two trees.

Ryan and Dante got ready. Ryan wondered for a moment, but it worked perfectly as Dante envisioned. The tank went between the two trees and could not pass. The shaft of the tank got caught in Dante's harpoon coil trap created between the trees, and parts of the tree began to collapse on the tank. It wasn't going anywhere. Dante took the time to use his sunspear to make a clean slice in the moving mechanism to ensure that was the case. Once the Black Dragon men tried to come out, Ryan's squadron finished them.

Dante, Ryan, and the smaller squadron moved to the next tank.

"This one hasn't gotten too close yet, and they won't expect the same thing again. We explode this one too."

"All right, we'll talk about your fascination with fire later. Go for it, Dante. We'll be watching the last tank."

Dante ran for the third tank, and Ryan kept his eye on the last tank. However, it did not change its focus to Dante. Moments later, the third tank burst into flames as well.

"Last one, Ryan. I'm going to disable it at closer range like last time. Where did they all come from?" It felt like more traffic to get to the last tank.

"They figured we're headed for the last tank." He kept up with Dante while alternating between his sword and blaster to make a path.

"Great, we ran into the smart squadron today." He got a look from Ryan. "Okay, I gave them too much credit."

Dante finally got his way to the tank. Climbing on top of it, he took a couple of slices off the shaft of the tank when he felt a blaster shot whiz past his leg. He turned to pinpoint where the blast originated, but almost too late before another one came close to finding its mark. They both missed, but he lost enough balance to drop from the tank. There, in front of him, stood the Black Dragon soldier that shot at him. From the ground on his back, Dante met the soldier's sword. The soldier smiled. Dante soon realized why as he heard the sound of the tank almost at this ear, and he heard Ryan yell at the same time, "Dante, get out of the way!" Dante took his sunspear and chopped the soldier at the legs. Dante rolled clear of the tank and jumped to his feet. The Black Dragon soldier no longer smiled as he met the fate intended for Dante. Dante sighed. They still needed to stop the tank. This time he would. He climbed on the tank again and created a hole in the top. Throwing the light crackers inside and dropping himself into the tank, he made quick work of the few soldiers inside. A minute later, the tank stopped.

"Ryan?"

"You're good. Come on out, Dante."

Dante climbed out and got off the tank. "Did you see that?" he asked, shaking his head.

"You almost getting squished with the tank? Yes, I couldn't miss it. The image will stay etched in my brain forever. It won't be a blaster shot or sword which kills me. You're going to give me a heart attack watching you. And I'm not much older than you, Dante." chuckled Ryan.

"I heard it the same time as you, and I got out of the way." Dante grinned. "They need more training on their driving."

"No, he meant to aim for you." Ryan shook his head and smiled at Dante. "Other individuals are concerned for your safety, but he wasn't one of them."

"Yeah, you're right." He knew both he and Ryan thought the same thing. Those individuals prepared to go on another dangerous operation soon if today went as planned.

Seth and Commander Gabe watched as the Black Dragon soldiers entered the lab. The soldiers began their process with the boxes, and the point came again in the process. Suddenly an alarm sounded, and there was a commotion outside again. Someone yelled of a fire outside the building, mixed with the sound of blaster shots.

The Black Dragon soldier in charge roared this time. "These colonists! I will take their heads off today." He started for the door, and the others followed him. Then he turned. "No, you three stay. The rest come with me."

One of the three asked, "Do you want us to start?"

"No, wait in case they come around here, and you need to cut them off," said the Black Dragon soldier in charge as he walked away and motioned for the others to follow him.

Seth and Commander Gabe exchanged a glance. Three left and little time. Seth and Commander Gabe had already put on their masks and made their way toward the three soldiers. While Commander Gabe concentrated on watching the three soldiers, Seth came around to the boxes. The two threw the liquid smoke, putting the whole room in a thick layer of fog. The Black Dragon men could not see, but Seth's and Commander Gabe's vision was clear. Seth quickly switched the carts. Rapidly moving over to the boxes the Black Dragon soldiers would be taking with them, he slipped one of the tracking devices in it. Seth and Commander Gabe returned to their hidden positions before the Black Dragon leader and his men came back in the door.

"What happened in here? I leave you here for less than five minutes, and this is how you take care of it? I asked you a question, and I'm waiting on an answer," thundered the lead Black Dragon soldier.

"We were here, and out of nowhere, all the smoke appeared," said one of the soldiers.

"Let me guess you didn't see anyone, though. Probably one of those security people came around who I told you to watch for to stop."

One of the soldiers peered in the general direction where Seth and Commander Gabe hid. "I think I saw something move over there." He raised his blaster to fire.

The lead Black Dragon soldier stopped him and yelled at him further. "You can't see anything that far with this smoke lingering. This is a lab. Half the stuff in here could probably blow up if you hit it. There will be no blasting here unless necessary. Put your blaster down this instant, you fool."

The lead Black Dragon soldier turned to them. "Get the good cart out of here before anything else happens today. Get the other one unloaded now." He waited until it was done and turned to the three soldiers. "We are not done. The three of you that could not keep the lab smoke-free for five minutes before me this instant." The three complied. He glared at them. "Consider your services no longer needed." He took his sword, and one by one, ended their lives. He turned to the others watching. "Lesson completed. Let's go now."

Seth and Commander Gabe waited until the Black Dragon soldiers left the building, and they received confirmation from their eyes outside. Then they came out of the building.

"It's done, and that is the last time it will work," said Seth.

"Yes, but we only needed this last time."

Seth stared out, knowing what came next. He hoped Alika's two spear-bearers were not sent on their last mission.

CHAPTER SEVEN

The girl continued going through the warehouse items with Christopher and was nearly finished. She reached for her water and realized she'd drank it all.

"Here, let me." He came back with more and handed it to her.

"I'm sorry this is taking so long, and the chemicals remain to go through."

"See, aren't you glad you got a drink this time?" He chuckled. "Considering what bets you're placing on these, you should be taking this kind of time," he said to her serious again as the girl studied the item in her hand. "Do you know the layout of where you're going?"

"No." She finished with the item, and he handed her the next one.

"What about the security?"

"No." She studied the next item.

Christopher watched her face. The girl was simply not telling him. He had enough experience with her to know she would not go into a situation seemingly this unprepared. Nevertheless, he sensed both answers rung true.

"Chris, this isn't like you at all. You're smart, smarter in ways others in this business will never be. I sensed that quickly about you."

"Hopefully, you're right. It would certainly help this one to go as planned." She shook her head as she remembered how badly Abigail's operation went off-script. Continuing to inspect the item in her hand, she scanned it with her data pad.

Christopher was perceptive, and he stared at her suspiciously. "Your last operation, not so smoothly?"

She looked up at him and bit her lip. "Not so much, and I don't want to do it again."

"Your friend, was she all right?"

"My friend was fine."

"I see," said Christopher softly. Obviously, the girl had been the one for which it had not gone well, and whatever happened, she did not want to recount the event. The girl continued with the item for a few more minutes as he watched.

She handed the item back to him and said, "Time for the chemicals."

The girl began, but it was slow going. She took a break between each of them, some longer than others. She glanced at Christopher after testing one.

Through her coughing, she asked, "Are you sure this isn't the real thing?"

"It's not, I promise. I made it like you and your friend wanted. Here." He handed her a rag, and she instantly recognized the scent on it. It had a soothing fragrance on it, often used to calm a cough. He lightly hit her on the back as well. In a moment, she felt better.

The relief didn't last long. One of the other chemicals, she felt like her eyes were on fire as soon as she took a whiff, and they watered profusely. He handed her a rag. She looked at him questioningly, and he smiled. "Different rag. It's only water."

She took it, put it on her eyes, and in a couple of minutes felt better. Her eyes returned to their usual clear blue calm.

A couple of others left her feeling queasy.

Christopher started to hand her one. "Okay, I said none would make you pass out. They won't. Although, this one is pretty strong, which is how you wanted it. I wished to warn you. My guess is this one could come close."

"Thanks for the warning. I'm sure it will be a treat." She reviewed the list to see which one it was. Good, they were almost finished. She took it from Christopher's hand and removed the lid from the tiny container. The second the container reached near her face, it hit her. She instantly felt dizzy and knew she needed to put it down. She barely got it back down on the table in time, her hand shaking in the effort.

"Are you still with me, Chris?" Christopher came over and placed a hand on her shoulder. The girl put her head in her hands for a moment, trying to stop the dizzy feeling.

"Yeah, it's a good thing I can trust you because you weren't kidding about this one."

He gazed at her sympathetically and continued to sit by her. In a couple of minutes, when she looked back up at him, the dazed look was mostly gone.

"Two more, right?"

"Yeah, you're almost done. Tell me when you're sure you're ready."

She closed her eyes and took a deep breath. "Okay, let's finish this."

Christopher got up and walked back over. He retrieved the next chemical and brought it to her. She got through the final two at last.

Sitting back for a moment, she rubbed her head and the back of her neck.

"Chris, what are you thinking?"

"I finished testing how authentic twelve chemicals were, and you ask me that? I'm not sure it's a wise question, Christopher." She couldn't help but laugh, and Christopher laughed as well. "I know what you meant."

"I know you did. I'm glad you don't appear like you're going to pass out anymore. You may have told me to do too good of a job. What do you want me to do?"

The girl was clearly in thought. "I don't know. It's got to be authentic. I'm hesitant to back down. I know what we give them won't hurt anyone. It'll make them miserable like it did me for a short time. This is our only entrance to get to what we need. If we don't get through the door, it's all for nothing."

Christopher listened to the girl. She was torn. He knew he could not help her. She talked aloud, trying to decide.

"Give me a minute, Christopher," said the girl. He realized she was discussing it with her friend. "Yeah, I'm okay. I don't know. Christopher and I are wondering too." The girl listened. "I know. I'm going back and forth too—one shot at it. I know. Okay. That's where I'm leaning." The girl turned back to Christopher. "Christopher, leave the chemicals as they are."

"Okay, it will be as you want, Chris."

The girl felt relief that she decided finally. "Thanks. I'm curious. Were you okay after doing this for us? I fell apart on your ship testing the samples."

"Oh, I wore equipment the whole time when I got to the chemicals. However, certain ones I got a faint whiff of still through the equipment."

"Gotcha. A disturbing picture of you entered my mind of what I put you through with this job. On a serious note, I'm sure you figured out by now, everything is good. We need you to do the rest of it and talk about the time frame as the time is running out for me and my friend to do our operation."

The girl pulled out the data pad and instantly sent something to Christopher's data pad. "Those are the quantities of the items we need." She pulled out a container. "Here's more of the other liquid to duplicate the other chemical. Of course, the topic of payment as well."

Christopher reviewed the list. "Four days is the soonest I see."

"No, that's good. I'm surprised so soon. I know you'll do longer nights to finish it in the time frame. Thank you."

"As far as payment, here is the amount."

"It appears too little for what we ask you to do and for the time."

"I told you I'm not going to raise the price for you. You're always more than fair with me, Chris. The payment is right. I'm more interested in seeing you and your friend come back safe than the profit made in this case."

"Thank you for your concern. Some now, all later, how do you wish it?"

"I'll see you in four days with the items, and we can do payment as well. I've no concerns about that part from you. I assume a lot of planning lies ahead to keep you busy. You told me what you don't know. What do you know about what you step into so you and your friend return safely?"

"You don't want to know, Christopher."

"You must know more than what you're saying." Yet as he stared in her face, his concern returned.

"At the moment, I don't possess a location. I hope in the next day or two to gain the information."

"Oh my, Chris."

The girl got up and smiled. "You're right. My friend and I have a lot to do, so I need to go. You have much work to do for us, so we can be ready. I'll see you in four days, lunchtime, right?"

"Yes, Chris."

"Hey, and don't worry about me so much. I don't want you to get one of those fake chemicals on you while you mix it up. You're an expert at your work." The girl laughed and gave him a light pat on the back.

"I'll try, Chris. Be careful."

She nodded and turned around. "Don't forget the cameras."

Christopher laughed as he walked over to the cockpit. "Yes, I know."

Christopher watched her head back to her ship and shook his head in worry.

"Let's head back," said the girl.

"We are on our way," said Alena. "How are you feeling afterward?"

"I should feel good because it was a success. Yet once again, the process to get there, not so pleasant. I'm still fighting a couple of battles with my stomach and head."

"Sorry."

"I'll be fine. Any word from Dante's crew?"

"Not directly to us yet, but Alika was monitoring it. I don't think he sent us anything because he wanted us to concentrate on this now."

"Using my own advice on me. Quite unfair." The girl grinned. "I guess we'll see when we return."

CHAPTER EIGHT

Lana sat and waited as the others began filing in. Caleb walked in with the other commanders first, then he walked over to her.

"Everything go okay?"

"In the air it did," said Caleb as he hugged his wife. "Normal stuff."

Dante and Ryan came in next. Lana peered at them.

"Don't ask," said Ryan.

"He didn't end up in medical today."

"Closer than you would imagine."

"I saw it and got out of the way in time. It went fine. That's all that counts."

"You're right. I don't want to know, Dante."

Seth and Commander Gabe arrived back last and sat. Everyone settled down around them, waiting.

Seth sighed. "The swap is done, and the devices are planted." Despite Seth's announcement, both Seth and Commander Gabe mirrored the same look of worry.

"Then why do both of you appear unhappy?" asked Dante.

"The one at the warehouse went well. The second at the lab did not go as smoothly," replied Commander Gabe.

"I thought as much, but how not so smoothly?" asked Lana.

Seth proceeded to tell them about the incident at the lab. "We are done with performing the box swap without incident after today. That much is guaranteed."

"We knew that part pretty much. We said only a couple of times. The question is how much will they figure out and maybe find the tracking devices," said Caleb.

"Alika's students could be on the operation before the Black Dragon soldiers begin to question the supplies," said Lana.

Seth and Commander Gabe looked at each other, and apparently, their discussions led them to believe otherwise.

"Say something, one of you. I can tell that's not what you think," said Dante.

"We don't, and you won't like it. The tracking device has just been placed. We don't know how long the Black Dragon is taking to get the supplies to their final destination. It could be a day if we're lucky, but I'm guessing a couple. I'm sure the students will make sure of its destination before they move. Once done, they scope out the place to see what they're up against. There's another day, at least. Then coming up with a plan and getting everything prepared for the operation itself adds at least a couple of days. I'm sure they have already begun preparing some plans. However, they can't make the final plans until they know the place. Also, if the supplies are going to two destinations, there are two separate operations. Either way, by this point, I'm sure another attack comes and finishes before they go on the operation. Based on today, I'm certain the Black Dragon Command will be alerted something is going on with the supplies."

"And that's the same time Alika's students will go in to do their operation," said Ryan finishing it for Seth.

"Yes, unfortunately, it's the timing Commander Gabe and I see."

"You know how it will end, Seth. There's no plan which can succeed. The Black Dragon soldiers will be alerted for anyone attempting to sneak into one of their locations. The students will be discovered the second they try."

"Dante, I would think so, but Alika's students surprise me in many ways. I do not understand how his younger one survived the last incident and is fine now. Alika must know the timetable and his students as well."

"But Seth, Alika didn't know how this would go today."

"He did not know for sure, Dante. He suspected how it would, though, as did his students."

"It's too dangerous. He can't send them in now." Dante pleaded the two students' case.

"Dante, it's not our choice to make," Seth said as he put a hand on Dante's shoulder. "We need to let Alika and his students know the devices are placed as they wished. We will warn them about how it went today, so they know what they face. It's their decision, but I'm sure it will change nothing for them. We will send the message to them now so that they can make some decisions."

Dante moved over to sit by Seth as he began the message. It could take time for them to respond as he remembered what they said about possibly being in the middle of something. He didn't care. He longed for them to say it was too dangerous, and they thought it best not to go through with it.

Seth wrote: *It is done as you requested.*

The girl and Alena got back and sat with Alika, listening to what he gathered from the monitoring of the attack. Alika had finished telling them he thought both of the tracking devices were placed, but he got the impression the swap did not go as smoothly as hoped. Alena and the girl shrugged as they all expected it. They watched the tracking devices at the moment, and both appeared to work perfectly. Directly, they received a transmission.

The girl glimpsed down at the data pad. "It's Seth." She projected it on the wall. "You wish to answer him?"

"I will, Alika."

Dante leaned over and read: *Thank you. We are receiving the information from your efforts. We will see where it takes us.*

Dante said to Seth, "That was fast."

"Yes." Seth projected it on the wall for everyone to see. Clearly, he did not expect an answer so quickly.

Seth continued to write: *However, it did not go as well as we wished. Do I need to elaborate as I know you monitor some activities of the day?*

The return message read: *No need to elaborate. We figured out the sequence from reviewing the monitoring later today. Sorry, we could not assist at the time, but we were in the middle of an operation which demanded our full attention.*

Dante looked puzzled. "They don't know where yet. I wonder what they were doing today?"

Seth glanced at Dante. "I don't know, but as I told you the other day, those two students are never idle."

Seth wrote: *We are concerned, especially one member of our party because of how things unfolded today you will be in too much danger to complete the original intent. Are you sure it is wise to continue?*

The return message read: *We anticipated we would need to deal with that factor by the time of the operation and are making plans to hopefully remedy it so it's not an issue, which is why we could not assist you today. We will continue as planned as it's too important not to do so. As far as the other, I have a good idea who is especially concerned about our safety. Dante, I will be fine and so will my friend. My fellow spear-bearer and Alika taught me well all this time. Stay safe and get ready for the task before you. I will do the same with those around me. Thank you always for your concern.*

"I thought Alika would answer, but that is the young spear-bearer."

"Clearly, it is. Remember, they all have access to the system. From what Alika said, I get the impression he leaves these types of tasks to his students. Apparently, the young spear-bearer took the lead in answering us today. I don't think there is anything further to say. Dante, if you wish, you can answer if you want to speak further to the young spear-bearer since part of the message is addressed to you." Seth took it off the projector, sent the last message to Dante's data pad, and smiled. Seth spoke to the others and said, "Why don't we break for about twenty minutes, and we'll readjourn?"

It felt strange now that Dante had the opportunity. He didn't know what to say at first, and he knew he must be careful what he communicated on the data pad. It should be secure, but still.

Dante sent a message: *It's Dante. I wish you would reconsider, but I understand. Were you safe today from your operation?*

The message back read: *This is a pleasant surprise, Dante. I'm glad you understand why I must go through with this. Today's operation was different from most operations, so I'm not sure how to answer about it. I was always safe during it. I'm still feeling the effects from it, but I'll be fine. One day I will be able to tell you about it, and my answer will make sense, I promise.*

Dante read the message and felt utterly perplexed by it. Seth saw his expression and was curious but didn't ask. Dante wrote back: *One day when I meet you, and you explain it to me, right?*

The message popped up a moment later: *Didn't miss a beat, did you, Dante? I don't know. I do know we both need to get through the tasks before us first. Then we'll go from there, okay?*

Dante answered back: *Okay, but I'm worried about your safety after the last time.*

The young spear-bearer continued: *Yes, I'm not sure how you pulled those details out of my teacher, but I wish I could undo it. I fear it will cause you unnecessary worry for the future. I enjoy talking with you. I could stay talking with you for some time if it were up to me, but I need to help my friend and Alika prepare for what we must do.*

Dante sent back: *I feel the same as I have spoken with you, but I understand. Be safe, please.*

The answer read: *I will. We will let you know what we find when we return. Please be safe as well. And Dante, stay clear of those tanks in the future, and yes, I found out about that incident. Goodbye until next time.*

Dante sat there and said aloud, "How?" He laughed. He glanced up to find Seth smiling at him. He smiled back. "Sorry, Seth, I guess it's time to get back to work."

"It's okay, Dante. You needed a break from thinking about it, and I thought you might enjoy speaking with the young spear-bearer for a bit."

"I did. It's strange since we haven't met, but it came naturally for me to do so."

"It's a curious connection you find with this one. We will see where it takes you, Dante."

"I guess you're right. I'm curious about the operation they did earlier today. I got a strange response when I asked about it."

"Really?"

"Yeah." Dante brought the data pad over to Seth. Seth looked at Dante questioningly, confirming it was okay for him to read. Dante nodded and pointed to the question he asked and the response he received.

Seth read it. "It's puzzling. I don't know what to make of it either. You'll wait until the young spear-bearer can explain it one day, Dante."

Seth peered down at his data pad as it blinked, and the messages disappeared. Dante sighed, waiting for his to do the same. To his surprise, they did not.

Another message appeared on his data pad: *Not forever will you keep them, but I think it's safe for now. I must get to work now, Dante.*

CHAPTER NINE

The girl put the data pad down and shook her head as she smiled.

"He couldn't resist," said Alena, laughing.

"Seth is the one who sent him the last message for him to began responding," said Alika smiling. "Dante needed no further encouragement. The mystery is driving him insane."

"Yes, and I let him keep them against every smart, careful bone in my body. Once I meet him, I'll clear them first thing."

Alena turned to her and started laughing again. "Yeah, I'm sure that will be your first thought when you meet him."

"Work, that's what we need to do," said the girl as she purposely avoided the implied meaning behind Alena's comment.

"Yes." Alika turned serious. "How are you feeling? Any more dizziness, nausea?"

"No, I'm fine, well mostly. I think it's sampling all of them back-to-back as I did. How is the tracking device coming?"

"It's still moving," said Alika. "It stopped and started a few times."

"We're looking at supplies going through various places before they get to a final destination?" pondered Alena.

"Yes and no. They're short stops, so I'm not sure how much we read into them yet. Both to this point are following the same route. That part is excellent news and a pattern I hope resumes to the end. It means only one place to break into, one operation," said the girl.

"I wonder how long before it gets to its final destination?" murmured Alena.

"I don't know," said the girl looking down at the data pad.

"You're wondering about those various pit stops, though," said Alika.

"I am, but it could be picking up other supplies or more personnel for what they're working on. I know we planned to check out all those stops the cloaked woman made too, but we need to concentrate on this operation now. There could be answers in those various places, but we should stick with the place with the biggest yield now. We're on a time factor, and we don't want to jeopardize this operation." The girl took a deep breath. "I'm frustrated at the moment."

"It's understandable, but if this operation yields what we hope, many of the other places will prove unnecessary," said Alena.

The girl nodded. "Then we do what we can to prepare until the tracking device stops for good."

—ℓℓ—

Late afternoon the next day, Alika rechecked the screen.

"Can the two of you come here for a moment?"

"Sure," said the girl as she and Alena came in from working inside the ship. "What do you see?"

"No movement to speak of since this morning," said Alika as the two students sat in front of the screen and checked as well.

"What movement there is appears to be in the same small space on the planet or a building," said the girl agreeing.

"The final destination?" said Alena.

"I believe so," said Alika.

"And they're both in the same place. We caught a break," said the girl.

"I assume you'll both want to leave tomorrow morning?"

"We will do so," said the girl to Alena, who nodded in agreement. "We'll go finish up with the ship."

—ℓℓ—

The next morning came, and Alena and the girl headed off to survey where they would try to do their operation.

"This whole region reeks of Black Dragon," said Alena.

"We figured as much. We should be okay as a transport ship. Be careful, and don't get too close. Let's just scope out the surroundings."

At first, there didn't appear to be much, but quickly it opened up to reveal lots of activity.

"Oh my," said Alena, and the girl gasped behind her.

They watched a few minutes and let the ship scan the area to obtain footage to examine when they got back.

"Where are the supplies going in all this?" asked the girl after getting over the activity from the scene before her.

"There." Alena scanned a gigantic ship with a floating structure attached to it at the center of the activity.

Ships went in and out of the large ship, but not immediately. So, they were probably taking their supplies and conducting whatever other business inside the ship. It had to be an enormous hangar. Neither one wanted to guess how many ships it could hold.

The floating structure attached looked as if the Dark Lord took a couple of his facilities and transported them into space. It was a huge spectacle there, churning a chasm of terror for the rest of the galaxy.

"Terrific." sighed the girl. Suddenly she said, "We need to leave now, Alena."

"We're gone," said Alena, and she turned them toward the portal. Seconds later, they came through it. This time they immediately switched the ship back from a Black Dragon ship to a friendly ship.

Alena turned to the girl.

"I know, Alena, Dante's argument sounds like the voice of reason now."

"Yeah, we sound like the crazy ones."

"I don't disagree with Dante, but there's no way around it. You know it, Alena."

"Yes, I know. Crazy is the way we roll lately. Rooftop rescues and all." Alena smiled and shook her head.

The girl read something behind the smile.

"What? You need to share something, I believe?"

"I hope Dante is ready for what's in store for him when you two meet."

"Dante handles everything he encounters quite nicely."

"But you're not something. You're someone. An individual who has a singular talent for somehow finding the most creative ways to get answers. However, you end up in situations where you have everyone around you holding their breath wondering if you're taking your last. You know craziness." Alena grinned at her.

"You're saying I prove a different challenge for Dante." The girl laughed.

"Yes, maybe a heart attack with your stunts, but your other redeeming qualities will cause him to overlook it, I'm sure." Alena laughed and cut the girl off before she could respond further to Alena's teasing. "Let's head back to Alika. He's going to love where we have to break into."

They sat at the table, studying the footage playing on the wall. They watched in silence for a while, making silent notes of what they saw.

"Quite busy, and you must get over there."

"It appears so, Alika," said the girl, staring at the image. "There is a route everything stays to once it arrives. I figure most of the other ships are delivering supplies as well."

"You are wondering if there is something more to the checkpoints it goes through," said Alika.

"Yeah, something like that," replied the girl, still following the ship's routes.

"If there is, we better figure it out. We can't cause any suspicion," said Alena.

"We have two resources now, this footage and the information from the tracking devices. Once the supplies get to this floating fortress, we should be able to go back and track its route. Between both pieces of information, we should see if there is a pattern and figure it out," said the girl.

CHAPTER TEN

Dante and Ryan sat and discussed the next attack. There would be no changes to their plan. They simply needed to continue changing the ways to get rid of the tanks.

Caleb and the other commanders saw nothing different from the skies, so there was no change in their attack plan.

Now everyone sat with Seth and Commander Gabe, going over the day's events. They all settled on the conclusion that there would be a confrontation to keep the Black Dragon soldiers from leaving with the supplies at some point in the next attack. They only question was if they should attempt a distraction or go ahead and ambush the Black Dragon as soon as they came to the next target. Maybe they should at least try one last time for the distraction as it might help Alika's students. Dante and the others didn't want to stir up anything if they could help it before the operation.

Nonetheless, everyone felt a full confrontation would not be avoided at the end of the day. Alika's students indicated they expected as much. Seth and Commander Gabe discussed it further. They knew what they would try for the distractions if they needed to bother with it. Maybe the game was up, and they should go straight to plan B, direct confrontation.

Either way, Lana decided there was nothing further to do. "I think it's time everyone got a chance to spend time back at home before the next attack. You are free to go whenever you wish."

Dante and Seth sat at the table. Most of the others left. Ryan remained speaking with Caleb and Lana.

"I wonder how they're coming. Do you think they know the location by now, Seth?"

"Yes, I would think so."

"They can finally start putting together a plan. I have no idea how they're going to do this."

"They're probably well into a plan by now, Dante. They will find a way. They proved stellar at getting in the facility when rescuing your mother, as I saw."

Dante glanced at him, puzzled. "What do you mean? I thought Alika simply relayed the information to you."

"No, Alika showed me the footage when he and I met."

"Do you have it?"

"I do."

"Can I view it?"

"Yes, I don't see why not. All the audio is gone and any views of his students as well."

"I figured as much."

"All right. You understand at the time we didn't mention it to you because we needed to give you the other information."

"Yes, I understand, Seth."

Seth pulled up the footage on the data pad with effort as it was clear he wasn't keeping it easily accessible on his device. He proceeded to project it on the wall for Dante. Ryan, Lana, and Caleb walked over and began watching as well. They glanced at Seth with a questioning look.

"It's from Abigail's rescue." They appeared surprised but resumed watching with Dante.

"All the blaster fire going to the one place, surely not, Seth?"

"No, you guessed correctly, that is where his students are in the room."

Dante continued watching. Knowing both students survived, he could make no sense of what he thought he saw next. He turned to Seth, horrified by what he imagined happened. The rest watching showed the same reaction.

"I know what you're thinking. I thought the same as I watched. Alika assured me of a ploy done which apparently worked," said Seth, and he saw Dante's look, "And no, he would not tell me the ploy used."

Dante went back to watching. It reached the final sequence. "So much blaster fire coming." He saw the door shut to the ship. He could see the sunspear, and it swung with incredible speed as the one behind it fought, deflecting the blasts and using it to mow down the guards. "The way his student must move and the skill with the sunspear, it's..."

"Much like watching you, Dante," said Seth.

Dante watched as the footage came to the final moments, and the angle turned strange. The young spear-bearer began to fall, and the footage went black.

They were quiet, comforted, knowing it did not end as it appeared.

Dante glanced at Seth. "Did they ever fix the problem with the ship?"

Seth stared back at him blankly. "What problem with the ship?"

"Alika said a problem occurred with the ship, which prevented them from returning for the young spear-bearer, remember?"

"Oh, yes. At the time, Alika found it easier to present it as he did. He wished the focus to be on the information he came to deliver, not on the rescue itself. It is what his student wished as well. He told me what happened with the ship on the rooftop that day." Seth paused. "There was no malfunction with the ship as they thought at first."

Dante and the others looked at each other and back at Seth, waiting.

Seth sighed and told them what actually happened.

"Alika and the other spear-bearer realized it after they got back home with my mother," said Dante quietly.

"Yes."

"But the young spear-bearer understood it on the rooftop."

"Yes. What are you thinking, Dante?"

"Who is this one who places such value on the lives of all others but gives no thought to one's own life repeatedly?" asked Dante softly.

"I do not know, Dante, but this one, along with the other student, are about to do so again soon. We can only hope their lives are spared another time."

⸺⁓⸺

Later Seth said, "Dante, let's go out and practice." Then he turned to Lana and Caleb. "Why don't you give Dante a bit of practice while Ryan and I observe. You two have not practiced in some time, and Dante is becoming accustomed to fighting only Black Dragon soldiers. Put protective gear on. I don't need anyone hurt before the next attack."

Dante had forgotten his cousin's mastery in fighting with the sunspear but regained his appreciation quickly. He suspected Lana did get practice in he didn't see, or perhaps it was one of those things which never left once it coursed through your veins. Of course, he and Caleb still came out and practiced despite the turmoil lately.

Seth grinned. "Lana, you gave your cousin something to think about this evening. My compliments. You lost nothing not being able to practice as you wish."

"Yes, it was entertaining." Ryan laughed. "I'm going to head off, though, before it gets too late, or Lana changes her mind." He smiled at her.

Lana returned his smile. "No, I told everyone they could go. We'll see you again soon, I'm sure."

"Till next time, Ryan," said Caleb.

Ryan nodded and smiled. Dante came over. "I'll see you soon, Ryan. There are always more tanks out there."

Ryan patted him on the back. "Dante, one day, this will stop, hopefully. We'll find you another interest."

Ryan walked to his ship, waving goodbye to them.

Seth came up to Dante. "Why don't you shower and get some sleep after all this?"

"That sounds great." He jogged off to his room.

Lana and Caleb glanced at Seth. Lana asked, "Did we all need practice, Seth?"

"He needed to begin training for the task before him."

"But he's not going to put a sunspear through his father, right?"

"No, beating his father will take different training, which begins immediately for him. However, I'm sure he will need to put a sharp object through the Dark Lord during the confrontation. The Dark Lord will not fight as a Black Dragon soldier when the time comes. He will try the other tactics first. Once Dante gets through those, the Dark Lord will fight back in the traditional sense, but with a mastery few can rival. Dante must be ready."

CHAPTER ELEVEN

The next day came, and it was uneventful. Seth supervised another practice with Dante, alternating sparring with Caleb and Lana in the morning. After going back to their quarters and showering, they ate lunch together. Seth went to his quarters. Dante felt strangely tired after another long practice session and had dozed off in his quarters when he was awakened by Seth calling him.

"Dante."

Dante started to get up. "I'm coming. It came quicker this time."

"There is no attack."

"Oh." Dante began to lay back down. "What is it, Seth?"

"I need you to come to my quarters."

"When?" Dante tried unsuccessfully to hold back a yawn.

"Now, please."

"Okay, I'm on my way, Seth." Hopefully, he hid his dismay. He didn't know why he was tired but could only figure all the events of the past days had caught up to him. Forcing himself to get up, he headed to Seth's quarters.

Seth sighed. The two back-to-back sessions found Dante tired, although he slept the night between them. He hoped no attack today. There had never been one this early, so he counted on that pattern continuing. Yet, he wanted Dante tired for this. He knew this was how the Dark Lord would find Dante as well, unfortunately.

Dante knocked, and the door opened. "Seth, I'm here."

"Come in, Dante. Sit down, please. Can I get you something to drink?"

"No, I guess I'm good."

"Are you sure? You sound like you're not feeling right."

"A little tired for some reason, but I'm fine. What did you need?"

"To speak with you for a while. We didn't get the chance to talk much more about all the information you received. A steady stream of attacks came since our friends left."

"I'm fine, Seth."

"How is your mother?"

Dante looked down at the floor. "She's the same. I check on her each night before I go to my quarters."

"You are a good son. I thought she would be awake by now. Dante, I know how much you want to hope, but has it occurred to you she took more damage than you first admitted? There is a possibility she will not awaken despite how much we hope otherwise."

Dante stared surprised at Seth. "It crossed my mind at the beginning, but I didn't think that way anymore. I figure if we got her back, there's a reason, especially at what the cost almost was. I believe at some point she must wake up."

"I'm not as optimistic as the days pass. You must prepare yourself."

"I suppose."

Seth could tell his words unsettled his student, but at the moment, it was his aim. "Dante, how are you feeling about the operation to come?"

"Anxious but determined."

"Have you thought about what you will say to your father to convince him of the truth?"

"I suppose I need to tell him what really happened with my brother, let him know what happened with mother, and show him the things from mother we possess to start off with."

"We tried to convince him the events were not as he saw them at the time of Collin's murder, and he did not believe us. He has now had years under the Dark Lord's corruption. You see what he has done with the time."

"We have my mother back now, the part we didn't have before."

"Your mother is asleep. She cannot speak to what happened. Besides, your father believed your mother in a moment slaughtered your brother. How could he believe such a thing?"

"I ... I don't know, Seth. I don't ..." Dante stumbled over his words, confused by Seth.

"What if he doesn't see? What do you do? Have you thought of the possibility? Are you going to be able to do it? You can end the Dark Lord's life with no problem, but where does that leave you with your father?"

"He will see. He must. Too much has been done, too much almost sacrificed for the chance to get him back. You're talking about throwing it away. No, I haven't thought about it because it's not coming to that."

"I'm not so sure anymore, Dante, the more I consider the task before you."

"The young spear-bearer said it could be done. Alika said it could be done. You were sure. What happened?"

"Alika said a lot, and I do trust him. His two students mean well, and I do not doubt their sincerity. Yet, he said it himself. He does not understand the visions totally. What if the vision is wrong or interpreted incorrectly? The vision saw you entering the room with your raised sunspear and seeing your father and the Dark Lord there. It could go a lot of ways after that point."

"I don't understand this change. You agreed with the visions before." Dante tried to reconcile what he heard.

"I thought about it further. Remember the young spear-bearer is the same one who almost died because of falling from the rooftop. Now they are on a new operation they hope will yield answers. They are willing to take numerous risks based on visions and inferences from those. I'm not sure I'm willing to stake your life as well. I believe your curiosity over these two students is clouding your judgment, particularly this strange connection you believe you feel with the younger one."

"The younger one saved my mother from further torture by the Dark Lord, Seth. The student didn't try to fall from the rooftop." Dante took a breath and forced himself to be calm. "And I don't imagine a connection with this younger student. I don't understand it or its purpose, but it's there."

"It doesn't matter. Perhaps you're not there to save your father. Maybe you're to kill both the Dark Lord and your father, and your father cannot be saved."

"I can't believe what I hear, Seth." Tears flowed from Dante's eyes. He rose from the chair and started toward the door.

"Dante, please do not walk out the door. Turn around and look at me." Seth said softly. He had gotten up from the chair and walked toward Dante.

Dante came close to walking out, but he recognized the change of tone in Seth's voice. He turned around, and Seth had made it to Dante. He put his hands on Dante's shoulders and looked him straight in the eyes.

"Why?" Dante searched Seth's face, tears still streaming down his face.

"Because this is how the Dark Lord will battle."

CHAPTER TWELVE

"All this was ...?"

"Yes, Dante." Seth gently guided Dante back to the chair to sit.

"You believed ...?"

"None of it, Dante, but you were confused at what you heard. You also started to believe portions of it or at least question it in your mind, did you not?"

"Yes, I did." Dante stared back at Seth unhappily.

"Why do you think, Dante?"

"I don't know, Seth."

"You do know. You don't want to think about it or admit it. I spoke in half-truths. You heard a grain of truth somewhere in it, and you grabbed it. Sometimes it rings true for a different reason. It speaks to a fear we hold, but we believe it buried in the deep recesses of our heart. Then it finds a voice and a power over us it should not. We act as if it is truth when it is not."

"Is this what the Dark Lord is going to use on me?"

"I do not know what he will use. His tactics have not changed as his master has not changed since time can be remembered. He will take something which looks clear to you at the moment, and he will find a way to twist it, so it no longer does. You must only look at your father to see how far the Dark Lord can twist truth. He can destroy relationships, families, and lives in a moment. He will find something to use, and once he finds it, he will keep going. You must not falter."

"How?"

"Truth must be clung to and reaffirmed. The young spear-bearer told you the Ancient One would guide you, and only with that will you be able to do the task before you. The young spear-bearer spoke truth to you as well."

"What do I do now?"

"Do not consider anything I said to you as truth before you almost walked out of my quarters because they were lies and falsehoods. We will talk about them further because something about them caused you to believe part of them. We need to figure it out because if I can use them, the Dark Lord could. The other part is to go back to your quarters and get more rest. You are still tired, but that was on purpose as well. I don't expect when you go for this operation you will be well-rested."

"I wondered why you needed me right away. We'll talk later, Seth. Unfortunately, today shows I'm not ready for the challenge ahead."

Seth gave Dante a hug. "We'll keep at it. You'll get through to your father, Dante. Go rest now."

Dante walked out and headed for his quarters.

Seth watched him leave, his heart full of concern for his student.

—ele—

"I don't see the supplies are leaving the ships until the final destination," said the girl.

"Me either. It appears the route they take once they get there, nothing more. Probably the way to keep the flow going," said Alena.

"You don't think there is extra checking which will happen with your supplies en route?"

"We all watched it several times, and we see the same thing, Alika," said the girl.

"It appears the final destination is where it passes inspection," said Alena.

"Now, by the time we do this, the inspection will be much more rigorous for the supplies considering how we expect the next attack to go." The girl stopped, and her eyes were somewhere else entirely.

"Are you all right?" asked Alika.

"I'm fine," she said softly, but something had happened.

"You saw something," said Alena. "We know that face."

"Dante. Seth is coming to the end of training with him."

"It apparently did not go as well as hoped," said Alika.

"I'm afraid not. Dante struggled, and I felt his confusion, his hurt. It was the first training of its kind. He's not ready to deal with the Dark Lord's tactics, and Seth knows it. I'm afraid for Dante." The girl sighed, feeling the weight returning once again of what she told Dante he must do.

"Seth will continue with Dante, my child. He will do everything he can to prepare Dante."

"Yes, you know Alika is right. You must trust."

"Seth is trying, and Dante is preparing. The time is short. I know somehow. The Darkness is so strong once it gains entrance. Dante doesn't realize how strong. In a moment, it can take you." The girl stopped, unable to continue. The memory became too strong of her own past, one which almost cost her everything. And Dante to face the same was unbearable to her spirit.

Alika gazed into her eyes and put a hand on her shoulder, speaking gently to her. "But it did not. It has been hard-fought before, and the battle won. You know. You must remember that, child. It can be done again. Dante holds the same source to fight the Darkness. The Ancient One will be there for him as He was for you and continues to be. You must not lose heart."

The girl reached over and hugged Alika as tears streamed down her face. "I know, but I'm so afraid for him, Alika."

"We all are, dear," whispered Alika.

CHAPTER THIRTEEN

The next morning Alena and the girl sat with Alika working out additional details of the operation to come until near lunchtime.

Alena said to the girl, "We need to head out for your lunch appointment."

"You're right. We better go."

Alika nodded to them and watched them go.

***

The girl walked through the local bar door and slid into the booth across from her lunch companion. "Hi," she said, dreading to see her friend's exhaustion.

Christopher glanced up at her, trying to hide his weariness. "Good to see you as always. Are you ready?"

"Of course."

"Please after you." He smiled as she quickly got up and smiled back at him. She walked beside him as he led her to his ship.

They both sat inside his ship. "I'm so sorry, Christopher. You must be about to fall over by now getting this done for me. Please tell me you're going to get sleep before you move on to another job."

He laughed. "You continue to amaze me, Chris. You're concerned about my lack of sleep when your thoughts center on much weightier matters, from what I can tell. Yes, I plan on getting sleep before I begin another job if the knowledge will put your mind at ease."

"It does, Christopher. I assume everything went well." The girl stopped. "I'm sorry, Christopher, a moment."

Christopher nodded, waiting. Evidently, it was her friend.

The girl's face changed. It mirrored the reaction from the last time she and Christopher met. "Yes, it's the right time frame. They prefer lunchtime the last few times to do it. I know. We must concentrate on our operation. They knew that to be the case. Continue to monitor it." She focused back on Christopher.

Christopher watched the girl's face and saw a range of emotions. None reflected happiness with the situation she was made aware of. However, her eyes still reflected calm.

"You don't look happy again, to put it mildly. Are you sure you don't need additional help?"

"No on both counts at this point." She tried to manage a weak smile, but it failed. "You did more than we hoped. This is the supplies, I assume?" She pointed to the boxes next to Christopher with the items inside.

"Yes, everything is there as you and your friend wanted, packaged as you wished." Christopher saw she quickly moved beyond what disturbed her.

"Thank you, Christopher." She got the payment for the supplies and handed it to him. "Why don't we go ahead and get these aboard my ship, and afterward, we can come back and speak further. We're parked right beside your ship as agreed. This part should go fast."

"As you wish, Chris."

Christopher and the girl got them to the door of Chris's ship, and Alena moved them the rest of the way into the ship.

Christopher offered to move the boxes on his own, but the girl laughed. "In all the time we've worked with each other now, do you believe I'd stand idle while you moved all the boxes yourself? Come now, Christopher, you should know me better by now."

Christopher laughed back. "You're right. I forget how stubborn you are."

The girl continued laughing. "You wouldn't be the first to call me such and won't be the last, I suspect."

Christopher didn't ask this time. He brought them both a glass of water since they had moved the boxes, and they sat back down on his ship.

"Is there anything I need to know about the items?"

"No, I don't think so. I marked them as you wanted only temporarily. I sent the list to you with the box numbers and the contents. You said you needed to take care of it the rest of the way."

"Yes, and it's already in the works. We'll label them when we get back. It's one of the final items to be prepared. Everything must match down to the way it's labeled. Is there anything else?"

"I encountered no problems with making the items. Once I created the initial samples, it went fast considering. I suppose one positive thing is they're not the actual harmful chemicals. We used things to mimic them. So, if you do end up getting into a firefight, you aren't transporting any chemicals which could cause an explosion if they got hit."

"That's something. However, if we get into a firefight early in the operation, it won't matter for us. The chemicals, real or fake, wouldn't end up being the death of me and my friend." She shook her head. "Hopefully, we're much further into it before any blaster fire begins, or it won't be worth any of the effort. It would be a shame at this point." She laughed.

He watched her. She said it with such ease, even laughing despite the worry she had to feel. She laughed off the fact she and her friend may not return from this operation. He did not begin to understand how she did it. "Do you know where you're going now? You didn't know before."

"Yes, we know now."

"Where?"

"Nowhere friendly as you guessed. It's better for you not to know. If someone found out, they cannot get information you don't know. If you did know, you would be most unhappy and give me all the reasons not to go."

He looked at her, concerned. "I'm sure you're right. Do you have a layout of the inside of it?"

"No, once we're inside, we'll work on that part. Christopher, these supplies should get us entrance. There is nothing more for you to do for us on this one. My friend and I must complete the rest of the task now."

Christopher stared into her eyes which reflected the same calm as usual. He spoke quietly to her. "You know how this could end, but you laughed a moment ago in the face of it. I don't know many who can do so. Is this something you must do? Is it this important it's worth the life of yourself and your friend? Can you truly say so, Chris?"

She met his eyes and smiled. "I have seen its face more times than you would believe, Christopher, and I know I will see it again. I never face death alone, and I know that for sure each time," she paused. "Yes, there is much more at stake than my life and my friend's life. If the exchange must be made, we are both prepared to do so. It's that important." The girl stood.

Christopher stood as well. He stared back at her and said softly, "Then it must be done. Be careful, and may the Ancient One continue to be with you and your friend. I will look forward to finding you both returned safely, Chris."

"Be safe as well, Christopher, and thank you for all your concern. May the Ancient One keep you as well, Christopher." The girl reached over and hugged Christopher goodbye this time.

She started to walk away and glanced back at him mischievously. "Christopher, don't forget ..."

Christopher chuckled as he walked over to the cockpit. "I know the cameras. Would you go before I come to my senses and prevent you and your friend from your own craziness?" Christopher could hear the girl laughing again as she started toward her ship.

"Ready?" The girl sat alongside Alena.

"Yes, we're headed out." Alena smiled over at her. "Christopher is a rare find in this business. You built a deep bond of friendship with him, another rarity in this business."

"It is. I feel more as if he's an older brother to me. I don't know since I don't have a sibling." She smiled at Alena and gave her a hug. "Many times, you feel much like I expect a sister would, so maybe I do know what it feels like."

Alena hugged her back. "You're right. It feels the same for me."

Alena and the girl returned to Alika and immediately sat at the table. Alika monitored everything as soon as the word came that another attack had started. Once done going over the monitoring, they would finish the preparations for their operation.

CHAPTER FOURTEEN

Dante, Seth, Lana, and Caleb sat down, eating a late breakfast.

"Have you heard anything yet, Seth?"

"I assume you refer to our friends, and the answer is no, Dante."

"I think, with the timetable you and Commander Gabe guessed, it would be in the next few days," said Lana, turning to Seth.

"Yes, but we only guessed."

"Depending on where those supplies ended up, they may take longer to come up with a way to sneak in. I don't know," said Caleb, deep in thought.

"Do you think the Black Dragon knows something is wrong with the boxes yet?" asked Dante.

"No way to know, but they must be suspicious with the confrontations they encountered with us at the sites. We're not doing our friends any favors, but there is no way around it," said Seth.

"But you both said Alika and his students are unconcerned about it," said Lana.

"They are completely unfazed by it, so we should not be worried about it affecting their operation."

They finished eating. Seth turned to Caleb and Lana. "If you don't mind, I'm going to speak with Dante over at the table. We started a conversation yesterday we need to resume."

"Of course, Seth. You and Dante go ahead," said Caleb.

Seth and Dante went over to the table.

"You appear well-rested again, Dante. Did you have time to think about yesterday?"

"I did, and I'm concerned about how easily I became confused. You were right. There are pieces of it I wonder about, perhaps fear they are somewhat true, which is why I didn't see it as false when you spoke."

"Name one, Dante."

"If my mother will awake. Everything you said has gone through my head. What I said back to you, I thought I believed. Then when I heard you say the other, it rang true because, at some point, I debated the same in my head."

"I don't have the answer to that one. We have not been given the answer your mother will awaken. However, I don't see she would be meant to struggle against the darkness for this long and rescued to these lengths to stay asleep. She was asleep for a long time, so now she is free from the darkness. My hope is it will take time for her to awaken because of what she endured. Perhaps there is another piece to the puzzle we are not aware of. Much is in motion, it appears, and sometimes we don't see it all. You must not give up hope for your mother to awaken."

"The other was convincing my father. What hope do I have if he couldn't be convinced when the Dark Lord had my brother killed?"

"Dante, you must be clear on that one when you face the Dark Lord. He can easily begin to twist you, make you doubt. He believes your father is under his control. At this moment, he is correct. Though you share all this new information, the Dark Lord will twist it somehow. I have no doubt your father will believe him over you at first, and I don't know how far into it. You must not give up. You cannot get your father to see if you let it become twisted for you. I don't know what it will take to convince your father, but it can be done."

"The part about having to kill my father. That was truly falsehood, I assume."

"Yes, it was a complete falsehood. If you go in believing you must kill your father, the battle is already lost. You will cost your father's life, and I fear your own. Alika and I both agree the battle for your father is not to be won with a sunspear. You must understand that. Every cherished memory of your father from childhood is what you must remember and what must guide you when you see him. You must speak from those memories to him. He must remember again who he truly is, not continue to see himself as what he has been deceived in thinking he has become now."

"Do you think that is all the Dark Lord will use on me?"

"No, it is different for each person, Dante. The tactics do not change, as said before, and he will probe until he finds an opening. For your father, he created and took a father's nightmare and grief and exploited it in the cruelest way. Many times, it's not an event so dramatic to twist to allow entrance. It begins small, and he causes one to doubt things which were once clear. There is no way your father would think he could be convinced his wife he loved killed his own child. Yet he did. He has ended the lives of many across countless worlds, and in his mind, he justifies it because of what he believes from the Dark Lord. I do not know what the Dark Lord will use on you. He will find something, and you cannot let him have entrance. That is why you must let the Ancient One guide you in this endeavor, unlike any other task before you. You must hear His voice, and remember what you have been taught from the beginning. It's the only way you will know how to free your father when you're in the midst of the battle. What are you thinking, Dante?"

"I'm thinking I have a lot to ponder, Seth. I believe the sunspear battling would be far less taxing than this."

"I do not doubt that, Dante. I believe you will need to use the sunspear as well, but it will be on the Dark Lord. He will not be happy when his tactics fail on you, and he loses his hold on your father. You will need training for that battle as well. That is more than enough for you to think upon today. Why don't we rejoin Caleb and Lana?"

Seth and Dante sat with Caleb and Lana for less than an hour when the advisor came into the room.

Dante said to the others as Lana sent the alert out, "I didn't care about lunch anyway." They all got up and headed out. The other commanders and their squadrons would be on their way to meet them at the planet under attack.

"Nice of everybody to join us today. Sorry to cut into lunch again. Someone needs to send a memo about adjusting these attacks." Caleb laughed. "Hope everyone is ready because here we go again."

CHAPTER FIFTEEN

Dante teased. "Hey Ryan, didn't we just do this?"

Ryan rolled his eyes. "Yes, and I'm sick of them doing this at lunch. You were right the other day." Ryan chuckled. "Let's get to it."

Dante and Ryan motioned for the soldiers to move forward. Dante's sunspear swung into action, and Ryan's sword did the same. Black Dragon soldiers quickly began falling to the ground as the two men pushed forward with the squadron. It was only a matter of time before the other would be coming into view.

Seth and Commander Gabe waited with their group, ready at the place the Black Dragon soldiers chose today. They watched as the Black Dragon soldiers approached the warehouse.

"There is a larger group today," said Seth turning to Commander Gabe.

"I see it too," said Commander Gabe, knowing he and Seth wondered the same thing.

Dante looked at Ryan and nodded. Right on time, the tanks came.

"It's been forever since I used one to blow up another, Ryan. They shouldn't expect it. I think I need to try," said Dante.

"I think you're right. Remember, careful."

"I know. I won't push it. Let's start off with that. I definitely will need it covered."

They headed for the first tank with the small group of soldiers.

Dante got to it with Ryan right behind him. Dante climbed on the tank while Ryan and the others watched the other tanks and cleared any soldiers around the tank attempting to hinder Dante. Dante made a hole in it with his sunspear and sent light crackers down the tank. He jumped inside and took care of the few soldiers he found. Dante stopped the tank and pointed the shaft toward the second tank. He let a blast off, and the second tank exploded into a fireball. Before he left the tank, he made one swipe with his sunspear across the control panel.

"Ryan, how is it looking?"

"You're clear, Dante."

Dante came out of the tank and climbed off. "Let's head to the next one."

⸺ꞒꞒ⸺

Seth and Commander spotted the Black Dragon soldier approaching the building and begin their normal routine. They watched the Black Dragon in charge of the operation today, sensing a difference in his command, in his mood. Seth and Commander Gabe exchanged looks again, both thinking the same. The point came for the swap, and the distraction started.

This time the Black Dragon in charge smiled. "The security team or perhaps the colonists again. This has happened a couple of times now. Everyone stop. Go no further with the boxes." The Black Dragon leader spoke into his earpiece. "Yes, we have a situation again. Have the small group come around and check on the source. Take care of it as instructed. We will remain here and finish this as planned. Let me know."

Commander Gabe mouthed Plan B to Seth. Seth nodded. Seth sent the information to the rest of the group.

The Black Dragon in charge said to the others, "Begin taking care of the boxes now. The others will handle the situation outside."

He didn't get to say more. Suddenly the room filled with blaster fire as a couple of his Black Dragon men fell beside him, and others struggled to deflect fire unsuccessfully. He roared, "We will cut every one of you down." He raised his sword and motioned for his soldiers to go further into the warehouse to carry out the threat. Seth and Commander Gabe and his soldiers came out from their places in the warehouse. They raised their swords, and Seth raised his staff, battling with the Black Dragon soldiers.

Seth eliminated another one of them when he found himself face to face with the Black Dragon soldier in charge.

Dante moved to the third tank. He disabled the tank from moving, and it slowed to a crawl. He finished spraying the adhesive to the side and quickly placed what he needed near the fuel source. Everyone in his camp knew what to do next. Fifteen seconds later, there was a second fireball.

"One more and done," said Ryan to Dante. They headed toward it. Five minutes later, Dante and Ryan wrapped a steel coil around the shaft of the tank and attached it to the charred remains of the third tank. It could go nowhere. The soldiers in the tank came out unable to move the tank or aim the shaft of the tank. They were met by the end of Dante's sunspear as they emerged. Dante quickly went inside, and a few swipes with the sunspear to the control panel later, and it was completely disabled.

Dante climbed out and said to Ryan. "The first tank."

Ryan understood. "Yeah, I get why you didn't want to hang out inside there long after the one time."

Dante went back to the first tank with Ryan watching. Dante went inside and, this time, gave it several swipes with the sunspear to make sure it was fully disabled. He climbed out and stood with Ryan.

"Looks like the squadron cleared out the rest of the Black Dragon soldiers as usual, so we're done for the day. You may be able to get back to lunch soon."

"Well, I'll be going back to your place for lunch now, Dante. Remember, we all still have to debrief. So, what's for lunch?" asked Ryan with a laugh.

◦◦◦

"You're mine. I'm going to put this sword straight through you. Your staff will not help you," said the Black Dragon soldier in charge.

"The Black Dragon Commander put you in charge of this operation, but you are like all the others. You will fall to my staff as your comrades did," said Seth quietly, watching the other's movements intently.

"I'm in charge because I'm better trained, and you will not live past today," snarled the Black Dragon in charge.

"No, I've watched you. You're not. I've trained many, and they could strike you down as easily as I will today. You will not terrorize another colony."

The Black Dragon soldier in command charged at Seth cutting off further conversation. He struck at Seth furiously, but Seth met each blow calmly. The Black Dragon leader plunged his blade at Seth another time, and he smiled as he dealt the blow to Seth. To his surprise, there was only air. He was no longer smiling because the sharp edge of Seth's staff found the opening as Seth dodged the Black Dragon soldier's sword. The soldier fell to the ground to join his comrades as Seth said he would at the end of the day. Seth surveyed the room. The others had cleared the rest of the Black Dragon men in the warehouse. Seth glanced at Commander Gabe.

"The diversion group heard the change of plans and did not leave when the Black Dragon soldiers approached them outside. That group took care of the Black Dragon soldiers outside as well." Commander Gabe said. "The Black Dragon left here with nothing today."

"Except the knowledge that we know what they were doing with the boxes, and it will no longer work." Seth sighed. "It could not be helped, though."

"You're right," said Commander Gabe. Then he peered over at Seth, smiling. "I don't believe the Black Dragon leader appreciated your comments. Was he truly no easier to beat than his comrades?"

"Perhaps, I should have given him slightly more credit, but no, I stand by my assessment of his training. All the students I train, or the one's work I've seen lately could eliminate him in the same time I did."

"We should get the boxes sorted back and returned now."

"Yes, let us do so."

—ℓℓ—

Lana sighed as she scanned through the information she could see from Seth's and Commander Gabe's operation. It appeared it had ended as they thought. She would see for sure when they arrived back.

They all began returning. Seth and Commander Gabe were the last to return as the previous time. There was silence from the others when the two finished their account of the events.

"They didn't leave with anything further, so we must be glad about that part," Ryan said, "They expended all those resources, and they didn't accomplish the entire purpose they came to the planet."

Lana nodded. "Ryan is right. Thank you, Seth and Commander Gabe, and to your squadron. It was good work."

Dante was clearly in thought. "We need to at least make our spear-bearer friends aware of what happened today. It's clear it won't change their minds, but the Dark Lord will be more alert of something tried after today's incident."

Seth nodded, and everyone else along with him. "You're right, Dante. I'm sure they did some monitoring unless they had already begun the operation. My guess is they know what happened, but yes, it's the least we can do. I need to stop and do it now."

Caleb peered over at Seth and Commander Gabe. "You both believe they're that close to doing the operation, don't you?"

Commander Gabe answered. "Yes, we're guessing, but I believe it's fairly accurate."

Seth pulled out the data pad and projected the screen on the wall. He placed the following message: *Were you able to monitor the activities today?*

Seth waited. After a moment, the answer came back: *Kind of. One of us did monitor the whole time. My friend and I ran an errand. We received a recap from the one when we returned.*

Seth wrote back: *So, you know what happened today?*

The answer came back: *Yes. It went as you expected. We all knew eventually such would be the outcome. We understand. It's okay.*

Seth wrote back: *We figured you knew, but we were reminded to make sure we let you know in case.*

The message back read: *We did know, but thank you for your concern. I don't have to guess who gave you the reminder. Tell Dante my friend and I will be fine. Tell him I'm glad he followed my advice today as well. He will know what I'm referring to. Please, none of you worry about us further. You won't hear from us for a time. We can have no more contact after this evening until we contact you. It will not be safe for us. We didn't want you to be alarmed. Goodbye and be safe. May the Ancient One continue to be with you.*

Seth glanced at Dante with a smile. "The young spear-bearer is apparently answering the messages again today and said you would understand the message to you, Dante."

"I do." grinned Dante.

"Is there something about the young spear-bearer we do not know yet?"

"They appear to have quite the sense of humor." Dante turned serious. "They haven't done the operation yet."

Caleb said, "But they told us they're going dark after tonight. Looks like Seth's and Commander Gabe's timetable pinpointed it."

Lana agreed. "It sounds like they go within the next couple of days, if not tomorrow." She put her arm around Dante's shoulder briefly. "Dante, there is nothing we can do to help them now. We have to wait until they contact us."

Seth watched as his data pad blinked, and the messages were gone as usual. "Yes, we must wait until they communicate again, Dante. They have a plan, no doubt. They said they ran some sort of errand today. No doubt it's connected with preparing for the operation. I can't imagine Alika would have them do something unrelated this close to it."

"You're right." He turned to Lana and tried to smile. "Okay, Lana, what do we need to do from today now?"

"You heard my cousin, let's get to it. First, though, I heard a request from someone about lunch. We'll get lunch and go from there."

Ryan laughed. "Hey, I wasn't the only one."

Caleb grinned. "You're right, Ryan. Don't let Lana get to you. She's giving you a hard time." Lana jabbed him lightly in the side at the comment. "See Ryan, how she does me." He wrapped his arm around his wife, reached over, and kissed her. Lana smiled at him and laughed.

Dante and Ryan sat and ate.

"You finally got lunch, Ryan."

"Yeah, and no mishaps for you today, Dante. I'm proud of you."

"You know the young spear-bearer found out about my near-miss with the tank from the last attack."

"How do you figure?"

Dante got his data pad out and pointed out the messages to Ryan. Ryan peered over at him, surprised. "I thought the policy was for Alika's crew to erase all correspondences."

"Normally, yes. Keep reading."

"You're sure?" asked Ryan. Dante nodded. Ryan read all the way down. "They let you keep them. How weird. It's not bad. I guess it makes sense with everything, with whatever this connection is between you and your family and Alika's student. No getting squished by tanks." Ryan laughed. "Dante, it's solid advice. I'm glad you followed it too."

Lana sat talking with Caleb. "I don't think there's much to discuss again. It appears the strategy will be the same next time. Seth and Commander Gabe will be the only ones who may need to discuss things further. They know the distraction will be unneeded now. It will be a straight-out confrontation from the beginning."

"They may need additional soldiers. The Dark Lord could send more to secure the supplies next time, but I think you're right. Once our friends get back, we hope for additional information which will be helpful to share. It's a waste of time trying to figure it out from the list of supplies."

"We'll let them know this evening, and they can head back tomorrow morning."

CHAPTER SIXTEEN

The Dark Lord and the Black Dragon Commander sat. They discussed the incident which occurred that day on the colony.

"We lost the whole group that went to retrieve the supplies and left with none of the supplies," said the Dark Lord.

"Yes, the attack was truly a complete waste of all resources," said the Black Dragon Commander.

"I wonder how they figured it out."

"We did it for a while now. Surely it was only a matter of time before they stumbled upon it."

"Perhaps you're right. I'm forced to give them some amount of intelligence. We should have seen this coming."

"The time before during the swap, an incident occurred at the time of the switch. There was no open confrontation at the boxes, so the incident was brushed off. Now that appears to have been unwise on our part."

"You are suggesting though the supplies were obtained, they may be compromised in some way."

"Yes, I believe so. The supplies need to be checked. I can send out the order while we speak. I would suggest starting with those from the latest planet of the attacks and going from there."

"Go ahead and send it out. I will give you time to do so, and afterward, we will continue."

The Black Dragon Commander sent the order out and turned back to the Dark Lord. "We also have the shipments coming in now, and we cannot afford any bad shipments to come and get mixed in with the good supplies. We don't know how big this problem has become."

"I agree. Alert the inspectors. Make sure they're aware of what happened, and everything coming in must go through a rigorous inspection. They are to open a random number of every shipment and test it before letting it go through. If it does not pass inspection, the one who brings it in is to be killed on the spot."

The Black Dragon Commander nodded and began the communication. It took some time, as he explained briefly, that there was a possible breach or issue with the supplies coming from the colonies, and there could be compromised supplies coming in as a result. He gave the order to begin the rigorous inspections and the punishment for those bringing in compromised supplies. Once the situation was made clear and the instructions were understood, the Black Dragon Commander turned back to the Dark Lord to resume their conversation.

"How do the lost supplies impact our plans?"

"In no way for what we discussed recently. It was almost completed with the supplies we obtained. Even if we find supplies compromised, we could complete it with no problem. We always knew we gathered the supplies for both things."

The Dark Lord laughed. "They believe they stopped us, but they only made us angry. It appears no more attacks are necessary. Although we do not need the supplies immediately, we will make one more attack to get supplies. They will remember this one."

"It sounds like you have specific orders for the way you wish it carried out."

"I do. Give me time to think about it, but an idea forms in my head. I will have it for you before the attack. They will pay for today, though."

The Dark Lord nodded to the Black Dragon Commander, signaling he could leave now. The Black Dragon Commander nodded back and walked out. He had more work to tend to after the incident on the colony.

The Dark Lord watched him go. He was unhappier than he admitted with the Black Dragon Commander about the past events. He only recently lost his prisoner Abigail and now this. They were totally separate operations, so the mishaps were probably unrelated. Duvessa was no closer to locating those two who rescued Abigail. Perhaps the Black Dragon Commander was right, and Dante and his group finally figured out what they were doing in the colonies. Either way, at the next attack, a surprise awaited them.

CHAPTER SEVENTEEN

"I don't believe there's anything left to do," said Alena.

"Yes, I agree everything is covered," said Alika.

"This will either work or not. We'll know soon enough if we live to see past tomorrow evening." The girl got up and stretched. "We just need to get some sleep now I suppose." She hugged both of them goodnight and headed to bed.

Alena got up and followed behind her. They had a big day tomorrow. Alika watched them both go and sighed. He hoped there was no repeat of Abigail's rescue. This operation must go smoother than that one.

The girl laid down and thought she would go straight to sleep. She couldn't as her mind wouldn't settle over the operation the next day. She told herself it would go better this time. It must. They were well-trained. The plan was sound. She had tested the supplies. They would pass inspection. Then the voice of doubt came. They were going to the Dark Lord's house again. The best-laid plans could collapse in a moment. They were outnumbered with no layout of the inside of what was in store for them. Again the two of them were going to take from the Dark Lord. It was Abigail's operation once more. It was craziness, but they had to go. There was no other way. It was just as she had said before when Alena mentioned Dante's worry about them going. Dante. She wondered what he was doing tonight. Hopefully, his concern had eased. Maybe he was spending time talking with Ryan. Ryan was a great friend to Dante and had a way of lifting his mood, kind of like Alena did her. Dante was probably making his nightly visit to his mother and had just finished. He had such a gentle heart. How she wished Abigail would awaken for him. She longed to see him happy but then realized she simply longed to see him. She hoped he wouldn't worry anymore for them, that he would get sleep tonight. His concern would prove unnecessary. It had to; they would be fine. She needed sleep, but her mind still refused to turn off for the night. It had to work tomorrow, but the echoes of the last operation kept coming back. What if it all fell apart like the last time? If they couldn't get it, or one of them couldn't get out? What if …?

Then she heard a whisper. "Why do you fear what tomorrow holds? I sent an eagle the last time. I will always be there, child." The girl smiled, finding herself sleepy suddenly as a calm settled over her, and the last image as she fell asleep was a diamond shimmering over the water.

—ele—

Morning came. Alika helped the girl and Alena get ready. The cargo was packed the night before with the essentials as well as fully supplied with any extra goodies needed in case they ran into trouble. They were always prepared in case of the unexpected happening, a lesson learned from enough operations.

Alika looked at both of them carefully and nodded with satisfaction. "I cannot recognize either one of you as my students. You both appear as Black Dragon soldiers from head to toe. I never think of that as a good thing to say, but for our purposes I know it is what you want. Let's hear you now."

They both said something. With the helmets totally covering them and the voice-changing device, they sounded like Black Dragon soldiers as well. "Excellent work. Now remove the helmets. I can't see the two of you off with those awful things on."

They did and laughed as they followed Alika's instructions. They walked out to the ship.

"We'll be back, I promise." The girl hugged Alika.

"I will hold you to your promise, child."

Alena hugged Alika. "That makes two of us, Alika." Alena stared at the girl. "Do you hear that? No repeats of last time."

The girl glanced at them and laughed. "I get it, you two."

"Wrap it up by dinner for you and Alena, would you?"

"We better head out if we're going to make that happen, Alika. Geez, the expectations around here." She laughed again, looking at Alika fondly. She turned serious and said softly. "Don't worry. We'll be back. You know I've always kept my promises to you." She gave him another hug and turned to Alena. "Ready."

"Ready," said Alena nodding at the girl and smiling back at Alika. "We'll be as safe as possible, considering, Alika."

"I understand, Alena. Take care of each other. May the Ancient One guide you in this."

He watched them as they turned around and walked into the ship, replacing the helmets back on their heads. Once they got on the ship, they checked each other to make sure they once again appeared as Black Dragon soldiers. They did. It was time.

They got to the portal. They stared at it for a moment. Once they went through the portal, they were all in. Last time they stayed on the outskirts. This time they were going into whatever the structure held. Alena and the girl took a deep breath. Alena disguised the ship as a Black Dragon vessel, and they passed through the portal.

"Here we go, and the line starts here," said the girl.

"A lot of ships in line today before lunch," said Alena.

"We've established the Black Dragon frequently work through lunch."

"You're right. How could I forget?"

"It appeared massive the first time, but I don't know. With the number of supplies they have accumulated over time ..." the girl's voice trailed off.

"You expected something bigger. Remember, we don't know what they're doing or how far they have left to go."

"Yeah, which is why we're here. Hopefully, it becomes apparent."

The girl watched. The part in the middle interested her. It was a strange configuration, almost like connected towers. She wondered what the string of structures were. A thought entered her mind of how much better she would feel to send a whole series of explosions right through it and flatten it. She knew they didn't have any capability to do so today, and that wasn't their purpose. A combined fleet could do damage to it. They would have to get through all the rest of the Black Dragon ships first. The girl sighed.

"We haven't gotten in, and you already sound despondent. Not like you at all."

"I wasn't thinking about this operation."

"I thought you weren't going to think about him while we were on an operation." Alena teased.

"Actually, I wasn't thinking about him. Now it's your fault I am." The girl shook her head, laughing.

"Likely story. So, what were you thinking about over there?"

"You won't believe me, but I thought how I would like to demolish the whole section in the middle they are busy doing. I'm curious what it is. It would take a fleet which we currently don't have with us, and we wouldn't be able to get past all the enemy ships anyway."

"Actually, I do believe you, and you're right, although it's fun teasing you about him. This line is not going any faster, and I scanned everything more times than I can count. I would see this layout in my sleep now."

"Yes, me too, and it's still a mystery."

It was almost thirty more minutes. Alena turned to the girl. "It's showtime. They're asking for it."

The girl sent it. She and Alena weren't worried about this part. They had hacked enough access recently from the data pads of the Black Dragon soldiers to get past here. The real work would begin once they made it inside and had to push the supplies past the inspection. A moment later, the Black Dragon in charge of clearance spoke, "Black Dragon ship #51443, you are cleared for landing in slot H4. Please continue to stay in line. Report to the inspector on duty as normal, and he will give you further instructions with the cargo."

Their ship entered the hangar of the structure ahead and landed with everything they needed on them. They had their sunspears safely concealed on their persons, along with other hidden surprises, none being standard Black Dragon gear. The two walked out of the ship, the military-style boots of their Black

Dragon uniform joining the rest of those in the hangar. So far, it worked, and they blended in perfectly. They walked up to the inspector and repeated the confirmation they gave upon entry. He checked his data pad and scanned the confirmation they showed him. He was satisfied.

"You have quite the list of supplies today. Bring them to me. I'll wait here for you to return. Hurry. This could take time to check-in," said the Black Dragon inspector.

The two nodded and walked back to the ship. They had the supplies ready on the ship, loaded on two carts. They wheeled them out, bringing them immediately to the inspector.

"Prompt and efficient. If all came to me as such, this would go much faster." He got his data pad out and finished scanning all twenty of the boxes. "Now, this part will take time. I will need to open some boxes. There are issues with items coming from the colonies recently. We need to ensure there has not been any mix-up in the chaos. Did any of these boxes leave your hands or sight anywhere in transport?"

Alena and the girl both shook their head and said in unison, "No, sir."

"Excellent news. The Black Dragon Commander is not happy about the current situation, which means the Dark Lord is not either. I hope your boxes check out. Neither one is in a forgiving mood."

Alena and the girl nodded as the inspector began opening the first box.

The inspector pulled the first item from the box. He inspected it closely, moving it from one hand to the other, and scanned it with the data pad as well. He was through as the girl was on Christopher's ship. Putting the item back in the box, he closed it and set it aside in a separate pile from the rest of the items. Not a word escaped his mouth.

The girl knew Alena was thinking the same thing. They had no idea if it was his way of simply designating which items he checked or if he slowly wrote their death certificate with each item. Either way, they both stood waiting, showing none of the anxiety they both felt.

The inspector pulled a few more boxes from the warehouse items and inspected them with the same level of care. He paused and sat. He stared down at this data pad, clearly in thought. Then he went to more of the stacked boxes he had not inspected yet. It was clear he searched for something. He picked out five boxes from the pile and began the same process as he had with the others. He opened them. The first one was a chemical.

The girl was glad they had the Black Dragon masks on now. It should block out most effects from the artificial chemicals. She had enough of testing them the one day.

The inspector pulled back as he got a whiff of the chemical. It didn't produce the same dramatic effect as on a human, but the Black Dragon soldiers were built to register basic sensations. So, the desired effect was achieved. That being the chemical passed the most basic test, the smell test. He scanned it, dipped a thin strip into the chemical, and watched the strip turn a certain color. Throwing the strip away, he resealed everything and moved to the next box he pulled from the pile. It was another chemical, as were the rest in the stack. The inspector went through the rest of the boxes he pulled in the same way in complete silence. Finally, he completed his inspection. He came over and set the data pad down on the table in front of them.

Alena and the girl waited. The inspector faced them. "You two impressed me with how efficient and quick you brought the supplies, but now after seeing them," the inspector slowly walked around while he talked, and he was now behind both Alena and the girl, "it's nice work from you two. You should be quite proud of yourself." Alena and the girl heard him getting it out. They both knew what he held in his hand, a sword to end both of them right there. They looked at each other and slowly turned around.

CHAPTER EIGHTEEN

The inspector continued, "I'm glad to see these items did not get involved in the unfortunate situation occurring in the colonies. The Black Dragon Commander and the Dark Lord will be pleased." He used a device he retrieved to reseal the boxes and secure them more to his liking.

Now that Alena and the girl could breathe again, as they realized they were not about to be cut in two, they quickly switched gears. The inspector's data pad sat right there. They needed to connect to it to get further into the building easily. They thought they might need to come up with a distraction to get it for a moment, but it didn't appear that would be the case now.

Alena said to the inspector, "Would you like us to assist you with stacking these back on the cart?"

"Yes, once I seal them further, you may do so since they passed inspection."

While Alena assisted the inspector and their back was turned, the girl started to move toward the other boxes. Before doing so, she quickly scanned the inspector's data pad with her own. Alika could start sorting through it now. When the inspector turned around, he saw the girl stacking boxes on carts.

"I simply need to signify these passed through inspection." He returned to the table and picked up the data pad. Within a few moments, each box received a seal, showing it had passed inspection. He glanced down on the data pad and back up at them. "Take all the supplies to Large Room One. They are expecting them."

"Yes, sir," said Alena and the girl in unison. The two headed toward Large Room One with the supplies. It was easier to get around now. Thanks to the inspector's data pad, they found they were afforded additional clearances. Their badges now opened the doors in the building without issue. They would get the supplies delivered first and see where to explore next. There could be a reason the room was called Large Room One.

"It was a box sealer device. Exactly what I thought the whole time." said the girl.

"Yeah, sure you did. For the record, I'm glad we were both wrong." Alena shook her head.

"You're right. The sealer I imagined he had would have enclosed us in a box in pieces once it had done its work. Let's get these supplies where they go."

Alena and the girl stood at the entrance of Large Room One. It appeared to be the only room on the whole hall, and it was heavily guarded. The guards saw their carts and the seal on them. One of the guards asked for their confirmation from the inspector to be sure. They showed it to him, and he opened the door to the room and motioned them inside. He pointed to the checkpoint below them.

Inside it was huge and busy. Everywhere guards were working. Alena and the girl made their way slowly, with the supplies taking in the scene. They could see what appeared to be the manufacturing of a handheld device of some type, but they were different from anything either had seen before.

Alena and the girl made it down to the checkpoint with the supplies. Again, a guard asked for the confirmation, and they supplied it. The guard scanned the boxes and took the shipments from Alena and the girl. He nodded to them, signaling his business was done with them, and they were free to go to the next task. Alena and the girl nodded, seeing he clearly had no idea what the next task was. They walked around trying to appear busy like the others. It wasn't hard, with as many in the room working at the moment, but it wasn't a room where they could download information unnoticed. However, they would be able to get a closer look at the handheld device being made in this room. They also had cameras on their person as usual, so Alika was seeing everything as they did now. Then they could all review the footage later.

Heading toward the beginning of the assembly of the strange handheld devices, they pretended to work with one like others around them. The center part was like nothing they had seen before. It was somewhat barrel-shaped, like a gun, but with the weaponry of a blaster. Yet it was like neither one. There was no clear answer as to what powered it. They continued to watch the assembly, and they worked with their piece. The girl held one of the pieces and stared at Alena. Alena took it from her hands and inspected it. It was disk-shaped. Alena's expression mirrored the girl's puzzlement as she put the item down. The disk-shaped part felt different from the rest of the weapon as if created of another material entirely. They went further down the assembly process and inspected one of the weapons. There was the disk piece toward the center of the weapon.

The two moved closer to the giant centerpiece of the room without appearing to do so. The structure was made from a shiny, metallic material, similar to the small containers used in a lab. It was not until they got closer that they saw the flexible metallic coils or hoses that came out at the bottom from all around it and went to stations all over the room where the devices were created. They stooped down to one of the hoses and tried unsuccessfully to see what was going through it.

Suddenly a shadow loomed over them. "Is there a problem?" A Black Dragon soldier questioned them with the air of one who wanted to be in charge of the room.

"No, we initially thought the hose was loose, but it's fine," said the girl standing up along with Alena.

"Are you sure? We don't want any of the substance leaking out."

"No, that would be unfortunate to the operation," said the girl. "If you would care to double-check it, do so. We don't want the Black Dragon Commander unhappy."

"You're right," answered the Black Dragon soldier, who reached down and inspected it for himself. "It's secure."

Alena and the girl nodded, and the Black Dragon soldier did the same before leaving them.

The girl and Alena moved away from the object and pretended to work on the data pad. They watched around them as they spoke in hushed voices.

"I thought this would be a suitable place for a couple of our goodies, but I'm reconsidering now," said the girl.

"Yes, I think we have guesses of what could be in those hoses," said Alena.

"An explosion could release it everywhere. Currently, it's contained."

"You're right. We can't set anything off in this room. We're also close to wearing out our welcome in this room."

"I agree. Anymore poking around, and we'll get in trouble. There's nothing else to see here."

They went down the hall. Once they got away from Large Room One, the activity died down to a lull along with the traffic. They waited to see where Alika wanted them to go next. By now, he had enough time to see the layout of the building.

Alika said, "There are two rooms, one is above you, and the other is back on the same floor as the hangar. Go to the one above you first. There is construction of some sort going on there too. It is room three. Then head to the other room back on the hangar. It is room eight. It usually only has a couple of people in it, but it's often abandoned as well. However, it has a control portal inside where you can access the information we need."

The two started toward the room above them as instructed and walked in. It was busy and large, but after the last room, it felt subdued. They walked around and picked up items, appearing to be busy again. It was apparent that there was some building of items that took place there. There were no signs of any chemicals or other substances. The two glanced at each other. They intended to put a dent in the progress.

The girl carefully got one of the small devices out from her bag, and Alena discreetly handed her the tiny adhesive spray. She quickly sprayed a bit on the bottom of the device, and it came out without a sound. She stuck the device upside down on the bottom of the assembly line surface and handed the spray back to Alena. They walked further down toward the middle of the assembly line, pretending to busy themselves with another item, and placed another device there. Finally, they placed another device toward the end of the assembly line. They nodded and walked out of the room.

They got back to the same floor as the ship and found themselves at room eight. Alika proved correct. There was only one Black Dragon soldier in the room. Immediately as they walked in, he turned. "Can I help you?"

"We're here for a bit to check on one of the systems," said the girl.

"I don't remember getting anything about that."

"Everything is busy now. I'm sure that's why," said Alena.

"I'm sure you're correct."

The girl couldn't believe their luck. She had thought they might have to produce something official or come up with a better story. Instead, they found the one Black Dragon soldier who had a bit of lazy in his programming, or this station was the pits. It was worth a try, and she plunged forward. "We can do this for a while if you need to attend to something else."

The Black Dragon soldier hesitated for only a moment. "I've been stuck here for a while, and I do have items to tend to in Large Room One. I'll go there now if you two are here for a while."

"Yes, take all the time you need. This system check could take considerable time. We'll stay till you return," said Alena.

The Black Dragon soldier nodded and went out the door.

"Wow, this must be the bottom of the barrel of jobs," said Alena.

"You're telling me. I've never taken such little effort to clear a room in my life." The girl started searching in the system.

Halfway to Large Room One, the Black Dragon soldier remembered he needed to do something for his commander in charge for the day. The commander in charge would find him soon. It would be fine. His comrades would direct his commander to Large Room One to locate him.

The girl said, "Time to hook this up to the portal." She pulled a small device out of her pocket and connected it to the portal. The information started going to the small device and straight to Alika in real-time. The girl and Alena scoured through the system. There were tons of lists of supplies which were mostly unhelpful because they already knew the type of things taken. Then they started getting somewhere.

"It's what we saw in the large room when we got here," said Alena, surveying the pictures.

"It is. It appears a little different, but it's pretty close, I suppose ..." She stared at it puzzled but brushed it aside. There was no time now. "There are the hoses like we saw." The girl picked through more diagrams and scanned the information quickly, knowing Alena read with her.

Then the girl stopped. Her hand drew away from the control panel as if it would somehow undo the image on the screen. Yet the display remained frozen as if mocking them, reveling in the threat it had brought into being. Both of their faces held the same expression of horror as they turned from the screen and stared at each other.

CHAPTER NINETEEN

"It's a dispersal device," said the girl softly.

"All this time and that's what they built," said Alena, stunned as her mind went to a million terrible places as well.

"When? Anywhere... is it here?" The girl forced her hand to begin moving again on the control panel. The image of the device stayed on the screen, but to the side of it, information began to scroll as the girl's gloved fingers continued to move over the panel.

"I didn't see, and I still ..."

Suddenly the door opened to reveal a Black Dragon soldier who quickly surveyed the scene. He saw the screen pulled up. "I came for soldier #789, but I'm much more interested now in what the two of you are doing."

Alena and the girl knew there were stories they could spin, but this soldier possessed the air of one in charge. It was also clear even to the most incompetent Black Dragon soldier a download was in progress, and the device remained in the port. To make matters worse, the Black Dragon soldier began advancing on them quickly. The only part in question was how quietly could they eliminate this Black Dragon soldier?

"We're analyzing the system. What does it look like?" said the girl sarcastically as she pulled out her sunspear, and so did Alena.

"Neither one of you will live to analyze it further." The Black Dragon soldier drew his sword.

It was two against one, though, and the two were masterful with the sunspears. He sparred with them for a minute, but he could not dodge the blow when it came. Yet, he sneered at them before he fell and said, "It doesn't matter. You will not make it out of here."

Alena knelt over the soldier staring at his data pad glowing red and looked up at the girl. "We're about to have company and lots of it. He made sure before we took care of him."

They heard commotion far in the hallway. Alena stood, reached over to the port, snatched the device out, and put it safely in her bag. "We must go now."

The girl turned back to the port, torn. "We only need a few more minutes, and maybe we could have the rest."

Alena grabbed the girl's arm and met her eyes. "Alika has what we could get, and what we retrieved is valuable. The little more we would get is not worth our lives." Alena pulled her blaster out and shot the screen of the control panel, ending the discussion. "I said we're leaving."

"You're right. I know you are. Let's go."

They ran out and sensed the soldiers approach from both sides. The only positive part was they were in the same hall as the ship. They got their sunspears back out as well but kept their blasters out too. It was the only way to deflect the blaster fire and get shots off. The girl didn't see how both of them would get out, but maybe there was a way.

The girl turned to Alena. "You go ahead. I'll hold them off."

Alena didn't let her say more. She grabbed the girl's arm again in a vice grip and held her eyes. "No, you're not doing that again to me. I'm not leaving you behind. We're both getting out of here. You promised me. Do you understand me?"

The girl gazed back at Alena. It had been a long time since Alena drew the line in such a way, but she understood. She said softly to Alena, "I get it. Both of us. Let's do this."

The blaster fire came from both sides, and it got closer. They were trapped.

Alena let go of her and nodded. "I'll take care of the ones coming behind, and you handle the ones in front. We need a path." Alena set to work.

The girl checked ahead. "There are a lot more ahead of us than I realized." She deflected the blaster shots as she cut down the soldiers.

"Stop with the survey. I've seen you with the sunspear. I helped train you, remember? You'll do a training session until you're too tired to swing your sunspear when we get back if I hear any further excuses from you. Now, a path, please."

The girl somehow kept from laughing despite the terrible situation they now found themselves in. "Let me make my teacher proud."

"Please do." Alena smiled as she swung the sunspear and fired with the blaster.

The girl swung the sunspear with new determination, and the Black Dragon soldiers met their end at its edge. Behind her, Alena continued fighting. The girl could not see Alena as their backs were turned, but she heard her saying softly, "a bit further." The girl knew what Alena was up to behind her. The corridor had a door in between it. Alena must be almost past it. A moment later, Alena crossed it and sent a shot to the controls with her blaster. The door shut, cutting off those soldiers from the hall and forcing them to find a way around. Alena turned around and ran up to the girl. "Now, let's both work on this path and get out of here."

They soon forged the path ahead to the end of the hall and opened the door to the ship hangar.

They stopped in their tracks. They had company.

CHAPTER TWENTY

"I think I'll take the all-day training session gladly right about now," said the girl quietly.

"I would conduct it happily for you," said Alena, softly surveying the scene.

A whole squadron stood in front of them, and above them, soldiers surrounded them.

The squadron leader stepped forward. "You are the two who have caused such havoc today, but this is where it ends for both of you."

"I don't think so," said Alena. "We're not out yet."

"Yeah, we went through a lot of trouble for today to have it end now," said the girl.

"Your spirit will help you none. You are surrounded. Every soldiers' blaster is pointed at the two of you. You have two options. The first is for me to kill you right here in the hangar. The second option is to take you both prisoner, torture you until you tell us why you are here today, and then kill you. I'm mildly interested in knowing why you came all this way today to die. But only mildly."

Alena and the girl knew they thought the same thing. The longer this went on, the more soldiers would fill the room, and their chances of escaping diminished further. It appeared hopeless now, but it would continue to get worse. They both saw the hangar door at the far end where their ship could still leave, and it was currently open. That could change in the blink of an eye, and they would be trapped. They needed to buy time until they could find a way out of their current situation. Yet, the more time they took, the worse the other two things got for them. It was just bad.

"We don't want to die in the hangar and not too crazy about torture," said Alena.

"Surely you must have a third option for us," said the girl.

"That's my offer for you two."

"How unfortunate. You have all these soldiers with you. On the other hand, we are at quite a disadvantage," said Alena.

"Yes, we neglected to bring our squadron along with us today," said the girl. "A little help would be great."

Immediately, they both heard a voice through their headpiece. "Ask, and you will receive. Explosion behind. Blasts in the middle."

The two exchanged a glance with each other. It was time to get ready, and they knew where to head once it began. They turned back to the squadron leader and made a motion to lower their sunspears in a surrender motion.

"It appears you two decided not to go out in a blaze of glory after all. I wondered. It's a shame with all your abilities and you waste ..."

He never finished his sentence. An explosion came from somewhere in the hall above them. Almost in the same instant, two huge blasts shot from somewhere in the hangar right through the center of the squadron. The blasts originated from the ship's guns, but the Black Dragon soldiers did not realize it.

As soon as the attention was diverted by the explosion from the upper hall, Alena and the girl ran with lightning speed around the side where no soldiers stood and headed for their ship.

Meanwhile, the Black Dragon soldiers scrambled to figure out what happened. They had lost their two prisoners. Adding to their difficulty was their prisoners were in Black Dragon uniforms like everyone else, so the Black Dragon soldiers searched for the two with sunspears in their hands. The Black Dragon soldiers in the middle, who were not dismantled by the shots, slowly got up and attempted to get reoriented.

Before reaching the ship, the two were spotted by a few soldiers attempting to intercept them. The Black Dragon soldiers got to them too late though, and a few swipes with the sunspear ended the dismal effort to recapture the two. Alena headed into the ship first with the girl at her heels. The girl sensed something as they entered the ship as one of the Black Dragon men followed them unnoticed. He shot his blaster off, and it headed for Alena. Alena didn't see it, but the girl did. She tried to put her sunspear in front of it, but she didn't see it in time to get the angle on it she needed. It missed Alena, but it hit the girl in the arm. She fell back right inside the ship from the impact. Alena turned, hearing the girl stumble. The Black Dragon soldier thought he had them and began making his way further into the ship. Alena started toward him, but the girl was already back up and advanced toward him.

The girl's eyes blazed with anger. "He's going to pay for that shot." With her bad arm, she sent a blaster shot through him, and with her uninjured arm, she sliced him straight across with her sunspear. He went toppling down to the floor of the hangar as the girl closed the door of the ship. "Let's go."

"Alika already charged it up. We're on our way," said Alena as she steered the ship.

They were taking fire and stared ahead in dismay.

"Alika, we have a problem. The doors are shutting. We're not going to make it at this rate," the girl said as she shook her head in rising frustration. "We're so close. No, this can't be how we get trapped. We keep going."

They got closer to the doors, but they continued to shut.

Suddenly the doors stopped closing as if they were stuck. Alika's voice came through, "I've gotten into the system and have control for the moment. I'm only the student in this area, so hurry."

It was enough for the ship to squeeze through the hangar.

"Your teacher is impressed, Alika," said the girl as she got ready to start firing the ship's guns.

***

Meanwhile, the Black Dragon squadron leader was furious. He thought they had the two spear-bearers. He watched the door closing, and then it stopped. "What is going on? Why is it stopping?"

"Sir, we don't know. There's a problem. We're trying to get control of it," said the soldier.

"They got away. I want every ship in pursuit of them!"

"Yes, sir. It's already happening."

"Why is the door shutting now? I said after them. Open the door back so our ships can leave, you fool!"

"They're opening now, sir. We gained control of them again."

⚬⚬⚬

"How long till the portal, Alena?" yelled the girl over the blaster fire.

"Several minutes," said Alena as she steered the ship for the portal and dodged blaster fire at the same time.

"Not good. A whole fleet is literally after us, and not all are bad shots." The girl continued to shoot furiously with the ship's guns.

The two tried, but the fleet steadily closed the gap, and the ship took hits. "How much more time?" asked the girl again.

"We're still minutes away, and we lost speed because of the damage we sustained."

"We can't go through the portal to where we planned. Not like this. We'll be dead as soon as we get to the other side with the condition of the ship, and once there, we'll be defenseless. We need somewhere with a fleet which is friendly to us. Not Dante's, especially not with Abigail there... Ryan's planet. Alika!"

"I'm on it. Head for Ryan's," answered Alika.

The girl blasted as she talked—a minute later, nothing. "No, no, this is not happening. We lost our weapons."

CHAPTER TWENTY-ONE

Seth and Dante sat at the table talking after finishing lunch about an hour earlier. Caleb and Lana sat at a nearby table discussing something as well.

Suddenly Seth's data pad flashed red and vibrated violently. Seth grabbed it instantly. There were few times he saw it work in such a manner. He checked it. The person on the other end did not wait to hear him respond.

"Seth, it's Alika."

"Alika ..."

"No time. My students are in serious trouble. They are headed for Ryan's planet, and they could have company with them. The ship is considerably damaged."

Dante had already pulled out his data pad. "I'm on it." The next moment he said, "Ryan, it's Dante. We're receiving a communication from Alika. His students are headed your way, and their ship is in bad shape. Sounds like they have ships on their tail too of the unfriendly kind."

Lana and Caleb rushed over and listened now.

"Got it, Dante. The fleet is in the air, and I'm joining them."

Dante heard Ryan giving the fleet orders. "Attention, this is Commander Ryan. We have a ship trying to come through the portal, and it may be heavily damaged. It may appear to be a Black Dragon ship, but it has friends inside. Also, they may be followed by enemy ships. Do not fire on anything coming out of the portal unless told to do so. I will give the command if any firing goes on. Is that understood?"

They could hear Alika communicating with his students. They could not hear his students' part of the conversation, but Alika's end of the conversation did not inspire any hope as they continued to listen.

Alika sighed. "It must have gotten hit. No weapons."

The girl sat there, her mind racing. She must get space between the fleet bearing down on them and their ship. They had no weapons, but they needed some way to disable the ships getting closest to them, an explosion ... but without weapons ... then she had it. She checked. "It's down too. I'm forced to do this manually." The girl got out what resembled four flat saucer devices. She pulled out four detonators and sprayed them with an adhesive substance, sticking one on each saucer.

Alena glanced back at her for a moment. "What are you up to?"

"Concentrate on the portal, Alena."

The girl took two of the saucers in her hand, climbed up to a small area of the ship, and opened a hatch.

"Why are you going outside the hatch door with detonators in your hands?"

"The portal, Alena. I got this, I promise." She put the two transporter devices with the detonators on the hatch platform and sent them outside. With the remote device in her hand, she sent them straight toward the two ships closest to them. It exploded right on the two ships disabling them. The girl got down and started working on two more to send out.

Alika heard Alena and felt alarm growing. "Going outside the ship with a detonator? What are you doing, young spear-bearer?"

Dante listened with the others in horror, and he peered at Seth with an expression that said something had to be done to stop them. Seth could only stare back at him, helpless as Alika was to stop his young spear-bearer.

Alika sighed. "I got this. Yes, how many times have I heard that one from you?"

"Not again, please. You're going to lose something you need in a moment with all the blaster going on out there."

"It disabled the two closest ships the last time. If you have a better idea, I'm listening, Alena." The girl climbed up to the hatch to send out the next two. "Get us to the portal."

The girl sent the next two out, but it proved harder this time. The blasts got better or closer or both. She could hear the hiss as they went past and the heat as they went close by her hand. She got it off, but as she got the fourth one off, she felt a shot whiz right off her hand. It burnt, and she let out a yelp of pain at the sting.

"Your hand, I told you not to do it again."

"Not the time, Alena. It's still attached to my wrist. It'll be fine."

Alika said, "I will be attaching body parts back before this is over."

Dante glanced at the others feeling worse after Alika's last comment.

"Well?" asked the girl.

"Your stunt did help considerably, but we're still almost two minutes away. We need to go faster, but I don't see how we make it."

"So close. They must make it," said Alika quietly.

The girl's eyes darted desperately. It could not end like this. They had fought all day too hard. They needed the extra push, the extra minute difference. For an instant, it was as if the button for the propulsion and navigation systems glowed, beckoned to her. She heard a voice whisper, "Put everything there." She knew to trust that voice.

"Everything, huh," the girl whispered. They only needed a minute. "Okay, Alena, it's time to give you the extra speed you need to get to the portal. I'm moving everything to the propulsion and navigation system."

"We're diverted a few things already."

"But now we're all in, everything," said the girl. The lights dimmed, so only the control panel was seen. "Alika, communications will be gone, and the air is about to get thin in here for a minute, Alena." The girl punched several more buttons on the console, and the ship went down to a quiet hum.

Alika said quietly, "Oh my."

Seth asked, "Alika, what is going on?"

"I don't know. They were a couple of minutes from the portal and unsure of making it. My young spear-bearer diverted all power to propulsion and navigation. I was told to expect no communication, and the air was to get thin in the ship."

Dante gasped. "Life support systems, no."

"Hopefully, my students emerge through the portal soon, Dante."

The Black Dragon squadron leader watched and smiled. "Oh, we have them now. Finish this."

Alena and the girl stared ahead, waiting for the portal. Suddenly they felt blasts near the ship. Alena and the girl stared at each other, thinking the same thing. They came so close, but it ended here. Thirty seconds from reaching the portal, they were blown into a thousand pieces. Both knew it could end this way. They had hoped not, but they had said they would make the exchange today, that it was too important not to do so. They surrendered to their fate now, ready to be received by the Ancient One. It would be up to the others to take Alika's knowledge and try to stop the imminent threat. The girl could not help but feel the sadness come over her that she would not meet Dante after all. And she had not kept her promise to Alika.

Alika felt sick and whispered, "It can't be."

"Alika?" Seth asked.

Alika choked back tears. "Several blasts ..." he could not hold back a sob, "struck at my students' ship."

Dante sat stunned, as did the others. He put his head in his hands, and tears streamed down his face. It could not be. They could not be gone.

CHAPTER TWENTY-TWO

Alena and the girl realized it at the same time. The blasts originated from their ship.

The Black Dragon squadron leader could not hold back his fury. "You said they had no weapons. Why is our ship now damaged because of blaster fire from their ship?"

The girl and Alena gazed at each other. The blasts that did not fire before now came online with a sudden fury, and they let loose on the Black Dragon squadron. It was only about ten stored up blasts, but they were well-targeted and perfectly timed.

The Black Dragon squadron leader could only watch, infuriated as the ship escaped through a portal seconds later.

Ryan spoke up suddenly, "Hey, their ship came ... through." The last word came out as one in disbelief at what was before him.

Dante's head sprang up, his face still streaked with tears. Yet a ray of hope sparked in him. "Ryan?"

"It's bad, Dante. Any word?"

"I'm trying now, but there is nothing yet," said Alika.

The girl and Alena held on despite the conditions on the ship. The girl positioned her hand, ready to push the button to redirect power to life support, but not until she saw Ryan's planet in front of her. Once she did, she pushed the button. She reached over to Alena to check on her, and Alena nodded weakly to her.

They sat there for several seconds, waiting for the ship to return to normal, but it wasn't getting better. Smoke filled the ship from something which finally gave way from the damage. Finding themselves coughing and their eyes stinging from the smoke, they knew they must get enough of the smoke cleared from inside before it overcame them. They also needed to get communication back up. Alika surely was in a full-scale panic by now. Now, though, the smoke in the ship commanded their full attention. The girl went over to Alena and pointed to something. Alena understood because neither one could still speak because they coughed so severely. The girl struggled as she coughed, with eyes stinging, but climbed up to the hatch and opened the door. Alena stood behind her, steadying her between her own coughing. The girl climbed down, and she and Alena slumped down in the chairs, exhausted. After a couple of minutes, the smoke cleared enough, so they managed a word out every few seconds without going into a coughing fit. The girl pushed a button on the control panel.

"Are you both all right? One of you say something, please." Alika listened for a moment. "That doesn't sound convincing."

"I finally heard a weak yes from one of them. They are coughing a great deal from a lot of smoke in the ship. They're trying to clear it out," said Alika to the others.

There was a collective silent cheer from everyone at the news. It was strange to be happy at Alika's announcement, but considering the thoughts only seconds before about the fate of his two students, it was understandable.

Ryan said, "Alika, the ship is leaking several things outside as well, so it doesn't surprise me."

Dante said softly, "At least we finally know they're alive, which is more than what we thought moments ago."

"Yes, we all thought the worst," said Seth.

"I wished this to go smoother than the last time, but it did not. This has been another long day." sighed Alika.

Several minutes later, they heard Alika speaking with his students again. This time the conversation sounded better. They still only heard Alika's end of it, but they figured out the responses of his students easily.

"You two sound much better now. Why did you not use the hatch opening before to clear the smoke out? Yes, that makes sense now. I suppose it proved difficult to locate things on the ship at first. Are you both all right?"

Alika paused for a bit, evidently getting a rather long answer to the question. "Did you take care of it, young spear-bearer? Only a scratch. Yes, somehow, I'm doubtful. You did not intend to tell me. Your counterpart had to do so. Another injury at the end. How bad is your arm? Yes, it sounds like he paid for the shot to you. I believe Dante and the others would have gladly dealt with one additional Black Dragon soldier rather than you absorb such a shot." Alika sighed. "Can you please take time and treat both of them now? Yes, I sense you will make it a high priority." Alika's tone reflected someone who finally gave up on the discussion.

Seth spoke, "Alika, I'm sure Ryan would be glad to offer medical assistance if needed."

"Oh, I know he would, Seth," Alika answered, "but my young spear-bearer is stubborn as we established on a previous occasion. I will admit only a temporary defeat on this battle with my student. I will see to it soon."

Alika went back to his students. "What is our next step?" He paused to hear his students' responses. "Yes, Commander Ryan agrees the ship will need considerable work after this trip, and I see the list of supplies you graciously sent me now, my young spear-bearer. It's quite long." He laughed. "I'm now reduced to your delivery service. Yes, I'm working on it as we speak. And quickly. I don't know that I can beat that time." He laughed again. "You forgot one of the first lessons of your training. Use other items when you do not possess what you need to make the repairs. You don't need to since I'm bringing you the correct supplies. My young spear-bearer, remember I remain your teacher. I foresee a long training day in your near future."

Dante and Seth listened and smiled at each other. Although they could not hear the young spear-bearer's part of the conversation, it sounded familiar. They imagined the two of them in a similar discussion back and forth.

Alika listened again, and this time his voice softened. "Yes, you kept your promise to me again, and I'm grateful. Yes, by dinner, my young spear-bearer. I'm glad you're both safe, and I'll see you both shortly."

Alika spoke to the group first, "They indicate to me they're ready to land the ship now." He paused. "Ryan, they may need help. Oh, and they both apologize for the detour to your planet. It was unneeded, but at the time, they thought they brought company through the portal with them."

"Alika, it's all right. I'm glad they're okay. That's the last thing they should think about now. What can we do to help?"

"They're unsure of how far the damage extends, so they're concerned about being able to safely land the ship. They want to land on the outermost empty hangar, and they request an escort around them in case the ship needs assistance during the landing process."

"Understood, Alika. We'll get the ship down safely."

"Thank you. I'll wait until it's done before I go further with my plans."

A few minutes later, the ship safely landed on Ryan's planet.

"Thank you, Ryan. They indicated it went smoothly with your assistance."

"Is there anything else? Alika, I'm the one looking at the ship, and it will need a lot of work, to put it mildly. I'll be glad to help with the repairs. Let us know what you need."

"I know you would as well as any of those listening, but my students will wish to take care of the repairs. I continued to gather the supplies for the repairs as we talked. My ship is a much smaller vessel, so please be sure no one shoots at it since it's unfamiliar to you." Alika chuckled.

"I promise you'll arrive to my planet's surface safely, Alika. The hangar next to your students' ship is set aside for you."

"Excellent, Ryan. I'm sorry to the rest of you for how the day transpired. I did not have a chance to greet you properly. Are Lana and Caleb there?"

"Yes, we're both here, Alika. We're thankful your students made it through today. We were so afraid earlier," Lana said.

"Yes, Alika. My wife speaks for both of us. It's good to hear from you. Even better to know you have heard your students' voices, and they're safe," said Caleb.

"Good to hear both of your voices as well. I wish it were not always in these circumstances, but it is the pattern. And, Seth, thank you for answering my alarm so quickly. I do wish our talks did not always begin as they do."

"I agree, but your students are safe, and that is what matters."

"Yes, they are. They can look forward to many more days of training." Alika laughed. "Speaking of students, how are you, young Dante?"

"I'm well, Alika."

"Good. You do tend to stay on our mind here frequently."

"I'll admit the same, but not during the attacks. I'm following the young spear-bearer's advice."

"My student will be relieved to hear, Dante."

"May I ask you something, Alika? You don't have to answer if you don't wish."

"Of course, Dante, you know you're free to ask me anything. I always give you an answer."

Dante smiled. That was undoubtedly true, even when the answer turned out he couldn't tell Dante. "You said something to the young spear-bearer about a promise, and your manner changed. Then you mentioned something about dinner, and you answered in the same manner. It was curious to me."

"Dante, you caught that, did you? Your spirit is sensitive, much like my young spear-bearer. My student promised me before they left for the rescue of your mother, and on this operation, they would return safely from the operations. Well, you know how the operation with your mother went for my young spear-bearer. This one today didn't go smoothly either, as you saw for them. That is what the promise entailed, and my student kept it again. When they left to rescue your mother, I also told both of them to be back by dinnertime. We tried to make light of it somewhat to calm each other's anxiety before leaving. Then the rescue went wrong, and we thought our young spear-bearer dead. Part of the message my young spear-bearer sent to us mentioned getting home by dinnertime. It was one of the ways we knew for sure the message came from our young spear-bearer. Today before they left me, they said the same thing."

"I understand. I'm glad the promise was kept as well."

"I believe we can all agree it was a well-kept promise. I gathered all the supplies, I think. There is something I know yet unspoken, so I will voice it before it drives the one insane. I feel there is one who would like to find himself headed toward Ryan's planet as well. Am I correct, young Dante?"

"I won't deny it as there's no point."

"Dante, you do understand, there will still be no meeting with my students and no helping with the repairs? Your curiosity will not be satisfied."

"I understand, Alika."

"I believe it's a good idea for you to come, Dante. Nonetheless, I defer to Lana and the others if you need to be there. I don't believe it's a wise idea for you to travel on your own with the state of affairs at present and with what lays ahead of you. However, someone else is there who does not need to be alone, and Lana should not be the only one left there with the one, considering the mystery surrounding that situation. My two students did leave with the crucial information they went to get and more, so your group will want to get all the information. I could not review it yet, considering the day's events. You need the intel relayed back to your group of what was found, which is why I encourage the trip you wish to make to Ryan's planet while I will be there."

Caleb spoke, "Alika, I will stay with Lana and keep everyone safe here."

"Alika, Dante and I will meet you at Ryan's planet."

"Very good. I will speak with my students first when I arrive. They will need the supplies to begin work on the ship. I also plan on checking on their condition to treat any injuries. I have certain students who tend to underestimate the extent of their injuries, so I will judge their condition myself when I arrive. Then I'll speak further with the two of you and Ryan."

CHAPTER TWENTY-THREE

Dante and Seth got to Ryan's planet first.

"How are you two?"

"Well. Ryan, has Alika arrived?" asked Seth.

"No, I figured you two would get here first. He has to load those supplies in his ship, which will take a minute," said Ryan, turning to Dante. "You okay?"

"Yeah, where's the ship?"

Ryan pointed to an area behind them. "Over there."

Dante turned around and stared back at Ryan in disbelief. "Dante, I didn't recognize it either. I'm glad you weren't the first to see it when it came through."

"Remember, Dante, we know they are all right despite the appearance of the ship." Seth touched Dante's shoulder in reassurance.

"You're right," said Dante, clearly trying to get over his horror at the look of the ship and separate in his mind it didn't reflect the condition of those inside the ship.

"Yes," said Ryan, stopping to respond to a communication. "Clear the vessel to land at the designated space as discussed. I'll meet the visitor and take it from there." Ryan turned back to Dante and Seth. "Alika arrived and is landing."

Alika walked out of his vessel and shook his head at the sight of his students' ship. He saw Ryan, Seth, and Dante over on the other side talking and continued over to them. "Ryan, thank you for all your help today and making sure we all got landed safely."

"Not a problem. How are your students?"

"I will check on them further in a moment. Seth, it's good to see you again."

"You as well."

"And you, young Dante. Your eyes still appear very concerned."

"I keep staring at the ship."

"It's hard to imagine they're all right, but they are. I'm going now to treat them, my stubborn young spear-bearer included, I promise."

Dante grinned. "We don't try to be difficult for our teachers, Alika."

"Yes, we know, but there are areas you and my younger student test your teachers." Alika grinned back, peering at Dante with the same fondness Seth did many times. "This may take some time with getting supplies in their ship, checking on their injuries, and discussing a few things with them."

"There's a small conference room immediately to your right when you come inside from the hangar. We'll go inside and wait for you there. Take all the time you need, Alika," Ryan stated. He gave Alika something. "This will get you wherever you need while you're here." He laughed. "I don't know why I'm bothering. I'm sure your group could find a way to access everything."

"You're probably right, but my young spear-bearer worked hard enough today obtaining clearances for the two of them. I'll be back."

Alika returned to his ship and got two containers of supplies out first. His students didn't call for either one of them. He placed both on the list and made them a priority. The ship door opened and shut behind him swiftly as he greeted his two students.

"I'm glad to see you two are much better than the outside of the ship."

The two of them got up from the floor, where they peered unhappily at one of the panels of the control portal of the ship.

"Us too," said Alena.

The girl stared unhappily back at the panel, but then she turned to Alika and smiled. "Yes, it was close again."

Alika smiled and hugged both of them. "I'm glad you're both safe, and I want to check your injuries before we go further. So, sit now." He gazed straight at the girl who began forming her protests. "Especially you. Did you even try to treat the injuries?" The girl did not answer. "Yes, as I thought." He shook his head and waited until the girl sat down as Alena had done before scanning them both with the medical scanner. He was not pleased with the reading and pulled something out from his supplies. "Each one of you put a mask on your face."

"Now, please." Alika stared at the girl, who reluctantly complied. Taking four tubes of liquid out of his bag, he broke off two tubes for Alena and poured them into a compartment in the lower part of her mask. Instantly the liquid reacted, and vapor began to circulate in the mask and into Alena's mouth. "Let your body breath it in. Do not talk. The task will be easier for some of us than others." He could not contain his laughter as he turned to the girl, and he pulled two more tubes out, repeating the same process for the her mask. He spoke to both of them, but his eyes locked on the girl. "This will take about ten minutes. If you talk during it, we will redo it. I brought plenty of tubes with me. I'm sure I make myself clear. While it's going, let me examine your hand and your arm, child."

The girl started to protest, but Alika locked eyes with her again. "Remember what I said, no talking while the medicine works, or you will be here for some time. I did it in this order on purpose. I know my student."

The girl smiled back at him. Her teacher had won this round.

Alika pulled both gloves and the outer covering of the Black Dragon suit off the girl so that he could see her arms better. "It's not a mere scratch on either count, and they both do need treatment. After your last ordeal, though, I can see where you consider it a scratch. You have learned to continue to operate at a high level when you should feel considerable levels of pain. You and young Dante both possess it. I'm not sure if it's a good way to be. I'm going to treat it, so it doesn't restrict you from any of the work you need to do on the ship," said Alika anticipating her protests. Alika finished treating the girl's injuries as the vapors completed doing their work for both students. "Wait before you take them off." He scanned both of them again with the medical scanners. This time he smiled, much happier with the result. "Now, you can remove them. I expect you both find you didn't realize how poorly you were still breathing."

Alena smiled. "You're right, Alika. I do feel better."

"Yes, I'm not sure why I was stubborn about it. I'm sorry I'm so difficult sometimes. I don't try, Alika."

Alika laughed. "My, the two of you are a pair."

The girl turned to Alena and back at Alika, puzzled.

"Oh, I don't think he was referring to the two of us."

"No, I wasn't. It is the second time today I heard almost the same comment from another person." Alika continued to laugh as the girl stared at him blankly. "Dante, my young spear-bearer."

"Dante?" said the girl, still puzzled. She didn't see how Alika could chat with anyone after today's events.

"Yes, an extremely concerned Dante with the well-being of the two individuals in this ship. It brings us to the next order of business. Dante and Seth arrived here, and I will meet with them after I get the two of you started repairing the ship. I'm to let them know what you learned in your operation, and they will take the information back to Lana and Caleb. Neither one of you can be seen here by Ryan or any others. Now that Dante himself is here, you need to be sure it does not happen, I assume."

The girl gazed back at him. "Dante is here?" She didn't know why she was having such trouble comprehending it, but she told herself to move beyond it. "I mean, yes, you're correct. It's not time yet. I'll somehow know when Dante and I are to meet."

Alika hid a smile as he watched his student try to conceal her happiness at knowing Dante was nearby. "Anyway, the two of you may need to do repairs outside the ship before I return to assist you. You cannot leave the ship in those, or else half the planet will shoot you. I brought you the change of wardrobe you need. No one will tell who you are, and the helmets also have voice changers. You will be the more friendly sort of fighters for this planet if you go outside the ship." He placed the bag down with two complete changes of disguise.

Alena remarked. "I assume the goal with the repairs is to get the ship in enough working order to get it back home safely."

"Alena's right. There's too much to repair here. We would be here for days. We also don't know when the next attack could happen either. And ..." The girl stopped with her thought.

Alika peered over at her. "You're thinking something else. What is it?"

"I have a bad feeling. The Dark Lord and Black Dragon Commander are unhappy about the whole incident at the colonies. Today's encounter only made it worse. Normally I don't care about their level of unhappiness. Yet, after what we saw today of what's in the works, I fear what happens since we made them angrier."

"I understand where your thinking went now, but as you also know, there is nothing we can do about it."

"That's true. We need to move on, Alika. Do you mind bringing the supplies? I'm sure Ryan, Seth, and Dante eagerly await to speak with you by now. Alena has the device for you with the information though I know you received it on your data pad as well. I suppose you'll want to make a copy for Seth and Dante to take back to Lana and Caleb."

"Yes, I was planning on doing so," Alika said as Alena handed him the device.

"Is there anything from what happened that I need to tell them which will not be apparent from the footage or the data from the device?"

Alena and the girl thought for a minute but ended up shaking their head. The girl said, "I can't think of anything, Alika. I mean, you normally take out the sound and images of us. You can check, but I don't believe it necessary this time. We were in Black Dragon uniform the whole time, and our voice sounded like Black Dragon soldier."

"I believe you're right." Alika got the supplies moved over as Alena and the girl began the task of figuring out where to start.

"Here is the last of them. Is there anything additional you need me to tell them, any messages to pass on?" His eyes rested on the girl.

"I suppose not. I need to concentrate on getting the ship back in order, not on a certain individual. I'm trying to take my own advice these days."

"Yes, but everyone is glad you're both safe. Dante wanted me to be sure to check on the injuries you incurred. He did not believe they were a mere scratch either. I could tell. Are you sure there is nothing more?"

The girl smiled and started to say no again but stopped herself. "Can you check on how his training is going, Alika?"

"I will as well as try to give him some guidance and encouragement while doing so. I know you're concerned after how the one session went." He turned and left.

CHAPTER TWENTY-FOUR

Dante watched as Alika disappeared into the ship after going back to his ship to get two large bags of supplies. He watched, waiting for Alika to come back out for the rest of the supplies, but he didn't.

"Dante, are you with us?" asked Ryan.

"Yeah, sure." Dante tried unsuccessfully to focus but gave up. "No, I'm not."

"What's bothering you, Dante?" asked Seth.

"Alika stayed in there for some time now. He got a couple of supplies, and that was it. Do you think one of the students was hurt worse than he thought?"

"I think you must stop worrying so much," said Seth. "If it were more than Alika could handle, he would request further medical assistance for them."

"Didn't the last time there was something like this, and you were close by, you felt something, Dante? It's all a part of the connection thing with the young spear-bearer," said Ryan.

"No, that was only with the vision part, and we still don't know how this connection thing works."

"How about we go inside and wait now before you go insane wondering, Dante?" said Seth as he and Ryan nudged Dante toward the inside conference room.

⸺ ℓℓ ⸺

After what felt like forever to Dante, Alika walked in. Dante immediately got up. "Alika, are they all right?"

Alika sat, reading Dante's concerned face. "They are treated, Dante, and began working on the ship."

"It was truly as they said." Dante sat back down, visibly relieved.

"I wouldn't go that far, Dante. I was more concerned about all the smoke they inhaled. It proved a greater challenge for the younger spear-bearer to get treated for as well."

"Did they breathe more of the smoke in somehow?"

Alika laughed, and Dante was taken aback by the reaction. Alika smiled at Dante. "I'm sorry, Dante, that's not what I meant. The treatment involves sitting for a whole ten minutes and not speaking during it so the medicine can work. Those are two things which are almost impossible for my younger student to do as a patient anyway."

Dante laughed. "I understand their difficulty. Did it take long?"

"Oh no. Only the required time, with a warning beforehand, we would repeat the treatment as many times as needed if either one of the requirements were broken during the ten minutes." Alika smiled. "I am difficult as well when I must be. I used the ten minutes to treat the injuries to the arm and hand simultaneously. It's much easier when the patient is forbidden to speak. It needed to be treated, but the injuries were minimal compared to the last time. I understand why my young spear-bearer was not concerned."

"We were worried about both of them. I'm glad it proved unwarranted." Dante paused. "You have the floor, Alika. We're ready to listen."

"I brought the data obtained, but I believe it will make more sense if you see the footage from the operation. You will be able to see both the surroundings and interior of the building where the Black Dragon is assembling their arsenal. Now, it is not clear this is where everything is happening. This is a large operation. I didn't get a chance to go through the data yet, so something may strike you I didn't notice yet. My students went in as Black Dragon soldiers. They fit the part in every way from wardrobe to voice changers in their helmets."

Alika began the footage toward the beginning when his two students stood in line to get in the hangar but intentionally past the part when Alena and the girl's conversation had turned to Dante. They watched it all the way through until the ship squeezed through the hangar doors. Alika quickly stopped it. He knew the girl began calling Alena by name shortly after.

A quiet settled on the group for a few minutes after watching. They were still processing the reality of the threat and the destruction it could mean for the galaxy if allowed to be unleashed. It could not be allowed to happen. Then, although it had been through the Black Dragon soldier voices, Dante and the others finally heard the two students. They heard the way they spoke back and forth during battle. They protected each other, joking around in what appeared a hopeless situation, and faced the prospect of death fearlessly.

Alika smiled at Seth. "They are much like Ryan and Dante at times during the attacks, are they not?"

"I thought the same thing."

"It's never gotten that bad for us, Ryan."

"That kind of comment sounds like one which would come from Alika's younger spear-bearer from everything I see. Dante, you have your own moments which are hard to forget. A chunk out of your back, half of the tank in your back, and the near-miss with the tank the time before last." He saw Seth glance at him and Dante. Alika showed no surprise because he knew about it. "Don't worry, Seth, it missed him. His words." Ryan peered over at Alika and laughed. "Are you sure they can't meet? They are so alike. It's crazy, Alika."

"I guess I do see the resemblance. I'm sorry, Ryan, but I'm glad you always have my back." He grinned at Alika. "Ryan needs to meet your other student when the time comes. They can trade pointers on how to keep me and the young spear-bearer out of harm's way."

"Ryan and my older student certainly have a whole other job managing the two of you."

Dante turned back to the footage and switched gears. "So, the whole delivery at the beginning. I know you wouldn't be crazy enough to give them real supplies, but they passed, and the inspector thoroughly examined them."

"As we knew they would. We assumed before we went on the operation where the state of things would be in that regard which is why we were not alarmed when we found out how the swap went at the last attack. We knew the supplies must pass a rigorous inspection. They had to be authentic fakes."

Ryan shook his head, amazed. "They were right on. Nothing like the stuff the Black Dragon tried to pass off on the colonies."

Seth said, "The time it took to create and package all those supplies and to prepare for the operation, I'm not sure how your students accomplished it, Alika."

"My students have their ways. However, they could not possibly do everything themselves needed for a mission of this magnitude with the urgent time frame laid before us. Part of their training, in the beginning, was to find out the different connections in the world they entered. That meant who the players were in the business, whose side they were on, how they operated, if they could be trusted, etc. They found a select few in a difficult business who fit the criteria my students knew they had to work within. There are certain situations like this where we find the need to outsource part of it. We did, and our source came through for us."

"I thought it was only the three of you."

"There are, Dante. You sound confused."

"Does your source know who your students are?" He hated himself for the question. It was silly. He felt like he had diminished in age by years.

Alika realized what swirled through Dante's head, and he also knew how terribly it bothered Dante. He felt awful for him. "No, in the shipping business, the norm is no one gives their true names. It's too dangerous. We have a name we know our source by, and he has a name he knows my young spear-bearer by. We have a few other individuals we use as well, and it is the same with them. They know my student by a different name. It's the only way to stay safe in that world and the role I asked my young spear-bearer to take on." Alika hoped he answered it so Dante would move to something else. He did not wish for the next question if Dante did not.

"But they still met your students though they don't know their true names." Dante hated himself for continuing this line of questioning and caring as he did.

Alika sighed inside. Dante did go there, and he hated it for Dante. "They have not met the older student as that one stays in the ship and is responsible for monitoring. As for the young spear-bearer, yes, they have. The one does all the deals and takes care of the interactions. The point of the original question was about the supplies. We did not give them any real items or real chemicals. They were excellent fakes. My young spear-bearer wanted to be sure, considering what was riding on them. My student examined them, tested the samples, and was satisfied they would pass inspection. Then we gave our source the green light to finish the order, and as you saw, they fooled the inspector."

"Did your students ever figure out about those handheld devices?" asked Ryan, genuinely curious and ready to change the subject.

Alika was relieved for the moment, although he still watched Dante. "No, but it was hooked up around the stations and hoses and the cylinder structure. The Black Dragon soldier indicated there was a substance going through the hoses, as you heard."

Seth said, "And with the size of the cylinder device, I imagine it could hold an incredible amount of something."

"There are the chemicals they got from the attacks," said Ryan.

"But there's another substance out there," said Dante, finally drawing himself back into the discussion, "the unknown substance your students brought back when they rescued my mother."

"That's true. The thought entered my mind, and I'm sure my students as well, Dante. The most logical is the chemicals from the colony attacks, but we know about the other substance."

"But we said Dante's father didn't know anything about the other operation with Dante's mother, so it must be the chemicals," said Ryan.

"I don't know. The Dark Lord is a master of deception. He could tell my father he's using the chemicals and instead make something with the other substance."

"You're right, Dante. That must also be remembered," said Alika as he pulled out something. "I made a copy of the data obtained from the download, and it also contains the footage we watched. This is for you to take back to Lana and Caleb. I don't want to forget to give it to you." He handed it to Dante.

"Alika, I didn't mean for you to rush off. Earlier ..." Dante shook his head, not sure what he tried to say. He felt he had upset Alika.

Alika stared at him strangely. "Dante, what are you talking about? I'm not leaving yet. I simply wanted to make sure I gave it to you for Lana and Caleb. We never know when another attack will strike." Alika smiled over at Dante. "You have nothing to apologize for, so I'm not sure why you felt the need."

"I'm not sure either. Thank you, Alika."

"You're welcome, Dante." Alika gazed back at Dante as one still mystified. "Now that we sorted that out." Alika laughed as he shook his head at Dante.

"You sound as if you expect an attack sooner than normal," said Seth.

"Something my young spear-bearer voiced earlier today got me thinking, and it concerns me."

"Did your student have another vision?" asked Dante.

"No, it wasn't like that." He proceeded to tell them about the discussion before he left to come to them.

"Two huge mishaps close together for them," said Seth mulling it over.

"Don't forget to factor in the Dark Lord's loss of Abigail. Dante's father doesn't know, but the Dark Lord is probably still seething over that one," said Ryan.

"With each time we hit and hurt them for a moment, they may answer us tenfold in wrath with this." Dante surveyed the screen, with the downloaded file appearing and showing the dispersal device. "We'll meet them in battle as we have, like your students have, Alika." He turned to Alika. "We will not fall."

"No, we must not, Dante." Alika's fear returned for Dante.

"No answer to the when question in the data. This appears to answer a great portion of the where they are doing the building. It also doesn't tell us where they attack with it first." said Seth as he studied the download.

"No, but the download contains a lot of information, much of which is yet to pour through, and so it may be there somewhere. You are taking a copy with you.

Of course, my students were interrupted and could go no further, so there is that possibility. This is what they obtained. Hopefully, the answers are somewhere on it."

"Your young spear-bearer tried to stay longer. They could have been killed, and they wouldn't have downloaded the rest. I don't understand why your student took such a risk." Dante shook his head but found everyone staring at him. "Why is everyone looking at me like that?"

Ryan chuckled. "Are you so sure? Do I need to review with you, Dante?"

Seth said, "Dante, I believe Ryan has you on that one." Seth glanced over at Alika and laughed. "I'm not sure it's a wise idea to pair Dante and your young spear-bearer up for an operation without supervision."

Dante laughed. "Hold on a minute. What are you doing, Seth? You'll ruin any chance for me to meet Alika's students with those comments."

Alika laughed. "I don't know, Seth. They could work well together. Their concern for each other's safety may keep them from taking all the risks they normally do. Or if one attempts to do so, the other one would stop them in their tracks. It could end up being a nice partnership," he saw Dante's look of hope, "which has not happened."

Dante watched Alika, and Alika did not say anything further at the moment about it. However, Dante had noticed it, as did the others. An unspoken yet ended his words.

"Is there anything further for now? I don't wish to leave your company, but I need to help my students with the repairs. I get the feeling they push to leave tomorrow."

Everyone's face mirrored the same expression of surprise. Ryan said, "There's no way the ship is repaired by tomorrow, even if your students work deep into the evening, Alika. After the day they lived through ..."

Alika said, "We understand. The intent was never to complete all the repairs here. The goal is to repair it enough to get back home without mishaps. We'll finish the repairs there." He turned to Dante and Seth. "We could end up leaving the same time as the two of you. I assume you want to return tomorrow to consult with Lana and Caleb about the findings."

"You're right, Alika. I don't believe there is anything else tonight," Seth said as Dante nodded in agreement.

"Before I go tonight, Seth, do you mind if I speak with Dante for a bit?" asked Alika.

"Of course not, Alika."

"We'll meet you back in my quarters, Dante," said Ryan.

"All right, you two." Dante remained seated, unsure of what to expect.

CHAPTER TWENTY-FIVE

A fter a moment, it was him and Alika in the room. To his surprise, Alika got up and smiled at Dante. "Come, I've heard Ryan's colony is quite nice. We sat long enough in this room. Let's take a walk and talk, young Dante." He laughed. "Really, you appear as if you were sent to the Elder's office for a lecture."

Dante laughed, got up, and followed Alika. "I did wonder."

Alika gave Dante a light pat on the back and shook his head. "I can't fathom why. Come, young Dante."

They got outside and walked away from the ship hangar around the complex. It felt refreshing to be out of the room.

"Someone requested me to ask you something, and I always try to keep my promises. Of course, I'm curious myself as well."

"Who is this request from, Alika?"

"I believe you can guess, young Dante."

"Your young spear-bearer. What is the question?"

"They wished me to ask about the progress of your training."

"How do they think it's coming along?" Dante wondered how far the connection went. Alika always answered honestly before when he could from what Dante sensed.

"We believe it's progressing in the right direction from what the young spear-bearer tells us. It sounds like one of the beginning sessions with Seth proved difficult from what they sensed." Alika sat on one of the seats outside the complex, and Dante sat in a chair beside him. "You must continue, and listen to what Seth tells you in this. You go to fight a difficult battle."

"What if I'm not ready?"

"You must be, young Dante. In truth, you possess all the resources on hand you need. You must now learn how to wield them in the battle to come. Young Dante, you are not the first to fight this battle and won't be the last. It has been won by others, and each time it is with great struggle. You can come through it as well. Victory does not always come in the form of the end of a sunspear."

"Did your young spear-bearer tell you to give me that message?"

Alika thought about it for a moment. "It was implied, so I told them I would encourage and advise you after I asked the question. I sensed they wished me to do so. Whether I succeeded, I'm not sure, but I did try, young Dante."

"Alika, I'm glad we got to see the footage tonight with your students with the voices. I know it wasn't their voices, but it was nice to see how they interacted, though it wasn't ideal circumstances. I feel like I finally got a peek at what they were like firsthand, although I still haven't met them. It sounds strange, I suppose."

"No, it doesn't sound strange at all, Dante. They were in formidable circumstances. However, they are both consistently as you saw them, as you and Ryan are consistent whether in a conference room or on the battlefield. They trained together for a number of years now and care like family for each other. They will do whatever they must to protect each other, as you saw, but somehow their lighter side surfaces even in the most stressful of circumstances. The two have laughed and cried together, depending upon their experience. Perhaps it was better to see them in the circumstances you did. That is when one's true character comes through many times—when our inner resources are pushed beyond what we believe its limits. It also reminds us we have the One beside us to get us through those circumstances, as my students did today."

"You're right, Alika," Dante said softly. "I could see all that as I watched them. I know the intended purpose of showing us, but it accomplished something much more valuable. Thank you." Dante paused. "Alika, earlier, you said with these sources no one actually knows who everyone is. Then how can you know your two students are safe?"

Alika smiled and was relieved this time by the question. It went in a totally different direction than last time. "I understand your concern from how you see it. Yet the process of finding this select group to work with did not happen overnight. It occurred over months, involving intel and monitoring every day. In that time, we also realized who to avoid any dealings with. My students also encountered the ugly side of this business, so they know the costs if one deals with the wrong individuals. There is another element to this. It was clear to us additional guidance led us to our first source, and the other few opened up from there. My young spear-bearer sensed the prompting from the Ancient One for the initial meeting with the first individual we work with the most. So, when I tell you we work with a select group, it is very much so. We do not know their names, and they do not know ours, but it's to keep everyone safe. Does that make you feel better, young Dante?"

"It does, Alika. I didn't see the time put into getting the sources established. I suppose because my mind jumped to something else as it should not have. Alika, I apologize. It's silly." Dante's face filled with regret.

"You're much too hard on yourself, Dante. You remind me of someone else. Yes, the two of you are alike in many ways. It's driving the other insane as well, Dante. You're not being silly."

"That was supposed to make me feel better." Dante smiled. "I don't understand. This strange connection. It binds me somehow to your young spear-bearer, but I can't meet them. They felt when the training didn't go well, but I knew before I asked you. I know I shouldn't care as I do. Yet, I care about what happens to this young spear-bearer of yours even if we haven't met. I feel I know them because I sense this connection that somehow is being created. I'm sorry, I'm not making any sense, Alika."

Alika smiled and stared into Dante's eyes. "No, you're making more sense than you realize, young Dante. You're in the center of a mystery yet to be revealed, and you are attempting to sort it out as best you can. I hear the same sentiments from my young spear-bearer. They have the visions additionally in connection with you, making the connection much stronger as you see. So, the difficulty in sorting it out is more confusing than what you find. Something is in motion, Dante, which neither one of you sees or understands yet. You both must continue to be patient."

"Your young spear-bearer wishes to meet me as well?"

"You know the answer. It has always been the case, young Dante. However, it's clear the time will become apparent when the meeting is to happen. The time is not upon the two of you."

"Yet."

"It is the assumption, but I don't know, Dante."

"And you can't tell me why and who?"

"No, I made a promise many years ago, and I must keep it. That is one way my student and I are alike. I practice what I teach. We keep our promises, Dante."

"I understand. I must be glad you both keep your promises, especially the young spear-bearer the last couple of times."

"Yes, I agree." He got up. "Come, Dante, let's head back so that you can relax with Ryan and Seth for a bit, and I can assist my students with the ship."

Dante got up and walked with Alika as they continued to talk until they reached the entrance of the building.

"Have a good evening, Dante. I will see you and Seth before we leave tomorrow."

"Alika, tell your young spear-bearer the message helped, and tell both your students we're glad they're safe."

"I will, young Dante."

"Thank you, Alika." Dante hugged Alika.

Dante walked inside for the night, and Alika walked toward the ship. Alika gazed out into the night sky. His fondness for Dante grew, as did his concern, even with the short time he spent with him. The boy could be one of his own children. It was that way with some students, and it had always been such with Alena and the girl. It felt like he lost his own child when he thought her dead when she fell from the rooftop. Then today, at the other end of the portal when he thought the ship blown to pieces, and he lost both of them. He died a million deaths, it seemed, monitoring their missions, thinking they would see their last moment, but thankfully they were saved from death. He always comforted himself, knowing he prepared both of them if the end came as well, knowing the Ancient One held them too. Turning back to the door Dante went through, he knew the Ancient One had that child as well, but how it would grieve his heart to see that son succumb to death at the end of the battle. He hoped it was not the ending. He found himself whispering, "You promised to go before him in this. You have never broken a promise, for You cannot break your promises. You are the fulfillment of every promise. Protect this son from the Darkness and shelter his spirit from the storm to come. Do not let it take him." Tears streamed down his face as he stood there, taking a final look at the night sky. A calm passed over him, accompanied by a breeze that dried his tear-stained face. He took a deep breath and walked back into the ship.

CHAPTER TWENTY-SIX

The two were hard at work on the ship as expected when Alika came aboard.

Alika smiled. "It appears much better already. What is most urgent to do on the outside of the ship?"

Alena and the girl came over to Alika, and after a few moments of discussion, Alika nodded and went outside with the needed supplies to begin work.

Dante entered Ryan's quarters and sat.

"Everything okay, Dante?" asked Ryan.

"Yeah, Alika asked about how the training was going and gave me assurance about what lay ahead," said Dante smiling.

"Being Alika to you, it sounds like," said Seth. "He is quite fond of you. I know we feel the same for his students though we have not met them face to face yet."

Ryan said, "How about I get dinner sent to the quarters, and we can review more of the download while we eat?"

"It sounds like an efficient use of time, Ryan," said Seth.

Dante looked at them both, and Seth didn't let him finish. "I'll ask now. I don't know how we could forget."

"No, we're fine, Seth," Alika replied, "I have dinner covered. Tell the others as well. We will be working well into the evening. See you in the morning."

"You heard. I tried you two."

The three began studying through the download as they ate.

"This isn't good," said Dante.

"I gather you mean something besides the obvious, Dante," said Seth.

"Yeah," said Dante, clearly in thought. "Remember when the two students thought about putting explosives in the Large Room and decided against doing it?"

Ryan answered, "They ended up using them in another room. It was a good move as it helped them later to escape from the hangar."

"Come back with me, Ryan. Remember why they didn't use them in the Large Room, though," Dante said.

"They were afraid of the substance in the cylinder, of the reaction if it was released." said Ryan.

"A battle in the air with lots of gunfire, with a huge dispersal device. How does that end for us, for the colonies anywhere near the device?" Dante asked.

"Not well," said Seth quietly.

"If we battle in the traditional sense, we could end up releasing it everywhere," said Ryan.

"Which is the thing we wish to prevent. How do we fight this?" asked Dante.

"I don't know," said Seth.

Dante kept studying it, and something else nagged at him.

"What is it?"

"I'm not sure, Seth. Kind of like with the attacks way in the beginning. The feeling we're missing a piece again. Like there's something else behind all this, big we haven't seen," said Dante.

It was eleven at night. Ryan showed Dante and Seth to their quarters for the evening. They peered outside to the two ships. They were still lit up. Alika was outside working on the ship. He asked something, and a moment later, someone in the ship switched something on. Alika scanned something outside the ship where he worked and nodded it was good. He closed the compartment and moved on to another panel.

"How much longer do you think they're going to be at it?" asked Ryan.

"I don't know. I wish Alika would call it a night for them," said Dante.

"I don't believe this is Alika's doing. I feel sure it's his students pushing themselves to a limit. Alika will continue to work with them until they're ready to stop." Seth sighed.

"If only they would allow us to help," said Dante.

"They know we are more than willing. There is no point in none of us getting rest tonight," said Seth.

◦ℓℓ◦

It was near one in the morning, and Alika came into the ship. The two still tried to work.

"Enough of this, you two. One of you is going to end up wiring something to blow the whole ship apart. It's time to get rest. We said the goal was to get the ship repaired to the point so it could safely leave here and get home. How close are we to our goal?"

The girl named something on the ship. Alika shook his head. "Not essential to getting back home. Try again." They went through the exercise a couple more times with the same result.

"I have definitely heard enough. It's time for us to get sleep. We will start again tomorrow morning, going from the most important systems to the least important to get us off the planet and back home." Alika's voice softened, and he looked at both of them with a deep fondness that could not be mistaken. "It has been a long day again, and I thought I lost both of you today. I am grateful you were both returned to me." He hugged them tightly.

Once he released the girl, he said to her, "I didn't get the chance to tell you yet, but I did ask Dante about his training as I promised. He was concerned about being ready. I guided him as I promised as well. He said to tell you what I told him helped, and he was glad you both came back safely."

The girl smiled back and gave Alika another hug. "Thank you, Alika." She headed off to her quarters.

Alena and Alika smiled as they watched her and headed for their separate quarters to get sleep.

——ell——

The next morning Dante and Seth met Ryan in his quarters around nine-thirty in the morning. They looked out into the hangar. Alika was already outside working on the ship.

Dante shook his head. "I wonder how long they were up last night."

Ryan said, "I don't know, Dante. When I got up a bit before eight-thirty this morning, Alika was already out there working."

——ell——

"How do we look?" asked Alika. It was near eleven in the morning. "I need essential things to get us from here to back home. Nothing else, you two."

The girl and Alena surveyed the ship, starting with the control panel.

"There are things which would be nice, but to get us from Ryan's planet to home, we should be safe," said Alena.

"We can't run into any trouble, or it's over," said the girl.

"We should be okay. The portal is almost right at Ryan's planet, and we are in friendly skies now." Alika hesitated. "The two of you never told me what actually happened at the moment before you entered the portal, but it's for another time. I'm going to meet with them for a bit, and afterward, we will leave. Is there anything else coming to mind I need to relay to them?" asked Alika.

Both shook their heads. "Are you sure there is nothing I need to tell them before I go?" Alika gazed at the girl. He was surprised. She was quiet, seeming lost in her thoughts. He didn't have to wonder whom her thoughts kept coming back to even as she tried to stop them. He smiled to himself. Yes, it would be interesting to see where this connection took the two of them. He walked off the ship to meet the others.

Alena and the girl began working on the ship again. Alena peered over at the girl too. She was absorbed in working on the ship.

⸺ele⸺

"Alika, how late were you and your students up working on the ship?" asked Seth, concerned.

"I finally made them quit at one this morning. They would have continued, one more than the other, of course," responded Alika. "They both agree it is fixed well enough to get safely home to complete the rest of the repairs. They are continuing with repairs now, but we could leave at the moment if need be. Is there anything else you came up with? Obviously, I was not able to delve further into the download after I left you last night."

Dante told him about the conclusion they came to about the difficulty in handling the dispersal device.

"I know my students well enough to know they reached the same conclusion. It's a situation where you want to think more in terms of disabling it, keeping it contained, or neutralizing the substance inside it since you don't know what is in the device. The time is running out."

Seth said to Alika, "Yes, and something else bothered Dante last night about it. He was correct the last time."

Alika looked at Dante and smiled. "I have learned to trust your instincts in these situations. Explain yourself, Dante."

Dante tried, but it didn't make sense to him. He felt lost trying to put it into words, but he did the best he could.

Alika listened and thought about it. "It sounds similar to something my young spear-bearer said about it. The first time they went to spy out the place, it seemed huge. Once they went in for the operation, my student said it didn't appear as large as what it should for all the supplies the Black Dragon accumulated all this time. Of course, there are the supplies we know they stole from the colonies, but we honestly do not think the colonies are the only ways the Black Dragon obtains their supplies. It is a guess from our knowledge of seeing the shipping business. There is a sense more is going on than what they found, as if they are missing something too."

"That was well-stated, much better than the way I stumbled around, Alika."

"You speak quite well, Dante. When you are in need of the words, they will come for the task ahead." Alika paused as if something else had come to him. "I believe you may be surprised at how well you speak if you find yourself so inspired, young Dante." Alika smiled.

Dante stared at him, thinking at first the comment referred to the task with his father, but he felt there was more to the last part of the comment. However, the expression from Alika told him he would receive no further clarification on it. He was left to wonder.

"As much as it pains me, I know Alika needs to get back, and we must get this information back to the others."

Alika got up. "Seth is correct. We'll finish the repairs to the ship at home. I'm not sure what the next move will be. I need a chance to review the download with my students. It may involve figuring out a way to disable the dispersal device. Yet, we don't know what time remains. The Dark Lord may launch his plan before anything further can be done. There is no way to know for sure. We will let you know if we find anything further, but everyone must be careful about communications. It will only become increasingly dangerous, so we'll initiate all communications after this point. Then we'll communicate back and forth thereafter. So, we will not answer if you call."

Dante, Ryan, and Seth followed Alika outside.

"This is where we part again. Take care of each other, please and be safe." He turned to Ryan. "Thank you for everything you did for the last couple of days for my students. Take care of Dante. Keep him out of trouble, please."

"I will do so, Alika. Tell your student to do the same with the young spear-bearer you have." Ryan grinned as he hugged Alika goodbye.

Alika laughed and turned to Seth. "It has been good company again, Seth, and I continue to be impressed with your student. One day our meetings will not always be like this."

"It will be a good day, Alika." Seth smiled as he hugged Alika goodbye.

Alika turned to Dante, and his eyes softened. "Young Dante, I wish to see you again safe. I feel very much as if you are one of my own students. Please remember my words from last night."

"Anything else?"

Alika knew what Dante hoped. There was always a message. Alika knew there had been one this morning, yearning to be given but unspoken. Thus, he delivered it.

"Yes, Dante," said Alika softly, "You were not the only one who had trouble with words this morning. My young spear-bearer did as well. So, I will deliver it as I believe it was meant for you. My young spear-bearer felt overwhelmed with concern for your safety, with what stands before you. They frequently think of the challenge ahead of you but have seen the Darkness you face beaten before. You must beat it, Dante. Please, you cannot allow it to overwhelm you. They could not bear to see that happen to you. The Ancient One will be with you and give you what you need during the battle to get your father back. My young spear-bearer will await your safe return, young Dante, and hopes the day to meet you indeed does come."

"Thank you, Alika. Tell your young spear-bearer I will return safely, and I keep my promises as well."

Alika smiled and hugged Dante goodbye. "I will do so. And young Dante, I already know my young spear-bearer will hold you to your promise."

Alika walked to the ship and disappeared inside.

***

"Are we ready?" asked Alika.

"I believe so," said Alena.

"Ah, yes," said the girl watching Dante and attempting to concentrate on the control panel.

Alena smiled. "I got this. Enjoy the view for a little longer. I'm not sure the next time you'll see him."

"You may be right," said the girl. She regretted now she left as she did, without a word to him. It probably didn't matter to him.

"I gave him your message," said Alika softly.

"I didn't give you a message. I told you I didn't have one," the girl said sadly, still gazing out the cockpit, her concern growing again for Dante.

"You did. You simply couldn't come up with it this morning. He knew you had a message. His young spear-bearer always has a message for him," said Alika.

They were now out of view. The girl turned to Alika, her eyes filled with tears, "I did. I just … I'm so afraid for him sometimes, Alika. I cannot lose him. He must come back."

Alika held her eyes. "He will. He said to tell his young spear-bearer he promises to come back safely, and he always keeps his promises."

The girl hugged Alika as tears streamed down her face. "I will hold him to that promise."

"I told him that as well, child," said Alika.

Dante, Ryan, and Seth watched as the ship left. Dante could feel the same eyes watching him from the ship. He knew for sure it was the young spear-bearer. Seth and Dante headed out.

"I'm sure I'll see you both soon again, probably in the next couple of days around lunchtime."

"You're probably right. See you then, Ryan." Dante shook his head and waved to Ryan as he followed Seth inside the ship.

Dante sat down and helped Seth get the ship lifted off.

Dante became lost in thought. "You know, Seth, Alika's two students, act like two siblings. They remind me a lot of how me and Collin used to be." He looked over at Seth.

"You're right. They do." Seth waited to see where Dante took it. He figured he already knew. The boy was still nowhere in the ballpark if so.

"I hope I get to meet them soon. It would be like having an older or younger brother again, especially since there's this strange connection thing going," said Dante, smiling at Seth.

"We'll see Dante," said Seth, returning Dante's smile. Seth kept from laughing. The boy would get a surprise, but Dante would not be disappointed at the unveiling from what Alika said.

CHAPTER TWENTY-SEVEN

"All this happened under your watch," demanded the Black Dragon Commander, listening to the squadron leader carefully. "Two spear-bearers did all that and escaped."

"Yes, we surrounded them in the hangar, but somehow they caused an explosion. Their ship was badly damaged. One minute they had no weapons, but then their ship starting firing."

"Enough, I do not want to hear excuses, and the Dark Lord will not either. Your services are no longer needed." He pulled out his sword and stopped the soldier's speech permanently.

The Black Dragon Commander made the call instantly. There was no point. The Dark Lord would want to know about this last incident.

"Another incident. Come immediately, and we will speak, Black Dragon Commander."

The Dark Lord listened as the Black Dragon Commander spoke. When he finished, the Dark Lord's eyes blazed fire.

"There is no footage of it." repeated the Dark Lord.

"None. I did not believe it when told, but no trace was left. I don't know how it could be possible."

"You would be surprised." The Dark Lord practically spat out the words. "No one has a clue who they are?"

"No, they were fully disguised. They came dressed in Black Dragon gear and even sounded like Black Dragon soldiers. My guess is they were equipped with a device to change their voice. They wielded sunspears. Few do so with the skill reported and would dare attempt something so bold. It must have been Dante and either Caleb or Lana with him. They came straight from the attack and went on the offensive with this operation."

"You must be right. It could only be one of them." The Dark Lord knew otherwise. It was those same two spear-bearers who rescued Abigail, and he still had no clue of their identity. "How did they get in the hangar in the first place?"

"Since the footage is cleared, I can't be sure. The assumption is they brought supplies."

"Those were being checked. The two intruders should have been eliminated on the spot."

"They were being checked. They prepared well. Whatever supplies they brought passed inspection. It makes sense with it being Dante and the others. They probably figured they would need to pass a thorough inspection by the point they tried to do their mission."

"A reasonable theory." Once again, the Dark Lord reached a different conclusion. The two spear-bearers accessed the information from the attacks. The Dark Lord smiled. Or better yet, contacted Dante and his crew. It appeared they were at least sharing information, possibly working together. He didn't know if it was that close, though, as the two didn't help with the attacks. He knew if two strangers fighting with sunspears appeared on the battlefield, his Black Dragon Commander would mention such an occurrence.

"Dante's group learned a new group of tricks. An astonishing work to create supplies to pass the inspection we now administer. They were extremely well done," said the Dark Lord, shaking his head in displeasure.

"It appears so. What do you wish to do, Dark Lord?"

"I assume you eliminated the squadron leader for this incident?"

"Yes, it has been done."

"There may be other cuts after this, but I will think about it. Are we still able to do everything as before, even after all the destruction the two caused in the building?"

"Yes, we are still on target for the one."

"Perfect because we will move up the operation as we discussed. I thought about it previously. After the incident with the colony, I was going to inform you I wished to move it up to the faster timetable we had spoken of. They have succeeded in sealing it with this incident."

"When do you wish, my Dark Lord?"

"We will do the one last attack as planned on one of the colonies for supplies because I want to make a point for what happened during the last attack." The Dark Lord smiled. "Then we will give them time to wonder, keep expecting another attack on a colony. It will appear not to come. They will soon find something so much worse lays in their near future." The Dark Lord laughed. "First though, the plans for the attack on the colony. I decided how I want it done."

"I'm listening to your orders."

"They care for the colonists so much. It will be their undoing the next time. The colonists will suffer for the Elders believing they could trick us as they did at the last attack."

The Black Dragon Commander listened as the Dark Lord instructed him on how the attack was to be conducted. "It will be carried out as you wish, Dark Lord."

CHAPTER TWENTY-EIGHT

The girl, Alena, and Alika returned home safely. They let the downloaded information run as they ate lunch. Then they headed to the ship and worked on more repairs. They talked about the findings as they worked. Then, as they ate dinner, they let the downloaded information continue to run as they ate again. Then they worked on the ship again after dinner. It would be their world for the next couple of days.

—ele—

Dante and Seth also found their way back home safely.

"You're back." Lana smiled and hugged them both.

Caleb greeted them too. "Yes, it's good to see you both back safely." He paused. "How were they really?"

They all sat.

Seth sighed. "It was as Ryan said. I'm amazed again."

Dante said softly, "Seth is right. It is only the Ancient One's hand that Alika's students were not seriously hurt. The ship was unrecognizable."

Lana asked quietly, "How did they get through at the end?"

Seth and Dante turned to each other and back to Lana and Caleb. Dante answered, "You know, Alika never said. Honestly, I don't think he asked."

Caleb said, "Strange, but from what you said, I guess he was just grateful they were okay, and he didn't get there yet. It sounds like they have an extended stay at Ryan's place to repair the ship."

Seth shook his head. "No, they left at the same as we did to go home." Lana and Caleb were obviously surprised. "We were in disbelief ourselves. They did the repairs essential to get them safely off the plane, and returned to do the rest at home."

Lana sighed. "They still would not allow any assistance, I assume. I suppose you saw what they went through such lengths to get. Was it worth the great risk they took once again?"

Seth said, "I believe it was. You won't feel any better knowing, though."

Dante agreed. "Seth is right. The question remains how to fight the threat created by the Dark Lord."

Lana and Caleb looked at each other, wondering what was found.

Seth turned to Dante. "The best way to do this is as Alika did."

"I agree, Seth. I'll start it." Dante turned to Lana and Caleb. "This is the footage exactly as Alika showed us of his students during the operation. Then we can move on to the downloaded material they obtained. We didn't go through all the downloaded material yet. His students are all in Black Dragon uniform, and they have voice-changing devices in their helmets to sound the part as well. As a result, the audio is present too. Here we go."

Lana and Caleb watched as Dante and Seth did so for the second time.

They were all silent as the footage ended.

"They should have met their end how many times in the sequence?" Lana stared at the wall where the footage ended and turned to gaze first at Caleb and then at Dante and Seth.

"Yeah, there was a whole army of Black Dragon soldiers," said Caleb shaking his head.

"How many times can they do it before it ends terribly?" Lana shook her head.

"I don't know, and I'm afraid to find the answer," said Seth.

Dante sighed and stared at the frozen screen, wondering the same thing.

"A dispersal device." Caleb shook his head.

"Yes," said Seth.

Lana turned to Caleb. "What are our options?"

"Not good ones, as I figure have already been concluded," The look from Dante and Seth confirmed his guess. "Talk to me about what you guys discussed, but I think I know how this conversation went."

Dante and Seth did, and Caleb and Lana found they were at the same place.

Caleb said, "Let's sort through more of the downloaded stuff and see if we find something about the device to help us fight it."

They ate dinner and continued to go through the download and talk simultaneously. Finally, they could study no more of the information for the evening.

"I need to go see my mother before I go to my quarters. I haven't checked on her since I got back."

"Would you like me to go with you, Dante?"

"If you don't mind, Seth, yeah, I would appreciate the company."

***

"How I wish she would awaken. She would know how to convince Father. She always knew the answer." Dante stared down into his mother's face.

"She possesses great wisdom along with a kind spirit. One day she will awaken to share both with us again, Dante," reassured Seth.

"I do hope so, Seth." Dante sat in a chair beside his mother's bed.

Seth sat in another chair. "Dante, tell me one of the best memories you have of you, your mother, your father, and your brother together."

"There are many to choose from, Seth."

"It should be easy to remember one and tell me all about it. Go ahead, Dante."

He chose one and told Seth all about it. It spoke of a time when they had all been happy, when no Dark Lord was known and seemed ahead only endless days of running out in the yard, enjoying time as a family. They had learned the ways of the Ancient One together, with the words of both of his parents reminding him and his brother the importance of keeping the words close to them.

"I see why you remember that one so fondly, Dante. Keep remembering those times."

"I will, but I sense another purpose from you."

"Perhaps I wanted you to remember something nice," said Seth, but Dante waited, "or perhaps a couple of other reasons. Maybe I thought it would do good for your mother to hear pleasant memories from your family after what she has been through. Also, I want those memories at the forefront of your mind as the time approaches for you to face your father."

"Now that sounds like the Seth I know." Dante got up and walked over to his mother's bedside. He kissed her goodnight on the forehead. He and Seth walked out of the room and headed for their separate quarters for the night.

⁓ℓℓ⁓

The next morning Lana and Caleb sat down to breakfast.

"You're right. They need to know," said Lana.

Caleb agreed and sent out the message while he talked to Lana. "They should begin arriving shortly. We need to begin working on this with the other commanders."

"I wonder what Alika's group is going to do after this. I mean, of course, they must get the ship repaired first."

"I thought about that as well. The impression I got was they want to obtain more information on the dispersal device, but I'm not sure they knew their next move after this last time."

"I know the time is running out, but I hope they give it a break. It was so close this last time. Another time so near and I don't see it working for them. If something happened, we would all be grieved, but Dante ..."

"I know. I don't want to see any more tears for your cousin."

At that moment, Dante and Seth entered the room.

Dante got to them first. "So serious you two. What's up?"

Lana got up, smiled, and hugged her cousin. "We were talking about how glad we were you and Seth returned, and Alika's crew got back safe. Did you sleep well?"

Dante's expression said he didn't think that was the extent of the conversation but let it pass. "Yeah, I did, and it's good to be back."

Caleb said, "The rest of the commanders are on their way. We need to let them know the results of Alika's operation."

Dante and Seth nodded in agreement, joined Lana and Caleb for breakfast, and continued to talk.

Ryan was the first to arrive, and the others quickly followed.

"Didn't I just see you?" asked Dante, laughing.

"Yeah, I thought the same. I wonder how Alika's crew is doing with those ship repairs. I don't envy them."

"Me either, but we wanted to help." Dante sighed. "Let's go join the others."

The commanders spent the day watching the footage, going through the downloaded information, and discussing it with Lana and the others.

CHAPTER TWENTY-NINE

The girl sat with Alena and Alika. She was the last to get a shower for the night. All three worked all day and into the evening on the ship and watching the download. They were exhausted. They took inventory of the ship repairs still left.

"The weapon system is not all the way up," said the girl.

"We also have work to do before the holographic system is completely stable," said Alena.

"Some backup systems remain to be repaired," said Alika.

"Yes, I'm afraid our quarters resemble as if a small tornado blew through most of it," Alena added.

"And don't forget little luxuries on the ship, like the drink dispenser. Although after this last time, it may not have been a luxury. We had small fires in the making on the ship." A smile started to play at the corner of the girl's mouth.

"Not funny," Alena said as she tried not to smile. "We'll repair the actual backup system to take care of that situation."

"Suit yourself, Alena." This time the girl's eyes twinkled.

"Yeah, your solutions are more creative, more entertaining, but I wish we wouldn't always try them out in such crucial times, like life and death situations. We had this discussion already. Your talent for it?" This time it was Alena's eyes that danced.

"I did walk right into that, didn't I? You enjoyed that immensely, Alena. You're right, I suppose. Entertaining solutions are not the ones we want to go to first in the situations we have found ourselves in lately. I'll try to make it less entertaining for you for a bit."

"It's all right. Just calm until we get the ship repaired. You do keep things interesting, and I wouldn't want you to change. After all, I have no doubt when the time comes, whatever challenge you provide him, he will make every effort to make it work. I can't think of anyone better matched to do so."

Alika watched the two as they teased each other back and forth. They grinned at each other as the girl finally shook her head at Alena, and neither one could contain their laughter any longer. Alika smiled. "That was entertaining to watch. I hope you two enjoyed yourselves. Alena got you at the last, but we were reminded tonight of your many redeeming qualities that no one can resist about you once they meet you, correct?"

Alena laughed harder at Alika's comment to the girl.

The girl grinned. "So, I've been told that I possess these qualities. I'll have to trust you're right. It also appears I've been reminded tonight of what a stellar job you do, Alika, of monitoring us during our operations. My compliments on your recall."

"The two of you are amusing at times. You said it yourself." Alika grinned.

"All right, in all seriousness, considering the damage, we should be happy with what it looks like after only a few days of work on it," said Alena.

"Agreed. You two have worked extremely hard, especially after what the two of you escaped. We all need to get sleep tonight, and we'll start in on it again tomorrow."

The girl asked, "Have we thought about our next move once we get the ship repaired in light of what we gained?"

"I have, but I don't know," said Alika as Alena shook her head too.

The girl stared out in thought, not saying anything.

Alika peered back at her. "Apparently, you have given it some thought."

"I have, but the time factor. It's rushing upon us. I have this feeling... I'm not sure." she paused as if far away for a moment. "Maybe we won't get the chance to decide."

"The time will run out on us," said Alena.

"Hopefully, not. We need more time to figure out how to stop it," said the girl.

Alika knew her instincts were right in the past, so he didn't feel good now.

The girl got up. "I'm exhausted, though, and of no use to either of you in this state." She hugged them both and headed to bed.

CHAPTER THIRTY

The next morning began.

The Black Dragon Commander stared down at the plans for the attack on the colony. It was set, ready, nothing remained to be done, and yet it didn't work as he told himself the words. The screen stared back at him. At last, he gave up and decided he needed to go over last-minute details for the attack on the colony. He called the squadron leader in charge of the small group of ground soldiers back in to see him.

"Yes, Black Dragon Commander, you wished to see me," said the squadron leader.

"Do you remember when we spoke earlier about the change of plans for this attack on the colony?" asked the Black Dragon Commander.

"Yes, sir, it will be done as you said the Dark Lord wanted."

"Yes, good." The Black Dragon Commander hesitated. "Some additional orders for today. No children." Something stirred in him again. "And no more than one from a household." Something stirred in him further, but he pushed it back. He could go no further modifying the instructions from the Dark Lord.

"Are you sure, Black Dragon Commander?"

The Black Dragon Commander got up and put his hand to his sword. "I'm your Commander, and it sounded like you questioned my orders. Do I need to put someone else in charge of this attack? I can end your service right here, right now."

"No, sir. I will carry it out exactly as you ordered. I will go immediately and make sure my squadron understands the rest of the instructions."

"See that they do. If not, I will hold you responsible, and any of those that do not follow instructions will also pay the penalty. I'm most unhappy with the way things have gone the last couple of weeks. You and your squadron cannot handle another incident. Do we understand each other?"

"Yes, sir." The squadron leader turned and walked away to relay the instructions to his squadron.

The Black Dragon Commander sat back down as the squadron leader walked out the door. He felt the stirring he sometimes got still. Each time he pushed it back down, thinking it buried, but it always resurfaced no matter what. Sometimes it was more like a whisper, but he tried to ignore it. He told himself it was the Elders' fault; they were the ones who caused all this for the colonies. He was forced to these tactics as the Dark Lord because of the lies of the Elders. Over and over again, this same record ran through his mind. He told himself it worked. That he felt better after he did so. Sometimes he did feel better. Other times like today, he found a harder time ignoring the whisper from deep inside.

CHAPTER THIRTY-ONE

The three sat down to a late breakfast. Exhaustion finally had taken over from working so late the last couple of days on the ship. They needed the extra sleep this morning. Then they resumed working on the ship.

◦◦◦

Dante's camp started work around nine in the morning, eating while they continued to discuss the information. Two hours later, a familiar sight entered the room. Lana nodded, and everyone groaned.

Caleb got up and quickly headed for the door. "Time to move out, everyone."

◦◦◦

Alika glanced down at his data pad and sighed. He stopped working. They had only worked for a little under an hour on the ship repairs. "You two, another attack is beginning. It just came up." The two stopped their work.

"We probably need to watch it for a bit," said the girl.

Alena and Alika both nodded in agreement, and they all went inside.

◦◦◦

Caleb was in the air with the fleet. "Looks like the normal. Everyone ready?"

Dante and Ryan were on the ground. Dante glanced at Ryan. "Is it my imagination, or am I seeing more soldiers?"

"I think they multiplied too, Dante."

Lana listened. "What? Are you sure? A whole army? On the other corner? Okay, let me see what we can do."

Ryan turned to Dante. "That sounds like tanks already."

"It does." Dante took out his scopes and peered through. His face went pale. "Ryan, more than four uglies are headed around the corner."

Lana said, "How many are you seeing? Okay, Dante, I hear, but we have another problem." Lana gasped. "They're doing what?" Lana held back a sob. She had no idea how to protect the colony at the moment.

⁓ℓℓ⁓

Alika, Alena, and the girl listened in horror as they already saw what was unfolding on the colony before all the reports came into Lana.

The girl stared back at Alika. "We must help them." She suited up.

Alika nodded, and Alena began preparing as well.

"I'll let Lana know you and Alena are headed to help," said Alika.

"We'll go help the colonists' army on the corner," said the girl. "I have an idea on how to help Dante and Ryan. They sent more tanks, but most of them are way back still. A couple of ships from Caleb's fleet with well-placed shots if they do it now could be the solution," said the girl to Alika as she finished getting the last bit of her covering and gear on.

"I understand," said Alika.

"We're gone," said the girl as she and Alena ran out the door. "We'll talk more on the ship if we come up with a plan to help Seth's situation."

⁓ℓℓ⁓

"Lana and Caleb, it's Alika. My two are on their way to help."

"Alika, you have no idea how good those words sound," answered Lana as she struggled for a solution.

"Lana and Caleb, we came up with a plan to get rid of most of the tanks. A couple of well-targeted shots from the fleet. Can they disable the tanks furthest from Dante's and Ryan's squadron?"

"Of course, Alika, it makes so much sense. Caleb, did you get that?"

"I did, and we should be able to do it. Let Dante and Ryan know so they move the squadron back. We should do it now before the tanks are too close."

"Dante and Ryan, move the squadron back now, way away from any of the tanks. Do it this second."

Dante and Ryan glanced at each other, but they had heard the tone before, and they knew Lana meant it. They gave the signal for the squadron to fall back immediately.

Alika continued to Lana, "My two should be there any moment to take care of the squadron attacking the colony army on the corner. They are in full covered uniform, but they display Freedom Fighter insignia on them, so they should be recognized as friendly."

"I'm letting the colony commander know now."

⸻ ℓℓ ⸻

The girl and Alena listened and talked as they got to the planet. The girl said, "We must get the one thing wrapped up so we can help Seth's group."

Alena said, "They're not going to take those colonists' prisoners all the way to their ship."

"I know, but they have to last long enough for us and Seth's group to come up with a plan. Hopefully, we don't run out of time."

"We've landed. Let's go."

The two ran out of the ship to the corner of the colony, where the battle had started a few minutes before.

"We're here to help, courtesy of Lana," said the girl to the colony commander, and Alena nodded next to her.

"What is the plan?" asked the colony commander.

Alena and the girl pulled their sunspears out, watching as they grew to their full length.

"Pretty simply," the girl said to the colony commander, "dismantle as many of them as possible, so they don't get to your colonists. Come on, let's go."

While the two got to work with their sunspears, the colony commander motioned for his squadron to continue pushing back the Black Dragon soldiers. The battle went much differently with the assistance Lana sent. The two slashed through the ranks with lightning speed. Pieces of metal and Black Dragon gear covering flew in the air as their sunspears cleaved through one Black Dragon soldier after the other. The colony army fought harder, inspired by the two spear-bearers. They knew the fighting force of a spear-bearer, but there were few with the skill of Dante and his group. That skill was a special one seldom seen, and they glimpsed moments of it when Dante would defend a colony. Now they saw two spear-bearers that had the same incredible mastery, the brilliance with the sunspear, and they fought at their side today. They witnessed it and understood.

Dante and Ryan waited. A minute passed. They continued to fight, but it was with the Black Dragon soldiers that came close range as Lana instructed.

"Okay, Dante and Ryan, Caleb is about to knock out some of those tanks to a manageable amount."

"What about the other army?" asked Ryan. "Do we need to split the squadron and get help over there?"

"No, it's taken care of. Two somebodies dropped in on us and are assisting there. That front is going much better."

Before Dante and Ryan could react to the news, several explosions marked the terrain in front of them, but far enough away from them and the squadron, it posed no threat to them.

"How many are you left with now?"

Ryan checked with the scopes. "Nice shooting by that husband of yours. Only three tanks left, but they gave us extra soldiers today, so it evens out. Back to a normal day in the neighborhood, Lana. We got this."

"I needed to hear that, you two. I've got another situation to figure out still. I'll let the two of you get to work."

"We better move. At least no more worrying about the other army," said Ryan.

"Yeah, with those two spear-bearers, they should have it knocked out soon. Man, they're busy." Dante shook his head. He and Ryan ran toward the remaining tanks and motioned for the squadron to follow them.

⁓

Seth and Commander Gabe listened to Lana.

"Are you sure?" asked Seth softly.

"Yes, It's the initial report coming from officials of the colony, and the Black Dragon soldiers are almost to your position."

"I told our soldiers to stand down. We cannot harm the colonists in a firefight," said Commander Gabe.

"What do you wish us to do, Lana?" said Seth.

"I don't know yet. Do what you must to keep the colonists alive until we come up with a plan. Help has arrived in the form of two somebodies, but they are assisting somewhere else now. The Dark Lord sent an extra army to the far end of the colony to deal with, so they are tied up at the moment. They indicated you would be their next stop once they can finish their current battle."

"I'm glad they dropped in on us today," Seth said.

Commander Gabe nodded and sighed. "Until then, it appears we must go along with this sick game the Dark Lord chooses to play with the lives of these colonists."

"The Dark Lord is cruel, and he again shows it," said Seth.

"Here they come," said Commander Gabe.

Almost forty soldiers approached Seth, Commander Gabe, and their squadron. In front of each soldier, they firmly held a scared colonist prisoner.

Normally, Seth and Commander Gabe would hide in the building, but this time they came out and openly faced the Black Dragon force.

"Why have you done this?" asked Seth quietly.

"He's right. Your battle is with us, not these innocent colonists. Let them go," said Commander Gabe quietly as well.

"They became a part of it after the incident at the last colony attack. The Dark Lord was most unhappy with the result. He guarantees today will be much more to his liking. We have business to tend to, and you will let us do it."

"Let them go, and we will let you take the supplies. Do not hurt the colonists." Seth saw the scared look in the eyes of the men and women.

The Black Dragon squadron leader laughed. "No, we will not let them go. You won't allow us to take the supplies without the colonists any longer. Come, do you think us fools? Besides, as you can see, we did not bring carts today. We do not need them. The colonists will be the carts today. One box for each colonist. Once the transport is done, you're smart enough to figure out the rest." He ran his hand fondly over the blade of his sword and laughed again.

"To use these colonists for such evil, one day your Dark Lord will pay. It's a horrible thing you're a part of," said Commander Gabe with controlled anger.

"Make a path now before we kill one of them right here. I'm looking for an excuse to make an exception. You are in no position to give any orders. I hold all the pieces. We both know this, so now move aside."

Seth and Commander Gabe got out of the way and let the Black Dragon squadron leader pass along with the rest of the squadron with their prisoners in front of them.

"Thank you for your cooperation. See that it continues."

CHAPTER THIRTY-TWO

The girl and Alena continued to make fast work of the squadron sent to overcome the small colony army. Although the Black Dragon sent a sizable extra force, there were no extra surprises to contend with as Dante and Ryan had found. The girl looked up and finally realized there were no swords coming in opposition with hers. She tried to seek one out, and there was none as well. She looked at Alena and got a tired nod from her too. Alena came over, and they found the colony commander.

"They are stopped, it appears," said the girl.

"Yes, thank you," said the colony commander, surveying the scene.

"You do have a few injured," said Alena.

"We will treat them immediately."

The girl heard a whisper, "Look." Her gaze went to a young man kneeling over a fallen body. "One of your men did not survive the battle. Who is the young man that grieves over him?"

"His name is Jonathan."

The voice whispered, "Go to him. I will make the time for both of you to do the other task."

"Thank you." The girl turned to Alena. "We need to go to him." Alena wondered the obvious question. "We have been given time," responded the girl. Alena followed her.

The girl went over to Jonathan and knelt beside him. Alena knelt across from both of them.

The girl looked at the body. He had been older than Jonathan, considerably older. The girl somehow understood, and tears came into her eyes.

"Jonathan, is it?" the girl asked softly.

"Yes." He stared up at her through his tears.

"This was your father?"

"Yes, how did you know?"

"I'm not sure. I'm sorry we didn't get here in time to save your father and spare you this grief, Jonathan."

"There is nothing you could have done. It happened in the first moments." His voice broke. "It should have been me. I was almost overpowered, and he got in front of me. He took the blow and fell." Tears flowed down his face again. He turned from his father's body and back to her.

Tears streamed from the girl's eyes, safely hidden from view by her visor. "Your father loved you and paid everything to protect you. Hold on to that part, Jonathan."

Alena said softly, "Yes, Jonathan, that is what he would want you to remember from this day."

"You're right. It is what he would wish. That was his spirit."

The girl said, "Grieve your father's loss but do not let what was done today turn into bitterness or anger. Your spirit is gentle. Let it stay such, Jonathan."

"I will. My father is with the Ancient One now. He has taught me in those paths, and I would not depart from them."

"Good. My spirit feels better about leaving you now. We grieve with you today in your loss, Jonathan." She placed a comforting hand on his shoulder.

"Thank you ..." He searched for a name and realized they had never given him one.

"We come to assist occasionally when the need presents itself. We are friends to Lana's and Dante's cause." The girl rose, and Alena did the same. "We must go now, Jonathan. The day is not won yet."

Alena patted Jonathan on the back as she walked past him as well. Jonathan watched them go and sadly stared down at his father.

The girl and Alena jogged quickly over to the colony commander. The girl talked to Alika on the way.

"How many soldiers are in the team which came for the supplies?" asked the girl.

"Seth says about forty."

"How many soldiers in his team?"

"About twenty-five."

"We need about fifteen more."

"You have a plan it sounds like."

"It's forming. Tell Seth and Lana we'll be in touch."

The girl and Alena reached the colony commander.

The girl said, "We have an additional situation involving another squadron of Black Dragon soldiers. We need your fifteen best shots from your army to come with us to assist. You know who those are, and we must have them standing in front of us ready to head out now, please."

"Give me two minutes, and they're all yours."

"Alika, can Seth hear us now?" asked the girl.

"Yes, I can, but you sound ..." said Seth trailing off.

"Full uniform, in the helmet too, Seth," the girl said with a laugh.

"Ah, continue. I will put this so Commander Gabe can hear as well," said Seth.

"That's fine. We're getting enough soldiers from the colony army to join your group to have the same amount of Freedom Fighter soldiers as Black Dragon soldiers now. We gathered they are using the colonists as human shields."

"Yes, it appears to be their plan."

"Are they finished getting the supplies?"

"Almost as they are starting to line up like they are about to head out momentarily."

"Did you get a feel for how long they plan to keep the colonists alive?"

"It sounds like until they get to the ship to load the supplies."

"Although the squadron leader made it clear he is eager to shed blood," said Commander Gabe.

"Yes, I understand, Commander Gabe, so unless something unexpected happens like one of the colonists tries something on the way, the colonists should continue to live. It makes sense which is good news for us if the time frame holds. Do you or any of your soldiers have any liquid smoke by chance?"

"I'm not sure. Seth or I didn't bring any since the distraction was no longer an element."

"It's all right, we did. If you can locate any among your soldiers, have it ready. The visors with the masks are standard equipment, so I hope your soldiers followed orders, and they wore those today because they will need them."

"They did."

"Good, tell them to put their A-game on when it comes to their shooting. They will need to make it count. If it's not right, it hits their colonist instead of the Black Dragon soldier. We want forty Black Dragon soldiers on the ground and zero colonists hurt when the smoke clears. I'll convey the same here as well. Of course, if you have a better plan, I'm all ears."

Seth and Commander Gabe turned to each other. Seth said, "Lana did you hear all this?"

"I have. It's solid. I don't have a better solution. The first priority must be the colonist's safety. There could still be a colonist hurt in the crossfire. However, the other way only ends in certain death for them."

"Yes, the worst physically with this will be coughing from the smoke, but it produces no lasting effects. Been there, done that recently. We'll talk later, Lana. Seth and Commander Gabe, we'll track their movements so as they get close to the end of the road for the supplies, we can do this. We'll keep the channel open so you can hear how close we are, and we can hear what goes on at your end. We will see you soon."

Alena looked at her with an unspoken message. "No names."

The girl returned her glance and nodded back, returning the unspoken message. "I know."

⸻ ℓℓℓ ⸻

The colony commander came up to them with the fifteen soldiers. "They're all yours to command."

"Thank you, Commander," said the girl. She turned to Alena. "You want to start briefing them while I speak with the Commander for a moment."

"Do you or your soldiers happen to have any liquid smoke, Commander?"

"Yes, a little." He pulled out what he had.

"Good, they'll need it for the operation with us." She accepted the vials from him. "I assume they have their visors with the masks attached." He nodded. "Those will be needed today as well." Her voice softened, and she gazed over at Jonathan. "Commander, watch over Jonathan. He has a gentle spirit. Make sure the grief over his father does not cause his spirit to turn. Stay by his side and comfort him at this time. You must take on a different role to him at this hour."

"I will do so now. My thanks to you and your companion today." He shook her hand and walked away toward Jonathan.

The girl walked up to Alena and the group of soldiers. "Let's roll. You can finish this briefing on the way."

Seth and Gabe could hear the girl's conversation with the commander. They glanced at each other, puzzled for the part involving whoever Jonathan was but decided it was a different matter unrelated to the current situation.

The Black Dragon squadron leader came over before leaving with the supplies and their prisoners. He smiled at Seth and Commander Gabe. "You behaved well today. The Dark Lord will be pleased. Do not cause any trouble for us today." He laughed. "Remember we bring precious cargo with us."

Seth and Commander Gabe glared at him coldly.

"No more words today," said the Black Dragon squadron leader. "Oh well. Remember what I have said. You would not want to be blamed for their blood being on your hands, at least not this early, right? Pleasant doing business with the two of you today." He laughed and walked away as he motioned the rest of the squadron to follow with the prisoners.

"He will not laugh for long. We'll make sure of it at the end of a blade," said the girl firmly, holding back her anger. Seth and Commander exchanged a glance as they heard the young spear-bearer's words come through their earpiece.

Commander Gabe said, "I would not want to be at the end of your sunspear when the time comes."

"Commander Gabe, you're correct. They wanted a fight today. They will get one," said the girl. "We'll see you and Seth soon with the squadron."

"You heard our friends. Let's stay on the Black Dragon soldiers' tracks with our squadron," said Seth. "We will brief them on the way. I agree, Commander Gabe. I'm not sure the Black Dragon leader realized what he unleashed today."

CHAPTER THIRTY-THREE

Dante and Ryan found getting to the tanks harder today because of the larger army the Black Dragon sent to fight, but they still managed to do so.

Dante and Ryan reached the first tank. Dante got close enough to it to throw several firestones into the shaft of it, and Ryan shot several blaster shots into the shaft at the same time. An instant later, an explosion blew the entire structure off the tank. The soldiers in the tank scrambled out, and Ryan's squadron made quick work of them.

Dante and Ryan went to the second tank. Dante saw one of the fallen Black Dragon swords lying there. "This will do nicely." He jammed it into the moving mechanism of the tank. It slowed the tank down, and it was all the opening Dante needed. He sprayed the adhesive on the explosive item, stuck it on the tank, and cleared the tank in time. There was a small explosion, enough for the tank to stop moving altogether. Once again, those in the tank began to come out, and they had company waiting. Dante climbed on the tank and used his sunspear to make the shaft of the tank inoperable. He would come back and do a more complete job later.

"One more," said Ryan.

"One more," responded Dante. "It got close, usually the case with the last one. I'll take it out from inside."

"Understood. We'll cover you out here."

Dante climbed on the tank and dodged the shaft of it. The soldiers in the tank tried to shoot the squadron with it. Dante took his sunspear and damaged it enough, so it was no longer an issue. He cut a hole in the top of the tank, dropped the light crackers inside, and quickly jumped into the tank. After eliminating the few soldiers inside, he was about to disable the tank when he realized he wasn't alone. He turned around in time to see a Black Dragon soldier almost upon him and three more coming toward him. They waited inside for Dante. The one swung his sword, and Dante got his sunspear up before the sword got him all the way. However, the move was not enough to keep the edge of the blade from catching his arm. To make matters worse, the others bore down on him, sword in hand, seeing they surprised him.

Meanwhile, Ryan watched as the tank continued to move. "He's been in there too long, and the tank is still moving full speed. Something is wrong. I'm going in." The others nodded as they covered Ryan.

Dante realized this wasn't going well. Normally it wasn't a problem, but they surprised him, and it was close quarters inside the tank. He saw them getting out their blasters as well in the other hand as they slowly pushed him in a corner, and he only succeeded in eliminating one of them. Working on the second one, he could feel the other two soldiers pressing their advantage. The tank continued to move as well, making it harder to fight. He finished off the second one and saw the other two point their blasters straight at him. He got the sunspear up to try to ward both blasts off and duck at the same time, but he already knew it was too late as he heard the blasts go off. To his amazement, the two Black Dragon soldiers fell before his feet.

"Would you get the tank stopped now, Dante?" said Ryan from above the tank with his blaster still in his hand pointed downwards toward the two fallen soldiers.

Dante breathed a sigh of relief. "Will do, Ryan." He took several swipes to the control panel with his sunspear, and the tank stopped.

CHAPTER THIRTY-FOUR

Seth, Commander Gabe, and their squadron followed the Black Dragon soldier at a safe distance. They needed to be close enough when the time came, but not too close to give the squadron leader a reason to take one of the colonists' lives early. The girl and Alena, with their squadron, closed in from the other side.

"I don't want to do this too close to the end destination, but we want to be sure it's clear of any other colonists. I'm afraid if we let them get too close to the end destination, it may be too late. They may decide to end the colonists' lives early. On the other hand, if we do it too early, they could take another group of colonists prisoners," said the girl.

Seth and Commander Gabe glanced at each other and nodded. Seth said, "We agree with your assessment. Do you have a place in mind?"

"We located a ship resembling a transport ship, so our guess is that's where they're headed. We need to find a location that fits the description I gave. Lana and Alika, do you think that's where they're going?" asked the girl.

"I believe so. Other ships are in the area, but the one fits, and it's the direction they're headed," said Lana. "What do you think, Alika?"

"I agree from what I see as well," said Alika. "I would say go with our current guess unless they change directions, or something else comes into play which changes our mind."

"Can you two map out the best place to put this into action?" asked the girl.

"Will do, and we'll get back to you in a couple of minutes," said Lana.

"My comrade has a valid point. Our soldiers need to start marking their Black Dragon soldier with Seth and Commander Gabe. Each soldier must know which one they're responsible for taking down. There can be no confusion once this begins. Tell me how you want it done so our squadron is prepared. They must work as one once we get there," said the girl as they continued to walk and talk.

"Understood," said Commander Gabe. Seth nodded. Commander Gabe and Seth started discussing it. They didn't get far, though. Lana's voice came back.

"I spoke with Alika. We located a place that fits and sent it to your data pads. What do you think?"

Commander Gabe and Seth nodded. Seth said, "We think it works, Lana."

The girl and Alena nodded as well, and the girl answered, "We are in agreement, Lana."

Alena and the girl listened carefully as Seth and Commander Gabe let them know how they wanted the soldiers to know who they were to take down when the time came. The girl said, "We'll take care of it on our end. Every Black Dragon soldier will have a target on their back, and it's up to our soldiers to make sure they make the shot today."

The girl, Alena, and their squadron got there first.

The girl addressed their squadron. "Get ready. Everyone, masks on now. Blasters ready. Everyone knows your shot. As soon as the liquid smoke is thrown, take the shot. Own it. There can be no hesitation, no mistakes, and no missed shots. They have used your fellow colonists today as pawns in a cruel game, and it stops here at this spot. We will make it so. May the Ancient One be with you as you finish this battle today."

The girl reported. "Our group is ready, Commander Gabe and Seth."

"I would say so," said Seth as he exchanged a smile with Commander Gabe.

Lana heard the young spear-bearer too and smiled. It sounded familiar. She had heard herself voice similar sentiments at certain points. She liked Alika's students more as the moments passed. "Alika, your students sound ready."

"Yes, indeed. Their fighting spirit is something I did not train. It's all them."

Seth and Commander Gabe prepared the soldiers as they approached the place to spring the ambush. They were there. The girl and Alena watched and waited with their group until the Black Dragon soldiers reached the place.

Instantly smoke filled the area, and blaster shots went off in unison. The Black Dragon soldiers scrambled in confusion. Screams filled the air, mixed with coughing. A furious roar erupted from the Black Dragon squadron leader as he watched most of his squadron decimated in a single moment. He realized what happened and tried to grab one of the colonists up, but he didn't get the chance. He had a sunspear in his face in an instant. Seth and Commander Gabe moved to take care of him but found one of Alika's students had beat them to it. It didn't take long for them to realize it was the young spear-bearer.

"Don't even think about it. Your reign of terror on these colonists ends now at the point of my sunspear."

"Actually, I enjoyed myself quite thoroughly until now. I planned forty bodies to give to my Dark Lord as a trophy." He sneered. "I'll happily settle for one spear-bearer instead. You will make quite the offering."

"Think again. This spear-bearer doesn't go down easily," said the girl coldly as her sunspear caught all his blows.

Meanwhile, every shot found their Black Dragon target. Some shots did better than others. Now the Freedom Fighter soldiers came closer, firing the second shot or using their swords to finish the job. Either way, the result was a success. The colonists escaped death. A couple of shots brushed a colonist's arm or leg, resulting in minor injuries. The Freedom Fighter soldiers moved the colonists out of harm's way as the young spear-bearer and the squadron commander continued to battle.

Alena watched with Seth and Commander Gabe. They wanted to help, but there was nothing to do. Alena had no doubt the girl would finish it.

"This is all you have?" asked the Black Dragon leader, laughing.

"No, the colonists are clear now. This is what I have. Now you will pay for the terror you have spread through these colonists today. You're about to join your comrades, I promise," said the girl with the same calmness but with fresh determination. Her sunspear moved with new energy, and her blows came smooth and with lightning speed. The Black Dragon squadron leader was forced back, and his smile disappeared. He tried to hit her with one of his sword thrusts and thought for a moment he got her, but it was nowhere close. She dodged expertly as she had done all along, and the next moment her sunspear cleaved right through him. He fell at her feet to join his comrades.

The girl glared down at him. "This spear-bearer will be no trophy for you this day or any day to come."

The girl turned around to Alena. Alena walked up to her. They approached Seth and Commander Gabe.

Seth looked at both of them. They were completely in gear. There was no way to tell their identities. Only he knew two women hid underneath all the gear.

The two reached out their hand to clasp Commander Gabe's hand in greeting.

"A pleasure to meet you, Commander Gabe," said Alena.

"Yes, Commander Gabe," said the girl.

"We have heard much about both of you. It's good to finally meet you two," said Commander Gabe.

"And Seth, very much the same," said Alena.

"Yes, Seth, Alika spoke nothing but good about you," said the girl.

"Both of you as well. I'm amazed at seeing both of your work first..." said Seth.

His words were cut off. They all heard it at the same time, and it was approaching from behind.

"That can only be trouble," said the girl. She took out her scopes and peered through them. "We have company coming, so we must send the colonists to safety." She and Alena ran over to them with Seth and Commander Gabe close behind them.

"Those who came with us. Three of you take the colonists. Get them out of here. Take them the same path back to your colony commander. Make sure they get there safely and receive the medical attention they need." She turned to Seth and Commander Gabe. "We need one from your squadron."

Commander Gabe motioned for one of his soldiers to come. "Do what the spear-bearer tells you."

"Go with them. You can communicate with Commander Gabe if there is trouble along the way, and we'll figure it out. I don't expect you to find any. If you need to do so, though, don't hesitate to call. Lana will hear and can figure something out. Go now. Once they're safe, let us know. Leave, now, hurry."

They did, and they were gone with the colonists.

The girl turned to Alena, "Ready again?"

"Always."

The girl turned to Commander Gabe and Seth. "I hope you and your squadron are ready for round two because here they come. Our sunspears are at your command."

Commander Gabe said, "Okay, everyone, get ready. We have company coming."

Seth said, "Lana, did you hear?"

"I did, and I think Alika's crew is right as far as the colonists. The path seems to be clear for them to get back safely, but I'll monitor and make sure they make it back to the colony commander. The Black Dragon squadron is almost upon you, though."

"Commander, we need to be careful. Try to move them further this way. We don't want to hit those supplies, as some contain volatile chemicals in them," said Alena.

"The spear-bearer is right. I forgot momentarily. Let's try to draw them away from the supplies if possible."

⌇

Dante got out of the tank and climbed off it.

"What happened?"

"Extra soldiers hid inside waiting on me, Ryan. My back was turned, and they surprised me."

Ryan said, "I meant your arm. It's bleeding. How did you manage that?"

Dante followed Ryan's eyes and saw he was right. "Oh, one of them scratched me with his sword."

"It's a scratch." Ryan sighed. "Where have I heard those words before? Okay, compared to the whole half of your back torn apart, yes. Here." Ryan took a cloth out and tied it tightly around Dante's arm. "Go run the sunspear through those other two tanks all the way, and we'll treat your arm with something correctly. Come on."

"You're overreacting,"

"No overreacting would be telling Lana and her coming to get you."

"You're right. We're good, Ryan. We'll do it your way and treat it in a minute." He laughed.

Dante went into each of the two tanks and made sure both control panels were completely destroyed.

Ryan took the cloth off and sprayed medicine on it for Dante, then tied another cloth on it. "Okay, it will do until we get back."

"Let's check in with Lana," said Dante. "Lana, everything is under control here now."

"Good to hear."

"You sound different, cous."

"We're still working out the other situation."

"The other army on the corner?"

"No, we took care of that a while ago. A situation with Seth's team now."

"Do we need to split up and go there?"

"No, we need to see how it plays out. The worst is over, and the colonists are safe, it appears. The Dark Lord's plan was foiled thanks to the help Seth and Commander Gabe received today."

Ryan said, "I thought they were helping with the army on the corner which appeared."

"They were. They finished and went and helped Seth and Commander Gabe. They're still there."

"What happened today, Lana?" asked Dante.

"The Dark Lord used colonists as human shields to try to get the supplies out."

Dante and Ryan stared at each other in horror. Dante asked, "How are the colonists?"

"All safe. However, another squadron arrived and is bearing down on Seth, Commander Gabe, our friends, and the small squadron with them. It's unclear how large it is."

"We need to go help them. It's too small a force to handle a Black Dragon Army," said Dante in a panic.

"You would not get to them in time. The battle is begun. Our friends triumphed once today with similar numbers. Seth and Commander Gabe are fierce on the battlefield, and their soldiers are well-trained. We must trust this will go our way as well. The Ancient One is with them."

"There's nothing we can do but sit as they fight outnumbered."

"At the moment, yes, Dante. I will let you both know if there is anything to be done. I need to see what can be done to help them now."

CHAPTER THIRTY-FIVE

"They keep coming," said Commander Gabe.

"Yeah, where's the source?" asked Alena.

"Do we have an answer to that beyond the obvious?" asked the girl as she continued to swing her sunspear.

"Lana, do we?" asked Alika.

"You know, perhaps we do, Alika. They were taking the items to a supply or transport ship."

"I see it too. The trail goes from the ship and another one right by it."

"There is nothing between those ships and that trail. Let's do it." Lana paused. "Caleb, we need more of your excellent shooting today and quickly."

"Anything for you. Where are we shooting this time?"

"I sent it to you, dear."

"Expect it in the next minute."

"We're giving you breathing room. The flow should stop in the next few minutes. We're cutting off the source. Hang in there a little longer, please," pleaded Lana.

They heard it but simply nodded as they fought and resisted the urge to count the minutes.

A minute later, they heard several large explosions nearby and could feel a couple of them under their feet. They ignored them and kept fighting. At the moment, it made no difference.

"Stop him!" yelled the girl. The girl ran in front of the Black Dragon soldier before he could bring his blade down on the soldier. "Not while I'm here."

Her sunspear came between the sword end of the Black Dragon soldier and the soldier's neck, and she took care of the Black Dragon soldier. She spoke to the injured soldier the Black Dragon soldier tried to finish off. "Get back now. Use your blaster if need be for defense. Encourage any of your injured comrades to do the same," shouted the girl. The soldier nodded and slowly got back out of the way.

"You heard the spear-bearer. We mean not to lose anyone today," hollered Seth.

"Continue fighting for a bit longer," said Alika quietly.

"Yes, hold on, the stream is almost done," said Lana softly.

"I got him," said Alena, taking down the Black Dragon soldier as the girl found herself overwhelmed when she jumped in to help a soldier almost overcome. One of the Black Dragon soldiers just about took off a piece of her shoulder through her protective gear in the fray.

"That was close." The girl continued to swing the sunspear as Alena did the same beside her. She could see Seth and the Commander Gabe nearby swinging with equal fury.

This must end soon, thought the girl. She knew they had injured soldiers, but she didn't know how many. Hopefully, it wasn't serious because now they must keep focused and going. She wasn't sure how much they had left in them. She also knew the colony soldiers weren't as well-trained, so they could be a fair portion of the injured soldiers.

More minutes passed, and they each watched as another Black Dragon soldier fell at their feet. They raised their sunspears, ready for the next one, but there was no one. They looked around them at Seth and Commander Gabe, who were catching their breath. Alena and the girl took a deep breath and nodded to each other. Could they be done?

Seth said, "Lana and Alika, tell us there's no more coming on our position. Several individuals long to hear those words."

Lana and Alika said in union, "There's no more."

"We will speak in a moment."

Seth and Commander Gabe walked over to the girl and Alena.

The girl said to them, "Some are injured, but I don't think it's serious." She heard Alika clear his throat when she said it, and Seth smiled at her. "However, I'm told I'm not always the best judge in that area, so it may be better for someone else to decide."

"You're told so because it's true. Although usually, it involves your own injuries. In most cases, you're a fair judge concerning everyone else's injuries." Alena shook her head at the girl and turned to Seth and Commander Gabe. "I don't think they're serious either, but they need to leave and be treated in case."

"I'm not sure which are your soldiers, Commander Gabe, and which are part of the colony army. We need to route them accordingly," said the girl.

Commander Gabe nodded and motioned for a few of his uninjured soldiers to come over. He explained what needed to be done.

Seth called to Lana. "You heard all that, I assume."

"Yes, I did. I'll send two ships to your positions now. One to take the soldiers for the colony army to be treated to their facility, and the other ship can bring Commander Gabe's soldiers here to be treated."

"What about the colonists?" asked Alena.

"Yes, my comrade is right. Any word if they got back safe?"

"I received confirmation they are safe. I contacted the colony commander to tell him they were on their way, and he immediately sent some of his soldiers to them to help the group get the rest of the way safely. They are already getting whatever medical attention they may need thanks to your efforts today."

"It is a relief to hear, Lana," said Commander Gabe.

"It is." the girl said as she walked over to the supplies. Alena, Seth, and Commander Gabe followed her. "Surprisingly, none of the supplies were damaged. These should be taken back to the warehouse and lab. We don't want the chemicals getting damaged and causing an explosion after we kept it from happening all day."

Seth replied, "We'll make sure the task gets done."

"There's something else before you leave the colony today. A favor. There were some injured today at the colony army before we got here. I'm sure they weren't serious, but since you're still here, if you could check by there. However, we did have one fallen soldier today in the colony army. The son is a soldier in the colony's army as well. The son's name is Jonathan."

"We heard you speaking of a Jonathan earlier with the colony commander," said Seth.

"Yes, we didn't arrive in time to stop his father from being slain. During the battle, his father got in front of him to keep him from being slain but paid with his life. We spoke with the son Jonathan for a bit before we came to help you, but we had to leave. Jonathan has a gentle spirit." The girl's voice turned soft. "I have seen grief turned into something dark. I don't think it would happen to Jonathan, but the grief is fresh. It would give comfort to me if you and Commander Gabe would check on Jonathan one last time before you leave since you're checking on the injured at the colony as well. Of course, this is a task. Dante and Ryan are free to go with you as well."

"We will check on this young man and give him whatever comfort we can," said Commander Gabe gently.

"Thank you. I know you'll want to check on the injured from today from our group, so I will leave you to do so, Commander Gabe. We'll leave in a few moments. It was a pleasure fighting with you today." The girl reached her hand out and clasped Commander Gabe's hand.

Alena reached her hand out as well to meet Commander Gabe's hand. "Yes, my comrade speaks for both of us, Commander Gabe. The Ancient One keep you until we meet again."

"Yes, well met friends. I'm glad after seeing the two of you today, you are helping us. I would not want to be on the other end of your sunspears." Commander Gabe laughed. "May the Ancient One keep both of you safe as well until we meet again." He walked away to take care of the task at hand.

The girl and Alena were left standing there with Seth staring at them.

CHAPTER THIRTY-SIX

The girl motioned with her hand for them to come over to the far side, so there was no chance of being heard by the rest of the group. She adjusted something on the data pad and then peered up. "Alika, I adjusted the communications so only what is said for this time can be heard by you, me, the other member of our circle, and Seth. I did not wish you to be alarmed. Oh, I'm also adjusting the voice devices as well."

"Understood."

The girl purposely positioned her and Alena so their back was to everyone in the squadron. She lifted her visor. Her blue eyes could be seen, but nothing else. She needed to feel open air for a moment.

Alena did the same. It had proved a long day.

Seth smiled and waited patiently. He heard her say she was adjusting the voice devices, and he knew what that meant. He admitted curiosity to finally hear the real voices of the two spear-bearers.

"It's nice to finally meet the two of you."

The girl smiled back at Seth. "Same here, Seth. I'm afraid you should not be entirely honest with your student. If he finds you spoke with us for more than what was necessary for battle, he won't be happy."

"She's right, Seth. You'll find a despondent student on your hands. She and Dante are difficult to manage without adding that element to the mix." Alena laughed, her eyes twinkling.

The girl shook her head at Alena. "We're not so difficult to manage." She laughed. "Perhaps you and Ryan need further training regarding the two of us."

The girl turned back to Seth. "She enjoys teasing me, but it's okay, especially after a day like this."

"I see that. Rest assured, I do not wish to see a despondent Dante, so he will receive an abbreviated version of today. Dante has no idea. He continues to believe he will meet someone who could be a younger or older brother to him when the time comes. He voiced that on the way back to me the last time."

"That means we did an excellent job hiding my identity, including that part. Perhaps he will see me as a sister when the time comes, and we meet." The girl shrugged her shoulders.

Alena laughed, and even Alika could be heard laughing softly. Seth smiled at her. "It sounds like you are the only one continuing in such thinking, young spear-bearer."

Alena finally stopped laughing. "She is, Seth. Dante is not the only one clueless in these matters. Although she is not clueless, but she simply pretends to be in denial about the whole thing."

"I'm afraid they have you there, young spear-bearer." Seth laughed. "I know Alika believes Dante's feelings will take a different form than those of sibling. Come young spear-bearer, surely you know as well once Dante and you meet."

The girl's eyes twinkled at Seth. "Even I know when I fight a losing battle, so I'll stop now. We'll see how it plays out with him."

"We will. When will we see the two of you again?"

Alena and the girl exchanged a glance. The girl turned back to Seth and answered, "I don't know, Seth. I haven't seen any visions of what is to happen, but I sense things as well. Things are unraveling fast, and they were before today. After today's events, we all know we made the Dark Lord angrier though I didn't believe it possible. I hoped to get more information to stop the threat to come and was worried before we would run out of time. It's certain now. I'm sorry as that's a long way of saying I don't know."

"Actually, I think you told me you believe the next time we hear from any of you, it could be to say the Dark Lord is upon us, and the time has run out."

"Yes, I fear that could be the next time you hear from us."

"And Dante will be to his task."

"Yes, Dante ... Dante will be to his task."

Seth saw and heard the change that instantly came over the girl, despite the heavy protective gear covering her. The girl said Dante's name with a gentleness that could not be mistaken. Everything about her form softened instantly. Seth gazed into her blue eyes and saw concern there, but something reached far deeper for Dante. Seth smiled. Yes, the girl could deny it all she wished, but when the moment came, it would not work. "I know you're afraid for Dante, but he will be prepared for the task before him. The Ancient One will be with him. He wishes to get his father back, and he will put everything into doing so," Seth paused and said to her softly, "You care for him deeply. I see it. There is no hiding it and no need to do so. Dante also cares for you in ways he does not realize yet. He will, though, once the two of you meet. He must return as he very much wishes to meet his young spear-bearer."

The girl looked down for a moment, and when she stared back into Seth's eyes, tears slid down her face. "I so very much wish to meet him as well when the time comes. Oh, Seth, you must prepare him well. Dante does not understand the Darkness he is about to encounter, its strength. The battle he must face will try to pull his spirit apart, his very core to pieces. Please, Seth, you must be sure Dante heeds your words, Alika's words, everything he has been taught, or Dante will be lost as well. To see Dante lost to me ... I cannot." The girl had reached out to clasp Seth's hands as she spoke but stopped, unable to continue. Tears continued to stream down her face.

Seth continued to look into her eyes. He thought he understood this young spear-bearer, the emotional connection between her and Dante, but he realized he had not begun to appreciate it. Remembering the conversation with Alika, he saw now what Alika meant. Alika had spoken of a battle this one fought, a battle which echoed the one Dante was about to fight. Seth had wondered about the mark it left on the young spear-bearer. He saw it now in her eyes as she pleaded with him for Dante, this one she had come to love, though it scared her to do so. He did not know about her battle, but he felt pain go through him for this one for whatever it had been. "You will meet your Dante, young spear-bearer, and it will be a sweet meeting for the two of you. He will not be lost to us. We will not allow it to be. No more tears, child. You have shed enough," he said softly.

The girl closed her eyes and opened them back up, regaining her composure. She nodded to Seth and smiled. "You're right. Thank you, Seth. We must go now. None of this conversation can be spoken of as long as I am still unknown to Dante."

"As you wish, dear," said Seth gently and turned to Alena.

Alena reached her hand out and clasped Seth's hand. "I enjoyed my time with you today as well. You're everything Alika told us and more. Please bring Dante back safe. We're all concerned for him, but this one," looking over at the girl, "must see him return safely. You're right. I've watched her cry many tears in the time I trained her. I wish no more for her."

"I believe you, dear." Seth glanced back at the girl and then turned his attention to Alena. "It was a pleasure meeting you as well today. Take care of each other as you do."

"Goodbye, Seth. We must finish the repairs on the ship. May the Ancient One be with all of you and keep you safe," said the girl. The girl and Alena quickly walked away.

Seth heard a beep, and a voice said, "All communications restored." He knew it meant everything could be heard again.

Seth quickly went over to Commander Gabe. "Where do we stand?"

"None of the injuries are serious, Seth. The two ships arrived. We loaded the injured, and the ship just left for the treatment facilities."

"We need to get these boxes back as well."

Lana answered their call, "You're right. I'll send another ship, Seth. Yes, everything wrapped up there a bit ago. I'll pick the two of them up on the way so they can assist you."

"Yeah, Lana," said Dante. "Okay, we'll be ready to go."

Dante and Ryan got out of the ship. They met a tired Seth, Commander Gabe, and the rest of their squadron.

"Everyone okay?" asked Ryan.

"We had some injuries, but nothing serious here. Those individuals were transported for treatment. Now we need to get all these supplies loaded and back to the warehouse and lab. The squadron is beyond tired after today," said Seth.

"We understand," said Ryan. "The Dark Lord got away with nothing today?"

Seth and Commander Gabe exchanged a glance. Seth said, "They did not leave with any supplies. Yet, today was not without its grief. They did claim one life."

Dante and Ryan both wondered. Dante realized he did not see either of Alika's students. Then he realized he wouldn't know if they were there since he didn't know what either looked like. Fear embraced him. "Who was it, Seth?"

"It was one of the colony's soldiers. I don't know his name. We only know the son left grieving," said Seth sadly. "We will take care of the supplies first, and afterward, we have a visit to make before we leave the colony. The visit concerns the son."

Dante and Ryan walked with Seth and Commander Gabe to load the supplies into the ship to take to the warehouse and lab. Dante could stand it no longer. "I thought Alika's two students were here with you. Where are they?"

"Oh yes, they were for some time. They are the ones who came up with the whole plan of how to save the colonists. It worked perfectly. They continued to fight with us when the Dark Lord sent a new army after the failed ploy with the colonists. I'm surprised they could lift their sunspear anymore after the fighting they did today," said Seth.

"They already left. I missed them."

"Dante, there remained repairs on their ship to complete. They rushed off to return to that task. Those were their last words to me before they left."

They continued to talk as they loaded the supplies.

"They were everything Alika said, though, Dante. Amazing with the sunspear, and they formulated a plan quickly to save the colonists. Incredible strategy, but we knew that with the operations they do," said Seth.

"Yes, and the squadron leader wished he never met the young spear-bearer today, Dante," said Commander Gabe laughing. "I'm glad we let the young spear-bearer take care of him. I should have known when we heard them speak to the squadron before we entered the ambush site. It was truly inspiring to hear, the battle speech of a commander. They made good on it too with the squadron leader."

Dante said to them curiously, "The young spear-bearer took care of him that well?"

Seth replied, "Oh yes, the Black Dragon squadron leader thought he would carry a young spear-bearer body back as a trophy today and said as much. He found out otherwise."

"That is what he said to them?" Dante felt the words hit him, and anger coursed through him.

"Yes, but don't worry. The young spear-bearer was unfazed and made it clear he would be unsuccessful with the endeavor. The squadron leader paid for his words to the one and joined his comrades. Our friend was quite spirited as usual today."

"That part stays consistent with them." Dante laughed.

They loaded the rest of the supplies, delivered them back to the warehouse and lab, and then unloaded the supplies to where they belonged. The four of them, with the rest of the squadron, headed to the medical facility on the colony. Those of the colony army headed home after the long day. Those of Commander Gabe's army waited for one of Caleb's ships to pick them up so they could leave the planet.

CHAPTER THIRTY-SEVEN

"What are we doing here?" asked Ryan.

"I received a request from the young spear-bearer before we left the planet today," said Seth. He proceeded to tell Dante and Ryan about the request.

Commander Gabe came up to them at the moment. "I found the colony commander, and he said Jonathan is next door. The military facility is the next building over. He'll ensure Jonathan stays until we check on those injured from today."

The four went through and did so. The injuries were minor, so the visits were quick. They headed over to see Jonathan.

"How?" asked Dante. He didn't need to finish the question.

"I'm not sure. There's a level of sensing, of seeing we have yet to appreciate from the young spear-bearer, Dante." Seth smiled. "Let us go meet Jonathan."

The four walked into the room. Jonathan sat in a chair, and his eyes showed one drowned in tears. He looked up when they entered the room. He saw their Freedom Fighter insignia and started to rise out of respect. Seth motioned for him there was no need for such, so Jonathan remained seated and watched them curiously.

"Jonathan, we were asked to come check on you after today before we take our leave of your colony," said Seth, "We are sorry to hear you lost your father today in battle."

They sat with Jonathan.

"Thank you. I know each of you. You're Seth, Commander Gabe, Commander Ryan, and Dante, right?" He focused on Dante last, and his eyes stayed on him. "Yes, the two spear-bearers who assisted us today, the one mentioned you when I tried to ask their names. They would only answer they were friends of Dante's and Lana's cause. They were both concerned for me. The one, I could tell, felt badly that they didn't get here sooner to perhaps prevent my father from being slain. I told them it happened so early in the battle they could not stop it, but I don't sense it eased their minds. The one figured out it was my father though I didn't tell them."

"That sounds like our two friends. Both of them were still concerned about you, but the one who spoke with you mostly asked us to check on you before we left. How are you considering?"

"I'm good, Dante. I don't feel any bitterness, only grief. The words from your friends did help, though. I'm grateful for their kindness. I needed to hear it. One doesn't sometimes realize at the time how much."

"They seem to come when help is needed for us."

"Yes, that's what they indicated. I could tell they wanted to stay longer, but they said they couldn't because another situation remained unresolved. The one said to me, the battle was not won for the day," Jonathan hesitated. "Did that battle go our way?"

"Yes, all the colonists' lives were saved, and the army the Dark Lord sent after was defeated. I wasn't there, but I'm told the one who spoke with you at length took care of the squadron leader quite nicely."

"I'm glad. The two were a force to be reckoned with when we fought with them. The same is spoken regarding you, Dante, with your sunspear." Jonathan laughed.

Dante laughed as well. "If so, I owe it all to years of training, courtesy of Seth here. I test his patience many times. As far as the other, I'll take you at your word, Jonathan, as I hope one day to have the pleasure of fighting beside them. Is there anything we can do, Jonathan?"

"I don't think so. I'm overwhelmed by the concern for my well-being. It means a great deal for your group to check on me again." Jonathan looked at them and settled back on Dante. "Please tell your two friends thank you again, and I'll be fine. Also, their words helped from earlier today."

"We'll do so one of the next times we speak with them."

Ryan said, "If you need anything, let us know. We mean it, Jonathan."

Commander Gabe agreed, "Yes, he's right. We're saddened we could not prevent the loss of your father today, but if you need something, we'll be here for you."

Seth said, "Continue to keep your gentle spirit, Jonathan, as you grieve. I'm glad our friends' words provided comfort to you today."

Jonathan smiled and rose from his chair. The others did the same. "I sense matters demand your attention after today's events, so I'll let you go. Thank you for checking on me."

Seth patted Jonathan on the shoulder as he left the room. The other clasped his hand and said goodbye. Jonathan smiled as they walked out of the room, feeling better despite the day's event.

CHAPTER THIRTY-EIGHT

The girl and Alena landed the ship back home.

"Still energized to start on those repairs," joked Alena.

"I'm rethinking those words." She got up from the cockpit seat, and Alena did the same.

Alika met them. "You both did exceptional work. Many lives were saved today because of what you did with the others. I'm proud of both of you."

"I believe this counts as the all-day training session I was warned about in the future," said the girl, her eyes twinkling. "I do feel I can hardly swing the sunspear further."

They all laughed.

"Come, let's get something to eat for you two. Then we'll see if you truly reserved any energy for the repairs. I am doubtful."

They finished eating, and the girl said, "Somehow something is left in me. Not much. A couple of hours at the most, and I'll stop. I won't ask you two to help with the repairs tonight just because something remains in me."

"No, I feel better now that we ate and sat for a bit. Maybe it's the fact I don't have a blaster being fired at me or a sword attempting to cleave me in half anymore. I agree, though. A couple of hours is all I'm good for as well."

✺

Lana peered up as everyone started arriving back. Caleb came over to stand with her. Exhaustion covered everyone's face as they entered the building. It had been a long day—no one needed to be asked to take a seat. Lana smiled at them. "I'm glad everyone is safe, and the battle was won today. Thank you for continuing to fight when you felt you had nothing left to continue, to give. The colonists' lives were spared today because of you. This evening, get some rest, and we will start again tomorrow."

The others left to rest. Dante and Seth stayed behind. Seth said, "And Lana, thank you for your leadership. It was beyond difficult today, but you did well. I know it was overwhelming at first."

"Alika's guidance was extremely helpful, and the assistance from his students proved invaluable. I'm not sure how this ended for the colonists without their quick thinking and their extra arms on the battlefield."

"Together, we protected the colony. It was a victorious day." Seth gave Lana a hug as he turned to Dante. "Let us go see your mother before you rest for the evening, Dante."

"Thanks, Seth." Dante gave his cousin a hug goodnight.

They finished seeing Dante's mother, and Dante said to Seth, "You ended up meeting Alika's students today. Ironic, isn't it?"

Seth shrugged it off. "It worked out that way with the circumstances. They were in full gear, so I would not recognize them if I passed them somewhere. I still have no idea who they are, Dante. I take it back as I believe I could recognize their fighting spirit with those two sunspears no matter how well disguised they were. It is only matched by your own, Lana, and Caleb."

"I'm glad they helped us today. That's what matters."

"It is. I know you desire to meet them one day, especially the younger one, since you feel this connection. I'm sure the time will come at some point, as I believe Alika feels as well. Now you must concentrate on accomplishing the task with your father, so you can return to meet the young spear-bearer whenever the time comes. I'm sure, in time, things will become clear, Dante. Go get sleep now."

⸺ℓℓ⸺

Seth sat in his quarters, reading before bed. His data pad lit up showing an incoming transmission, but it showed no great urgency to be seen. Once he finished reading, he checked and found the sender to be unknown. He knew though who it had to be and quickly opened it. He read it and sat back in the chair. That's where the two had almost made their last mission. It was a close escape. Now his group had the information, depending on what they decided to do next. He understood why they sent it. With everything, they were still scrambling to figure out their next move.

∼ele∽

"Did you send it?" asked Alika.

"Yes, I just did," said the girl.

"At least they have it now," said Alena.

"They'll have to make decisions soon about it. For that matter, so will we. We're too exhausted to think about it now. The only move in my head this second has me going toward my bed," replied the girl as she could not hold back a yawn.

CHAPTER THIRTY-NINE

Alena, the girl, and Alika started another day. They worked all day and into the evening, stopping only to eat something and take well-deserved showers in the evenings. They were determined to get the ship back to its original working order. They didn't know what lay ahead, but they remained convinced it would come soon. Time was not on their side, and no vision needed to tell them that truth.

❧

Lana sat with the others. "Everyone looks much better. I hope everyone slept well."

Commander Gabe responded, "I don't believe anyone had trouble getting right to sleep after yesterday, Lana."

"I expect not. We have to plan for every attack like they will be as yesterday, unfortunately."

Seth said, "With an important exception. We cannot count on two crucial individuals who assisted yesterday."

"Yes, and they were masterful at their work," said Commander Gabe.

"That will certainly be a gap which must be planned for from what we heard," said Ryan.

Commander Conrad said, "We can route some air support down to ground soldiers."

Caleb nodded. "Yes, it's the only area which remained unchanged, so that's a possible adjustment."

"Remember until today all the areas appeared the same, then the battlefield changed on several fronts. We should prepare to modify things quickly. We can't get comfortable again. The next time it could be the air battle they change," said Dante.

Lana agreed. "He's right. The other part we can count on is surprise by the Dark Lord's strategy."

Seth said, "Yes, but there's something else to consider." He sighed.

Dante studied him. "Seth?" It was clear Seth toyed with saying whatever it was.

"We need to prepare for another attack, but we must begin thinking beyond it. This device, the threat from it, we must begin to address it. I'm not suggesting we don't prepare to protect the colonies. However, if we ignore the other by not addressing it, whatever they plan with it will crush all those it touches."

"You believe it's that soon, don't you?"

"I've come to believe so, Dante. I thought about it more after this attack. It began to feel like these latest attacks were almost as in the beginning."

Dante and Ryan said it at the same time. "A distraction."

"Yes, I'm not saying it was meant to be, but it is accomplishing the same purpose now. We stay so consumed with getting ready for one attack after the other that we are left no time to develop a plan to address the other. What information we accumulated is not from our efforts but our spear-bearer friends."

Caleb sighed. "Seth's right. We must find a way to address both threats somehow. Continuing to sit idly by while they point this dagger at us isn't an option. A plan must be formulated from something we find in the download our friends got us. We're growing accustomed to them doing the work, and it's not right."

"We expect them to be an army, and though they fight as such, they are only two," said Lana.

"She's right. They almost paid with their lives for the information they confiscated the last time. The next time it may not end with their life spared," said Dante quietly.

Commander Gabe said, "Why don't we get the plan for the next attack out of the way and then begin to work on the other? We all understand there are no more pauses between attacks. We must work out a plan to confront the other threat looming over us. We must stretch our resources in a way beyond what we ever did before."

Everyone nodded—time to get to work.

CHAPTER FORTY

The next day, the three worked all day on the ship again. Evening came, and Alena and the girl finished the last repairs to the holographic system. Alika went inside about an hour before, after completing the repairs on the ship's quarters. It was finally back together again.

The two did a visual scan around the ship and walked it. It seemed good. They went outside and walked around it together.

"We can check again tomorrow with the daylight, but I think it's done," said Alena.

"Yeah, we can test the systems too, to make sure the repairs are all good. We'll save that for tomorrow." She looked over at the lake. The moon shone full on it, and the sky displayed a clear night. "It's nice tonight. I'm going to sit for a bit before we go in. You want to come, Alena?"

"Yeah, you're right. It's a clear night." They walked out to the lakeside and sat.

"I thought we were never going to finish, Alena. We couldn't afford to leave again without the ship back in shape. I don't know what the next trip will bring."

"Yes, you seem sure when we spoke with Seth that things are coming fast. I know you're right."

"Yes, and I don't know that we gave them enough to stop it. Although you were right, I'm not convinced any more of the download would provide them the additional knowledge. We'll see."

"I'm not trying to give you a hard time when I ask you this. I honestly want to know. When we spoke with Seth about Dante, you know how this will go when you and Dante meet. You know how he'll feel for you once he meets you. You know how you truly feel for him. Why do you continue to act as if it's not so?"

"I know, and it does seem silly. I sometimes wish it was a passing thing with Dante that I would forget. I know it's not the case, though. This is unfamiliar territory for me and the strangest of circumstances, but I know what I feel for him. It won't fade or go away. I know what he must face, though. A part of me wonders what happens if he doesn't come through this task. Maybe if I don't think about him in that way, it won't hurt as much ..." she stopped and stared out at the lake. She closed her eyes and opened them back again, attempting to regain her composure, her voice soft. "I know that could never be the case, though. I'm all in with Dante. I love him, Alena, and I have for some time now."

Alena put her arm around the girl's shoulders. "I know you do, and he'll come back. You'll have worried for no reason."

"You seem so sure, Alena. I watched my mother slaughtered by the blade. Seeing Dante's mother tortured all this time and still asleep is like seeing my mother die a second death. Ethan lives, but in a cruel bondage, a slave to the Darkness as he has forgotten the truth he once knew. To see Dante meet his end, I cannot bear it. And I will be the one who sent him."

"He won't fail. He is strong, well-trained with the sunspear. He will not fall to the sword of the Dark Lord."

"Alena, it's not the only death. The other is far crueler. Ethan suffers under it for years now." The girl stopped. Tears fell from her eyes. "If Dante falls to the Darkness, that would be a dagger to my spirit. I can't fight against him, but I cannot follow him in the Darkness."

"You would go to him as he goes to his father now."

"I would in a moment to get him back, Alena."

"You won't have to; he will not fall. His spirit would not succumb to it. You know that as you know him better than any of us. You see his heart. He sees what the Darkness has done to his father, to his entire family."

"And it matters not at the moment when the Darkness gains entrance and ensnares you, Alena. I knew all that as well not long ago in the Darkness. I didn't care," said the girl bitterly as the tears continued to flow.

"But you didn't fall to it. You keep forgetting that part."

"But I did, Alena. I took those steps. In my heart, I was already traveling the path. I threw everything aside, as Ethan did. It was not me that stopped it, but the encounter from the Ancient One which stopped me further, made me see. Ethan and I are no different, Alena. Are Dante and I so different? His spirit is gentle, and he has seen all the destruction the Darkness can do. How could he embrace such Darkness, you ask? Did you and Alika not think the same of me that night when I told you to leave me? What did I do? I did embrace it even after all I saw, after the path I knew it led. Would Dante choose this path? I ... " The girl began to weep uncontrollably.

Alena reached over and gently leaned the girl into her as the girl cried on her shoulder. She had no words for her because she knew the girl spoke truth. She did wonder that very thing to Alika that night. Alena could not fathom the girl choosing such a path after what she had seen, but in the girl's mind, she allowed it to take her for that single moment. That was the only part the girl remembered. It haunted her how close she came to taking the path of Darkness, and the strength of the memory remained with her.

"I love him, Alena. I would give my life to save him if I had to."

Tears streamed down Alena's face, "I know you would," as the girl continued to weep on Alena's shoulder.

After a while, the girl's tears slowed and finally stopped. "I was honest with you. Now you know."

"I would prefer you not end up in tears."

"It seems to be the way." The girl shrugged. "Even if everything goes as planned for his task, I don't know that Dante gets all the answers he wishes from me. We have no way of knowing how everything will play out. Depending on the outcome, there are questions I may not be able to answer."

"We know some answers cannot be told until the proper time. So, you're right, but he'll find enough answered that he'll be satisfied."

"We'll see. Everyone is convinced he won't care once we meet."

Alena's eyes twinkled. "You're the only one unconvinced."

The girl laughed. "Okay, I'm not as clueless as I pretend about Dante's reaction to me." Alena eyed her, waiting. "And yes, I'm not as blind as I pretend to be. Let's say the long trainings have served to keep him in ... excellent physical condition." She saw Alena still watching her. "Okay, Alena, yes, yes, Dante is handsome, oh extremely handsome."

Alena started laughing. "Finally. Was it so hard to admit?"

"No." The girl laughed again as she cast a sideways glance at Alena. "I think more of the other things that make Dante who he is because I got to know him so closely with the visions. Those are the things that drew me so deeply to him. I didn't dwell on his physical appearance as much." The girl's eyes twinkled at Alena. "However, I admit to appreciating his good looks more as time goes on. He certainly ... " The girl shook her head. "Alena, we did enough of this honesty thing tonight. I fear what else may come out if we speak much longer, especially as I become more tired." The girl grinned at Alena as they both got up to go inside, and she hugged her. "Thank you for listening."

"Always."

CHAPTER FORTY-ONE

The next day, the girl and Alena went through the ship, checking systems and doing test flights to make sure all systems worked properly. There could be no glitches. They were relieved they did. The holographic system still didn't operate all the way, so they located the problem and retested it. A couple of other minor issues cropped up, mainly in the wiring. Apparently, a few places incurred further damage from the firefight and necessitated replacing the wiring. Everything appeared completely repaired finally. They sat and discussed the download again from the last operation.

"I don't know our next move. If we wait until it comes, it's too late," said Alena.

"But we don't know how to disable it," said Alika.

The girl had been strangely quiet, but she finally spoke, "Disabling it involves another operation. We're missing several crucial elements, with time being the biggest one. We don't have it, and we're not the only ones. The others know it's running short as well."

"Speaking of time, I can't believe how late it got," said Alena as she noticed the display as they continued to analyze the download of the dispersal device.

"Yes, time slipped away, and we're no closer to an answer. We remain stuck."

"We'll study more of it tomorrow, you two. At least the ship is finally repaired."

"Yeah, tomorrow, I suppose." The girl wondered how many more tomorrows lay ahead before the time ran out.

The girl stared out before her. She had known. Felt it. Hoped she was wrong. She closed her eyes at the image, but it did no good. It had come. All around her, there was no denying its venomous touch, its destructive power unleashed upon all life on the surface. She looked at Alena and Alika as they both shook their head. They all knew it was coming, but they still were powerless to stop it. The others could not either. At least not before this. There was the sound of one in agony near her. A pain that could not be soothed, could not be helped, but only echoed seemingly endlessly on as the night shadows crept closer. It was only the beginning. The girl turned away. She could not look upon it, listen to the cries anymore. She dropped down, overcome by the scene, and wept.

—elle—

Alena woke from a sound sleep. Did she imagine it? No, it was crying coming from the girl's room. She was sure now. She got up and went to the girl's bedside. The girl's head went from side to side as she cried in her sleep. Alena realized the girl must be receiving a vision.

"Lights on," said Alena softly as the lights came on in the room.

Alena gently nudged the girl and spoke to her. "Come, awaken. You're safe. It's only one of the visions. I'm here beside you."

The girl opened her eyes and saw Alena. She responded by throwing her arms around Alena and weeping. Alena could do nothing but try to comfort the girl again as she did the previous evening. Alika walked in with the obvious question, but Alena's eyes told him she didn't know the answer yet.

Alika came over and sat on the other side of the girl's bedside, waiting silently as she cried in Alena's arms. Finally, the girl quieted, and she hugged her knees in the bed. She stared out into space for several minutes.

The girl turned to them and said softly, "Time has run out."

"You're sure?" asked Alika.

"I am." The girl choked back a sob. "I only wish I could unsee it."

"If it's set and can't be stopped, why show you the vision?" asked Alena.

"To give us our next task for the coming storm. We won't stop it."

"And the others won't either?" asked Alika.

The girl did not answer at first, staring at both of them, and said quietly, "I'll tell you what I saw."

The girl went through the images, describing the scenes. She stopped frequently as the images overcame her, and she struggled to regain her composure. When she finished, she said, "I'll let you answer your earlier question."

"They'll try," said Alika softly.

"But in the end," said Alena quietly.

"I don't know, honestly. They either fail completely or not in time before ..." the girl did not finish as the scenes replayed in her mind.

For several minutes they all sat there in silence. The girl peered at the clock. It read three in the morning, and she groaned.

Alika said, "You need to go back to sleep. We pick this up in the morning." The girl stared back at him. "At an acceptable time, child. You told us the vision revealed the time frame too. A few more hours will not make the difference in what we need to do." Alika got up and came back with something. "Take this to help you get to sleep." The girl looked at him. "Don't worry. It will not put you out for a long time. Just make you drowsy for a few hours, enough to finish your night's sleep. I promise you, child. I know you will not get back to sleep easily with what you saw. Please take it as I ask."

The girl took it gratefully from Alika. For the first time, she gave him none of her usual stubbornness about such matters. He was right, and she desperately wanted sleep. She longed to leave the images behind that terrorized her sleep, even if for a few short hours. "Thank you, Alika, and thank you, Alena." She laid down, and Alena pulled the covers back up to her. "Alena."

"Yes."

"Do you mind staying in here for the night and sleeping in the extra bed? I know it's silly, but I can't get the images from my head this time."

"I don't mind at all. I'll be over here if you need something."

"And I will be in the next room, child."

"You two are so good to me. Goodnight to both of you." The next second she fell asleep.

Alika and Alena glanced at each other, hoping the girl would get a few hours of peaceful sleep. They got up from her bedside and attempted to do the same.

CHAPTER FORTY-TWO

The next day Alika, Alena, and the girl got up. They ate breakfast and began working.

"We did this before, but on a much smaller scale," said Alika.

"We do have more time, but not by much. It doesn't help, though, because as Alika pointed out, this is on a larger scale," said Alena.

"Yes, it worries me too, but I think we could get one more person to assist us with this."

Alena and Alika both thought about it and nodded.

Alika asked, "When do you wish to go check?"

"Immediately. The arrangements need to begin with the time we have left." The girl glanced over at Alena, who indicated her agreement.

"All right. We must make some preparations to present to him before you two speak with him. Let's get the preliminaries worked out."

***

"We'll return shortly, Alika. This shouldn't be complicated. Either he'll assist us or not," said the girl as she and Alena got on the ship.

"I'll be back." The girl walked off the ship as it finished landing. She stepped inside the bar doorway and slid into a booth.

A friendly face glanced up, and a smile lit up the man's face. "I'm glad to see you again." He got up from the booth and signaled her to come with him. "Please after you."

The girl followed him out the door and inside his ship.

Christopher motioned her to sit and brought her something to drink. He sat across from her. "You're really all right? And your friend?"

"Yes, Christopher, we're fine."

"I began to wonder. No problems?"

"I didn't say that, Christopher, but we both got out. We got a good portion of what we went to obtain. We spent a considerable amount of time repairing the ship, which is why I'm only now getting to you. There was also another delay, but most of the time was spent repairing the ship."

"The supply thing didn't go well?"

"Oh, no, that went perfectly. Those supplies are probably still mixed up with the real ones. No, we got deep into the operation before we were discovered and had to fight our way back to the ship. We weren't terribly concerned until we got to the ship hangar, and a welcoming party awaited us. From that point forward, that's how we ended up with all the repairs we just completed. Like I said, none of it was due to you. You did your role splendidly, Christopher."

Christopher listened carefully. Days of repairs. It spoke of an ugly firefight. A hangar full of enemy soldiers against two individuals. "You said both of you are fine. I have a hard time believing that after what you described. Are you sure neither one of you was injured?"

"Nothing serious, I promise, Christopher. We ended up with considerable smoke in the ship when something blew after the attack on the ship. We took care of it, and we both breathed smoke-free in no time. One of the blasters got me in the arm slightly, and one grazed me on the hand when I was setting up the detonator, but it was only a scratch."

"A scratch, huh?" He held out his hands, made a motion, and stared back up at her.

She laughed. "You're serious, aren't you? You remind me of someone else I know. To ease your mind, Christopher." She held out her hands and arms to him and turned them over. "There are no marks. You can't see or feel the injury anymore. Do you feel better now, Christopher?"

"I suppose I must be convinced, Chris. What were you doing with a detonator in your hand and getting fired on? Those are not recommended combinations."

"You won't be happy when I tell you, so let's not."

"Let's do, Chris," Each time he thought he figured out this girl, he knew there was more than met the eye.

"We headed to the portal with most of the fleet on our tail. All our weapons were gone, or we thought at the time. My comrade worked on getting us to the portal with the damage to the ship. I used remote detonators we brought in the ship to get space between us and the ships behind us. Unfortunately, I had to do it manually because that mechanism in the ship was also damaged. You can figure out the rest."

"One shot from one of those ships and the whole detonator would blow up in your hand and face, or the shot takes your whole hand off." Christopher shook his head at her.

"Yes, I heard all those sentiments during and after it. At the moment, we thought we might end up shot into a million pieces before the ship made it through the portal. The important thing is, none of those terrible things that could happen did. My comrade and I are fine. Neither one of us was injured in any real way. In fact, both of us were in another battle, which is the delay I spoke of earlier. We took care of business in the battle with no problem, I assure you." The girl actually said it with a smile.

"I believe you, and I don't even think the battle was close."

"It wasn't, Christopher."

"There's more to you than what you say, Chris. I'm not sure what to make of it."

"I'm about to tell you a piece of the puzzle which will clear some of it up for you, Christopher."

"I'm listening."

"This must stay between the two of us, you understand."

"I understand, and it will."

"I received a unique gift from the Ancient One. I'm able to sense things, see things vividly at times. It's helpful to my comrades and me. Sometimes it doesn't feel like a gift because what I sense is not always the happiest of things to come. Nevertheless, it's a gift because there's always a purpose for being shown, whatever it may be. Is this making sense to you, Christopher?"

"Yes, it's starting to, but I wonder why you choose to disclose it now."

"Because I have sensed something important. Events are about to unfold. A task lies ahead. I'm not sure with the time left if me and my comrades can accomplish it. I again come and ask for your assistance." The girl started to continue.

Christopher stopped her. "I'll help you. What do you need?"

"Christopher, you didn't hear what I'm asking of you, and there's no payment for this. I ask as a friend, not as a business partner."

"I understand, and I'll help you. Chris, I don't know what it is, but I'm sure it's related to what you came back from doing. You and your friend were willing to risk your life to accomplish it, and it sounds like it was close. It's that important to the both of you. This task must be as well. I'll help the two of you with it. There's no question in my mind."

"All right, we tried to figure out for some time what the Dark Lord is planning. He's building something and gathering supplies to do so. We discovered he's building a dispersal device."

"And he obtained all those chemicals to use with it. For how long has this been going on?"

"It's hard to say. It appears seriously for at least nine months."

"Where did they get all the supplies?"

"Attacks on the colonies it would appear for a large portion, but my comrades and I believe he also works through the shipping business. You know some will work with anyone if the price is right. So that part of their supply line has always been and continues even now. The question is, when did they start using that part of their supply line to obtain these supplies to build this device. That I can't answer."

"You're right. Everyone in the shipping business knows there are those bold enough or a better word would be foolish enough to do business with the Black Dragon and those like them. They believe the payoff is worth the risk. It's why such care must be taken in all dealings in this business. What chemical has he created with it? If you know, there may be a way to counter it."

The girl sighed. "We don't know, and that's only one of the problems. One of the other operations revealed there's a second substance out there, and so it could be that in the dispersal device."

"What is the second substance?"

The girl gazed up at Christopher with fear in her eyes. "I don't know. I inspected the sample many times now. It's not anything I encountered before. It's not made from any chemicals we can find in existence. Also, a great Darkness is bound to it. Every time I begin working with it, I feel it, and it's not just me. Both of my comrades felt it when they tried to figure it out, and they don't possess the gift from the Ancient One as I do."

Christopher looked at her. She mentioned comrades a couple of times now. He thought it was only her and her friend. He would ask her later. "It could be either substance in the device, but it helps you none since both substances are a mystery."

"Exactly."

"Are you wanting to go find out the nature of the substances to try to disable it?"

The girl met his eyes and shook her head. "We come to the other problem in this. We ran out of time, Christopher."

"How can you know?"

"The gift, Christopher."

"You do nothing to stop it. That doesn't sound like you."

"We gave everything we learned to the key players in the Freedom Fighters. You know them, Lana, Caleb, Seth, and Dante. They have more resources to develop a plan to disable it with the time left. We tried, but I don't think we succeeded in getting what they needed before the time runs out."

"It makes sense now what you've been doing. You said comrades several times today. I thought there were only two of you. Are there more?"

"Yes. There is the one that trained both of us, whom you'll meet when you help us."

"Trained you? There's some training for this business, but I don't get the sense that's what you speak of."

The girl reached from behind her and pulled out something. "There are times I use a different weapon, Christopher."

Christopher recognized it instantly as the handle of a sunspear. "You are one who wields a sunspear which explains how your arm reaches much further than the shipping business. Chris, I should have guessed."

The girl replaced her weapon. "Christopher, you cannot say a word. We, along with Lana's group, have caused considerable problems for the Dark Lord recently, and he's angry. He knows Lana's group, but he is trying to locate the two spear-bearers who caused him all the problems. He doesn't know who we are or our appearance, and neither does the other dangerous agent he has searching for us. So far, we have dodged both. Though the Dark Lord cannot find us at the moment, he does know we're spear-bearers. If he gets close to us, it'll put in danger everything we're doing, and it could put others in danger as well. All the mishaps he encountered are probably part of the reason the time ran out as well, but it couldn't be helped."

"I thought I understood the importance before, but now I truly do. I'll keep you and your comrades safe. None of this will be heard from me, Chris. I once said you traveled in dangerous circles for one so young. I now only realize the truth of those words. If we're leaving it up to the others to stop it, what are we doing? What is this task I'm to help you with?"

"Let's begin."

———

"It can be done?" asked Christopher after she explained it.

"Yes, the Ancient One wouldn't tell me in the vision if it were not so. The visions are never wrong as the source of the visions is never wrong."

"Are the images you see always this terrible?"

"It's hard to answer, Christopher. The ones where it involves acting on them immediately, yes, always. It's the state of things now. It's a miserable way to wake up at three or six in the morning or so on. However, I continue to see it as a gift as it yields valuable information. It's okay. Are we good with the plans for the task?"

"Yes, it looks in order." Christopher watched her. She appeared unsure about something. "I'm not the one who appears unhappy."

The girl leaned back in her seat. "No, I'm fine. A battle will wage at this time somewhere else with the dispersal device and the Dark Lord's army in play. My sunspear and my companion's sunspear would be of help to the Freedom Fighters, but the Ancient One doesn't wish that to be my battlefield. At least as long as our task goes as planned, and we make the time frame. If it doesn't, it could be the exact opposite. I think our task must go as planned. We wouldn't accomplish our task by the Ancient One if we found ourselves in the middle of trouble. I've learned not to question the Ancient One's plan. It never ended well for me. His plan is far better as is than what I envision. Sometimes it's hard to still not wonder about it, to trust. We'll see how it plays out."

"To be honest, I'm not unhappy about it. You might be out of harm's way for a change."

"I'm well-trained to handle most situations I encounter, Christopher, as you learned today. I would be fine."

"Those were close calls, Chris."

"I've only told you about ..." the girl stopped in mid-sentence, "and we'll leave it at that. We're all set?"

"You need to be more careful, seriously."

"Are you auditioning for the part of my older sibling?" The girl laughed.

"Is it taken? Because if not, yes, because you desperately need more supervision, Chris."

"My comrade is like an older sibling to me, but I was told I could probably use another one for all the trouble I get in." She laughed again but then turned serious. "Christopher, I promise you I don't take it as lightly as I appear. We do try to be safe, but the situations turned ugly quickly of late. We had solid plans with the information we went in with, but the best plans don't always go as on paper. Each time the risk has been worth it because what was at stake was too important not to go through with it." she gazed at him sadly and said softly. "I cried many tears, Christopher, when I received this image. I did it many other times in recent months. We hoped to stop the Dark Lord, but I'm not sure it will be done now."

"Well, sis," he smiled at her, and she smiled back, "you must not be so hard on yourself. You and your comrade do not bear all the weight on your shoulders though you try. Perhaps the image is not clear in its meaning. The others could come up with a plan that succeeds." He reached out and clasped her hand. "We'll keep hoping. I do not wish to hear of any more tears from you."

"Nor I, brother." She shook her head. "You'll regret soon taking on this new role. The task I brought you will be much easier than trying to manage me. I'm told by several people already."

"I'll take my chances. I'm glad you and your friend got back safe, though."

"Thanks for all your concern. As much as I enjoy your company, I must be off now." She stood up.

"Because a lot must be done." He got up as well and followed her eyes. "The encryption is all set on my data pad for this. I know it only works for this task. We'll make sure any communication has encryption. We'll be in the same place most of the time, but for the instances we're not we can't take any chances."

"Agreed. We'll see you soon. The race to beat the clock begins." She reached over and hugged Christopher goodbye this time. "Thank you."

"Anytime. Hey, and try to stay out of trouble, at least until I see you again. Surely even you can manage such a short length of time."

"I promise I will, and I always keep my promises."

"She didn't even make sure I took care of this. She's slipping." He walked over to clear the cameras on the cockpit.

"Because I knew surely you wouldn't forget after all this time." Her voice floated back.

The girl climbed aboard the ship. "Alena, time to head back to Alika. There's a lot to get in motion."

***

Alika, Alena, and the girl worked on getting everything in place. They watched the screen at different intervals.

"There will still be many," said the girl quietly.

"It cannot be helped. We do what is given to us, child," said Alika.

"And which is worse ..."

"In a sense, the other would be kinder than the fate seen," said Alika.

"You must not place this on your shoulders as you do. Someone reminded you of that today, and it was sound advice. You only saw the vision. You're not the one who brings it to pass."

"You're right, Alena." She peered back at the screen. "It appears good so far. We need it to keep looking like this. Let's continue and make sure it will play out right for the real thing."

It was late when they felt they had finished. They were prepared now to put it into action.

"We are ready to begin first thing in the morning," said Alika. The other two nodded and headed for bed.

***

The girl laid down to sleep. Suddenly, she heard a whisper and thought at first she imagined it. Yet it came again. She smiled. There was no mistaking the whisper, and she whispered back, "I'm here and listening."

The voice whispered, "You have long been confused by something, even fearful at times because you did not understand. No longer be so, my child. I have put this in motion. It's a gift I give to the both of you, one which cast out all fear. When it reaches its fulfillment, both of you will find its full joy."

"You can only mean ..."

"Yes, you know. There is more, my child. Soon you will be asked to make a promise in connection with the same. You will know what is asked of you. Do not hesitate to make the promise. You will know what the promise entails, and the one who asks you will know as well. The one it concerns will not understand what is promised at the time, but as time goes on, it will become clear to the one as well. You will fulfill that promise, and it will bring great happiness to you and the one it concerns as the promise is kept."

"I will."

"Sleep, sweet dreams, my precious child, and I promise them for tonight."

The girl found herself asleep a moment later. Her visions were sweet that night for the first time in a while as she found herself staring into the gentle brown eyes of the one she had come to love. She also found all the visions were ones intended only for her to keep.

CHAPTER FORTY-THREE

Lana sat with the others after breakfast the next day. "Does everyone feel sure about the plans to cover the next attack with the understanding we may have to do modifications quickly if we get thrown another curve from the Dark Lord?"

Seth spoke, "There is only one thing I would bring up we didn't consider yesterday in our plans. We may have another key player missing. We cannot be sure."

Everyone appeared confused.

Seth turned to Dante. "It could be you, Dante. We do not know when you are to go for your task. I feel the time approaches." Seth turned to the others. "We must take that into consideration when we decide what part Dante plays. It should be one where someone else could easily take his place. He must be ready to accomplish the other task he is to do."

"Do you think it would be in the middle of this?" asked Ryan.

"It was in the middle of a large operation the fleet was engaged. I don't think it is an attack on the colony. However, this last attack proved different from any previous encounters. I strongly believe it involves the dispersal device. Since I expect those plans to be the next order of business, I figured it best to bring it up now."

"I hate to not help with this task. It feels wrong."

"Although, that is exactly what we saw went through your mind as you went to face your father and the Dark Lord. You could not assist at the moment though you wished to do so because the time came for the task with your father. There is another way to think of this, Dante. If you complete your task, not only do you get your father back, but a second part is accomplished."

Dante peered at him, puzzled, trying to understand how he should feel good about not assisting the others.

"Dante, you destroy the Dark Lord. You cut off the head."

"He has an excellent point, Dante. Definitely helpful to the galaxy," said Ryan.

"We make sure Dante is somewhere he can detach himself easily, or someone else can jump in for him. Got it," said Caleb.

"That has moved us to the dispersal device," said Lana, "Any ideas? Nothing is off the table."

There was silence.

Caleb glimpsed around and focused back on Lana. "Okay, you said nothing is off the table, but maybe we start there. I think we do have things we need to eliminate. One is we wait until they use it, and we deal with it after the fact. Also, anything which involves shooting at the device itself because we risk releasing whatever it contains."

"We come back to only two options, disable it or neutralize it."

"Same problems too. We don't know what is in it to neutralize it, and we don't know how to disable it," pointed out Commander Aegeus.

Caleb flashed the download up with the pictures of the device and, next to it, put the footage up when the two spear-bearers were in the room with the big cylinder object.

"We assume the device in the download and the device in this room are the same. I still don't see any clue how to disable it either," said Caleb.

Dante studied it in deep thought. Seth watched him. "I've seen that look. What are you thinking?"

"The young spear-bearer is right."

"Can you elaborate, Dante? They have been right about a great many things."

"I could sense something didn't sit right with the young spear-bearer when they saw the download, but there was no time to explore it because of the interruption by the Black Dragon soldier. Caleb, can you go to the point where the two of them began watching the download to the point where the Black Dragon soldier enters the room?"

Caleb did and froze it at the beginning. "Dante, sorry, but which one is the young spear-bearer? I figure you know."

Dante pointed. "That one."

Seth smiled. Dante had his eye trained on the one.

Caleb started it up, and they listened. Caleb turned to Dante. "I heard a pause, but nothing important about what was said. You're the expert, Dante."

"You really didn't?" Dante shook his head. "I heard a mood change, like puzzlement or confusion maybe between the information in the download and what they saw in the room. The young spear-bearer tried to push it aside momentarily. It worked at the time because everything went into chaos not long after."

"Caleb, play it again for us. I have come to trust Dante's instincts when it comes to our friend."

Caleb played it again. This time it was apparent. "What do you think it means?" asked Commander Gabe.

"I don't know, and I don't know that they ever figured out why the disconnect was felt. Dante is right, though. They spotted something that did not appear right between the two. Their instincts were correct so far, but I'm not sure what we do with it," said Seth.

"They are similar looking, but I don't know that they are the same exact device. Is it disabled in the same way?" Something else bothered Dante about it, but he couldn't put his finger on it.

"Probably close enough they can be," said Commander Conrad.

"Perhaps the one in the download is an earlier version of the finished product, and that's why they appear different, Dante," said Lana.

"I suppose."

"You're not convinced, Dante. I can tell."

"No, the other one is busier. I don't know. It seems more involved in the diagram, I think, Seth."

"Then the opposite, which would be excellent news. We can stop them before they finish," said Commander Cepheus.

It still didn't feel right to Dante, but he chose to push it aside much as the young spear-bearer did.

"I feel we're leaning toward going to their place. Very dangerous," said Caleb.

"Isn't that what our spear-bearer friends have already done, but they knew the costs if they didn't? I'm sorry, I didn't mean for it to sound as it did. I shouldn't have input in this discussion. The task suggested would clearly not be one I'll be a part of. It wouldn't leave me free to go on the other task I need to do."

"No, Dante, please continue in the discussion as I, for one, value your insight. Although you may not be a part of the operation to go in for the dispersal device, you will play a part as you always do, I'm sure. You're also right that we cannot ask less of ourselves than what our spear-bearer friends have done. They put themselves in great danger several times we know of, probably many more times we don't know. I fought at their side this last time. They didn't hesitate a moment. If any fear existed, it couldn't be found. We have been on the defense in this battle for too long. It is time we went on the offense. The young spear-bearer said it at some point this last time. They said to us the Dark Lord wanted a fight, they would get one," said Commander Gabe firmly.

Seth agreed, "Commander Gabe is right. They have continually brought the fight to the Dark Lord, to his very doorstep. You saw footage when they obtained the download for us, but Commander Gabe and I had the pleasure of battling beside them. A moment occurred when the squadron leader tried to reclaim one of the colonists as prisoners, and the young spear-bearer stopped it in its tracks. They made it clear the line was drawn, one found at the point of the sunspear. That is how they fought from the beginning, from their speech to the wielding of their sunspear in battle. We must fight like it now. Our time is running short."

Suddenly a sound of audio could be heard starting, and footage followed. Lana smiled. "I found it." She remembered with Alika and her working together that they shared information that day to keep up with how things went for their groups. Lana forgot until now, but she had the transmissions and the whole encounter from start to finish when the ambush was being arranged until after the second attack ended. Lana started it with the communication that Commander Gabe indicated to where the young spear-bearer told her group to prepare themselves and informed Seth and Commander Gabe her group was ready and played the audio all the way through her confrontation with the squadron leader.

There was silence as it finished. There was authority from the young spear-bearer and a fighting spirit that would not be vanquished. It spoke volumes, better than any encouraging speech could. It had served its purpose today.

"That doesn't need any expert explanation from Dante about the young spear-bearer's mood after listening." Caleb glanced at Dante, who smiled back after hearing them take care of the squadron leader. "Although it's good to be reminded of some things from our spear-bearer friend."

"You're right, Caleb," said Ryan smiling. "We're looking at an operation to go to the device and disable it or neutralize it. We assume it's the cylinder thing. There's another big problem. They never told us where it is and said no further communications."

Seth interjected, "Actually, they did tell us, or they told me to be more exact. Sorry, I was told to wait. I believe they were thinking about doing another operation independently, but they were unsure of their next move. They sent me the location depending on what we decided to do. That part will not be a problem."

"Did they communicate with you on what they're doing instead?" asked Dante.

"No, they did not. I'm not certain what avenue they will decide to pursue to stop the imminent threat."

Dante appeared concerned, but he knew he needed to focus on helping here.

"Once we get there, we need to know how to disable or neutralize it," said Commander Conrad.

Ryan shook his head. "We viewed the download and the footage. We still don't know. We face the real possibility we get there and figure out how to do so."

"That's craziness. We can't. It goes against every sane strategy," said Commander Austin.

"It's just like with the operations from the spear-bearers so far, but it's what they did with the limited knowledge they had going into the situation. The other option is to wait until we sort it out. We don't have that time. If we run out of time, we're stuck with the other scenario, an unthinkable one for our homelands. That being a dispersal device literally pointed at us or a planet somewhere in space, and there's no chance of disabling it," said Ryan.

Everyone was silent. They knew he was right.

"Are we doing what I believe I hear?" asked Commander Gabe, unfazed.

Caleb glanced at Lana. She nodded back. "I believe so. We take over one of the Dark Lord's facilities. We figure out how to disable the device before they can use it. If we can't disable it there, we formulate a way to transport it here safely and disable it. Either way, there's a Black Dragon fleet to get through and plenty of Black Dragon soldiers once inside."

Seth spoke, "It's a lot, but remember how we got the current information from the facility. An operation of a mere two individuals. Two highly trained individuals whose trust rested in the Ancient One. We can continue to learn much from them. We also have a huge advantage they did not have going into their operation, that being a complete layout of the building, footage of the device, etc. These are all benefits we reaped from the labor of their last operation."

"We have to plan our resources carefully. If there is an attack, we must be able to meet that threat as well. Although enough should be sent for the other operation to be successful. It's going to be a tight line," said Lana.

"I don't think our resources are as bad as we think. I mean, they're nowhere near what the Dark Lord has. However, we don't use all our forces during the attacks on the colonies. We didn't need more soldiers until this last attack, but we didn't realize it until after the attack began. We know going into this from now on we need more soldiers to cover the attacks. The last attack also showed the colony armies should be on alert if the battle comes to them. I'm more concerned about mobilizing the soldiers in time, depending on how quickly we go in for the device," said Ryan.

"Yes, it's going to be pushing it, Ryan. You and Lana are both right about the other, so we'll have to be aware of how we divide our soldiers. Yet, if this is what we decide, we must all be agreed for it to work," said Caleb looking around at everyone. Everyone met his eyes and nodded. "This evening, Commanders, communicate with all colonies in your region about both matters. No details about what's going on as far as the Dark Lord. The Dark Lord cannot be alerted to the fact that we know anything. You can blame it on the last attack if you wish. Also, make it clear the colony armies should be prepared if they're attacked, and we go to full squadrons. We need every soldier ready and ask them to report. I'd say as soon as tomorrow afternoon. Let's get started and pull up the footage from the facility again. We'll study the layout outside and go to the footage inside to see how the soldiers are situated. I'm sure that part didn't change much."

CHAPTER FORTY-FOUR

The Dark Lord sat as he finished listening to the Black Dragon Commander. His eyes went between flashing red with anger and turning black as night. His fist clenched that rested on the armrest.

"No supplies back, and all the colonists survived today," said the Dark Lord in fury.

"We cannot be sure about the colonists, but it is the assumption. All our ground soldiers were lost as both transport ships were destroyed. We assume the outcome since no soldiers remain to get a report from now," said the Black Dragon Commander.

"The only thing we have is the scattered transmission during the battle and what we can summarize from it?"

"Yes."

"And two spear-bearers helped them with the attack this time." The Dark Lord silently fumed. Who were they? This is the first time they helped with one of the attacks. Why this attack?

"Yes, it must be Caleb and Lana. Dante was over on the side where the tanks were engaged from the scattered communications by the soldiers."

"The two were in full uniform again, and so they hid their identity."

"But Lana and Caleb make sense. It appears they came after the others in their group were already there. I'm guessing once they saw the state of things, we forced them to rearrange their defense."

"Of course, that makes sense." Inside, the Dark Lord continued to have his thoughts. It made sense if the two monitored the attack. They saw the trouble Dante's group found themselves in, and the two took it upon themselves to lend their aid. Still, he didn't know who these two were. He grew tired of them for all the trouble they caused. He wanted both of them dead before they ruined anything else, but they made sure not to expose themselves. And that worthless Duvessa had gotten nowhere with tracking them. He got up from the chair and stomped throughout the room. "The attack was to make them sorry for humiliating us for the last attack, for siding with the Elders. Instead, they shoved it down our throats again. I will not be made a fool further. They will pay, every one of them. Their tears will flow and never stop when we are done. They will wish for death if they manage to escape it." The Dark Lord spat out in fury. His eyes turned as black as the abyss. "I am done with these attacks on the colonies as they have been. It is time to go ahead with the operation as agreed. Can we be ready as we discussed?"

"We can, my Dark Lord."

He settled back in his chair, his eyes still smoldering. "Good. Make the preparations. It's time we try out our masterpiece on them. They will be sorry for what they started. They saved those colonists in the attack yesterday, but it will be short-lived. What is our time frame? I'm eager to do this, but I want no mistakes. Everything must be in place perfectly, from the soldiers to the ships."

"A week. I know it sounds long, but ..."

"No, it doesn't, considering the operation. Although you and I will watch it from somewhere else, as we discussed, we will not be leaving the command ship without a strong leadership presence during it."

"You still haven't told Duvessa?"

"No, I haven't. She will not be happy, but I don't care. Surely she knows I will not put this in her hands." Other ideas surfaced of what she would be sent to do. He was also most unhappy with her now, so he wondered if he would allow her to live that long at her current rate of failure. He also knew she did not hold the degree of respect from the squadron to command such a large operation though she thought so highly of herself. "I will communicate my changed timetable. He can make the arrangements to report to the command ship."

"I will take care of the communication with the squadrons so there will be no misunderstanding during the operation."

CHAPTER FORTY-FIVE

Another day started for Lana and the others. Caleb met with the other commanders to ensure all their personnel arrived as requested. Their personnel reported to their command centers on the commander's home regions at the moment. The commanders did not want them all gathering at the fortress as doing so could alert the Dark Lord. The commanders all received confirmation their squadrons were assembling as requested. Repairs were done to ships as needed and equipment prepared.

Seth would stay behind to help on the ground with an attack on a colony if it occurred at the same time along with Lana to coordinate the group's efforts. Of course, Dante would probably be to his own task. Another of the commanders would remain behind to coordinate the forces in the air if an attack on the colonies happened.

A small portion of soldiers would stay as well to assist with protecting against an attack on the colony. All the rest of the squadrons would be sent to take over the Dark Lord's facility.

Seth and Dante wanted to help, but they knew they were not a part of the plan to get the dispersal device back. Lana and Caleb came to them.

"Dante, the time for your task approaches, and you must be ready. We don't want to be the cause of you not completing the task or harm coming to you," Lana said.

"Lana's right, Dante. We want you to come back safe, and we're worried about how little time you had to prepare."

"We need to help you, the other commanders. Tell them, Seth."

"Lana and Caleb are wise as always, Dante. I know you're concerned for them, the commanders, and the colonies, and that is where your words spring from. In this case, though, I agree with them. You must prepare for your task as they currently plan for the mission they are about to do."

Seth turned to Lana and Caleb. "Dante and I will continue his preparation for his task. We will be close by and can break from it to come to you if need be." Seth turned back to Dante. "You are overruled, Dante. Time to get to work."

"All right, but I may wish to return helping here rather than your preparation, Seth."

"That is probably true, Dante, but come anyway."

The two walked off toward Seth's quarters.

Lana and Caleb looked at each other.

"Do you think my cousin is given enough time for what he must face, Caleb?"

"I hope so, but if anyone can equip him, it's Seth. We trust now, sweetheart." Caleb wrapped his arms around Lana's waist and leaned down to kiss her softly.

———𝓔𝓔———

Another day wrapped up for Caleb and their group, and evening came. Seth and Dante went through a training session much like the one Dante struggled through not long ago. This one seemed to go smoother simply because Dante knew Seth tested him as his enemy would. However, Dante still struggled through it as he and Seth realized he held on to falsehoods found in it.

"How am I to be ready for this, Seth? I knew what you did and still I feel I was beaten?" Tears sprung up in Dante's eyes, a mixture of pain and frustration.

"Because you're not alone in any battle, including the one to come. You must continue to battle this with the only weapon which will win it. Truth. And you cannot give up. It's like when you're in one of the attacks on the colony. You continue to swing the sunspear and cleave down one Black Dragon soldier after the other until there are no more. No matter how tired you are, no matter how many there are before you, you cannot stop until the battle is won. This must be the same, Dante. The lies will keep coming, but they will be wrapped in a layer of seeming truth. You must be able to see through them and break them apart again and again. At some point, all the lies and falsehoods will lay waste at your feet if you endure through the battle's end. This is what the Ancient One said you would do to win your father back and to keep your own spirit safe in the battle ahead. That is how you will be able to do this, Dante," said Seth softly as he hugged Dante.

They debriefed for longer and went to see Dante's mother together before bed. Seth had Dante tell him of another good memory of his father as the previous night.

❧

Another day started for Caleb's group. They continued with their plans for taking over the dispersal device. Dante and Seth came in for the first bit with the group to see the progress made and give input. They soon broke off from the rest of the group and went back to preparing for Dante's task. It was another long day for both groups. Lunchtime passed, and early afternoon began.

Lana and Caleb stood away from the group and talked.

"Caleb, there was no one. It's beyond the time."

"I know. I noticed too."

"I should be happy finally. We all should be."

"Yeah, you would think."

"Why am I not, Caleb?" Lana already knew the answer before Caleb spoke it.

"Because every time they do the unexpected, it keeps getting uglier."

"What will this storm look like, Caleb?" Lana's eyes filled with worry.

"I don't know, but we'll face it together as we always do, and we'll get through it." Caleb smiled down at her. He kissed her, and she leaned up against him, wrapped up in his arms even if for a few moments as she tried not to think about the storm to come.

CHAPTER FORTY-SIX

The girl, Alena, and Alika were up early the next morning. Last night they packed everything they thought they needed in the ships, so this morning there was little left to do. Alena and the girl went into the one ship while Alika took his ship for this trip too.

The girl said, "Something occurred to me last night. Considering what the others are doing, knowing the clearance codes to get around the facility and hangar would be useful. I should send the information over to Seth. The download is ready to send with a message. I'll wait a little later this morning. He and Dante prepared intensely for the last couple of days for Dante's task."

Alena agreed. "Yes, you're right. It should save them time. They'll need everything to help them once they get in."

"Hopefully, it still works. So far, getting access in that area isn't a problem once gained. If it doesn't work, they're right back where they started. The only place which provided a challenge was the facility they kept Abigail, and it wasn't Black Dragon security."

"Yes, when they obtain outside help is when they get quality in that area. Fortunately for us, they don't outsource often. I think you're right, and the information will be useful to the others. Go ahead and send it to Seth in a bit."

They walked out toward the ships. They were all dressed in casual clothing this time, far from the typical battle-ready attire they expected for the coming events. Even so, their weapons were concealed and ready on them if needed.

"Ready," said the girl as she turned to Alena. "I've secured it while we're gone."

"I'm right behind you," said Alika from his ship.

A few minutes later, they passed through the portal.

"There it is. Our reserved spots are waiting," stated the girl.

"Looks like Christopher beat us here," said Alena.

The girl sent a communication. "Yeah, it's him. It doesn't sound like he waited long, though."

They landed, and the girl sent another message to Christopher. A moment later, the ship door opened, and the words, "identity verified" could be heard from the computer as Christopher slowly walked through the door.

"Come in, Christopher."

"It's good to see you as always, Chris."

The girl hugged him. "Thank you for helping us again."

"Anytime, you know by now."

"I do, Christopher. This is Alena, my friend and adopted older sister, who forever bears the thankless role of keeping me out of trouble."

They all laughed.

"It's nice to finally meet you, Christopher. I'm not sure what to do with Chris's introduction, but it's accurate."

"It's a pleasure to finally meet you as well, Alena. My compliments to you as I believe the task is quite daunting and demands your full attention."

"Hey, I did keep my promise to you, Christopher. I should get some credit."

Christopher shook his head, smiling at Chris, and looked around as if searching for someone else. The girl knew who he searched for. "Oh, he should be here any second," the girl said as the door reopened, and the computer announced, "Identity verified." Alika walked onto the ship at that moment.

"And here he is. Christopher, this is Alika."

Alika smiled at Christopher. "It's good to meet you, Christopher. We can't tell you how grateful we are for your help."

"I'm glad I can and I'm relieved to find Alena and Chris made it back safely. I know you trained them well, but I was concerned."

"You were not the only one, Christopher. I have grown fond of them over the years." he laughed. "They are well-trained though for battle, and that I claim a part in. The fighting spirit you caught glimpses of is all them."

"Now we are all introduced in a sense. Outside of the ship, Alena and Alika may find new names to introduce themselves, considering the events we know about to take place. I'll leave that to them, and we'll follow their lead. Are we ready to jump into this?"

"I believe so," replied Christopher.

They all observed the screen the girl pulled up.

Alena said, "That's where it's located here? Well, done. We're not far at all."

"Yes, we should be there in no time. Alika, are you ready as well?" asked the girl.

"Yes, let's go."

All four got off the ship and talked as they walked along together. Activity abounded inside and outside when they arrived. Someone approached them curious. Alika went ahead and took the lead. The other three stood back and waited. After several minutes, Alika motioned them to follow the man and him inside. The girl came up to Alika as they walked inside. "I'm sending this message to Seth now before it gets later."

"Yes, now should be fine. Seth and the others need any help they can receive. I read the message too with it. It is excellent. It will encourage them. You have a way with words when you are so inspired. I don't believe you are the only one."

⸎

Seth and Dante sat with the others as the morning began. Seth stopped in mid-sentence when his data pad signaled a message arriving. It displayed a standard alert. Dante glanced over at Seth curiously but waited for Seth to check on it. Seth calmly picked it up, but his face showed surprise.

"It's from our friends, Dante." Seth felt relief. He expected the next message to say the Dark Lord was upon them, but the message did not come with the urgency for such a threat.

Dante tried his best not to appear as impatient as he felt. "What does it say, Seth?"

"It's a communication for all of us." Seth turned to Lana, who nodded. Seth put it up on the wall so it could be read:

Hello Seth,

Please share this communication with all those organizing the task at hand. We did not think about it until later but realized there is another piece of information that may be helpful in the task your comrades are undertaking. We attached it and sent it to you. It's the clearances and access to get into the different doors throughout the facility where we visited recently, courtesy of the inspector's data pad. I suppose it's possible they changed the accesses, but fortunately, I find them lax with that sort of thing. It has served us many times so far, and we hope it does the same for you. If it doesn't, you are simply back where you started. Once it's downloaded, you should maneuver quite nicely throughout the facility. Some of it may allow you to control the hangar door as well, but it will be only briefly. We found they figured out how to take control of it rather quickly again. Hopefully, this is helpful as we want to do anything possible to see you come back safely from this task.

Seth, on a side note, tell Dante he is thought of frequently in the task ahead of him. I know he wishes to help the others, but he must focus on his task. Tell him to remember everything you taught him, everything my Elder

told him, all the training from the Ancient One, and even the scattered messages I relayed to him through others. I was once told our struggles can make us stronger if we allow them. I must continue to believe it to be true, or I suppose I would be quite unhappy by now given how smoothly a few of the operations have not gone. The struggles are given to prepare us, so one does not fall but will stand victorious on the day of battle. When the day is done, we can look upon it and know it's worth all the struggles we encountered and came through. It will be so for Dante and his comrades. The Ancient One will be beside each of them in the battle to come, wherever the battlefield may be.

I look forward to finding everyone returned safely. I will trust you received this message as we cannot communicate further for a while. Goodbye.

The message ended. As it did, the symbol of the Ancient One appeared, two sunspears crossed and a dove in the middle. In the middle, a message scrolled across which read:

The Ancient One will go before you in battle, my friends. We never fight alone.

It stayed for a moment, and then it disappeared.

There was silence. No one said anything for a couple of minutes but smiled.

Lana finally came over to Dante. "We all feel better after hearing those words from your young spear-bearer, Dante."

"Yes, the young spear-bearer has a way of speaking, that is ..."

"Yes, I'm not sure what the word is either, Dante, but it is encouraging." Seth pushed something on the data pad and sent the download to Lana and Caleb. They could disperse it to the others.

Seth and Dante got up to leave a few minutes later.

Ryan came over. "Dante, you know the young spear-bearer is right. Your task is important. Do you realize how big it will be once you accomplish your task? I know personally, you'll be happy because you have your father back, and he's no longer a slave to the Dark Lord. For the galaxy, though, he won't be working for the Dark Lord anymore. The next part is killing the Dark Lord. The army will be stripped of its leaders completely. Without any leadership, it won't stand for long. We'll do our task, and you take care of yours. They are both part of the same goal. See it like that, Dante. We all come back safe, though, like the young spear-bearer says, deal?"

"Deal, Ryan. Time for us to continue preparing, right?"

"Definitely, Dante." Ryan went back to the commanders, and Seth patted Dante on the back as they headed in the other direction for a while.

"You know they never said what they're doing now, but whatever it is, they can't communicate further," said Dante.

"Yes, I caught that as well."

"They said that last time before they went on the operation to get this information, and it almost ended them."

"Yes, I'm not sure what path they take to approach this threat. Clearly, they are not going straight for the dispersal device. They are also not going to the Dark Lord or your father. I can't guess what angle is left to approach it. I would say no one is going on a task which does not involve a great deal of danger. We will trust they heed their own advice."

"Yeah, I'm sure they are." Dante tried to sound confident, but it missed its mark.

CHAPTER FORTY-SEVEN

Evening came. It was late. Christopher, the girl, Alena, and Alika sat in the girl's ship, exhausted after the day.

"I admit that I harbored doubts, Chris. I'm not sure why. I suppose it went as you said."

"Actually, I understand, Christopher. Things haven't gone as scripted for the last few times. I'm pleasantly surprised myself when it goes as planned now."

"If the other couple of days goes like this, we'll be fine," said Alena.

"I think it will. The Ancient One truly goes before us in an apparent way for this task to work. We must continue to see ourselves as the facilitators in this process," said Alika. He turned to the girl. "Do you know how the others are doing with their tasks? You are usually able to sense how these things go."

"They continue to work on it. The full squadrons are assembling on schedule. Lana and Seth will remain behind in case there's a standard attack on one of the colonies. Of course, there will be a small portion of soldiers left with them. A commander will stay as well. The rest go with the fleet for the dispersal task. Lana, Caleb, and the commanders work together, while Dante and Seth prepare Dante for his task. All that we gathered from the monitoring we can tap into. As far as the other... Lana is worried since there was no attack as the unexpected from the Dark Lord usually means worse. She's right, of course. I wish it were not the case. No doubt Caleb will reassure her as always. Dante still struggles with the training, but they press on. It's hard. There's no way to know what will be used against him. He knows that by now. I can only hope he'll be ready."

Christopher looked at them and said, "I think I missed something."

Alika said to the girl, "It's your choice. I will do it, or you may."

The girl nodded and turned to Christopher. "The more you know, the more dangerous it becomes. You cannot speak of it. It can put those we care for in great danger, Christopher."

Christopher stared back at her. Her eyes were intense. He heard the way she spoke of the individuals before. They were dear to her. "Chris, I've learned a great many things about you. One is once someone becomes dear to you, there's no truer friend to be found than you. You would pay whatever price for them, including your own life. I won't put them in danger. Whatever you tell, it will not leave me ever, I promise you."

"I believe you, Christopher. I assume your question refers to Dante as you're aware of the other task."

"Yes, I mean, I know Dante is well-known as a spear-bearer. There are few who can match him in that area."

"You're right. Dante is exceptional with the sunspear. Normally, he's in the center of any operation the group undertakes. His skills and well ..." she started to say something else and then didn't. "He'll be missed during the operation for sure. The other task he goes to complete he must do alone. Do you know the story behind Dante as far as his family, Christopher? It's common knowledge, but I don't know it's spoken of often now."

"Yeah, I think I remember. I mean, everyone knows, unfortunately, his father is the Black Dragon Commander. I imagine he doesn't like to be reminded of that one. It must be harsh. I seem to remember Dante's sibling was killed, a brother perhaps, and they blamed his mother in the child's death. It was far-fetched to me she would do such a thing. I never heard anything else about her, though. Then, it seemed like there was Dante and the Black Dragon Commander in an instant. Everything happened fast."

"That is probably a pretty good memory. I think most people would recall the same if asked, and they really had to remember what they could. The Elders always believed the story far-fetched as well, that Dante's mother could not kill her own son. They also always believed the Dark Lord's handprint could be found somewhere in it. We recently learned the depth of the Dark Lord's involvement.

He stood there, in fact overseeing it, and one of his agents disguised as Dante's mother killed Dante's brother. All these years, Dante's father is deceived by the Dark Lord, and thus we know him as the Black Dragon Commander. Dante has been told this, of course, and his task is connected to this information."

Christopher stared at her as the words sunk in, and he scrambled to process their meaning. "Oh, Chris, poor Dante, and his father. I never thought I would feel sympathy for the Black Dragon Commander, but I do after hearing this."

"I know. It certainly puts the Black Dragon Commander in a different light. He's used by the Dark Lord cruelly, but he doesn't realize it."

"And Dante's mother. The Dark Lord would kill her after to cover his tracks." Christopher shook his head, but he stopped at the strange expression on her face.

"I sometimes wonder if that may have been kinder, Christopher. Instead, the Dark Lord kept her prisoner, tortured in a half coma state, for who knows what purpose. Dante's father never knew. Alena and I rescued her recently. It was one of the operations which didn't go smoothly. She is with Dante and the others now, but she remains asleep. We couldn't awaken her, and Dante and the others could not do so either. Dante is a good son too. Every night since she arrived there, he checks on her, sits at her bedside, and hopes she will awaken. Dante's father still believes she is dead and murdered his child."

"Such pain for one family, Chris. How does Dante bear under it?"

"With many tears, Christopher," whispered the girl.

"I'm sorry, Chris. You cried many tears along with him, haven't you?"

The girl nodded and took a deep breath. "Yes, but Dante doesn't see them as we have never met face to face. I fear I'll cry many more tears in the days ahead, Christopher. The task Dante goes to do is to get his father back. We already know the Dark Lord will also be there."

"Can Dante really do it?" Christopher's eyes searched hers.

"Yes, Dante can. He wouldn't be given the task by the Ancient One if not. The training is difficult for him, and he struggles with it. The time is running short before he must do it, and he feels it."

So much stirred underneath the surface with her. He saw a new depth of feeling with her as they spoke about Dante and this task. "Chris, how do you know all this about what Dante must do and what's going on inside his head?"

"All part of the gift from the Ancient One, Christopher. For some reason, the Ancient One chose to center the images I received on Dante and his family for a while. The last several months, they centered especially on Dante. The images created a connection with Dante. It's one of those things we haven't understood yet. It's a strange experience for Dante and me. Hopefully, he accomplishes the task and comes back safely. It's what I hope for them all. Now there's nothing further we have been shown we can do to help any of them."

"Is there anything I can do, Chris?"

"It is forever the question it seems. My comrades asked the same question many times to me. At the moment, though, no. The task before us is what is given. We must accomplish it. The Ancient One will show us what is next." The girl got up. "Speaking of that, we should get rest, so everything goes smoothly again tomorrow. I'm sorry, Christopher, I didn't ask you. Did everything make sense to you?"

"No apologies. I'm going to break you of that, Chris. Yes, it all made sense, and I'll keep every word safe, I promise you. I'm in agreement with the rest thing now, though."

Alena asked, "Are you ready for another long day tomorrow, Christopher?"

"I will be, Alena."

"We will look forward to another day of working with you, Christopher. We'll let you get rest."

"You as well, Alika. Goodnight."

The girl reached over and clasped Christopher's hand. "Thank you for everything. I hope we didn't place too much on you, especially after this evening."

"No, I'm fine. You, on the other hand, I'm continuously astonished at what is held behind those eyes. The others will return safely, Chris. All of them. You'll see. Make sure you take your own advice and get sleep too."

Christopher walked out the ship's door to return to his vessel for the night.

Alika hugged the two goodnight and headed for his ship to do the same. Alena and the girl each got a shower before bed and needed no urging going straight to sleep in their quarters. They were exhausted.

CHAPTER FORTY-EIGHT

Another day dawned.

Alika, Alena, the girl, and Christopher arrived at the next destination for the day. Again, they checked the screen and found where they needed to go on the planet. Again, it was not too far from the landing area. They walked along until they came to the place. Alika went ahead and spoke to the one who came out to greet them. As the day before, after a few minutes, they were motioned inside. The busy day began soon after that, and it did not finish until evening as before.

Lana and her group continued making their plans. Seth and Dante resumed training. Everyone felt things coming together even as they felt the time slip away.

Morning came too early again for both groups.

Alika, Alena, the girl, and Christopher came through the portal and arrived at the next destination for the day. They gathered on the girl's ship and surveyed the screen for the third morning in a row. They found their destination on the planet and followed the same process as before.

Alika and the girl assisted in one area while Christopher and Alena worked together close by with another group.

"This proceeds as smoothly as we hope," said Alika.

"It does. We must continue so with the time frame we have remaining," said the girl.

"I believe someone wishes to get our attention."

"Excuse me," said a voice.

The girl realized it at the same time and turned around in the direction of the voice. The girl smiled as she located the source.

ele

Caleb listened and nodded as the commanders walked through the attack scheme once they arrived at the location of the device. Lana listened quietly, her face trying to hide the worry creeping up for her husband as well as the others about to leave for the task ahead. On the data pad, it displayed a well-orchestrated plan. Yet, everyone knew things could quickly change, and they could find themselves in a terrible spot. They told themselves two people breached the place and escaped, and here a whole army would be going to face the place this time. Reason dictated they would accomplish the operation. They attempted every argument to make themselves feel better. It still came down to the fact that they were going straight into the Dark Lord's territory, and no amount of words took away that truth.

ele

Seth and Dante worked together again.

"I still feel unprepared. What am I to do, Seth?"

"Dante, this is something no matter what we do, you will never feel fully prepared to complete it. You had everything you needed from the beginning to do this task. You will use all of it when the time comes."

"The Dark Lord will be there, Seth. How am I to get through to my father?"

"I don't know, Dante, but you are not there for the Dark Lord. You are there for your father first and foremost. The Ancient One entrusts you with this task, and He will show you how to accomplish it. You must trust." Seth paused. "Dante, we are not always given the entire plan step by step to get us to the end, but we can trust The One who holds it. Remember your young spear-bearer and the long journey from the rooftop back to Alika and the other student. Certainly, no one could guess the plan to get them back home. I know whatever brave front they put on at times, it could not quench the fear felt that day."

"I know you're right. Although I saw no fear when they faced the squadron leader and during the battle with the Black Dragon soldiers."

"I see no fear from you when you face the attacks on the colonies. You face the Black Dragon soldiers as if they are nothing as well."

"Well, the words from the young spear-bearer show no fear."

"No, Dante, you are wrong about that one."

"How, Seth? Their words encouraged everyone."

"They have, Dante. I will not disagree with that part. However, the messages to you, Dante, there is fear entwined in each one of them. The greatest fear of the young spear-bearer has never come from the sword or a blaster shot from a Black Dragon soldier to their own person. Their greatest fear is for you, Dante, and it's conveyed in every message sent to you. It is the fear you will not return safely, either by the sword itself or the same bondage your father now finds himself in."

"I could never join the Dark Lord as my father has done, Seth. The thought…"

"I know it sounds like there is no way, Dante. However, no one thought your father could ever do the things he does. He has, though. The Darkness is strong. The young spear-bearer understands this and fears it for you, which is why you are reminded repeatedly to beware of the Dark Lord's tactics. So yes, one does not look far to see the young spear-bearer's fear. I would guess it will be a long evening tonight and tomorrow for them as well since it will be the same for you. I feel sure you will be very much in their thoughts now and until you come back safely."

"I didn't think about it like that, Seth." Dante sat quietly for a moment. "You're right, though. I know how I felt when we sat there, thinking the ship and everyone in it blown up on the other side of the portal. The same fear gripped me. Well, I have a promise to keep. I must come back, and I plan on doing so with my father. Let's continue, Seth."

"As you wish, Dante."

Evening came, and they all sat down to pretend it was a normal night. It hung in the room. Finally, Ryan could take it no longer. "Okay, can everyone stop acting like this is our last meal together?"

Dante laughed. "Technically, there's an early breakfast together. That would be the last."

Ryan laughed. "Dante, I don't know that you helped, buddy."

Everyone laughed, though, and the tension evaporated from the room.

Caleb agreed. "Dante and Ryan are right. It can be done, and it will be. We will be back before we know it. All of us."

"Agreed," said Commander Gabe. "We cannot lose as we know The One who goes before us."

Lana said, "Yes, but it's always good to be reminded."

CHAPTER FORTY-NINE

Dante checked on his mother for the evening. This time Seth and Ryan both went with him. "Maybe when you get back with your father, she'll be awake. It would be perfect, right?" said Ryan.

"Yeah, it would, Ryan. Perhaps that's what the Ancient One is waiting on."

"Don't give up, Dante. She fought for as long as she did. She's going to keep fighting. There's no if she'll wake up. It's only when."

"Thanks, Ryan. I know you're right. Seth keeps telling me the same each night too. I'm grateful for both of you keeping me encouraged."

Dante walked closer to his mother's side and spoke to her gently. "Mother, I'm going tomorrow to bring father back. You'll soon hold your Ethan again. I'll get him to remember and won't stop trying until he does, I promise. I'm going to borrow a couple of things from you to help me get him back, but I'll keep them safe and bring them back to you." Dante pulled out a slender silver secure container and laid it on the table next to his mother. He gently slipped the wedding band off her finger and put it in the container. Just as gently, he unclasped her necklace and slipped it from her neck. He placed it in the container as well. The container closed tightly, and he secured it with his sunspear.

"Thank you, Mother." He continued to look at her, but her form remained silent. "Don't worry about me, please. There are enough people to do that for you. Seth prepared me well, and you and Father always taught me from the beginning. I have everything I need to get him back and both of us to come home to you. Ryan is right. It would make everything perfect for us to come back to find you awake. Please, Mother, won't you do it for me?" Tears streamed down Dante's face. "It's all right. I know you would awaken if you could by now. Keep trying, okay? I love you." He reached down and kissed her cheek. He wiped his face with his hand and turned around to Ryan and Seth. "It's time to get rest before tomorrow."

The three headed out toward their quarters for the night. Ryan said goodnight to Seth and Dante.

"Get some sleep, Dante. You will need it for tomorrow. Everyone will, I feel sure."

"I will, Seth, and thank you."

"I did nothing but remind you of what you already knew."

Dante hugged Seth goodnight. Seth smiled as he hugged Dante back. "Now go rest, Dante. You leave after the others, but I know your heart. You will want to see them off."

~oℓℓ~

Lana and Caleb returned to their quarters, exhausted for the night. They laid down to get sleep, but to no avail yet. Lana got something to drink and took a sip of it as she came back to bed. She tried to block out tomorrow and tell herself not to worry. Caleb went out all the time on the attacks, and he returned safely every time. This was no different. She put the glass down on the nightstand.

"Hey, I know that look. What's going on in your head?"

"Nothing, Just tired. All the planning and everything wore me out."

"Do you really think that's going to work? Come here." He continued to search her eyes and saw the tears behind them she could not hide. He pulled her over to him. "You're strong all day for everyone. Now you can stop. I'm here, and I'll be back to you as soon as we get this task done."

Lana could not control the flood of tears anymore. "I'm so afraid of something happening to you, of you not coming back, Caleb."

"I know you are, but I told you we would face this together. We will. I'm not leaving you to do this alone. We may fight on a different battlefield for a bit, but we fight the same battle." He wrapped his arms around her and pulled her close as he gently kissed her.

"I can't lose you too, Caleb," whispered Lana as she kissed him back.

"You won't. I promised to stay by you for life. I still have a lot of life left to spend with you, my Lana," he smiled at her again as he whispered, "and it keeps getting sweeter. Let me show you how sweet it can be." He continued kissing her. Suddenly Lana and Caleb forgot about the storm tomorrow held, even if for one night.

*

The girl, Alika, Alena, and Christopher, sat on the girl's ship that evening after another long day.

"It has been a long three days," said Alena in a tired voice.

"Yes, but it went as you all said. I stand amazed."

"There is still work to do. The phase which required our supervision and management is completed, though," said Alika.

Alika saw Christopher focused on the girl. They all noticed it, her strangely quiet manner the last bit. Alika touched the girl's arm lightly. "You have been preoccupied, to say the least. Are you all right?"

"Yeah, I'm okay."

"That sounded hardly convincing."

"I'm sorry. My thoughts drifted to what the others must do tomorrow. I'm concerned for them. Tonight will be difficult for them." The girl was somewhere else, but she forced herself to come back to the conversation at hand. "Yes, as for us, I don't know about tomorrow. We go with our instructions so far. It's an easier role than what we did the past three days. Seemingly we could still assist with our task for tomorrow and leave it if we needed to for a space of time, and it should continue reasonably well." The girl received a surprised look from Alika. "I'm not suggesting we leave the location at all. We simply possess more freedom to monitor the others as that would have been impossible with this task and the time frame laid before us. Unless we get a signal from the Ancient One to help them, we wait."

"Do you believe we're to help them tomorrow?" asked Alena.

"No, I guess not."

"You don't sound convinced, Chris," said Christopher.

"I haven't received any images or anything, so at this point, I must say no. Tomorrow, we go forward with the task before us."

"At the moment we all need sleep for whatever tomorrow holds," said Alika as he stood, and the others followed suit. Christopher said goodnight to them as the girl hugged him goodnight. He tried to assure her the others would be fine and not to worry. The girl smiled as he left for the night to sleep on his ship.

Alika hugged his two students goodnight.

"You're not fine. You're beyond worried. Are you going to get any sleep tonight?" asked Alika to the girl, "I don't have to wonder who the worry is centered upon."

"Actually, I sense Dante and Lana are both struggling tonight. Caleb will give Lana the assurance she needs. Tomorrow when it all comes at once, it'll be hard again, but she'll pull it together. For Dante, it'll be a long night, and tomorrow will be longer."

"What can I do?" asked Alika to the girl.

"I can try tea. I'll make a cup now." She shrugged her shoulder as she walked over to do it.

"I'll do it for you."

"Okay, Alika."

"How did his training go?" asked Alena.

"Much better. He still doesn't feel ready, though. There's no way he could feel ready for what lays before him." The girl's voice bordered on despondent.

Alika handed her the tea, and she put it down in front of her, while staring out into space. "The tea will only help if you drink it, child."

"Oh yeah, I will." She ran a hand through her hair.

"Is Dante getting any sleep?" asked Alika.

"I don't know." Her eyes got the faraway look again. "No, he's not either. How did it come so fast? If only there were another way. He can tell his father everything, show him the things from Abigail. The Dark Lord will be there to twist it. He can make it sound so convincing. Dante doesn't understand. If he listens long enough, it'll wear him down. It'll be all over. Why did I tell him to do this? Why?" The girl could not stop. The words kept spilling out, and she covered her face with her hands.

"Stop, child. Don't do this to yourself." He wrapped his arm around the girl's shoulder as Alena rubbed the girl's back. "Dante does not go alone, and you know that. You must not let your fear rule over you like this. You also must not shoulder a burden that is not yours to do so. The Ancient One sends him to do this, not you. You are simply a part of how the Ancient One chose to deliver the message to Dante." Alika took her face and gently lifted it, gazing into her eyes. "Look at me. Dante will return. We all know by now this is not the end of the story. Once Dante meets the messenger, he will be very pleased. It is about time you and Dante had a nice surprise."

"I wish I could believe such a perfect ending, but I cannot see it tonight."

"Then we'll see it for you," replied Alena.

"What can we do for you, child?" Alika asked as he gently wiped a tear from her face.

"It's not a day away now. It's only counted in hours now, and he must face them." The girl's eyes came back to the present, and she finally responded to Alika's question. "There's nothing to be done." She got up and paced. She picked up the tea and drank it down. It didn't burn. It was lukewarm now, but she didn't notice. She walked over to the cockpit and gazed out into the night sky. It displayed a clear night with lots of stars, but she saw none of the beauty from the night sky, only the darkness that lay before her. "I'll go to bed soon, I promise."

Alika and Alena went over, hugged the girl goodnight, and left her to be. Clearly, she would go to bed when ready, and nothing said to her would comfort her tonight.

⸙

Dante laid down as soon as he came in from leaving Seth, but he couldn't sleep. He got up and made a cup of tea, one of Seth's recipes that sometimes helped when sleep alluded one. Going over to the small window in his quarters, he stared out into the night sky while he drank the tea.

The girl turned back to the night sky. She felt pain go through her as the thought of losing Dante came with renewed force. She could feel his worry tonight. For a moment, she felt as if he was as close as the other side of the cockpit window. She whispered, "Dante, please come back to me." A sob escaped her.

Dante continued to stare out the window. Suddenly he felt something strange. It felt as when he was awakened the morning at the same time as the young spear-bearer experienced the vision of him in the Elders Hall or when he felt them watch him from the ship. He sensed the same presence, the same connection now. It felt burdened, concerned, but beyond that. He understood. Somehow, he could sense their fear for him this evening. He found himself answer aloud before he realized it, "I will return, I promised you, my young spear-bearer."

"You always keep your promises, my Dante. You must keep this one." She continued to cry.

"I cannot fail to keep this promise. I cannot break a promise to you, any more than this bond between us can ever be broken."

"I cannot lose you, Dante. It scares me more than you know."

"I know your fear and how great it is, but you do not need to fear. I won't be lost to the sword or the Darkness, but I'll come back safely. I must meet you as promised. Now let's both get to sleep."

Her tears stopped, and she took a deep breath. "Goodnight, Dante."

"Goodnight, my young spear-bearer." He shook his head and wondered if he imagined the whole presence he felt, but he knew he hadn't. He laid down, and this time he went straight to sleep.

She turned the main lights out in the ship and went into her quarters. She laid down, and this time sleep overcame her.

CHAPTER FIFTY

Morning came early for Lana's group, and a bustle of activity rapidly filled the daybreak. The commanders prepared to leave to assemble with the rest of their squadron and brief them on the plan. The process would probably take the hour to ensure everyone was on the same page before heading out to where the dispersal device lay. They did not dare assemble all where Lana and Caleb were and alert the Dark Lord of the operation today. As previously decided, one of the commanders would stay behind with Lana and Seth to direct an attack if it came on one of the colonies in the meantime. That commander's entire squadron would now be traveling there. The other commanders would be headed out with Caleb for the operation.

Dante and Seth were up as well. Dante would leave soon after Caleb and the commanders left to begin the operation for the device. They wanted to see Caleb and the others off, so Dante and Seth got up with the others.

Dante went to Caleb first. He knew Caleb and Lana would want the last few minutes to say goodbye for the day.

"Be careful, Caleb." He hugged Caleb goodbye.

"You too, Dante." He hugged Dante back. "Neither one of us has an easy task in front of us."

"We'll both get it done. We must, Caleb."

"Yeah, Lana is worried this time, though, as I know you sensed. There's no way to pretend this is business as usual."

"I know. I wish I could be here for her. At least Seth will be. He'll be strong for her no matter how hard it gets."

"Yes, he will. I'll see you back here when the battle is won, Dante."

"My cousin will have it no other way."

"It must be so as I promised her. There's none like my Lana. You better make sure you get yourself back here safe as well. She won't be happy with you otherwise. Then there's Seth and Ryan off the top of my head." He paused with his eyes twinkling. "And don't forget Alika and his students."

"I get it." Dante laughed softly. "I'm serious, though. Safely back, Caleb."

"Safely back, Dante." Caleb walked off to finish the last bit before he left.

Dante went to say goodbye to the rest of the commanders. He came to Ryan last.

"Are you ready, Dante?"

"I could ask you the same."

"We're about to find out. The plan sounds a lot better when you form them than when you try to carry them out. We'll see what curves we get handed today."

"Hopefully, nothing too drastic, Ryan."

"Yeah, if two can make it in and out, I keep thinking there's no way we can't do this. How are you feeling after the time you worked with Seth?"

"Better. I didn't realize how many ways there are for someone to get inside your head until Seth and I started the training. Give me a sunspear and an army of Black Dragon soldiers any day after this."

"Don't let the Dark Lord get inside your head. Remember all the training you've done. We each go to win our battlefield, but we need to come back safe as well."

"We will, Ryan."

"You better. You promised that young spear-bearer you would, and you don't want to make that one upset, Dante." Ryan laughed.

"Yeah, I would definitely meet my match, but I don't think I could ever make that one upset with me."

"No, I think you're right. They're all quite fond of you. Try to stay out of medical too, would you, Dante? I won't be right there today to watch your back. You'll have to be careful for a change."

"Hey, I'm always careful, Ryan."

"I don't know what you call it, but it's not careful. I need you to use my definition of careful, so you come back safe and with everything still connected. So, none of your careful or the young spear-bearer's careful. Got it, Dante?" Ryan shook his head.

"I got it, Ryan, I promise."

"Good. I'll see you when you and your dad get back safely, okay, Dante?"

"We will see you then, Ryan." Dante and Ryan hugged goodbye and headed in separate directions. Ryan headed toward the commanders to assemble with the rest of the squadron before heading for the device.

Dante walked over to stand with Seth.

"It appears everyone is almost ready to fly. I'm glad you'll be here with Lana."

"I as well, but she'll be fine. Her hands will be full managing the different fronts once everything begins. How are you, Dante? You appear well-rested. I admit I doubted last night how you would sleep when you left."

"It was a strange evening. I couldn't sleep at first. I made your tea to help me sleep. Then I got to sleep. I'd like to credit the tea, but I know I can't. You're going to think I'm ... no, I didn't imagine it."

"Dante, go ahead. It can't be any stranger than events we already encountered."

"You're right. I felt a presence in my room. It was like when I woke up at the same time with the young spear-bearer's vision or when they left those times, and I felt them watching me from the ship. No, it was stronger than that. The young spear-bearer was there, but they weren't close by as in past times. Yet, they felt so near suddenly. The presence felt burdened, concerned, the fear we talked about for my safety earlier. I had not felt it as I did last night. See, I told you it makes no sense."

"No, it does make sense, Dante. Go ahead."

"It was so intense. I could sense the essence of what they thought as far as the fear concerning me. I found myself answering aloud the thoughts I felt from them. It wasn't awkward, though. It felt natural. When I finished assuring them and alleviating their fears, I found I dispelled my own fears for the night. I laid down and went straight to sleep. The presence of the young spear-bearer didn't feel burdened anymore either. I feel assured to the point they found sleep as well, but I guess it's wishful thinking. After all, there's no way I could know that. I told you it got stranger."

"No, it appears the connection between the two of you was strong last night due to the challenge you face today. It's a good thing. You ended up reassuring each other, and in the process, you both got the rest you will need to get through whatever task you both must do today. Sometimes it's not important for us to understand how every detail of something works from the Ancient One to appreciate the beauty it simply works, Dante."

Seth and Dante turned to where Lana and Caleb stood as he got ready to leave. "We should head over there so when Caleb leaves, we're there for Lana. As strong as my cousin appears, she's worried about Caleb."

"I agree. We will make sure Lana is not alone when Caleb leaves today."

❧

Lana and Caleb stood facing each other.

"Everything ready?"

"Yes, it's time for me to join them. I'll be back soon, as I always am, Lana."

"Of course, this is no different from the other times." Tears started down her face.

Caleb reached over and wrapped her in his arms. "I know. We're lying to keep telling ourselves that, but I'm coming right back to your arms like I always do. I promise you, sweetheart."

"You have never broken a promise to me. I must believe you won't now. Come back to me safe, please, Caleb."

"I will, my sweet Lana." Caleb reached down and gave her a gentle, long kiss. He gave her hand a final soft squeeze and walked away.

On cue, Dante and Seth walked up to Lana. Dante wrapped his arms around Lana's shoulders. "He'll be back with you safely before you know it."

"You sound so sure."

"It's my turn to be comforting to you, cousin. You always must be the one pulling me back together lately."

Lana couldn't help but smile. "It does seem that way recently, but I appreciate it anyway, cous." Lana's face turned serious again, and she sighed. "You head out soon for your battlefield, Dante. There is no end to the worry for today."

"I'll be back. Lana. I received a thorough speech from Ryan about coming back safely. He made it clear he doesn't want to see me in medical. He also made it clear what safe looks like. I'm told my image is not to Ryan's liking."

Lana and Seth both laughed. Lana shook her head. "I happen to agree with Ryan, so I hope you heed his advice."

"As soon as they all clear the space, I'll head out too."

"We expected as much. They have almost done so. We will walk you to your ship. Do you have everything you need?" asked Seth.

"Yeah, weapons, the items from mother, and my data pad on me. Everything else is on the ship which might come in handy."

They arrived at Dante's ship.

"Are you sure about this? That you're ready to do this?" asked Lana.

"I'll be no more ready today than I would be with more days of training with Seth. It's time to do this. I know it to be true."

"Then I would not stop you, cousin. The Ancient One will be with you. Please, Dante, come back to us safely. I can't bear for something to happen to you."

"I know, Lana. I intend to cause you no grief. I'll return safely."

Dante reached over and hugged his cousin warmly. Lana hugged him back warmly in return.

"We'll see how ready I am, Seth."

"You're ready, Dante. Continue to fight today. Do not give up hope, no matter how many times it takes, no matter how long the battle wages."

"I will, Seth. I'll use everything I learned over the years from you. I know I will need it like never before today."

"You will. Dante, you must come back safely. Dante, you are as a son to me. Surely you know by now. However, I would gladly give up some of your training to your father when you return safely with him. I would rejoice with you to see you mend some of your family back together."

"I know you will, Seth. You always protected and cared for me as a father. You are my family, Seth, as much as my father and mother, and Lana and Caleb. I will see you when I return safely with father."

Dante reached over and hugged Seth tightly, and Seth hugged Dante back as well.

Seth looked at Dante with tears in his eyes. "Now go and get your father back, child. The Ancient One will be beside you and bring you back to us."

Dante got into his ship, and seconds later, it lifted off.

Seth and Lana watched quietly until it flew out of sight. Seth peered over at Lana and saw tears stream down her face again. He reached over and hugged her. After a moment, they walked back into the building. Commander Austin waited on them. It was time to begin managing the rest of the day.

CHAPTER FIFTY-ONE

The girl, Alena, Alika, and Christopher sat in the girl's ship.

"Has everyone left with Lana's group?" asked Alika.

"No, not yet. They're working on it. Lana is about to speak with them before they start going their separate ways." The girl pushed something on the data pad, and an audio transmission began. The sound of bustle in the background ensued for a couple of minutes. Then it settled down. Lana's voice could be heard, getting everyone's attention as the room became quiet. Her voice was firm but gentle as she spoke, "The task we do today will be difficult, but we have faced this foe before. We will do so again. The Dark Lord threatens every individual, every colony, and wishes to put his fear in every heart. He has been allowed to do so for too long, and now we must stop this threat further. We never go alone in any battle, and today's battle is no different. The Ancient One goes before us, and He fights for us. Let us go into battle with the confidence the battle is already won for us, not as one unsure of the outcome. The Ancient One promises to be with us and guide us in the path we are to go. He will never break His promises. Now go wherever your battlefield may be today and return safely at the battle's end." There could be heard the bustle of activity returning. The girl pushed something, and she ended the connection for the moment.

"Lana is much better than I expected," said Alena.

"Lana has always been smart too. She purposely did the address to the group before she said goodbye to her husband for this operation," said the girl quietly.

"Getting through the speech would be difficult, to say the least, if she had waited," said Christopher softly.

"Yes, I'm sure Lana would have found it so." The girl's mind was still with Lana, but she forced herself to shift to the task at hand. "Let's go ahead and get started. We'll monitor everything to an extent while we do our task."

They walked out of the ship and over to where they needed to be for the day. They spoke with the others there, and they understood. The next phase of the task began.

Alika came over to the girl. "Have you heard anything yet? How close are they to get?"

"I don't know, but the Ancient One will let me know when it's time to alert Lana and Seth. They have a fleet prepared to handle an attack if it comes, so they won't need much time. They'll simply use it for a different attack than what they expected. As soon as I'm told to inform them, it's literally a push of a button to send."

"I know you're right."

"I get it, believe me, but it's the Ancient One's prompting. There's a reason we're to wait."

CHAPTER FIFTY-TWO

Caleb's group went through the portal with the entire squadrons. In a moment, they saw what awaited them. For once, though, they held the advantage. They surprised the Dark Lord's army rather than getting surprised.

"Okay, let's stay on script. It looks like what our friends encountered. They already scouted it out for us. Let's do this."

The firefight began. Half the squadron engaged those ships now speeding toward them. The rest of the squadron tried to get closer to the ship hangar. Some aimed their shots close enough inside the hangar to stop the flow of more ships coming out if possible. They needed the hangar clear of Black Dragon ships as eventually, they would enter the hangar with their ships to get to the device. This time the Black Dragon ships didn't seem to be bringing any supplies in and out of the area but instead sat there at the facility.

"It's busy, but don't get bunched up. We can't get surrounded. Keep moving closer to the target, though."

"They're keeping the hangar door open so far," said Commander Gabe.

"Yeah, because they keep sending more ships at us," said Commander Ryan. "That's one way to clear the space for us to land ours. The footage showed a large hangar."

"We get to appreciate how huge now," said Caleb. "Keep at it, everyone. We won't let up on them."

Dante got through the portal, coming through on the other side of the planet where it appeared he needed to be. As suspected, he discovered he had made a wise decision. The scanners immediately picked up a few ships overhead on the other side of the planet from where he came through. If he had gone through the closest way, he would likely have been shot right out of the sky. The device on his ship would help divert his ship's signal for a little while. It should give him the time to land closer to where he needed to be on the planet and power down. Where he landed would take him a little longer to get to the Elders Hall, but he would get there. It was preferable to being shot out of the sky as soon as he emerged from the portal. He had the other advantage of knowing this planet like the back of his hand. He spent his entire childhood here before the Dark Lord ravished it. Quickly landing the ship and powering it down, he did a last-minute visual around the ship, trying to see if anything else remained he might need. He had a blaster, his sunspear, the items from his mother, his data pad, and additional items that came in helpful in battle at times. He reasoned you never knew when you might need a distraction or a small explosion. Unable to think of anything else he needed, he walked out of the ship as the door closed behind him. He got his data pad out and scanned. It showed in about an hour or less, he would be in the center of the action.

ele

"Sir, we received a report a huge fleet emerged and is attacking the same facility of the incident recently with those spear-bearers," said a Black Dragon soldier.

"How large of a fleet?" asked the one sitting on the command ship.

"It appears to be several of their entire squadrons. It's an enormous force to be reckoned with, sir."

"They are going on the offense and today of all days. Interesting and unlike them. I will let the Dark Lord and the Black Dragon Commander know. I believe I know their answer, but they may surprise me. Hold our position." In a few minutes, he returned and sat back down. He smiled. "It does not alter our plans. Continue to our first destination for the day. We must stay on schedule. The Dark

Lord and the Black Dragon Commander want no mistakes today, and they told me to remind everyone."

"Yes, sir."

"How long until we reach the first one?"

"It should be approximately four minutes, sir."

"Right on schedule. I will remind everyone the Dark Lord and the Black Dragon Commander want no welcome of our coming. First order of business is to close down their ability to communicate to the outside world, to call for help in any way. No one is to know what is happening there. After all, we have a couple more stops to make after we are done there. Does everyone understand?"

Silence greeted his announcement. However, in this case, the collective silence meant everyone understood the message perfectly.

"Excellent because the Dark Lord and the Black Dragon Commander are not in a forgiving mood. They will not take another failure, and they made that abundantly clear to me before they left. Let's get started, shall we?"

⁓ ✏ ⁓

Lana and Seth sat with Commander Austin, monitoring everything.

"I feel useless now."

"You should not. Everything is going as planned. Your husband and his crew are engaged in an air battle as they expected. Dante landed safely and approaches where he needs to be to get to his father in a matter of minutes."

"Yes, nothing unusual so far, Lana. All is going as we hoped," said Commander Austin.

"And they both have the element of surprise on their side for once rather than the way it normally is for us. They also aren't going in blind. Your husband and his group have a layout of the facility and, thanks to the footage, saw the inside of it. Dante is going back to his home, so he knows the landscape better than anyone in the Dark Lord's forces. Dante's father is the only one who knows the landscape as well as Dante."

The girl, Alena, Alika, and Christopher, worked together with the others. The girl instantly felt it, like a gentle nudge inside. She stopped in mid-sentence to Christopher.

"You okay?" Christopher reached out and touched her arm.

Alika and Alena looked over at the girl. They knew the look. They excused themselves from their task and turned to her.

"Yeah, I'm fine. It's time to send the message to Seth and Lana."

Seth, Lana, and Commander Austin continued to monitor. Suddenly, Seth's and Lana's data pads found a life of their own. The devices flashed a red alarm and vibrated violently. They both snatched up their data pads.

The same message was displayed for both of them:

The Dark Lord sends an army to attack you, Lana and Seth. It's on its way as this message is sent. You are the colony today. Prepare Commander Austin and his group for battle now. The Ancient One will be at your side.

Seth and Lana turned to each other and then to Commander Austin.

"Commander Austin, read the screen, please. The message is from our friends." She put it on the screen for Commander Austin.

Commander Austin read it and didn't blink. "Understood. Today, this is our battlefield. We will defend it. They will not get through, Lana." He ran out the door.

"I'll take care of the ground soldiers as agreed, Lana," said Seth as he hurried out the door.

"Did they get it?" asked Alika.

"Yes, they acted on it instantly as expected. Their battlefront will begin soon."

All four of them looked at each other. The girl finally said, "Let us get back to our task."

❦

Caleb's group fired furiously. They were making headway as shots began reaching into the hangar. They incurred a few heavily damaged ships, but those they sent back through the portal to Lana. It was better for them to come out than to continue fighting in the damaged state. They eliminated many Black Dragon ships, so they felt confident about how the battle progressed.

"We're getting close to the hangar, Commander Caleb," said Commander Gabe, "We could almost ..." he stopped in mid-sentence. "Oh no, we located the modification we'll be making in our plans for today."

"I saw it too," said Commander Conrad, "The shot did not come from a ship. So where then?"

"All right, everybody, we found out what the middle section does. We find a way to knock it out," said Caleb. "Watch your back from it until we do."

Commander Ryan sighed. "There's the curve today from the Dark Lord."

❦

Dante stood at the edge of the clearing. Several minutes ahead would be the Elders Hall. As expected, some Black Dragon ships and soldiers lay in the path between him and the Elders Hall. Considering the two people inside the Elders Hall, the outside wasn't bad. Perhaps since the real battle lay elsewhere, it made sense after all. Probably most of the soldiers accompanied the dispersal device, ready to launch it on a helpless colony. Unfortunately, Caleb and his group would get the full force of the Black Dragon's forces. Dante forced himself to push the thought out of his mind and concentrate on the task at hand. As much as his first instinct wanted to take his sunspear and cleave through every last Black Dragon soldier, he resisted the urge. His aim was to reach his father. Being discovered before would not help him with his goal.

Dante used the Black Dragon ships around the Elders Hall to slowly creep closer to the building. It wouldn't be a problem once he could get there. He knew ways in the Elders Hall few were aware of, and once inside, it was true as well, the advantage of training in there for his entire childhood. Dante knelt behind another Black Dragon ship and waited for an opening. It would get more complicated the closer he got as it meant more Black Dragon soldiers. He heard something and groaned inside. He turned around quietly, and as he did, his sunspear responded to him in his one hand, and his blaster poised ready in his other hand. The Black Dragon soldier came up behind him and brought the sword down on him. Dante used his sunspear to block the Black Dragon's sword. At the same time, Dante reached out and put the blaster right up against the Black Dragon soldier and a couple of shots silently fired. The Black Dragon soldier quietly crumbled to the ground.

Dante peeked around. It went unnoticed so far. Dante closed up his sunspear again. He got ready to get closer. He reached the next ship without incident. The next ship ahead of him where he needed to be had a Black Dragon soldier behind it. Dante kept waiting for him to move but finally concluded the soldier would be there for a little while. The Black Dragon soldier studied something on his data pad. Dante couldn't stay in one place for long, or he would be discovered. He quietly moved to the next ship. Once he got there, his sunspear responded to him again as he got behind the Black Dragon soldier. The troop turned around and swung his sword, but too late. Dante ducked, and his sunspear blocked the blow as before, and he reached out with the blaster again. He needed this to keep going quietly.

Dante arrived at the last ship in front of the Elders Hall but purposely ignored the front entrance since he knew another way inside. Proceeding carefully from the last ship to the building, he continued towards the back window of the building. He got closer and, this time, found three Black Dragon soldiers near where he wanted to be. Seeing no other soldiers in the back of the fortress, he was confident he could finish this fast and get inside the Elders Hall. His sunspear flashed into action. The Black Dragon soldiers tried to fight back, but Dante took them off guard. With one swipe of the sunspear, Dante cleaved both of the Black Dragon soldiers' legs before they could react. Dante turned to the third Black Dragon soldier, and a minute later, he found the end of Dante's sunspear. Dante checked and could see none of them had time to alert anyone, and no additional soldiers wandered around to his position. He quickly climbed through the window entrance and into the building now. Time to make his way to the Elders Hall. Strange, though he had not been here for years, he could still do this with his eyes closed. He trained in these halls for years, but he also played games with Collin, Caleb, and Lana here. They used to drive Seth up the wall. The games of hide-and-seek and tag and one they created called maze finder came back to him. Yes, he knew less-trodden paths in this place that would help him today. The Dark Lord and his father chose this location for their reasons, but it ended up giving him the advantage.

CHAPTER FIFTY-THREE

Lana watched and waited. She could see her husband's group still working furiously on the battlefield as she monitored their progress. They sent back the damaged ships through the portal. After taking one look at the ships, Lana knew they could not be repaired enough to send them back out. Once she found out about the approaching attack here, she rerouted those soldiers to join the ground forces with Seth. Commander Austin stood ready with the fleet in the air, and Seth the same with the ground forces. Lana continued watching the screen and waited. Maybe their friends got it wrong for once as only the calm hum of the communication system could be heard. Then it was as if the sky exploded. Through the portal came the Dark Lord's fleet. It had begun.

"Commander Caleb's group, I need to let you know, one of the Dark Lord's fleets arrived here. Any ships you send back due to damage must be aware when coming in. We don't want them shot out of the sky by mistake. That's all," stated Lana.

"Okay, everyone, no one gets through. The others fight their own battlefield. We are it here. It is up to us to hold it. The Ancient One goes before us. Let us not forget it as Lana reminded us earlier," said Commander Austin.

Commander Austin's fleet did not hesitate. They met the Dark Lord's army furiously. The sky lit up with explosion after explosion.

Seth stood firmly with the ground forces, his staff in his hand. The Dark Lord's forces approached. Seth met the eyes of his squadron leaders, and he motioned them forward. They would wait no longer.

"We have to do something about the middle section. We can't keep dodging it and get rid of these Black Dragon ships. Who wants to tackle the middle section?"

"I'll volunteer my squadron, Caleb," said Commander Ryan. "My squadron, follow me now."

Commander Ryan and his squadron concentrated their fire on the middle section, but it didn't work. Even worse, a couple of their ships now left because they didn't fare well under its fire.

"Hey, guys, it fires back, remember that. Geez, too close," Commander Ryan yelled.

"Are you okay, Ryan?"

"Yeah, just wonderful, Caleb," he replied, visibly frustrated by the situation.

A silence passed over the group. "Everyone heard what Lana said, right?" asked Caleb.

"Yes, do we need to send help there?" asked Commander Gabe.

"It's going to be hard, but we can't leave them too short-handed. Do we know how big of a force the Dark Lord sent?" asked Commander Cepheus.

"I'm finding out," replied Caleb. He answered back a moment later. "She says no. They'll handle it. Take care of our battlefield. She just didn't want our damaged ship coming through and getting blown out of the sky. Okay, Ryan, back to the middle section."

"Usually, there's one part of something like that, if you target it, you can overload it or disable it. Maybe if we can hit it at the same time. I tried scanning it from here to figure out where the target could be. I came up with a couple of ideas. It's worth a try," said Ryan.

"Go for it, Ryan."

"My squadron, follow me again. This time dodge better. Fire at the spot, I say, when I say. Let's do this."

Commander Ryan and his squadron sped through, dodging the blaster fire coming through the middle section, and fired all at once on his signal.

Commander Ryan's voice came through again irritated. "No effect. That's not the sweet spot, apparently. Let's try again. Another pass. This time fire at the next spot you were relayed."

Commander Ryan and his squadron sped through again, firing at his instruction.

Commander Ryan's voice came through again, and his frustration continued to rise. "This one may not work that way. Let's do this again. Another pass. Another spot."

Commander Ryan and his squadron sped through again, firing again on his signal.

"We finally got something. I picked up a big power fluctuation this last time, but it settled back down. The squadron hit it with everything at once, and all we got was a power fluctuation. I don't know how to disable it. We need to get close and personal to it, and we can't. By the time we do, the fleet will be destroyed if we don't get rid of it soon."

"There has to be a way to knock it out."

"You would think with all the time spent with Dante creating new ways to disable tanks, an idea to stop this would come now when we need it."

"Something quick needs to surface."

"I know, Caleb. No press ..." Ryan didn't finish his sentence, "Too close again!" He yelled as something exploded close to his ship. "We've got to dodge till we come up with it. We at least know where we need to aim."

"How are we coming getting to the hangar?" asked Caleb.

"The progress slowed down tremendously with the middle section of artillery structure firing at us," reported Commander Gabe.

"However, we're still holding our own without too much loss of ships on our side. We just aren't making any headway into the hangar, and we're not knocking them down like before," said Commander Conrad.

"This is going to catch up to us soon," said Caleb, clearly not liking the direction the battle was turning.

"Close and personal without the person." Commander Ryan could be heard mumbling. "Of course, the young spear-bearer did it, and Dante does it many times, essentially with the tanks. Caleb, I have an idea. Remember when the young spear-bearer did the whole thing with the detonators and explosions before they hit the portal?"

"Yeah, I don't believe any of us could forget as much as we've tried."

"I agree, but if we can get one at the exact spot and cause an explosion, it might disable it enough. Then I think the squadron's fire would work as expected on it. We all brought devices, so I'll use the ones on my ship."

"Try it. The worst that can happen is it doesn't work."

"I'm on it." He shook his head. He never thought remembering the crazy stunt from the young spear-bearer would help today, but if so, they had another reason to thank Alika's group if they ever got to meet. A couple of his squadron covered him as he briefly moved his ship away from the worst of the fire. He got the detonators ready and inserted them on the saucers. Thankfully the mechanism on his ship worked, so he didn't have to consider losing his hand to get the detonators sent from the ship to its destination. He put it on the platform, and the ship's system automatically directed it back up and released it. Ryan sent it where he wanted with the only challenge being it reaching its final destination without it getting hit by fire on its way. He got it there, though. It stuck on the target spot. He set it off and watched as it exploded on the structure. Ryan used the scanners.

Ryan's smile could be heard through the system. "The power level in the one tower section plummeted. Let's finish the one off. My guess is it can recover, probably a backup system. We won't give it the chance. My squadron, follow me, fire on the spot all at once on my mark. I think it will work now."

Ryan and his squadron went around for a pass and fired on the spot. A large explosion followed from the structure. "There won't be any more blasts coming from that section of tower."

"Can we see that, let's say five more times, Ryan?"

Ryan laughed. "It will be my pleasure. I'm on it. It'll be like exploding tanks with Dante. All right, squadron, you heard Commander Caleb. Let's make the rest of these inoperable." Ryan got the next detonator and sent it out for the second section of the tower.

⁓℮ℓℓ⁓

Lana watched as the firefight continued above the sky in front of her. Commander Austin kept his promise. Nothing got past. It appeared their forces held the Dark Lord's Army back. She could hear the explosions, but none of them hit near the fortress.

Seth and his group continued making good work of the Black Dragon ground forces. So far, they had not encountered anything unusual, and Seth was thankful, especially after the last attack.

CHAPTER FIFTY-FOUR

The girl, Alena, Alika, and Christopher, continued to work at their task with the others. The girl and Alena worked together, and a few feet away, Alika and Christopher did likewise.

The girl stopped, and her eyes got a faraway look. She heard a whisper. "It is time to put this task down. The day changes."

Alena glanced at the girl and touched her arm. "What is it?"

"I'm not entirely sure, but it's time to shift our focus for the day. We need to take our leave of this. I don't know for how long. We need to return to the ship."

Alena motioned for Christopher and Alika. They came over and nodded after they conferred together.

"Alena and I will go ahead back to the ship. You two let the others know we'll need to be away from this, and we don't yet know for how long we'll be gone. You should be able to wrap it up with them in about twenty minutes."

"In about twenty, then," said Christopher.

Alena and the girl got back to the ship. The girl started to sit but didn't get far.

The whisper came again to her. "The battlefield changes now. Go, refresh yourself, and make ready for the battle ahead."

"And?" asked Alena.

The girl told her the message.

Alena looked puzzled.

The girl shook her head. "Yeah, me too, but I learned a long time ago not to question certain things, just do it. One painful bouncing off the side of a building proved enough for me."

The girl went toward her quarters, and Alena followed behind her, still wondering about the message. "Hey Alena, come here for a minute, would you?"

"Sure."

The girl held something up on a hanger. "Did you pack this for me by mistake? I don't remember packing it or it even being here the whole trip. It's hanging on the door. It's mine, but it's completely unsuitable clothing for carrying out an operation."

"No, I didn't pack it for you."

"How strange."

The whisper came again. "I chose it. I told you the battlefield changes. The time approaches."

Alena saw the understanding come to the girl's eyes. "You better get to it, dear. It appears this day will get stranger."

"Yeah, let me get the rest of my things, get showered, and changed." The girl quickly did and had finished getting ready when Alika and Christopher entered the ship. They looked at her, puzzled.

"I don't know either. I just follow instructions." She repeated to them the instructions.

"Strange, it doesn't seem the time for a dress, even a simple one like you're wearing." Alika smiled at her.

"You do look very nice though, Chris," said Christopher smiling at her as well.

"Yes, she does, but she always does no matter what," said Alika.

"Okay, are we done now?" said the girl.

"You better get used to it once Dante meets you." Alena laughed.

"Yes, Dante," said the girl softly. "He should be close to the Elders Hall by now."

"He encountered no trouble getting into the building?" asked Alika.

"No, the location helped him as well. He knows the planet and the building since it's his childhood home. He knew ways to navigate both that the Dark Lord and the Black Dragon Commander were unaware."

"I didn't think about that part," said Alena.

"Doesn't sound like the Dark Lord did either," said Christopher.

"Supposedly, he didn't know of Dante's coming. Although we never fully determined that part." Without warning, the girl stumbled. She grabbed ahold of the cockpit control panel to steady herself, and her eyes filled with panic.

Alena gently took her arm. "What is it?"

The girl reached for her data pad, but her hand shook too badly.

CHAPTER FIFTY-FIVE

"The Dark Lord's companion is coming for Abigail. Lana and Seth must get to Abigail's room." The girl held out her shaking data pad to Alika. Alika rushed to reach Seth and Lana in time as he took the data pad from her.

"Is she trying to recapture her?" asked Alika as he alerted Lana and Seth at the same time.

"No, she is there to kill her, and she is already in the building, Alika." Her voice shook, and tears began to form in her eyes.

***

Seth could feel his data pad go off. There could be only one source who would send something now, so it must be important. He finished chopping down the Black Dragon soldier he was engaged in combat with and moved out of the heat of battle.

Lana was monitoring when her data pad flashed red and began to shake violently. She picked it up instantly.

"Lana and Seth, it's Alika. You and Seth get to Abigail's room now. The Dark Lord's agent is there and means to kill Abigail. Hurry before it's too late."

"Got it, Alika. I'm going now. Seth will join me." Lana ran for Abigail's room, pulling her sunspear out as she went. "Seth, did you hear?"

"I did, and I'm on my way, Lana." He turned quickly to one of the squadron leaders. "The three of you are in charge. Keep this going until I return." Seth ran inside for Abigail's room.

***

Alena guided the girl to sit on the couch. Alika and Christopher joined them.

"You heard them. The Dark Lord's agent will not succeed. Abigail will not die today, child." Alika handed her back the data pad.

The girl took it from him. "I saw it. It's going to be so close, Alika." More tears ran down her face. "I don't know if they make it."

"They will," said Alika.

"We still have the monitoring in Abigail's room, right?"

"Yes," said Alena.

The girl appeared perplexed. "I'm going to need it later."

"For?"

"I don't know, Alena."

"Let's put it on screen. We'll make sure it gets to your data pad," said Alika.

"This is quite a battlefield," said Christopher.

"Yes, and it keeps growing," said Alena.

~ele~

Dante quietly made his way through the building to reach the Elders Hall. It twisted and turned seemingly, but Dante knew exactly where he stood in it. He peeked around a corner. A lone Black Dragon soldier leaned against a wall. Dante was surprised he would be here. Probably skipping out on somewhere else he should be, or he didn't appear to take his guard duties too seriously. Strange, for mostly machine, they had a few in the batch that didn't follow the blueprint quite right, or there was a glitch in parts of the programming. Dante came up behind the Black Dragon soldier and cut him down with the sunspear before he could react. Dante kept going. He knew as he got closer to the Elders Hall it would be harder to avoid the soldiers, but he knew ways to get there that didn't involve the front door. He came to another room but needed to leave the room and go momentarily into the hallway. Two guards blocked the entrance, but not for long. He hid in the shadows behind something in the room and made a slight shuffling sound. He heard one of the guards shift and say something. The guard began to walk over, and the other one followed over predictably. Dante waited until both of them got close enough to him. Then he pulled his sunspear out and quickly took care of both of them. This time he would be keeping his sunspear out. He was almost next door to the Elders Hall now.

Dante waited a couple of minutes to make sure no one missed the two guards he caused to disappear from the door. Dante took his data pad out to get an idea of what the immediate hallway looked like as far as soldiers. As he suspected, a small concentration of them congregated near the front door of the Elders Hall. He didn't plan on going in the front door, though. He checked down the hall. There were guards down at the side doors on this side to the Elders Hall. He went over to the other door in the room and peeked out. The view revealed an unguarded back entrance into the Elders Hall. He kept expecting more guards around the place but painfully reminded himself again they were all probably bearing down on his friends. He hoped his friends fared successful and safe but forced himself to come back to his own task. Still no guards at the back door. The guard could be in the room itself for some reason or wandered away for a moment.

Either way, a clear path to the Elders Hall remained, and he would get no better chance. He quietly went out of the room and came around the corner. Opening the back door of the Elders Hall, he quietly walked in the room and felt waves of sadness wash over him. He spent many days happily training here before it all fell apart. The emblem of the Ancient One, two sunspears crossed with a dove in the middle on the wall, caught his eye. The banner was tattered but managed to stay hanging at the front of the hall. He felt anger touch him as he remembered what his father and the Dark Lord watched here today, but in their minds, this was a perfect location. He forced himself to brush it aside. It would not help him with what he needed to do today. He continued to step forward on alert. Suddenly, the door closed behind him.

Dante knew what came next. He saw the preview already.

Two figures entered the room ahead of him and stared up at him.

"Well, well, young Dante, we did not expect you today," said the Dark Lord.

"It has been too long, son," said the Black Dragon Commander.

Dante pointed his sunspear at the Dark Lord.

CHAPTER FIFTY-SIX

"There's one more to finish. They know what we're doing now. Guys, be careful. They do catch on to patterns." Ryan muttered under his breath. "It's like talking to Dante. I hope he's okay."

Ryan sent the last detonator device out, and it blew. The levels plummeted again. He drummed his fingers on the side of the control panel of his ship. He felt nervous about hitting it the same way. The last time was too close. "Okay, we're going to knock this one out like the others but different formation and come in from a different direction. We did it too many times the same way." Ryan gave the new instructions, and they did the flyby and took the shot. It worked perfectly. Ryan breathed a sigh of relief as he watched because he realized the move saved more than a few of his squadron.

"I don't know what made you change it, Ryan, but I'm glad you did. We would need to send several of your ships through the portal to Lana."

"You can thank Dante. The image of half his back taken off with the tank incident came to me. I had the same feeling before this last pass. They figured out the pattern."

"Inspiration has come from strange places today for you, Ryan."

"You're telling me, but it worked."

"Okay, everybody, we should be more successful at getting to the hangar now. We've been playing around with these Black Dragon ships long enough. Let's get to what we came here to do. We need progress clearing an entrance to the hangar."

"You heard Commander Caleb. Thanks to Commander Ryan and his squadron, the extra artillery system they welcomed us with was eliminated. No more excuses. Let's knock Black Dragon ships out of the sky," said Commander Gabe with fresh determination in his voice.

Caleb grinned as he fired a shot, and it hit its target perfectly. They would be inside the hangar in no time now. They were back in business.

∼ℓℓ∼

The figure found the hallway she needed to be on, and Abigail's room lay ahead of her. Surprisingly the hall was quiet. She thought they would surely be treating injured soldiers by now. They probably were just in a different area. They apparently attempted to keep their precious Abigail protected from the rest of the patients. After all, she was a long-term resident now. That wouldn't be the case for much longer. The room would be free for use again soon enough.

The figure approached the door. Two armed guards stood on each side of the door. She smiled at them.

"Hello, I need to check on Abigail. Can you open the door, please?"

The guard looked at her, puzzled. "Lana, you know the rules. You should have no problem getting inside. Go ahead."

"Sorry, it has been a long day, I guess." She waited another moment, hoping they would go ahead and open the door. They didn't budge, though.

Now they both watched her strangely. The other guard said, "Go ahead, Lana. Open the door. He's right." He moved aside to enable her easier access to the door mechanism to press her finger on it and activate the voice recognition.

"Of course." The figure paused and said, "Lana."

The guard continued scrutinizing her. "It's still waiting, Lana. Your fingerprints too. Come on, Lana. You know even Dante must do this."

"It seems unneeded after all this time." She reached her hand out but didn't quite place her entire hand on it. "It doesn't appear to be working properly now. One of the blasts probably caused a glitch in it. Why don't you open the door for me?"

"Lana, put your hand all the way on the handprint station now, please."

"I did the last time. It's not working correctly. Open the door now, gentlemen."

"No, stand back from the door now, Lana." Both guards had their hands reaching for their blasters. They didn't know the identity of the figure, but they both decided it wasn't Lana.

"All right, I'm stepping back. This is crazy, though." She hadn't moved. Instead, she got two blasters out, one for each hand. The one guard, she made sure the shot killed him instantly. The second guard, she only needed the shot to disable him. She shot the hand going to his blaster. Then she got her knife out and put it at his throat.

"Now, soldier whoever you are. I want in the room, and you're going to get me there. You must have access. Your friend here paid with his life. Surely this woman's life is not worth yours as well. Now put your handprint there, speak your name into the device, and get me in the room. I'm growing impatient."

"Never. You're going to kill me anyway after you're done. Even if not, I won't do it to Dante. I swore I would protect his mother, and I will."

"Then I will make you." She forced the man's hand on the device. It waited for his name to be spoken. "Say your name now."

The soldier shook his head.

"I will kill you right here. Speak your name for the device."

The soldier continued glaring at her coldly and spoke not a word.

"Nice try, but no." She saw him use his other hand to attempt to reach his other blaster. She took his blaster and threw it aside. He tried to wrestle the knife away as well, but she firmly rested it against his throat. Her tone held controlled fury. "No more games. Do what I'm asking, or you will not live any longer."

The soldier stared at her and did not move a muscle.

"Your choice." She ran the knife across the soldier's throat, and he crumbled to the ground, dead.

"No." The girl moaned, and a sob escaped her. She watched the soldier's blood spilled on the floor as he fell to the ground.

The others watched in equal horror at the scene which transpired.

Instantly the figure changed. Her voice and appearance no longer matched that of Lana. "Such a waste. These Freedom Fighters with their high ideals. Look where it got you." The figure eyed the device on the door. "It appears we will do this the noisier way." She took out some items, including a sword and a device. "This door will need to come down forcefully, but it will only take a moment. I know you're dying to see me again, Abigail."

True to her word, the figure quickly had the door down in a mangled heap on the floor. Now no barrier stood between Abigail and her.

The girl and the others continued to watch, helpless. Where were Lana and Seth?

The cloaked figure approached Abigail's bedside. "Abigail, you have not changed any since I last saw you. Did you miss me? I have missed you. Your relocation caused me much grief, but you have been found now. It appears your time is up." The cloaked figure regarded Abigail for another minute as one savoring the moment and smiled cruelly. Finally, she got her knife back out.

—ℓℓ—

Lana and Seth rushed down the hall toward Abigail's room. They could see the two bodies of the soldiers before they got there.

"Oh, no, it can't be," said Lana as she and Seth continued to run full speed to Abigail's room, seeing the door destroyed to it. They ran in and to Abigail's bedside.

CHAPTER FIFTY-SEVEN

Seth and Lana made a crisscross with their sunspear and staff inches above Abigail's chest before the cloaked figure's knife could sink its point into Abigail. The cloaked figure gaped up at them with fury from the other side of Abigail's bedside.

The girl finally breathed again, not realizing she had held her breath as she watched. Alena wrapped her arm around the girl's shoulders.

Lana and Seth pushed their weapons up so the knife no longer hovered over Abigail.

"Get away from Abigail now," said Lana firmly.

"You two this time. Is there no end to it for her? Fine, you saved her this round, but it doesn't matter. The Dark Lord has already won today."

"It doesn't appear that way from here," said Seth.

"Are you sure? I admit I'm unhappy about Abigail. I was told to either re-capture or eliminate her. Recapturing her would be so much trouble, too much bother. I hoped to simply kill her today. It would end this whole obsession the Dark Lord possesses with her, really her whole family. However, it's not meant to be. I'm disappointed about it." She smiled at them. "You have far from won, though. Try to tell your two soldiers at the door. Where is their victory?"

"They died honorably to keep Abigail safe. We don't expect you to understand such things," said Lana coldly.

"You're right. I don't, and I hope I never do. This honor only got your friends killed. Either way, this is only the beginning of your pain. The next one will slice you to the bone. Where is your dear cousin, Lana, and your student who you care so dearly for, Seth?"

Lana's and Seth's faces froze.

"Yes, my Dark Lord, let me know as I got the door down. Dante just walked into the Elders Hall. The Dark Lord is beyond happy to see young Dante. Oh, the plans for Dante are already spinning in the Dark Lord's mind. I hope you said your goodbyes to Dante because you will not see him again. If you do, you will no longer be on the same side. My Dark Lord has done this for some time now. Dante's father is already under his control. Now he means to gain the son too. Do you still see victory?"

"The Dark Lord will not take Dante. Dante is ready and will not fall."

"You believe in your training to the last, don't you? You are a fool. I have seen the Dark Lord's work with Dante's father for years. He is the master of taking a gentle spirit, and well, you see the Black Dragon Commander's work since his service under the Dark Lord's control. Dante is not ready for what the Dark Lord will do to his mind and spirit today. You are lying to yourself to think differently. Go ahead, though. It is amusing from where I stand."

"My cousin would not join you or the Dark Lord. You're wrong. His spirit will not be twisted."

"We will see who is right. I believe you will find yourselves on the losing side of this one as well. I think I could get used to having young Dante around. Actually, I could grow quite fond of him. Maybe I could personally assist him with training, help him tap into some undiscovered set of skills. Certain training takes a different teacher, more direct, hands-on training than what he has encountered. I bet he would excel in it as with his other training, and I would enjoy helping him with it." The cloaked woman laughed. "Oh my, if you could only see your faces now."

"Don't you touch Dante."

"Time will tell, Seth. I'll tell Dante you will miss him. I'll be going now. Another time I'm sure." The cloaked woman turned and ran out of the room. She didn't have far to go. She had slowly inched backward to the door during her confrontation with Seth and Lana.

"We should go after her, Seth." Lana couldn't move, though. The encounter, the words from the agent, left her shaken to the core and sickened.

"No, we would not defeat her today, not with the other going on."

"What about Abigail?" Lana looked at the door.

"I think the Dark Lord's agent is done for today with Abigail, but we'll get the other two guards in here and the doctor. They'll figure it out." Seth did something on his data pad, and seconds later, the doctor came in and several guards. The doctor surveyed the scene in shock before him. Seth explained what happened quickly.

"I understand, Seth. We will take care of it," said the doctor. The soldiers nodded.

"We must get back. We have been gone way too long," said Seth.

"You and Lana go," said the doctor.

Lana and Seth walked out. Lana stooped down outside the door as the soldiers began the grisly work of taking away the bodies of their dead comrades. She stared at the bodies and the scene left behind, shaking her head.

"They saved Abigail. They would not let the agent in. She had to tear the door down. They didn't give in, even though this was the cost."

Stooping down with Lana, Seth said quietly, "They represented the best of the Freedom Fighter, of the Ancient One. They lived it out today before us. Abigail is still safe because of it."

Lana slowly got up but continued to stare at the scene. "Taking their lives meant nothing to her, Seth. And how she did it … she didn't blink. I could see it in her eyes."

"Lana, she is the same one that took Collin's life, the life of a child, in the same way. For her, this …"

"Really was nothing."

"Lana, are you all right?" Lana buried her head in her hands for a moment.

"I can't get it out of my head what she said about Dante. About the Dark Lord and if she touches my cousin … Seth, I don't want to believe it, but she sounded …" Her eyes glistened.

"Convincing. I know. More than unnerving. I understand why Alika's group kept warning us about her now."

Seth gave Lana a hug as she took a deep breath. "Let's go catch up, Seth." They ran to the command center.

Lana checked the screen with Seth. "What is that ship which left a few minutes ago, Seth? It's not ours. It has to be enemy, but they're leaving, not coming to the planet with an attack."

"My guess is that would be our intruder. She is truly done with us for the day. At least it appears Abigail will be safe for now."

CHAPTER FIFTY-EIGHT

"The ground forces are holding, but they need help," said Seth observing the screen.

"Let's go help them, Seth."

"Don't you need to stay here?"

"I think I need to go assist for a bit."

Lana turned to the soldier. "If something comes through that demands my attention before I come back up, notify me, and I'll disengage myself."

"Yes, ma'am," said the Freedom Fighter leader at the communications center.

Seth stared at her.

Lana put a helmet and basic protective gear on. "You're right. I don't want to go out with a target on my back. Now, let's go, Seth." She pulled her sunspear back out.

⁓ℓℓ⁓

Alena glanced over at the girl. "See, everything is okay." Alena stopped. The girl's eyes were far away again, with something else yet calming. Alena didn't need to guess the source of the something else. Alena felt it from the girl when the cloaked woman teased of seducing Dante. The girl's anger was still subsiding at the thought.

Alika and Christopher turned to the girl as well at Alena's reaction.

Christopher reached over and touched the girl's arm lightly, "Chris, are you all right?"

"I am." Although her voice sounded miles away, her face held a strange expression like one trying to sort out a puzzle.

"What is going on, child?"

"The Dark Lord's agent spoke true on the one thing, Alika. Hopefully, nothing else. Dante had just arrived before the Dark Lord and his father. I can hear and see it through Dante's vision, a help granted by the Ancient One today. It started at the same time while the Dark Lord's agent confronted Lana and Seth. I tried to keep up with both conversations. It's easier now. There's only the one to listen to." Her eyes were as one watching a scene far away.

"How's it going so far?" asked Alena.

"The Dark Lord is searching for an entrance with Dante. He'll find all the places he can go first, and I sense he's already probing to find out which will give him the best yield. Dante must tread carefully. He can easily allow the Dark Lord too much room, and he'll not see it until the opening cannot be closed."

~ele~

Dante took a few more steps and stopped.

Dante was indeed alone. How strange. Time to find out what brought the boy here today. Surprises never ceased. "This is certainly a pleasant surprise, Dante. Please, put the sunspear away. I do not intend to hurt you, and of course, your father would not do so."

"It's fine where it's at, pointed straight at you."

"Suit yourself, Dante. There is no need, but I can see you are not convinced yet. I suppose it's expected with all the time you spent training with the Elder."

"Yes, the Elder trained me well, and I'm grateful for it. Seth protected me many times from you."

"Still clinging to that, are you, Dante? Many others do as well. Some see through it. I hope one day you will as well, Dante, as does your father."

"I do, Dante. The Elders do not help you. I thought for years they helped us and found out too late it's the opposite."

"How can you believe such a thing, Father? It's all a lie from the Dark Lord."

"No, you are the one lied to, Dante. The Elders took away everything from us, stole you from me, and fed you all these lies now."

"No, Father, they rescued me from a horrible enslavement. The Elders did none of this destruction to our family. All of it, every bit of it was done by him." Dante made a stabbing motion with the sunspear at the Dark Lord.

The Dark Lord did not flinch but sighed sadly as a parent watching a confused child. "Dante, I'm not the person the Elders paint me out to be."

"You are not the cruel, ruthless one I see played out across the galaxy? The Elders made it up? My own family's destruction, you had nothing to do with any of it?"

"Dante, I didn't. It was all the Elders. Your father long established that years ago."

"Yes, all formed on lies and falsehoods. I found out what happened, and I'm here to tell my father."

That was the boy's angle. The Dark Lord forced himself to keep from laughing. Tried and failed many years ago, but it could provide amusement. "All right, Dante, tell us the account again. It's the same as what happened those years ago. I'm not sure why you came all this way to recount such a painful memory for yourself and your father."

"You're going to play this all the way, aren't you? It's all right. I don't care. I didn't come here for you. I came here for my father."

Dante turned to his father. "Father, Mother didn't kill Collin, and no Elder ordered it. The Dark Lord's agent, disguised herself as Mother and killed Collin. The Dark Lord dressed as an Elder and ordered the murder."

Dante's father sighed and peered over at the Dark Lord. The Dark Lord shook his head sadly at the Black Dragon Commander.

"Father, say something. Look at me, not him."

"Son, I heard this story and many variations of it. The Elders attempted ever since they killed your brother to come up with lies to hide their deed."

"See Dante, I told you. This has been done. The only part which is a mystery to us is why the Elders chose to now send you on such, well, I'm not trying to be mean to you, but nothing short of a fool's errand after all this time?"

"It's not a fool's errand. Would you like to tell my father what really happened to my mother?" Dante asked, his voice edged with anger.

"Is this what this is about, Dante? I'm sorry as I know how horrible all this must be for you. I can't imagine. No one knows what happened to your mother. Theories abounded, but I mean, no one ever knew."

"Liar!" Dante burst out in frustration. "You know exactly what happened to her because you took her and kept her prisoner all this time. She was rescued, and she is safe with us now."

The Dark Lord stared unfazed at Dante. The truth emerged, his plan for today. It might have possibilities, except the Dark Lord had a ready-made solution. "Your mother is alive? I didn't have any idea, Dante. I would not do anything to hurt her or anyone in your family, despite what you are led to believe. If you rescued her, why did you not bring her? It would give her a chance to explain herself, maybe sort out everything. Perhaps finally mend your family back together."

The Dark Lord glanced over at the Black Dragon Commander. "What do you think? I know how painful it was and still is for your family, but perhaps it's something to consider?"

"Yes, he is right. Why did you not bring her with you if this is true, my son?"

"You're not listening to anything I'm saying. Father, she was kept prisoner for years. Yes, I said years by your friend." Dante spoke the word like it was poison. "Why would I bring her back? So, he could recapture her for who knows what he plans? Even if I wanted to, I couldn't. Whatever he did to her, it was terrible. When she was rescued, she was in some type of tortured coma state, hooked to all sorts of things. Even after the rescue, we can't get her to awaken. Whatever he did to her, I don't know how severe the damage, but we don't know how to wake her up."

"I'm sorry, Dante, but this is quite a tale. Your mother is alive after all this time, but she cannot be awakened. You conveniently can't bring her here to your father, which means there is still no one to verify a different account of what happened with Collin. Again, why would the Elders make you do this today? This is quite an elaborate ploy."

"It's not a ploy. I brought proof Mother is with us now." Dante took his data pad out and projected the pictures. "Look, Father, here is where the Dark Lord kept her prisoner. See all the stuff she is hooked up to. Here she is now, safe in a room but still asleep. This is what your friend over there did to her." Dante put his data pad up and got out the container. "He forgot to take everything from her." Dante opened the container and took the items out. "Do you recognize them, Father? You should as you gave them to her. Both of your names are inscribed on the band." Dante opened the necklace. "Do you still recognize your own family after all this time?"

His father studied the items, and his face softened. "Son, these are certainly Abigail's things. There is no doubt of that." He was plainly disturbed by what Dante revealed and pondered what to do with it now.

Dante put the items away and waited.

The Dark Lord did give credit to Dante. He tried to come prepared, but the Dark Lord sensed the boy had shown most of his cards now. The Dark Lord needed to get one more piece from him, and he would know where to go with him. He also didn't want to give his Commander time to question Dante further about Abigail.

"Dante, I apologize for doubting you. It appears you did rescue your mother, and she is with you as you say. It was such an unbelievable tale. How did you rescue her?"

"You know how she was freed. You were the one keeping her prisoner. Stop this game you're playing." Dante's voice rose again, trying to hold back his anger.

"Dante, I don't know about your mother. This is all news to me."

"Stop it! Stop it! You know I didn't rescue her, but the two spear-bearers."

"Dante, I'm not aware of this. You need to calm down."

"You're more than aware of it. One of them almost died after falling from the rooftop to rescue mother."

"Oh my, did they recover from their injuries? It sounds quite traumatic, Dante." said the Dark Lord, sounding concerned.

"They're both fine. You don't care what happens to either of them. Why act like it?"

"I do care. I know you must care for them, being they are fellow spear-bearers. You claim they pulled off this amazing rescue at great cost to them. You must know them well by now. I'm wondering if we know them. There is Lana and Caleb, and you. So, who are these two?"

"I don't know. It doesn't matter. They helped get my mother back, so they're friends."

The Dark Lord observed Dante's face, and he was sure he guessed right, but let's see. "Dante, you are telling me you didn't meet these two who rescued your mother?"

Dante glared at the Dark Lord coldly. "It's not important."

The Dark Lord smiled to himself. Oh, but it was. Let's see how much Dante didn't know about the two of them. "I think it is. How do you know they exist if you never met them?"

Dante gaped backed at him like he was crazy. "Just because I didn't see them yet doesn't mean others have not. Seth fought beside them, as did one of the commanders."

"What did they look like? What are their names?"

"We don't know." Dante appeared perplexed. He didn't see the point of it.

"But you said they fought with Seth and one of the commanders. Dante, I'm trying to understand."

"They were in full uniform, covered. We don't know who they are. It DOES NOT matter." Dante shook his head, beyond frustrated.

"Okay, Dante, it is strange to me. With your mother, did they just drop her off? I mean, you said you never met them, but you possess an abundant amount of information you placed enormous trust in today."

"No, they didn't just drop her off." Dante was mentally tired.

The Dark Lord smiled. He didn't need the answer. Behind every spear-bearer stood a trainer, an Elder. "You met their Elder, who trained them, didn't you? That is where you received all your information and whatever you were told about the two spear-bearers. I'm sure this Elder is very kind, just like Seth."

"Yeah, he is. So what? Are you happy?"

The Dark Lord shrugged his shoulders. "It doesn't matter to me, Dante." Inside he smiled as it mattered a great deal to him. He watched Dante lay everything out for him. Time to begin his attack, and the boy was already tired. The Dark Lord stopped himself from laughing again today. Now, time to break the boy.

The girl shook her head, and her eyes were deeply troubled. "No, not good."

Christopher asked, "Is he okay?"

"I'm not sure how to answer that."

Alika asked, "Is his father convinced at all?"

"No, not all. Dante is mentally tired already, and I sense the battle has begun. Dante succeeded in giving the Dark Lord all the information he needed to begin the real battle." The girl put her head in her hands and took a deep breath. Her eyes were far away again, and she listened. The girl whispered, "Dante, you must continue to fight, please." This time she sensed he could not hear her.

CHAPTER FIFTY-NINE

Dante watched the Dark Lord and his father, feeling unsure where to go from here. Nothing he presented to his father seemed to matter.

The Dark Lord turned to the Black Dragon Commander. "I feel terrible for your son, Commander. It's obvious what happened."

"Yes, it appears so."

The Dark Lord smiled gently at Dante. "This is most unfortunate everything you endured. We could be here for some time sorting this out. I'm going to sit and would invite you to finally do the same and put your sunspear away. You will not need it." The Dark Lord pulled up a chair and sat. He offered a chair to his Black Dragon Commander, who sat. He pulled one out for Dante and moved it in his direction, but Dante shook his head. Shrugging his shoulders, the Dark Lord gave up and left it in front of him. The Dark Lord settled back in the chair and gazed up at Dante. "Dante, this will not be easy for you to accept, but you must begin to see what has truly been done to you."

Dante looked at both of them. His mind whirred. What was going on?

"Dante, you must accept you have been lied to all this time by those who claim to care for you. They set you up today. It's okay, though. We see through it, as with your father. I'm not going to hurt you. Their ploy will not succeed."

"Do you seriously think this is going to work?" Dante stared at him in shock.

"It's the truth, Dante. Is that not what you care about, what you always cared about finding out? I give it to you."

"I can't believe this," said Dante looking at the Dark Lord. Dante turned to his father. "You really believe him. How?"

The Black Dragon Commander did not answer Dante audibly, but his silence served as an answer in itself.

"Dante, if you will but give me a chance and hear me out. It will make much more sense than this tale the Elders fed you. Come, young Dante, we heard your version of what they told you, and your father is not convinced. Is it not fair to hear my version and see why your father is convinced of my account of the events? Also, I think it only fair we ask more questions about this account you bring us. Or Dante, are you not interested in getting to the truth as you say?"

"You know I am."

"Then we all want the same thing, and we can move forward. If your version is the truth, you should have no fear. However, if I'm indeed telling the truth, you will be happy today because I will free you as well." The Dark Lord took a moment to smile over at the Black Dragon Commander. He turned back to Dante. "What do you have to lose, young Dante?"

"You're right, I suppose. I know I have the truth. I'm not concerned." Yet he felt as if in a moment he lost much.

The girl put her head in her hands again and whispered, "Dante, do not play this dangerous game with him. He is the master of it. You cannot win this game." A single tear fell. The girl sighed, and her eyes continued to be far away.

Alena, Christopher, and Alika looked at each other helplessly.

Dante started to say something, but the Dark Lord gently cut him off.

"Dante, we heard your rendering of the events already. I said it is time you heard my version, and questions remain about what you told us. We can talk about your account once I get my chance if you are still convinced you are correct. That was the deal, I believe."

"Yes, it was." He felt less sure of his decision.

"My version says the Elders are the ones behind everything that happened to your family. The Elders became quite powerful at the time of your father, and they ran everything. Your father and mother were well-known and one of the ruling families on their planet. Your father is also exceptional with the sunspear as you are, young Dante. I don't know if the Elders saw your family as a threat or what, but for whatever reason, they murdered your brother. We found footage of the whole thing. Your father saw it, clear as day. The Elders denied it and wanted to investigate. We all knew it would not be a fair investigation. How could the one behind the murder fairly investigate the crime? One does not ask the murderer to investigate his own crime. He would come back and say not guilty. Your father told them no. Of course, they became quite upset. I came to your father's aid. It was horrible. He tried to get you away from it. Before he could do so, the Elders kidnapped you as well. It only added to your father's grief."

"It's a nice revision of the truth, but it doesn't work. My mother didn't do it. We saw what really happened, and your agent killed my brother."

"Dante, I'm genuinely puzzled. Your father and I both saw it. It was your mother on the footage. Even so, I can't begin to know where the footage would be after all this time, but you insist you saw it. You say it showed something different. This can't be. Where is this proof of the different events? Show us, so we can all see it."

"I didn't see it myself. I was told."

"Dante, that is not proof at all. You could be told all kinds of things. You made clear the source, an Elder. They are the ones I told you were behind all this. Of course, they would come up with such a story. The Elder showed you no proof."

"He didn't have that kind of proof. The Ancient One showed them."

"Dante, that is what they all fall back on. Surely you figured it out by now. The Elder has no real proof, so the Ancient One showed him the truth."

"It wasn't to him."

"To one of the students then. Dante, that's only cause to doubt further. You said you don't know either student, know nothing about them. You haven't talked to either student to question them to be sure what they saw in the vision. How can you trust such a source?"

"They wouldn't lie to me!"

"You are so sure, Dante. I don't know why." Then the Dark Lord's tone softened. "I'm sorry, Dante. I do understand why. Seth, the Elder raised you for some time now. I understand you trust him. The other Elder is equally kind to you. They are all like that to their students. It must be part of it. To face the reality of what I'm telling you about someone so dear to you, I cannot imagine. So, I do understand why you can't fathom they lied to you. However, your father and I are here for you, Dante, to help you with this."

Dante stared at the Dark Lord. His face displayed concern almost like Seth's did at times. Dante reminded himself the Dark Lord stood before him, not Seth, not Alika. What was he doing listening to this? "You expect me to believe my mother killed my little brother?"

"I admit it is a horrible thing to accept, but the footage did show it, Dante. The part you must remember is we always wanted to entertain another possibility for why your mother would do such a thing. We never got the chance, though, as she could not be found after your brother was killed. No, Dante, no one believed your mother would simply do such a thing on her own. The question always came back to who else was involved in the incident. In the footage, an Elder clearly stood there as she did the heinous deed. Your mother is a kind woman with a sweet spirit. She would never hurt either of you without being provoked, forced, or even drugged. In any case, I always believed she was not in her right mind to do such a thing. We never got the chance to find out, though. From what you said, we still will not," said the Dark Lord sadly.

Dante didn't know what to say. The Dark Lord provided an explanation, and it made sense. He shook his head. "No, you kidnapped and kept her all this time. We saw the footage of the rescue. You were behind all this not, not the Elders."

"Dante, I did not know your mother's whereabouts since her disappearance, just as everyone else. This information today concerning her is news to me just as it is to your father." The Dark Lord's voice became soft. "Dante, you said she was brought to you by this Elder. Dante, by an Elder. Do you hear yourself? An Elder shows up out of nowhere with your long-lost mother. Your mother is asleep, and she cannot be awakened to tell what happened. You are given a story that she survived captivity all these years with the terrible Dark Lord who the Elders hate. How is she rescued? Single-handedly by two spear-bearers, you do not know, never heard of them. Logically, you want to thank them for doing such a thing. You are told no. Even more, the Elder says they received this whole revelation about your past, and still, you cannot speak with them. Rather, you are to put your entire trust in this information relayed to you." The Dark Lord paused and stared into Dante's eyes. "Dante, put your feelings and your loyalty to the Elders and the Ancient One aside. Look at it now. It does not make sense as you examine it. Come, Dante, try seeing it through my eyes for a change. Does it not seem clearer?"

Dante stared back at the Dark Lord. It didn't make sense the Dark Lord made such sense. They were all questions he had asked, wondered the answer.

—ℓℓ—

"Dante, why did you keep listening to him? I'm begging you to stop, Dante." The girl whispered, staring out into space, tears streaming down her face.

"My child, what of Dante?" Alika anxiously grasped her hand and searched her eyes.

The girl shook her head. "The words of the Dark Lord ring truer to Dante as the moments pass. I fear ..." She could not finish.

—ℓℓ—

Dante shook his head. Pieces remained he couldn't reconcile, too much to throw away so easily. "No, we saw the footage from the facility where they rescued my mother. It was one of your facilities. I told you one student almost died rescuing my mother. Your story doesn't work for an Elder to hold my mother prisoner this whole time with the rescue attempt. You can't pull out a cover story for everything."

"It's not a cover story, Dante. It's the truth. I don't know about your mother. I assume this footage you saw is from the Elder as well. All your information again is through this Elder. No contact again from the students to hear their account of what happened."

"You're trying to say the rescue never happened. We saw it!"

"Then that's worse, and it's exactly who I told you the Elders truly are, Dante. The Elder lied to his own students and sent them into this facility. He falsely told his students I took your mother prisoner and played with the lives of his own students. If one almost died of falling from the rooftop, he truly cares nothing for them. If he plays with his own students' lives with such ease and counts them as nothing, how can you trust anything he spoke to you?"

Dante gasped at the Dark Lord in shock, registering what he suggested.

⁓ℓℓ⁓

The girl's eyes streamed with tears, but in her eyes flashed a new emotion as she listened. Anger. "No, no stop! Dante, you can't possibly believe this! Stop listening!" She could sit no longer. She got up from the couch and stared out the cockpit window. Her frame shook.

Alika walked quickly over to her. Alena and Christopher glanced at each other, concerned, and waited.

Alika spoke to her gently, "Look at me, child."

The girl could not. The words rang in her head, and the dialogue continued. She could feel the anger flashing in her eyes. She wasn't sure who she felt angrier with now, the Dark Lord for suggesting such a thing or Dante for listening to it. If she were there now, she would run the sunspear through the Dark Lord and resist the urge to shake Dante not so gently. She could feel her body shaking still.

"Child, please, it's okay." The girl reluctantly turned to him. Alika saw it. Anger there, trying to be calmed, but it was not working. "Child, what did he say?"

"You don't wish to know, and he's still going, and Dante continues to listen." The girl stared back out the cockpit window.

CHAPTER SIXTY

"No, it can't be. He would not do such a thing." Dante shook his head in disbelief.

"Why would he not? Dante, the only reason you think not is that you continue to cling to this belief the Elders are good, and I'm bad. This pieces together perfectly if you switch it for a moment. All the questions that didn't make sense in your mind, they work. It will hurt because it means people you care about a great deal lied to you, which is why you feel it cannot be. It was terrible for your father as well when he came to the realization, but he did. I was here for him. I will be here for you as well, young Dante," said the Dark Lord kindly.

"No, you're the one lying. You must be. You didn't want my father to know about what you did to mother because you knew what would happen if he ever found out. That's why you hired another group to take care of the facility."

"My, if only I were half as devious as the Elders made me out to be. Dante, your father is aware of all my operations. I trust him completely. I would not use another group for anything. We use Black Dragon soldiers for all our operations. There's no reason to do otherwise. Now, I know a group that would use an outside source. Let's see, Dante, who might they be?"

"You're suggesting ..." Dante's voice trailed off.

"That is exactly who I'm suggesting. The Elders. This Elder is busy training, not one, but two spear-bearers we know of. Who knows if it's more? That leaves no time to secretly keep your mother captive. That is also if he is the only one involved. You may believe so, but I can't imagine it is the case. Either way, again, my explanation makes much more sense, Dante."

Dante tried to think of something else to question him. He stared at the Dark Lord. He had been told all his life this was a horrible man who single-handedly destroyed his family. However, the Dark Lord gave a reasonable explanation for everything Dante presented him. Dante's father served him for many years now and believed him completely too.

Nevertheless, nothing could take away what Dante had seen in his lifetime. Destruction repeatedly in the name of the Dark Lord, and countless lives cut down across galaxies. There could be no explanation from the Dark Lord for it.

"You surprised me today, not in the way I thought. You gave an explanation for everything I asked. I'm not sure how, but it'll never take away the fact everything your hand touches ends in pain and destruction. I've seen it span across the galaxy for so long now as I stood in the colonies and defended them against your attacks. How do you expect me to believe you're the good one and the Elders are the bad ones in this fight?"

The Dark Lord smiled sadly at Dante. "I can see where it appears strange through your eyes. Let me try to explain it to you. Tell me, Dante, when you see your father, do you see good or bad?"

Dante gazed at his father, and his face softened instantly. "I still see my father. I still see good."

"I thought so. If not, I suspect you would not be here today."

"Yes, I am here to free him from you."

"He does not need any freeing, Dante. He can leave at any time he pleases. He chooses to help me because he sees what I've tried to show you since you entered the Elders Hall. So, Dante, if you believe your father is still the kind father who raised you, how can he carry out these attacks with me, which are so terrible?"

"You deceived him and twisted him. He's confused."

"Really, Dante?" The Dark Lord sounded puzzled. "He does not sound such to me." The Dark Lord turned to the Black Dragon Commander. "Does that sound like you?"

"No, it does not." He turned to Dante. "My son, I know the purpose. It is done as plainly as you believe your purpose with the Elders. I'm sorry you believe otherwise."

"See, Dante. Now I think the question is, do your father or I enjoy the process to get to the purpose? That is an entirely different question. If I am as the Elders portrayed me, and your father by extension, the answer is yes. Yet, if it is not as the Elders portray us, the answer to the question must be different. So, you said you believe your father to still be the one you knew as a boy. Can you believe then he takes joy in attacking the colonies?"

"No, that doesn't make sense." He felt so tired. It was a never-ending chase in his head.

"Then, if there is another way to accomplish the same purpose without the attacks on the colonies, we would do it by now."

"There must be another way. There can be no reason for the lives of the colonists being sacrificed."

"We tried other ways, Dante. It seldom works. It worked on your father. I'm hoping it works on you today. Yet many colonies remain under the sway of the Elders and their teachings. We tried to give them the truth of what the Elders do to them. We are the ones trying to free them, Dante. You say you are defending the colonies, but you are not doing so. You keep them under the hold of the Elders."

"No, you're speaking insanity. There's no way."

"Yes, Dante. Do you realize how it pains your father each time he orders an attack? He wishes for another way. It's even worse to see you fight on the side of the Elders. I know he hopes you survive each encounter though you fight on the opposite side. You are his son, after all. He cannot wish you ill. It breaks his heart to see you fight against him, worried you will meet your end and knowing it could be during one of the attacks."

"Then don't order them," said Dante weakly as his head spun.

"That is not an option, Dante. The colonies stay under the tyranny of the Elders' control and all their lies. We are trying to save them from themselves." The

Dark Lord paused and spoke gently to Dante. "Young Dante, can you see now you have been fighting on the wrong side for all this time?"

⸻ ℓℓ ⸻

The anger left the girl's face. Pain stretched across it as tears flowed anew down it. "No Dante, please no, none of this is true."

"Child, what is happening?"

The girl reached over and cried on Alika's shoulder in response.

Alena and Christopher got up and came over.

⸻ ℓℓ ⸻

Dante stared at him. "It can't be. They would not lie to me. I trusted them. The Elders. The Ancient One. I defended them. The two spear-bearers defended them. I staked so much on it, on what they told me. I believed it. On what the Elder told me. It couldn't be wrong. There's no way. Now, I ..." Dante saw it all come apart in front of him as his sunspear dropped.

"I'm so sorry, Dante, as I know what you wanted to believe. It pains me how you were so used by the Elders as well as how they manipulated these two spear-bearers. You wondered why they kept you from each other all this time. It appears we uncovered the answer. It is a shame. Dante, you are not alone, though. Come, let us help you. Your father waited a long time for your return, and I will be here for you as well. Whenever you are ready, Dante, we are waiting." The Dark Lord smiled.

CHAPTER SIXTY-ONE

The girl sank to the floor on her knees, and the others ran over to her.

Alika's eyes asked the question.

"The Dark Lord turned Dante's heart against the Elders and the Ancient One."

"How, child?"

"Many ways. One was us." Her voice broke. "He could never meet us. The Dark Lord twisted it."

"Oh no. It can't be." Alika's voice broke.

"It didn't matter, Alika. Even if he did, it wouldn't matter. The Dark Lord would twist it somehow. We both know I couldn't …" Her voice broke again. "It's a battle Dante's young spear-bearer could never win from the start." Another sob escaped her.

"What is happening?"

"Dante is lost to us. He falls … to one knee … before them." The girl sobbed.

"I'm sorry." Christopher softly put his hand on the girl's back.

❦

Dante closed up his sunspear. He was so confused, so lost. He had nothing left inside to figure it all out. His world had fallen apart before him, everything he understood so clearly gone. One knee buckled where he stood as tears continued to slide down his face.

❦

"What can we do?" asked Alika.

The girl stumbled out to Alika. "Plead for Dante with the Ancient One like you once did for another student. Only the Ancient One's intervention can help Dante now."

Suddenly the girl heard a gentle whisper, "Your battlefield begins, child. Rise, now. Dante needs you. Speak to him. He is not lost to us."

The girl rose and said to them. "I'm to speak to Dante."

"There's no way to get to him," said Alena.

"No, he'll hear from here. I don't know how, but the Ancient One will enable it."

The girl stared out the cockpit window as tears continued to pour down her face. He could be reached. She must get through to him. He had shaken her world to its core, and he didn't even know it. She could not lose him. She could see the scene still. Dante was so empty, adrift as a ship in the darkness, unable to find its bearing again. His spirit hurt so much. She could feel it, and her spirit hurt with him. The Dark Lord and Black Dragon Commander sat. The Dark Lord truly waited on Dante. He showed no concern for allowing Dante to struggle. Apparently, he figured the longer he permitted Dante, the better. He knew Dante's mind was tired, so he reasoned it could serve to create a stronger hold. The girl realized the Dark Lord's inattention to Dante was a gift from the Ancient One. She knew Dante would hear her this time, and the Ancient One would give her the words she needed.

The girl would speak to Dante as if she knelt right there with him, looking into his soft brown eyes. So, she did. Her voice was gentle as she began. "Dante ..."

⸎

Tears continued to stream down Dante's face. He wanted to be away from here, not to think about any of it, but he could not do that. Then he felt it, and even with the day's events, he knew he did not imagine it. It was the presence he knew. He shouldn't have this, but he could not give up this connection with the young spear-bearer. Then it came. A voice, neither male nor female. This time he did not just hear the essence of the message as last night. The message came through to him word for word gently.

"Dante, why did you listen for so long to the Darkness? This is what I feared would happen. I know you're tired and confused, but I need you to listen to me, Dante. This is not you, Dante. Everything the Dark Lord said to you, as well as the concern he shows for you, was a lie from the moment you stepped into the Elders Hall. He did everything we told you he would do. And he laughs in his victory as he watches your spirit breaking as he did many years ago when he did the same with your father. Dante, you could ask him where his cloaked agent has been when we are done talking. I promise you there will be no honest answer from him as he only knows how to lie. Let me tell you where she has been as the Ancient One, who is always true, alerted me in a vision. The Dark Lord's agent was in your mother's room today, sent to end your mother's life."

Dante felt fear strike through him, and his body shake anew.

The voice continued gently, "Your mother is safe, so do not fear, Dante. It's only due to Seth and Lana getting there in time, with Alika sending the message immediately for me. However, the two soldiers guarding the door paid with their lives. They would not betray you and let the agent in the door. The whole scene is on your data pad to play for your father. The Dark Lord will find a way to twist it though the cloaked woman admits the Dark Lord sent her today to do the deed. She even mentions what the Dark Lord planned for you today, Dante, as you had just arrived before your father and the Dark Lord. It appears everything is going as the Dark Lord planned for you, much to my pain."

The voice pressed on softly, "Dante, I could try to reason out everything as the Dark Lord, but he'll find a way to turn it. That is what he is the master of. I'll speak to you the only way I ever speak to you, Dante, with truth and from my heart. We share a connection that neither one understands, but it still binds us. Dante, the Dark Lord said we have not met, so how could you know the truth of what you were told? Dante, we have met. We may not have seen each other face to face, but we know each other in a way few do. I have seen your heart, your spirit. It is always gentle. I have seen it happy and laughing, but I've seen it broken as it is now. My spirit has been in pain with you, shared in your brokenness. I've seen it concerned for me after learning of my rooftop fall and scared wondering if I laid scattered in a million pieces on the other side of a portal. I have seen you, Dante. You have seen me. I rescued your mother without a second thought. I think about her frequently, hoping she will awaken because I care for her, but also because I know how much joy it would give you to see her awakened. My spirit broke for you every time Alika or Seth burdened you with more the first time we came with your mother. I felt every time you cried and struggled. Everything I have done has been for you in some way, Dante. Can you truly say you have not met me? Do you truly not know your young spear-bearer after all this time? Do you not know my spirit by now? What else would I say or do for you to feel you know me? I'll do it if it is within my power. You know I would in a moment for you, Dante."

Dante looked down. Tears continued to spill down. He didn't know what he needed, but he wanted to hear the young spear-bearer. He had listened to the Dark Lord for so long today, and it was like poison to his spirit. The young spear-bearer's voice brought a calm to his struggling spirit, and he longed for calm now.

The voice continued gently, "Dante, it's okay. I know how strong the Darkness is. You have seen my heart, and I promise you it reflects the heart of Alika and Seth. I have never broken a promise to you and would not do so now. The Elders haven't betrayed you. The visions I am given are from the Ancient One, and I always relayed them to you truthfully. Dante, the Dark Lord tried to get you to see him as something he is not today. He wants you to see his heart as pure and full of light. Dante, you have seen his heart as well. You know it. Do not be blinded by his words today. His heart is as black as the abyss. It was when you walked into the Elders Hall, and it remains the same now. He sheds the blood of many men, women, and children, and he delights in every drop, every moment. There is no noble purpose in what he does. He corrupted your father's heart into doing the same. However, your father does not share in the joy of it. It bothers him because the Ancient One still whispers to him, pursuing him to return to the truth he knows. That is why you can get your father back. Be not confused anymore on what side you need to be on, Dante. You knew when you walked in today. It's time for you to know again. Find it again, Dante. You cannot look at Jonathan grieving over his slain father and tell him the Dark Lord is good. Dante, can you look into Emily's eyes and convince her the Dark Lord is goodness? Dante, there is no amount of persuasion you could do to have Emily believe such a thing. Even a child can recognize evil when it is as plain as the Dark Lord. Dante, it's time to take the blinders off the Dark Lord placed on you. He is what he has always been. He is a liar, and his master is the Darkness. It's time you stopped listening to his voice today, Dante."

Dante felt a sob escape him. He saw the little girl's face. He promised to protect her and others in the colony. Then Lana and Caleb and Ryan and countless others. Here he knelt today, thinking about helping the Dark Lord. He came to get his father back, and he made a mess of the whole thing.

The voice continued, "Dante, you're not alone. It's not too late. Do not speak with the Dark Lord anymore. He is not why you came. You came here for your father. Speak to your father. Speak from your heart. Help him remember. Dante, please do not fall to the Darkness. You have seen my spirit. I have seen yours. I feel how broken it is today. It cuts me to the core because of the bond we share. One which can never be broken. That is what I heard you say last night to me, and I still believe your words. I believe you do as well, Dante, and I cannot see this bond broken from you. I care deeply for you, more than what you imagine. If I could take away the pain you have seen, Dante, I would and take it as my own. Please do not go on this path of Darkness. I cannot bear to see you do this. My spirit has broken for you many times, but it has never broken as it does for you now. If you take this path of Darkness, though, I should have died when I fell from the top of the roof. Please, Dante, you are breaking my heart."

The girl fell on her knees and sobbed uncontrollably. She had no words left to plead with Dante.

Dante heard the young spear-bearer's words. The last words broke his own heart anew as he heard this one ask for death rather than see him go to Darkness. And he felt it. All the pain, brokenness, tears, and grief from the young spear-bearer for him suddenly joined his own pain for the day. He had never felt the weight of it before now, but he felt the full force of the connection for the first time. Dante felt himself bent to the ground from its weight and found himself on both of his knees. His chest hurt as he sobbed anew.

The girl could feel the weight of it hit Dante. She felt her spirit broken anew for him, but she understood why he was made to feel the full weight of it. The Ancient One needed him to do so. The others were down with her, trying to be a comfort. All they could do was wait.

Dante continued to sob. No more words came from the young spear-bearer, but there did not need to be. The young spear-bearer was there, her broken spirit reaching out to meet his own, bound by the connection neither one understood. Finally, Dante felt a calm come over him. He said gently, "I can't believe it."

The Dark Lord looked over at Dante. He smiled. His victory finally complete. Dante would be coming to him any moment now.

Dante shook his head as he stared at the ground. After everything, from the teachings of his mother and his father and Seth and Alika, and in what amounted to mere moments he came close to throwing it all aside. It didn't make sense. Dante smiled and said softly, "I will not break your heart, my young spear-bearer." Dante could almost feel a sigh of relief go through them.

The Dark Lord heard it too, and his face changed. He was no longer happy.

CHAPTER SIXTY-TWO

Dante heard another gentle whisper, and he recognized it as well. "Dante, I will give you new strength for this battle. You are never alone. I go before you as I promised. Your father's deliverance is near. Rise, my child."

Dante smiled. He stood and looked straight at his father and ignored the Dark Lord.

The girl closed her eyes for a moment and wiped the tears away. She smiled and got to her feet. The others watched her. Her eyes held a different look in them. Determination. She turned to them. "Dante found his way again, and he's on his feet. He won't be swayed again. It's a different battle now." The girl turned back to the cockpit window, her eyes intense as she watched through Dante's eyes again.

Dante stepped to the side to face closer to his father and further from the Dark Lord. He smiled at his father. "Father, it's time we talked, the reason I came today."

The Dark Lord began. "Dante, your father ..."

Dante cut the Dark Lord off but never turned to look at him. "I'm not talking to you anymore today. This is between my Father and me. You've said quite enough."

"Father, I know you can answer for yourself. It's time you stop allowing the Dark Lord to answer for you. I'll speak with you only now."

"All right, son, but it will change nothing."

"I'm willing to try as I believe differently. I know you don't believe anything I told you. I admit a whole new understanding of why after the last bit. I received warnings of the power of the Dark Lord's tactics, but I now experienced them. It can be broken through, and I mean to help you do it."

"Dante, there is nothing to break through."

"Sometimes, we don't realize the blinders on us. Father, I need to show you something. This happened since I got here with you and the Dark Lord. I found out about it moments ago. I want to show you what the Dark Lord sent his agent to do while we talked here. It was only due to the spear-bearer, the Elders, and Lana it didn't succeed. Watch, Father, please, with your own eyes."

Dante pulled out his data pad.

The Dark Lord said, "You are going to amuse us now."

"You're not a part of this conversation," said Dante coldly.

The Dark Lord tried to appear to shrug it off, but it irritated him.

Dante pulled the footage and audio up, and it projected in front of them. It started as the agent finished getting the door torn apart. As she came in, the two bodies of the guards could be seen in the background and the pool of blood spreading from the one. She approached the bed and spoke to the still figure in the bed. It was, without a doubt Abigail's form. The footage continued as she began the downward plunge of the knife into Abigail to Lana and Seth saving Abigail's life. The footage did not end until the agent ran out the door. It included the whole conversation between the cloaked woman and Lana and Seth.

Dante turned it off. He felt his stomach turn as he listened to the words of the cloaked woman, especially the ending about him if she got the chance to get near him. Dante peered back up at his father.

Dante's father watched the footage, his eyes visibly troubled at its images. Several emotions went through his eyes. He experienced relief to see his wife's life spared. However, he could not reconcile what he saw with what he knew about his friend, the Dark Lord. "Dante, there must be a mistake. This cannot be."

"Your father is right. The Elders tampered with the footage."

"Not talking to you," said Dante coldly, his comment clearly directed again at the Dark Lord.

Dante continued with his father again. "There's no mistake. This is what is happening behind your back, Father. It's what I tried to tell you. The Dark Lord planned this down to what he intended for me today once he saw me step inside the hall, and he almost succeeded."

Dante's father remained silent, still turning it over.

"Father, did you hear what the Dark Lord thinks of you? This is the person you call friend? You're not his friend. Rather, you're a pawn in his game, much like he used those colonists in the last attack to get the supplies out. You're no different to him. He used you cruelly from the beginning and continues to do so. This agent and him laugh about it every chance they get. Father, this is no friend. I need you to see. This is an enslavement and has continued on for years."

"No, it cannot be. You don't know him. You think the Elders care for you? They treat you with caring words when you are around. What do they say when you are not around? They stab you in the back, Dante."

Dante shook his head, and his eyes regarded his father with sadness at the words. "No, Father, they don't. I see their heart countless times, and I know it to be true. It's the same when I'm with them as when I'm apart from them. They are true friends, those who care for me deeply, and I for them. They would never speak of me in such a way as this agent says the Dark Lord speaks of you. I don't serve Seth or any other Elder. I serve beside them because that is friendship. The only one I serve or they serve is the Ancient One because He is worthy of my allegiance and the cornerstone of everything we hold dear. You once understood that, Father. You and Mother first taught me."

"I was wrong, son. I learned of my folly since those years."

"No, I don't believe that. You were right in the beginning. Your mind is now clouded because you listened to the Darkness for so long. You need to but listen to me. You can still hear it. The Ancient One continues to speak to you. You try to bury the whispers, but it doesn't work, does it?"

"You don't know what you're talking about, my son. The Ancient One is dead to me." His voice shook.

"How many times must you try to convince yourself, Father? Is it every time you order an attack on a colony? The last one must have been hard for you, using the colonists as human shields. I can't imagine. Was the whisper louder to you? Was it hard to block out? Tell me, because I believe the father who taught me as a boy remains there."

"I must do what I do. It is the only way, Dante. Why do you not understand?"

"You do hear it. You cannot bury it enough times no matter how many times you try. It will always come back because this is not who you are. I need you to remember who you are. Father, remember when Collin and I wandered away while we played one day? It got dark before we realized it. We got turned around out in the clearing we played and couldn't find our way back home. We were scared. It was strange. Before that, we spent the whole day pretending branches from the Zora tree were sunspears, and in our minds, we were the bravest, strongest, best spear-bearers ever to be. Yet, we were reduced to helpless, frightened, huddled-up little ones crying under a tree in a moment. We heard something and feared the worst. It must be an animal come to tear us to pieces, and it would have. We would sit there, unable to move because we were so afraid at the moment already from being lost. Then we looked up, and it was you, Father. You found us. We didn't call for you because our minds couldn't think of what we needed to do. All we saw was how lost we were. You went and searched for us, though, determined to find your two children who lost their way in the darkness. Hearing Collin and me faintly crying afar off, you followed the sound. You scooped us up and dried our tears and brought us back home. Do you remember what you told us, Father?"

Dante's father looked at him. He could only nod.

"I do as well, Father. You said we were never alone. That you would always be there for us, to protect us. We never needed to be afraid again. That we could never go too far, could never be so lost to where you could not be found. Because you loved us, and you were our father." Dante took a step toward his father. "Do you still believe those words you told me and Collin, Father?"

"Yes, my son. I longed for you to come back. The Elders destroyed it."

"No, Father, you were taken from us. You found Collin and me when we were lost in the woods so long ago. Can you find your way back to me? You have wandered around lost for so long in the Darkness, Father. I'm the one who knows the way out this time. Let me help you now, guide you out, please, Father. I long to have my father back." He gently held out his hand to his father.

CHAPTER SIXTY-THREE

Dante's father gazed at his son, struggling visibly now.

The Dark Lord watched, and he grew more uneasy as the moments passed. He felt the Black Dragon Commander slipping from his grasp. He must do something rapidly before he lost his servant for good. "Can you not see what he is doing, Commander? This is an elaborate ploy, from the video to this whole act. You must…"

"Father, don't listen to him. It's not about him. It's about you and me and our family. You listened to him for far too long. Listen to my voice, Father. I speak only truth to you."

"No, Commander, Dante is corrupted. The Elders turned your own son against you, as I told you. It is the ultimate betrayal. How can you…"

"Father, no listen to me only. I came here for you, to bring you back. I'm not corrupted. If you search deep in the recesses of your heart, you will know that to be true. The whispers you still hear that you try to bury, but cannot, are whispers of that truth that still remain. You're not lost completely. You can find your way again. I have been told so. Please father, listen to me …"

"You cannot let this stand. Your son allowed to do this. To continue to turn on you like this. You must choose, Commander."

"Father, please, remember, who you are, not who you think you have become because of the Dark Lord. Listen to the voice that still whispers to you, still calls to you in the quiet of your heart, please, Father."

The Dark Lord continued with an angry edge. "This boy must be stopped, Commander. He is like the others now, no better than the Elders. He will always war against you and our purpose. There is only one remedy for his kind."

— ele —

The girl heard and knew where it was going. The fear returned to her. Tears sprung in her eyes, and she felt weak. She slowly sunk to the ground again.

The others reached down to her, anxious. Alika asked her, "What is it?"

The girl watched the cockpit window, and the others followed her gaze. She was not the only one who could see the scene. Somehow, they could all see Dante, Ethan, and the Dark Lord. The Ancient One was allowing it for a short time.

— ele —

Dante held his father's eyes and said gently, "Father, please, I'm not your enemy. I need you to find your way back to me. I know you can find the path. Don't do as the Dark Lord urges you. It's not your heart. I'm your son."

"Commander, he is no longer your son. He is a traitor. Remedy this, I order you. Destroy him with your sunspear now."

Dante saw his father struggle, but his father took out his sunspear. It responded instantly to him. The weapon was black as the abyss, changing over time to reflect the effect of the years of the Dark Lord's influence on Dante's father. The Dark Lord smiled at Dante, barely hiding his glee at the turn of events. Dante thought he should be scared but found he felt no fear. He would not, could not, fight his father. He knew what he must do. It was out of his control, as it had been all along. He would do as the Ancient One led him to do.

The girl understood, but she began to weep again as she watched Ethan approach Dante with the blackened sunspear edging closer to his chest.

Dante fell to his knees before his father and gazed up at him. He smiled at his father through his tears and spoke gently to him, "Father, I am not guilty if any of what the Dark Lord spoke of me. Your wife, my mother, whom I know you still love, did not kill your son, my brother. I spoke only the truth. However, if you truly believe after searching your heart I betrayed you, your wife betrayed you, I am not worthy to be called your son, and I deserve to die by your hand. Then kill me, Father. If you are wrong, you shed your own son's blood, and I leave this world heartbroken. For I'm so sorry because I failed you, Father, as you remain in the same bondage to this darkness. Father, no matter what, even if I must die by your hand today, I will always see you as the father of my childhood who taught me of the Ancient One, who rescued his lost child, who promised I would never be alone, and who loved me. Father, I love you, even as you do this. Do what you must, my Father."

The shaking blade point stood at Dante's chest, and Dante winced as he felt the end scrape the skin of his chest through his shirt.

The girl pleaded as she cried, "No, please, no." The others watched in horror at the scene before them. Alena put her arms around the girl as tears streamed down Alena's face as well.

The Dark Lord smiled as he tasted victory again and said to the Black Dragon Commander, "I said do it now. Wait no longer. Finish him."

CHAPTER SIXTY-FOUR

Caleb yelled, "How's the hangar look?"

Commander Gabe said, "It's cleared out now as far as their ships. There's still plenty of soldiers to contend with for sure, but no more ships, though."

Ryan said, "We need to start landing ships inside and making our way into the facility."

"That's what I see as well. We need the three fleets moving toward the hangars and the other fleets staying outside to keep fighting the ships out here. We've got to get inside to that device. Once we get inside the hangar, discontinue firing inside it. We don't want to hit one of our own."

Caleb, Ryan, and Gabe's fleet got closer to the hangar, determined to get inside. Conrad's, Aegeus', and Cephas's fleets continued to fight outside the hangar.

"We only managed about six ships in the hangar, and we encountered a welcoming party. We need help, NOW!" shouted Caleb.

"I'm going to try to get out," said one of Caleb's men.

"No, don't. You won't last. Use your ship's gun to clear space. We wait for more of our squad or some of Ryan's or Gabe's group to make it in."

On cue, Ryan's ship made it into the hangar. "Let me take some off the top for you." Ryan fired up at the top-level, where a whole row of Black Dragon soldiers were shooting down. He did a few more quick shots like it in succession, and the whole upper guardrail came apart. The soldiers came crashing down like dominoes onto the hangar floor, some in better shape than others.

Suddenly Ryan called out, "Hey, where did that shot come from?"

"From a ship," said Caleb frustrated. "No firing in the hangar once our ships start landing, guys."

"It wasn't from our ships. It's the Dark Lord. They are attempting to destroy the ships once they get inside the hangar," said Ryan.

Commander Gabe spoke up, "It won't work. My squad will be the barrier for you, Caleb, and Ryan. We'll keep them situated between the other three commanders' army and mine. We'll hold off going into the hangar until it can be stopped."

"Sounds like a plan, Commander Gabe." Caleb hollered over the explosions. "My squad and Commander Ryan's squad, stick with the original plan. Into the hangar, and let's get to the device. Most of the fleet is finding their way inside the hangar. I need everyone to start making their way out of their ships. We got enough inside now to give them a proper welcome back. Let's move."

Caleb ran out of his ship, blaster in one hand and sunspear in the other. Ryan was at his side, weapons in hand as well, already using both. They both motioned for the fleet to push ahead and engage the Black Dragon soldiers.

"Looks like about the same size welcoming party as our friends encountered."

"That's a good sign, Caleb. It means they didn't know we were coming. Not that it's a small welcoming party, but still."

The floating facility shook from the explosions as the ships continued their firefight outside.

Ryan found his sword blade cleaving through one Black Dragon soldier after the other. They kept coming. He saw Caleb making fast work near him with the sunspear. Ryan smiled despite being in the middle of a battle as he was reminded again of how good all three in that family handled those sunspears. He wondered how Dante fared and then sighed as he continued to press on with his sword as another Black Dragon soldier lay in pieces at his feet.

Ryan and Caleb finally made it to the other side of the hangar to the door leading to the hallway entrance for the rooms. There remained a substantial number of soldiers in the hangars to deal with, but they both wanted to get to this entrance.

"Cover me, Ryan."

"I got your back."

"Let's see if the Dark Lord changes his locks." Caleb got his data pad out and scanned it over the portal for the door. Immediately, the door opened.

Caleb and Ryan barely got out of the way in time.

"Another welcoming party." Caleb shoved his data pad away and got his sunspear up instantly to begin round two. Ryan put his sword between Caleb and the edge of a waiting Black Dragon soldier's sword in the nick of time.

"We expect nothing less."

"At least we answered the one question." Caleb's sunspear blocked a blow from a Black Dragon soldier.

"In a moment, it'll feel important again, but now not so much." Ryan ducked and dodged the edge of a Black Dragon sword, and then Ryan took his own sword and cleaved through the legs of the Black Dragon soldier.

~*~

Lana and Seth ran to the ground forces. The squadron held during Seth's leave, but the squadron leaders' faces registered relief when he returned. They were clearly surprised to see Lana but glad as well. They did not recognize her at first with the helmet, but once they saw the raised sunspear, they knew it could only be her.

"I'm sorry we took so long. The Dark Lord sent one of his agents here, and we spent longer than we anticipated. You did well holding them, but now it's time to push them back," said Lana.

"She's right. Come on." Seth motioned to the squadron to move forward.

Her eyes reflected a determination seldom seen as she set to work with her sunspear. The squadron had forgotten Dante was not the only one who could wield a sunspear with the best of them. The squadron found new energy to continue as Lana fought with them, and Seth rejoined the fight as well.

She fought furiously, her sunspear finding its mark repeatedly, seemingly everywhere at once on the battlefield. The Black Dragon soldiers assumed it to be Dante at first, but as they got closer, they too recognized their error. It didn't make any difference because Lana caused the same damage to their ranks as her cousin. Then Lana heard it, something in her helmet, but she was engaged with the fighter at the moment. "Give me a minute," she yelled. She knew Seth heard the transmission too.

Once Lana finished off the fighter, she backed away from the action and found Seth did the same. Lana said, catching her breath, "What is it?"

The soldier at the command post answered, "Not sure, but you said to tell you. I'm sending the coordinates and the visual. It's strange. I thought a tank at first, but I don't know."

Lana and Seth checked on their data pads and studied the image, puzzled as well. "Seth, it doesn't look like anything good, and they're dispatching it." Moments later, something else popped up, another image. "Oh yeah, that's not a tank, and neither is the other one."

"It appears only to be two of them, but they will be enough."

"I agree. Commander Austin, we need help. I'm sending you something. I need you to fire shots at it and see if you can knock it out."

As Commander Austin viewed the image and got over his surprise, there was a pause. "They took the dragon part literally, Lana. Those are ugly. We'll see what we can do."

Commander Austin ordered, "Okay, you four soldiers, break off your attack for a minute. We received a new target, and I sent it to you. Let's see what we can do."

Lana and Seth watched the data pad as the ships fired a succession of shots at one of the walking dragons. They watched unhappily as it left no mark. It simply bounced off the armor.

"Lana, it didn't faze it. We'll do another pass."

"Go ahead, but I think you're right."

Commander Austin and his group did another pass, but again the shots bounced off the armor to Lana's and Seth's dismay.

"What do you want us to do next, Lana?"

"Go back to the air battle for now. We'll let you know."

"Did you see what happened the second time, Seth?"

"I think not, Lana. You sound as if you saw something to help us."

"I'm not sure, but watch." Lana replayed it and pointed to something. "We are focusing there, but I believe our advantage is here."

"I see now. We won't get it by blasting the armor, but it did become slightly unsteady on its feet and with the proper help …"

"That unsteadiness could send it crashing down. It's like a built-in Achilles heel without realizing it."

"The ships can't get that far down, not safely for sure anyway, and you need to get close to disrupt it."

"If only the ground could explode from under them, it would be perfect." Lana grinned.

"A landmine."

"But our time is short, and it's going to be different from a traditional landmine. We better get to it. Because if it doesn't work, I haven't come up with a plan B yet." She and Seth ran to the squadron leaders. Moments later, Lana and Seth got on a couple of speed glider vehicles to get a few extra supplies to create the trap they needed.

Lana put the last item in. "I think we gathered everything and more."

"I must trust we did. I have an idea of what you formed in your head, but you see the complete picture."

"Let's get back and hope the trap goes as I created in my head, Seth."

Lana and Seth made it back to the squadron leaders. "You must keep them pushed back as we have. Seth and I will rid us of these dragon creation machines. We're taking about twenty of your men. You still have to hold your ground, but it should be no problem doing so. We cut considerably into their numbers, and it doesn't appear they sent more." Lana and Seth went into motion, with the small group of twenty soldiers following them. Lana and Seth took the speed glider vehicles as well. They might end up needing them.

Lana and Seth and the group maneuvered around the fighting. "They should pass here at their current path, Seth. This is a good place." Lana spoke to the group. "You ten get rid of any enemy soldier that happens along while we do this. You other ten help us get this together. We'll tell you what to do."

They set to work. The trap came together.

"Not a moment too soon," said Seth to Lana, pointing a little way in the distance.

Lana nodded and motioned to all the soldiers to move to the side, close enough to see but far enough away to be out of the path.

One of the Black dragon soldiers in front of the two dragon machines stopped. He felt something. "What is this?" He bent down to examine it. The sun caught it and revealed a thin silver wire going across the ground. The other soldiers came over to inspect it as well. They tried to figure out the source. "It goes a pretty good length, sir."

One of the other Black Dragon soldiers followed it to what appeared to be one end of it and touched it lightly, "One end ..."

He never finished as immediately a thicker coil popped up from the ground with a harpoon quickness and wrapped around everything near the group, including one of the dragon machine legs.

Lana nodded at Seth. He pushed something on the data pad. A series of explosions erupted on the coil wrapped around the dragon legs and ended with a massive explosion that erupted in the underside of the dragon machine. The dragon machine stopped. It had no fire left.

"Wonderfully executed, but I believe you hoped to disable both."

"I did, but only one left to go. On to plan B."

"I thought you didn't have one, my dear."

"I've come up with one. I'm going to need to get up close and personal to it, and I'll need one of the speed gliders we brought."

"Lana, I don't like the sound of that. I will be the one in trouble with Caleb if something happens to you."

"I'll be fine. You'll cover me. I know what safe looks like, unlike my cousin Dante." She wondered if he was okay. She forced herself back to the task at hand.

"I'm sure he's fine." Seth read her thoughts and tried to convince himself. "Lana, let's hurry before this thing gets any closer."

CHAPTER SIXTY-FIVE

Ryan and Caleb tried to fight their way to the entrance again. Over half of Commander Gabe's group had landed in the hangar now too. Although Black Dragon soldiers came through the entrance to the hangar, Commander Gabe's group now helped with the flood.

"They keep coming. How many can this place hold?" asked Caleb.

"A lot. We got a preview, remember?" said Ryan.

"Yeah, but still."

"The more we get rid of here, the less we deal with in the hallway and in the room."

"Always seeing the bright side. I'm not feeling better, Ryan."

"I tried, Caleb. It's all I got." Ryan finished sending another Black Dragon soldier to the ground.

Commander Gabe could hear Ryan and Caleb. "You two said no shots into the hangar, but what about a single, nice shot down the entrance to clear the hallway?"

"Sounds perfect, but a tough shot to land."

"They stopped firing inside the hangar for the most part. One of the other commanders can take over now. I was about to land inside the hangar. I'll make the shot, Caleb. You two are the closest to the entrance, I believe. As long as you two back up, we should be fine."

"We heard you. We're making room," said Ryan.

"He's right. Go ahead. Take the shot."

Ryan and Caleb moved back and motioned their soldiers to do the same. Commander Gabe's ship entered the hangar, and an explosion went right down the center of the hallway.

"Give it one more shot," yelled Caleb.

A second later, another explosion ripped through the hallway.

"Nicely done, Gabe. I never doubted you for a minute." Ryan laughed. "Now come join us."

"I am. I can't let the two of you do it all."

Caleb and Ryan motioned the soldiers to move forward again and engage the Black Dragon soldiers.

Commander Gabe came beside them. "It appears that helped."

Caleb said, "A beauty of a shot. The hallway is a lot different now."

"Much emptier." Ryan laughed. "Let's say we try to get through the entrance and tour a couple of those rooms."

The three pushed forward with new determination, with their soldiers doing the same. They found themselves through the entrance and continued to fight. Still, they found they stepped over more Black Dragon soldier debris now than actually fighting them, thanks to Commander Gabe's shots announcing his arrival in the hangar. They would be in the target room soon.

CHAPTER SIXTY-SIX

The girl continued to cry. She could do nothing. Dante had struggled, given everything he had, yet this is how the battle ended. He did not succumb to the Darkness, but death still found him as she feared. He would be with the Ancient One, but Ethan would remain a prisoner. She felt the weight as the one who gave Dante the message to do this, assuring him he could accomplish it. Now here he knelt, his blood about to be spilled out by the blade, as his brother's blood before him. She could not bear to watch her Dante lost to her, but she could not turn away. She had always been there with him in all his tears, in his pain, and so she could not leave him now as he took his last breath. I'm so sorry, my Dante. In the end, she had failed him, the one she loved, her Dante.

Dante gazed at his father through his tears as he felt the blade shaking as it hesitantly dug into his chest. Dante still felt no hate for his father, only sadness. Despite his efforts, he could not free his father from the Darkness. He tried, said all the words given to him. He knew his father had come so close to breaking the hold. Dante understood, though, from the brief time he felt it from the Dark Lord. His father had been under it for so long. How could he expect him to see through it so quickly? His spirit broke for his father, with the knowledge of the bondage his father would remain yet a prisoner. So long he had endured this imprisonment, and there was no end to it. Today it was to be broken, but I failed him. I'm so sorry, Father. Dante saw a single drop of blood stain his shirt.

Then, a gentle but firm voice sounded in the Elders Hall.

"Ethan, lower the sunspear. I will not allow you to end your son's life. It's time you heard my voice again, Ethan. Your son did well today."

Ethan's hand slowly lowered until his sunspear dropped to his side. His eyes darted around the Elders Hall as one searching, but he knew he would not see anyone. He recognized to whom the voice belonged.

The Dark Lord's eyes turned black as the abyss, and he was furious. He started toward Ethan to take the sunspear from him and finish Dante but did not get anywhere with his effort.

The voice came again, and this time no kindness, only controlled anger was heard in it. "You will not interfere any further for the moment. I will make sure of it. You are bound and will stay that way as long as I see fit."

The Dark Lord tried to speak but found he could say nothing. He tried to move, but it was as if invisible chains wrapped around him.

The voice came again, returning to His gentle tone. "Rise, young Dante. It's time to help your father find the path back. We will do it together."

Dante smiled, got up, and met his father's eyes.

*　　ele　*

The girl turned to Alena. "He's ..." she couldn't finish. She sighed with relief and hugged Alena tightly.

"He's okay. The Ancient One is with him. You will get to hold your Dante yet," said Alena softly. "You will see."

Alika and Christopher smiled.

The girl got up again with Alena to watch.

Suddenly the window ended at the cockpit. The others stared at the girl, puzzled. "It's okay. I can still see through Dante's eyes."

*　　ele　*

The voice continued gently. "Ethan, your son told you the truth. He tried to get you to remember. You are seeing everything through a blurred vision. It's time to restore your sight. Are you ready, Ethan?"

"How?"

"I will give you the moment in time which changed your world. You will face it. This time you will see it as it was. There will be no interference from other individuals, and your vision will be clear. It's a bittersweet gift, for it's a painful moment for you and Dante. Dante will be here to face it with you this time. I will be here also as I have always been."

Dante moved closer to his father. "I'm here, Father. We will do this together."

His father nodded with tears in his eyes to his son.

Before them, a window of sorts opened. It seemed solid, yet it was not. They both recognized the scene instantly. It was outside their home in the evening, and Collin was there happily playing. He appeared to be hunting for something.

Ethan watched and murmured. "My boy. He was so sweet."

Dante watched as well, knowing what came next.

The moment in time continued. Collin heard someone coming but showed no alarm. Clearly, he expected it to be certain individuals since he was at home. The person approached him, and he looked up. He smiled at first, and then his face changed to one of horror. The dagger came, and he held up his hands to no avail.

Ethan watched, and tears streamed down his face. "Collin, my innocent child." He gazed up at the figure and spoke to it. "My sweet Abigail, how could you do it?" He stopped, his face full of tears. "What was that? Stop the vision."

The voice asked gently, "What do you need, Ethan?"

"Something's not right. I thought the woman was Abigail, but something in the eyes to begin with, and then ... I need to see it again."

"If that is what you ask, I will do so. I know how painful this is for you to see again, Ethan."

The moment went back to when the person approached Collin, and this time Ethan watched the one who came as Abigail. His face went pale. "It's not Abigail.

It's Duvessa, the Dark Lord's lady. She changed herself to be as my wife. It wasn't my Abigail."

Dante came closer to his father and touched him gently on the arm. "Father, are you all right? I'm here."

His father gazed up at him, tears pouring from his face. "How could I think for a moment my sweet Abigail could do such a thing? What have I done?"

"You know the truth now. That's what matters," Dante said with tears in his own eyes.

"But there is more." He continued to watch, his grief threatening to overwhelm him.

Collin lay on the ground, his blood pouring out to soak the ground. The Dark Lord's agent stood over him and turned around. In the background, a figure emerged. By all appearances, it was an Elder. He wore the garb of one, including the hood part of the robe. His head stayed bowed, so he could not be identified. He never looked up, but he watched the deed and did nothing to stop it. It was clear he was the one the Dark Lord's agent was waiting upon.

"Show me your face," Ethan demanded to the image of the Elder.

The image of the Elder stayed with his head bowed, refusing to listen.

The Ancient One spoke again, and His tone changed. He spoke to the hooded figure in the image harshly. "Do as Ethan says. Remove your hood and show your face to him as he wishes. I command you."

The figure appeared angry as one wanting to refuse the request but knowing it had no power to resist The One who commanded it now. The figure removed his hood and glared at Ethan. Ethan went pale again as he found himself looking straight into the angry face of the Dark Lord.

Ethan watched as the figure of the Dark Lord and his agent walked away from the scene. Collin's body was simply left there, lying in an ever-larger spreading pool of blood. Ethan fell to his knees beside the image of his child's lifeless body and began to sob. Dante knelt next to his father and put his arm around his shoulder.

"What have I done? Collin, my son, where are you now? I should have protected you. I promised you. How could I let this happen?" sobbed Ethan.

The voice said gently, "Oh. Ethan, your son Collin is with me. He is safe in my arms. He is happy. There is no pain from the moment. He does not blame you. He loves you. Look only into the eyes of your son, Dante, and you will see the same love that shines for you, Ethan."

Suddenly the image of Collin's bloody body began to fade. His body became bathed in light, and the blood was gone. His body floated above them for a moment, and it was gone as well. The sound of his faint laughter could be heard. Ethan watched.

Ethan turned to Dante. "My son, I'm so sorry. To think I almost spilled your blood today." He cried anew.

"Father, it's okay. It's as the Ancient One said. I feel nothing but love for you. You are returned to me. It's what I came for today." Dante's voice broke as tears streamed down his face.

"And my sweet Abigail, Forgive me. What she endured all this time, I ..." He could not finish as the image of his wife's still figure came to him, and he continued crying.

"Father, you know mother's spirit, and she has only love for you as well. It will be the same when she awakens. She is safe now and will remain so."

Ethan reached over and hugged his son, and Dante hugged his father back. They wept in each other's arms.

The girl sighed and smiled. The others looked at her waiting as she turned to them. "Ethan saw Collin's death again, but his vision was clear this time, and Dante stood with him. Dante finally has his father back."

CHAPTER SIXTY-SEVEN

Lana and Seth surveyed their finished work with satisfaction.

"It should work, Seth."

"I still don't entirely like this. You need to be careful."

"I got this, Seth."

"Oh no. You even sound like your cousin right before I'm bandaging up something."

Lana grinned. "The difference is I do have it." She patted Seth on the back. "Are you ready for your part?"

"Yes, let's do this." Seth shook his head.

Everyone in their group put their masks and visors on. Lana got on the speed glider vehicle and got in place. They moved until they were out of sight but in front of the path of the second dragon creature again.

The second dragon creature came forward along with a group of Black Dragon soldiers. Immediately, smoke filled the air around them, leaving the Black Dragon soldiers completely surprised, trying to find their bearing.

Lana sprang into action as soon as her team threw the liquid smoke. Driving the speed glider vehicle straight toward the legs of the dragon creature, she released the harpoon coil, and it attached to one leg. She circled the dragon creature until she wrapped the coil around both of the creature's lower extremities. Then she released the other end, and it stuck to the beast. Lana started to clear the creature when she saw something swinging toward the back end of her vehicle at the last moment.

Really, that part moves on it too, thought Lana, as she unsuccessfully dodged the tail of the mechanical dragon. It didn't get a clear shot of her vehicle, but enough to throw it off balance and send it for an ugly landing. Lana found herself falling off the vehicle right before it hit the ground. She heard a yell from Seth. "He's right there, Lana."

Lana saw the sword coming down and rolled over, dodging it with a second to spare. She reached for her sunspear and met the sword of the Black Dragon soldier, this time from her position on the ground when she turned back over. She used her feet to push him away and throw him off balance. It worked with enough time to get on her feet. She disengaged herself from him, ran clear, and shouted to Seth, "Do it now, Seth, before it gets loose." A moment later, a series of explosions erupted, and the underside of the second dragon creature was a ball of fire. It was destroyed.

Seth ran up to her. "Are you all right, Lana?"

Her eyes flashed a fire that matched her red hair. "I'm fine. Where is the Black Dragon soldier that tried to get a piece of me? We'll see how he fares with a sunspear through him."

Seth laughed. "Lana, I believe he ran away in fear when he saw you coming back for him. At least he should have. You remind me of another spear-bearer I know."

Lana laughed back. "I do like that spear-bearer's spirit. I'm sure we'll get along well when we finally meet. Dante is not the only one looking forward to the meeting. Let's rejoin the rest of the group near the fortress, and we'll take care of any soldiers we see along the way."

Lana and Seth motioned for the group to follow them back to the squadron near the fortress.

Lana peered up at the sky as they walked along. "Commander Austin is still doing well on that front."

"Yes, but I would let him know we took care of the two dragon creatures, so he's not wondering."

She did as they continued toward the fortress.

CHAPTER SIXTY-EIGHT

Caleb, Ryan, and Gabe, along with part of the squadron, continued to make their way to the room containing the dispersal device. The rest of the squadron stayed in the hangar and continued to deal with the Black Dragon soldiers. The commanders didn't want to find themselves or the squadron ambushed in the dispersal device room.

"Finally," said Caleb as they found themselves at the door. "Here we go." He made sure Ryan and Gabe stood ready behind him. Caleb scanned the data pad at the door, and it opened. To their surprise, there was no army of Black Dragon soldiers waiting at the entrance as before.

They went in and saw Black Dragon soldiers in the room, but it was minimal. It only took a few minutes of carefully targeted blaster shots, and they easily cleared the room.

"This is weird," said Ryan.

"Earlier, you said they all came running to the hangar to kill us," said Caleb.

"Yeah, but I didn't really buy into my theory."

They moved closer to the device, the metal-shaped cylinder in the picture.

Ryan shook his head. "This room is different too."

Gabe's eyes searched the room. "Those strange-looking devices on the stations around the cylinder ..." his voice trailed off.

Caleb turned around, surveying the room. "You're right. I don't see a one of them or any traces of them."

Ryan's face was troubled, but he sighed. "We need to inspect this device closer. I don't have a good feeling about this."

They started examining it, but it didn't get them anywhere.

"I don't see a control panel or anything on it. It doesn't make sense," said Caleb.

"The blueprints made no sense either as far as the disabling part," said Gabe.

"But we didn't get all the download. The room being empty is a surprise. There's a port right here." Ryan held up the download chip he had brought with him.

"Plug it in and be sure and get it out before we leave. We'll let it run while we work with the device more," said Caleb.

Ryan did and came back over to the device. "The hoses. The Black Dragon soldier said to be careful with the hoses. It could be the connection to disable the device also lies with them."

"Could be." Caleb put on his mask and visor and motioned everyone else to do the same. He reached down and scanned one of the hoses carefully. He paused, puzzled as he scanned again. "I don't understand this. It reads nothing is going through the hose. It's only residue of something having gone through it."

"Perhaps not all are in use," said Gabe. "Let's check a few more."

They did, and it showed the same reading. Ryan asked, "Should we take one of the hoses off to see how it works, maybe give us a clue?"

"It's worth a try," said Caleb. "Give me gloves. I still don't want to get this stuff on me, even residue, since we don't know what it is."

"Here's gloves. Use this Black Dragon sword to cut the hose. He doesn't need it anymore," said Gabe.

Caleb stepped back a little and cut through one end of the hose with the Black Dragon sword. He waited, wondering if the scanner displayed wrong, but nothing sprayed out of the hose. Caleb bent down and checked closer once he knew there wasn't anything fresh in the hose. He produced a portable light beam and activated it to see through the hose and around the connection. "There is a valve that opens up to the cylinder on one end and the same on the other end where these stations are. As far as I can tell, it looks like nothing is going through these hoses. Whatever the substance is, it's all in the device now."

"We must find the means to disable it," said Ryan. "There's a control panel somewhere for it. Everything possesses a way to control it."

"There is always plan B. Take it and continue to disable it back on our territory," said Gabe.

"Yeah, but Ryan's right. There's a means to control it. From a ship to a detonator ..." Caleb's voice trailed off. "What if it's not on the device itself? What if it's from somewhere else?"

"It should put off a signal, and it can be matched possibly," said Ryan, nodding. He got out his data pad and started scanning the cylinder device. The data pad beeped. "It picked up a signal. Let's try scanning this into the portal and see if there is a match to anything current. It could tell us how to disable it."

CHAPTER SIXTY-NINE

Dante and his father slowly got up.

"My son, the Dark Lord will never stop now. He will make it his mission to destroy both of us after today."

"I'm aware of that, Father, and I fully expected it to be the case. However, he deals with both of us now."

The Ancient One's voice spoke gently, "The Dark Lord must be stopped today. Ethan and Dante, are you ready to finish this battle together?"

Ethan and Dante smiled at each other and nodded. They got their sunspears ready again and turned toward the Dark Lord. Ethan stared at his sunspear in surprise. It appeared as when he first fashioned it. It was back to its color and radiance, down to the clear stone in the handle. Dante smiled at his father, and they turned back around to face the Dark Lord.

The Dark Lord found himself unbound by the invisible chains, and he could speak again. He glared at both of them with nothing but hatred in his eyes. There was no act, no pretense any longer. He eyed Ethan first and spat out the words in fury. "You turned now as well. I don't care. I will make you pay all the way finally. Yes, I had your little Collin killed, and I had your wife prisoner all this time right under your nose. Oh, what wonderful plans I had for her until the Elder and his two spear-bearers ruined it. It doesn't matter. There is no hope she will ever awaken."

Ethan's eyes blazed fire. "You're a monster. I can't believe all this time ..."

The Dark Lord cut him off and laughed. "Save it, Ethan. I used you for so long. I came close to having your son as well today." The Dark Lord turned to

Dante. "Didn't I, Dante? So close, Dante. Then the Ancient One interfered, and it appears he somehow enlisted one of those spear-bearers to help you. Those two keep causing problems for me, but I'll figure out who they are eventually. Then I'll take care of them, and quite painfully when the time comes. If not for that, you would be mine like your father. How did it feel to fail so miserably and so quickly, Dante? Seth will be disappointed in you. Such a waste of time training you."

Dante stared at the Dark Lord coldly, and he answered back perfectly calm. "It won't work. I don't care what you say anymore today. I have my father back. That is the first part of what I came to do. The second part of my task is now in progress. None of my tasks involve any further conversation with you. We're done talking with you."

"Ethan, your son does not wish to speak further with me. You called me a monster, Ethan. I am, and I took great joy in all the pain I caused for you and your family over the years as well as for the colonies. Remember, I brought you along for the ride. You were a part of all those attacks. The blood drips from your hands as well. Do you think you can walk away from your guilt, from your part in the crimes? Come do you think ...?"

"Enough of this. You deceived my father and kept him in a cruel bondage for all this time. Today he broke free. The Ancient One does not accuse him, and you won't continue to do so. No more talk with you for me or my father."

Dante turned to his father. "Father, we listen and speak with him no more. It's time to do this. Are you ready?"

"You are wiser than I today, my son. Yes, let us do this."

The Dark Lord realized his tactics had failed. He smiled. It was all right. He pulled out his sword. He would destroy Ethan's family line before the day was done.

Dante and Ethan advanced on the Dark Lord, and his sword rang from the sound of their sunspears. The Dark Lord furiously struck back blow after blow as Ethan and Dante tried to find an opening to sink their sunspears into him. He proved lightning fast with his sword as if possessed by a dark unseen power as his eyes flashed from black as the abyss to red as fire. Dante and Ethan would advance and seemingly overpower him, but he surged back, almost knocking them off their feet. At times, he appeared to become a shadow in the room, darting unseen in a flash from one part of the room to the other. Then he was there again, sword meeting theirs as if the battle had never paused.

Dante turned to his father, looking around. "Where did he go?"

They both heard it. A door closing. Dante knew what he heard, but he didn't think so.

Ethan shook his head. "No, he remains in this room. I can feel it from him as you can."

They saw it the same split-second. Dante dove and pushed his father with him. It barely missed them.

"Are you all right, Father?" They moved for cover.

"Yes, thanks to you, Son. I'm not mistaken. An arrow, correct?"

"Yes, and I know what we heard now. The door to the weapon arsenal in the Elders Hall. Some weapons are still in working order." Dante had to smile. "You know Seth shared the Elder's philosophy with training."

"That his students should be prepared for everything. Today shows he did well continuing your training."

The two moved quickly as another arrow came uncomfortably close to them. "We have to stop him, Father. Eventually, something will find its mark. As I remember, the arsenal is well-equipped."

"I recall that as well."

"We need a distraction." They moved again as another arrow whizzed nearby and exploded. "Great, now he's adding an extra zip to it."

"You thought of an idea, though." Ethan smiled at his son.

"I did. We'll get him stirred up in that room. It will be like exploding one of your tanks again." Dante motioned to an item in his bag and said something to his father. His father smiled back and nodded. They continued moving toward the weapons arsenal.

"Who would think the harpoon thing still works? I'll compliment Seth when I get back on the workmanship." Dante laughed softly under his breath as he and Ethan continued to dodge the Dark Lord's attack.

Ethan followed, amazed by his son. Even in the midst of this, his son's manner did not change. He had a feeling his son was the same while fighting during the attacks. Ethan began to realize how much he had missed with his son, but he became more and more grateful to the Elders for saving Dante those years ago.

"Put these on, Father. I've got mine on. We're about to need them."

Ethan took part of his helmet off to put the visor and mask on that Dante handed him. They were close now, and the barrage of artillery became much heavier.

They reached it. Dante met his father's eyes, and his father nodded. Dante threw liquid smoke outside the entrance of the weapon arsenal and, at the same time, opened the door to it. Ethan threw more liquid smoke ready in his hand inside the room from his position. Dante had gotten out a detonator, sprayed the bottom, and stuck it on the door. He kept expecting the Dark Lord to rush out, but he didn't yet. After racing from the door toward his father, Dante hit something on his data pad, and the weapon arsenal room exploded.

"Now there's a distraction and an explosion," said Dante.

"You are quite good at that. I'm glad all those tanks were put to good use." Ethan laughed softly.

"Let's go find the Dark Lord in the rumble and finish this," said Dante firmly with his sunspear raised.

"Yes, let us." Ethan followed him with his own sunspear ready.

Dante carefully stepped through the entrance, his father behind him to cover him. The explosion did its work well. Dante checked, but he didn't see the Dark Lord in the room in any form, dead, dying, or waiting on him. Dante continued, eyes forward, but he called back to his father, "Father, I don't see him anywhere. I don't know where he could be." Dante's eyes moved to the other side. The weapon room had two doors, one to enter and one to exit. How did he forget that detail? Dante stepped carefully but quickly back toward his father. "He went out the other door. He could be anywhere now."

"It's okay, Son. Keep coming as you are. I'm watching for us. We will find him." Ethan kept one eye on his son and the other around the Elders Hall.

Dante reached the entrance to stand beside his father. "I can't believe I forgot about the second entrance."

"Son, you can't remember every detail. You haven't been here since you were a boy." Ethan patted his son on the back. "At least, the Dark Lord doesn't have a whole weapon arsenal to shoot anymore at us. You did well."

"No, we did well." Dante smiled at his father. He turned and searched carefully through the Elders Hall. "He must be here, but there are numerous places to hide. I also remember that. I didn't just train here. Lana, Caleb, Collin, and I played here at times, much to Seth's irritation."

"Yes, I'm sure." Ethan smiled at his son. "You're right, though. He's still here."

The two started to walk carefully side by side through the Elders Hall, their sunspears ready. Suddenly successive shots fired. Surprisingly none of them appeared aimed at them. They soon realized why. They found themselves in the dark as all the lamps in the Elders Hall went out.

"Father."

"I'm here, my son."

"This isn't good. The Darkness is the Dark Lord's domain in many ways. He has the advantage."

"I know, but I won't let him harm you. I'll protect you as I promised, my son."

A whisper could be heard. "I will be your light in the Darkness. Do not fear, my children."

Suddenly their sunspears caught an unseen light, and it encircled them. As long as they stayed near each other, their combined sunspears lit the area around them as well.

"Thank you, Ancient One," said Ethan softly, smiling.

Dante smiled to hear his father say those words.

There was a rustle, a stirring. It originated on the other side from them, not far from the opposite entrance of the weapon room. Dante turned to his father and motioned. His father nodded. They moved closer. Dante sighed as they reached it. It was a good hiding place with several things there to provide excellent cover. Dante began to tread carefully. He had only gone a little way when he stopped, and he heard something and realized the source. He spun around the same time as his father, sunspear raised.

The Dark Lord stood, his sword making the downward swing toward them.

The Dark Lord had come around the other side, maneuvering behind Ethan and Dante. Another moment and his sword would have ended both of them. Now though, they stopped his blow in time, and the battle resumed. The two sunspears and the Dark Lord's sword clashed furiously. The unseen light from the two sunspears continued to blaze with every strike from the Dark Lord. They found themselves at the front of the hall where the tapestry of the Ancient One struggled to hang. The front had a table, chairs, and ornate items arranged on the tabletop. The Dark Lord toppled the table, and it came crashing down toward them. Dante kept toward the Dark Lord, but stumbled on one of the many items that came crashing down on the floor. He was in the process of gaining his footing again when he saw it and realized he would be too late. Dante saw the Dark Lord smiling at him.

The girl watched in horror and screamed, "Noooo ...!"

Ethan saw it too. He promised to protect his son, and yet he knew he would not make it in time with his sunspear.

The Dark Lord's sword found its mark. Dante looked down.

CHAPTER SEVENTY

He saw his father sink down in front of him. At the same time, the tapestry of the Ancient One fell, and the Dark Lord became tangled in it. Somehow, Dante found his sunspear moving, and he plunged it deep into the Dark Lord who remained trapped in the tapestry of the Ancient One emblem. The Dark Lord finally lay dead from Dante's sunspear.

The lamps in the Elders Hall suddenly lit up again. Dante knelt by his father, tears streaming down his face.

Ethan smiled at Dante through his tears. "I promised to protect you, my son. I did so."

"Father, perhaps ..."

Ethan shook his head, smiling sadly at his son.

A gentle whisper could be heard. "Ethan will soon be with his son, Collin."

*

The girl murmured. "Oh Ethan, I'm so sorry." She collapsed to the cockpit floor.

The others knelt by her side, and Alika held her eyes. "What happened to them?"

"Ethan lies dying in Dante's arms from the Dark Lord's sword point, one meant for Dante. Dante's sunspear has defeated the Dark Lord, but the cost will be Dante's father." The girl's voice broke as she continued to sob. "This is not how it was supposed to be, Alika."

"Oh, my child." Alika reached over and held the girl.

Dante saw some tapestry beside them. He used his sunspear to cut a large piece of it off and placed it on the wound from the sword of the Dark Lord. "Here, this will slow the bleeding, father."

Ethan smiled. "Thank you, my son. I never thought I would see you again like this. It has been a good day."

"Father, this is not how I planned to end this day. I'm so sorry." Dante's voice broke.

Ethan sighed. So much time missed with Dante, and no one but himself to blame. He made the terrible choice so many years ago, and it cost him everything. He had fought on the wrong side all this time. Oh, what he had done in the time. Tears streamed down his face as he heard echoes and images come to his mind now. "My son, you have nothing to be sorry for. This is all my fault."

"Father, no. It is cruel what was done to us."

"My son, there's so much, though." The echoes became stronger with the images. He did so much as the Black Dragon Commander. The Ancient One called him his child still, but He couldn't possibly after what he had done. The blood cried out to him that he had shed, and the echoes, the whispers screamed out now, refusing to be ignored for longer. His heart sank. He couldn't fathom the Ancient One could see him with such love after the blood he had poured out. He stared up at Dante. How could his son still hold such love for him? He saw his sunspear lying there. He would die anyway. Why prolong it?

The girl murmured sadly, "Ethan, no, do not think such things. Dante is right." She turned to the others. "I can hear Ethan's thoughts as well now."

Suddenly the girl heard a gentle whisper, "Yes, and this is not how Ethan is to come to me or to spend his last moments with Dante. He must be comforted, reminded of My love for him. The second part of your task begins today. You are to speak with Ethan. This time, you will be heard and seen by Ethan," there was a pause, "and Dante as well. Rise, my child."

The girl got up and told the others. "I'm to speak to Ethan as I did Dante, except I will be seen by both of them."

~ele~

Caleb, Ryan, and Gabe observed the portal. The screen popped up a status update.

The status read: *Current status: Activated.*

"That's strange," said Caleb, "Why would it say activated?"

"That could be its way of saying it's online, ready to disperse," said Ryan.

"Maybe," said Gabe, his voice sounding doubtful. "I don't know. This whole room felt off since we entered."

"I agree, but the device is right here. We're staring at it. It's not dispersing anything. We checked the hoses. The valves going to the stations are closed currently. Those strange devices at the stations are gone." Caleb eyed the bottom of the cylinder device. "Could something be going underneath it?"

The three bent down.

Ryan shook his head. "It's hard to tell for sure, but it appears to be a solid base. Down below this is another level, another open room. There is no indication of any system continuing from this room to somewhere else. We said it could be controlled elsewhere, maybe another room."

~ele~

"Sir, reports are indicating the Freedom Fighters broke into the hangar and the facility. They are in Large Room One. Do you wish us to do anything further?" asked a Black Dragon soldier.

The one sitting in the command chair spoke, "We expected from what we saw earlier today they would eventually make their way throughout the facility. It's no surprise. I will let the Dark Lord and Black Dragon Commander know. I don't see it will change anything."

He got up and left for several minutes. He returned and sat back down, clearly puzzled. "I'm not able to reach either one. How strange. Nevertheless, we will proceed as I was directed. This is about wrapped up anyway. How much more time?"

"Less than a half-hour, sir.

"Excellent. Go ahead and begin gathering what is left of the fleet. We did what we wished today."

"What about the Freedom Fighters at the facility?"

"What about them?" The one sitting at the command chair laughed. "They can stay and tour the facility as long as they wish. It did not stop us all day."

∼ꝒꝒ∼

Lana and Seth made it back to their squadron near the fortress. They fought beside the squadron, but the Black Dragon soldiers began to clear out.

"Lana, it's Commander Austin, we got rid of a bunch, but the rest of the Black Dragon ships are retreating."

"I hear you, Commander Austin. It started to thin out here quickly as well. I guess they all got the same order. Keep doing what you're doing until you see there's nothing to shoot."

"Will do, Lana."

Seth turned to Lana. "Why don't you go back to the command center and see if you get anything from the others? If it's winding down here, perhaps we'll hear something soon from your husband and cousin."

"I'm hoping you're right, and it's good news."

Seth tried to smile. "Yes, I as well."

Lana hurried off to the command center.

∼ꝒꝒ∼

"It's promising," said Gabe. "I'll go down to the room below this one with a squadron and see."

Caleb and Ryan nodded. Ryan said, "We'll stay put and talk with you from here. We'll see if it changes anything up here."

Gabe made his way down with the squadron. They ran into little traffic, surprisingly. It appeared their forces did good work clearing out the rest of the hallway. They got to the room and expected trouble but found only a handful of soldiers. From all appearances, they were already in the process of leaving the room.

"We're in the room," said Gabe.

"That was fast," said Ryan glancing at Caleb.

"Yes, I'm surprised by how little we ran into on the way here, and there were few soldiers in the room." Gabe sounded puzzled. "I see what is a large control panel in the room with coils reaching down into it. This could be a good guess. I'm trying to get access now."

Caleb and Ryan waited. The screen they watched on their end suddenly changed.

"Do you see it?"

"Yeah, we do," replied Caleb. "Those are some major connections."

Ryan wondered aloud, "What about overpowering the system? A surge through it?"

"It would need to be big, but maybe it works," said Caleb.

"Enough to disable it." finished Gabe.

"Can we do it?" asked Caleb.

"Yeah, we need to reconfigure things here. You two will want to get out of the way up there. We'll tell you when it's coming," said Gabe.

Caleb glanced at Ryan. "He does know you and I and the squadron are sitting on a cylinder of who knows what chemicals up here, right?"

"If it's a surge, the metal cylinder should be fine. Now explosion, not so much." Ryan peered back over at Caleb. "Yeah, I'm sure Gabe remembers the cylinder-filled chemical part, or at least I'm hoping so."

Less than ten minutes later, Gabe said, "You two and the squadron get back. Here it comes."

Ryan and Caleb stepped back and motioned the squadron to do the same. Suddenly it was as if lightning came from the floor. It started at the cylinder and circled all the stations surrounding the cylinders where the handheld weapons had been assembled and back to where it began. The stations around the cylinders went dark.

"Well?"

"You disabled something over there. It's dark now," said Ryan.

"We're checking it," said Caleb.

They went toward the port, which still crackled. The screen attempted to come up. They tried their access, but the screen finally went blank and died.

"It's gone, Gabe. We can't tell," said Caleb.

"Is there another port in the room?"

"Yeah, Gabe. It's on the other side from the device, but maybe it will pull up," said Caleb.

They went to it and accessed the port. It struggled too, but finally, the screen recovered for a moment. It read: *Status: Disabled.*

"Do you see that, Gabe?" said Caleb, his smile coming through his voice as he reached over and gave Ryan a hug.

"I do," Gabe said, happy as well. "I will be up there in a moment."

"This cylinder is still full of a container of chemicals that we don't know how to neutralize yet, which can't be left here," said Ryan.

"We go with the original plan with that part," said Caleb. "We transport it from here and deal with neutralizing it back home."

"Let's check with the other commanders and see how hard the transport will be while we wait on Gabe," said Ryan.

"This is Commander Caleb. The dispersal device is reading disabled, but the chemicals are not neutralized. We're at the next stage, and we need to know how it's going out your way."

Gabe walked in at that moment and made his way over to Caleb and Ryan to listen.

"This is Commander Conrad. We should not encounter any problems with the transport. The remaining Black Dragon Army began retreating a short while ago, including the ones from the hangar. Some left in escape pods or others tried to retreat in transport-type ships. It's pretty clear out here now."

"We'll proceed as planned. I need to let someone know we're headed home with this. Have the squad ready when I call."

"You're puzzled," said Ryan.

"Now you know how I've felt all day," said Gabe.

"Yeah, but I don't know what to make of it." Caleb smiled at them. "If you don't mind, I'll make this next call back home."

They grinned back at him as Ryan patted him on the back. "You go right ahead, Caleb."

___ele___

Lana finally sat and tried to get a grip on where everything stood again. She checked to make sure Abigail remained still safe. The injuries had piled up. Still no word from Caleb and the other commanders, nor from Dante. She got ready to tap into Caleb's and the commander's communications to make sense of their status when a voice came through.

"Hey, I'm about ready to come home to you, sweetheart."

"Caleb, it's really you!"

"Of course, it is," said Caleb softly. "I'll be home soon. We got to the dispersal device, and the port shows disabled."

Lana could not contain her happiness. "You disabled it, you and all the commanders. That's incredible, Caleb."

"We're pretty happy here too. We still don't know how to neutralize the chemicals in it, so we're bringing it there like we agreed to figure it out. Strangely it shouldn't be hard. The Black Dragon fleet started retreating a little while ago. There's no danger of it getting fired on during transport."

"Good. It's weird, though. We experienced the same scene here too. One minute, Commander Austin was shooting furiously, and then he said the fleet retreated as well. Seth and I witnessed the same. We were chopping down Black Dragon soldiers with the sunspear and staff, and then nothing."

"Wait, did they get in the fortress?" asked Caleb as he heard the last part about the sunspear.

"No, Caleb. You can't always be the one to battle. I got bored after a while in here today."

Ryan and Gabe stared back at each other and grinned as they saw Caleb's expression. Caleb broke out into laughter. "I had no doubts I left everything in good hands, but now it's no mystery to me why they retreated from there. I'll see you soon, and you can tell me all about it."

"Okay, Caleb, I'm sure that's the first thing which will come to mind when you return," said Lana softly, "Hurry back to me, Caleb."

"I'll be back safely in your arms again, my Lana, as I promised," said Caleb softly.

Caleb turned to Ryan and Gabe. "Let's get this out of here and transported. Once we get it far enough away and through the portal, part of the squadron stays to ensure the Dark Lord doesn't ever get use of this place again."

CHAPTER SEVENTY-ONE

The girl felt a peace wash over her, and she knew it came from the Ancient One. She turned to the others and smiled. Her eyes reflected calm and softness, none of the turmoil created by the day's events. She turned back around to the cockpit window.

Alika smiled at Alena and Christopher.

Alena said, "Yes, she has never looked more beautiful despite everything today."

❧

Dante still knelt with his father as he saw a strange look pass in his father's eyes. It was fear, with a mixture of regret and shame perhaps. He wasn't sure. At the same time, Dante knew they were no longer alone in the room. There was no mistaking the familiar presence, but it couldn't be, he thought. He followed his father's eyes and almost fell over in his astonishment as he beheld the enchanting figure standing before them. His own heart skipped a beat, but it was not due to fear as he became lost in the beautiful, gentle blue eyes now focused upon them.

It was as with the image before. The figure appeared solid like the person stood there, but clearly, the girl was not really in the Elders Hall. However, she was in the present and able to somehow be seen by them. Although they realized she was aware of both Ethan and Dante, at the moment, her attention focused on Ethan.

"Hello, Ethan," said the girl softly, smiling at Ethan.

Dante did not need to look down at his father to know the fear, regret, and shame melted from him. The gentleness of the girl's voice could only be matched by the gentleness which radiated from her blue eyes. Dante found himself unable to take his eyes from her, content to continue to gaze happily upon the figure before him.

Ethan nodded and smiled back at the girl.

"Why, dear Ethan, are you letting such thoughts enter your mind with the time left with your son? The Ancient One does not wish this for you."

"There is so much I did, such terrible things."

"Ethan, the past cannot be changed. The consequences cannot either. They are done. You are not the first to see moments in time they wish they could change, but it cannot be. Ethan, this is the Darkness that tries to pursue you at the end, to take away precious moments from you and your son. Do not allow it to do so. You're not a child of the Darkness. You must stop listening to its echoes."

"I thought I did, and then ..." His voice broke.

"Ethan, I know, but you're not a part of the Darkness. The Ancient One claimed you for His own. You remember the moment in time when you became His, Ethan. For a time, you wandered on a different path. True, you feel you lingered on it for a while. The Ancient One was always there, though, whispering to you, drawing you back. He never gives up on one of His children. No matter how far a child wanders, the Ancient One will bring His child back. Just as a father, with his wandering son when he hears his cries. Does that not sound familiar, Ethan?"

He stared at her with tears in his eyes and met Dante's eyes. Ethan turned back to her and could only nod.

"Yes, Ethan, just as there is no distance you would not go to find your own children, the Ancient One pursues with the same relentless love. He has you in His Hand, and He never let you go. The Ancient One has wandering children at times but never lost children, and it will never happen, Ethan. Once they are claimed as His, they are secured forever."

Ethan looked down, and he felt something in the palm of his hand. He opened his hand to uncover his locket. On the front displayed the image of his royal house, and in the background shone the emblem of the Ancient One. Turning it over, it revealed his name scrolled across it. He opened it, but he knew inside would be a picture of Abigail and him on one side and Collin and Dante on the other side. He and Abigail got matching ones during their marriage. Dante brought Abigail's locket today to show. Ethan peered back up at the girl in surprise, "How? I threw it in the ocean after I denounced the Elders and turned from the Ancient One. I thought I lost it forever."

"It was never lost as you thought. Almost as if it never left your hand. You thought to bury it beneath the ocean sand those years ago, never to be found again. It could still be found after all this time. It returned to you, Ethan. Nothing or no one can be lost by the Ancient One." she paused. "You cannot even tell it was buried after all this time. It shines as beautifully as the first day when it was created."

Tears streamed down his face anew. "The Ancient One loves me truly."

"Yes, Ethan, so much. The lengths He has gone to pursue you, to have you returned to Him. He sent your son to you to bring you back to Him. Do you need to know further how much He loves you, who you are?"

He knew, but he longed to hear the words even so.

The girl smiled. "I will tell you, Ethan. Another forced you to take a name years ago, but it was a lie, Ethan. You were never to be called that name. This is who you are. You are Ethan, the enduring love and husband of Abigail, the loving father of Collin and Dante, and the treasured child of the Ancient One."

Ethan let the words fill his spirit, like a balm soothing him. "It is true, then?"

Dante was puzzled, but the girl knew what Ethan asked.

"Yes, Ethan, He sees none of it. It is as your son said earlier. The Ancient One does not accuse you."

"None of it?" pleaded Ethan, tears pouring from his eyes still.

"Forgiven. All of it, dear Ethan. No one accuses you. The Ancient One took care of it for His children as He promises."

Ethan felt a wave of peace settle on him as the words washed over him. He smiled up at his son as Dante smiled back at him. Ethan stared back at the girl. "I did not believe it possible to see my son look at me with such love again, and yet he does each time today."

The girl said softly, "It should not surprise you, Ethan. Dante is as His Father, in spirit and heart."

Ethan met the girl's eyes. Tears rolled down his face.

Dante thought he understood the comment, but somehow, he understood another meaning laid in it as he saw the comfort it gave his father.

Ethan turned back at his son and said softly, "You saw me today as I forgot myself, my son. You almost gave your life today because of it."

"You paid with your life instead, Father," said Dante with tears in his eyes. "This is no better."

"No, no, my son," said Ethan, brushing his hand to his son's face. "I'm your father. I promised to protect you, and I did so. Your life is spared. I would have it no other way." Ethan smiled. "It's what any parent would do for their child in a moment, without hesitation. There is never a regret. It's not a hard choice. To know our child lives and is spared, the parent surrenders their life freely. There is no pain in the giving. Do not ever think otherwise. Ever." Ethan looked at Dante, but then he locked eyes with the girl's and smiled at her.

The girl felt tears stream down her face at Ethan's words as he held her eyes. She understood. She said to him in almost a whisper, "It is as you say, Ethan."

Dante watched the girl and his father. He saw her face as she smiled at Ethan through her tears. Dante didn't understand it, but he could feel from her whatever Ethan said spoke to her in a way she needed that only the two of them understood. For his father's part, he saw the girl provide comfort all day from what seemed a never-ending reservoir of strength, and here he received the chance to give her solace, reassurance of some kind. Ethan did it, and a silent thank you passed between them.

Ethan eyed Dante, who continued staring at the girl. Dante clearly tried to figure what had just happened, or perhaps he remained mesmerized by her. Ethan smiled. Dante had been entranced by her since the moment she appeared before them. Ethan understood because he had seen the look before. He saw it in his own eyes many years ago when he gazed upon his Abigail and the happy days they spent with each other afterward. He had watched the girl, and though she did not focus on Dante directly, it was clear to Ethan Dante's feelings were far from one-sided. Somehow, he also knew this was the spear-bearer the Ancient One sent earlier to intervene. Ethan felt a prompting by the Ancient One, and he knew what to do next.

"I'm concerned for Dante."

Dante looked surprised, but he said nothing. He sensed though he was the center of the conversation, he did not need to input into it. It was a strange feeling.

"There is no need to be so, Ethan. Dante is well-trained in the sunspear to handle anything he encounters. You saw who Dante has become as you fought by his side and in each word he spoke to you today. His heart and spirit cannot be matched. There is none like your son Dante. The Ancient One is with him in everything."

Ethan said softly, "You understand, I meant ..." He did not finish but watched her, waiting.

Dante kept waiting for his father to finish, but he did not.

Her eyes said she understood the rest. She said gently to him, "Ethan... I do." Then, as she said it, she turned from Ethan and gazed into Dante's eyes for the first time. She smiled at Dante. He smiled back at her and felt his heart skip a beat again.

The girl turned back to Ethan again as she sensed he was not done. "Promise me."

Again, Dante waited for his father to finish, but he did not.

She did not need any further explanation, and she did not hesitate. She said softly, "Dante is never alone. Ethan, I promise you I will always take care of Dante." As she ended the words, she met Dante's eyes again and smiled at him.

This time Dante held her eyes for longer, searching them. He could see a fondness, a deep caring for him, but something so much more. Even as he dared to hope he saw what he thought, he wondered what lay in the promise made.

The girl felt her eyes held by Dante's. She felt him ask how far her care went for him, hoping to find the answer he sought, the answer he already knew. The girl finally took her eyes from Dante, but she could have kept staring into his soft brown eyes. They pulled her in, but she reminded herself she was here for Ethan.

"My heart is assured now when the moment comes to meet the Ancient One."

"Then my heart is as well, Ethan, for the Ancient One sent me today to give you comfort. May peace rule your heart as you finish this journey and enter the arms of the Ancient One. Ethan, the rest of the time is given for you and your son." She stayed in the room but stepped back from them.

Ethan smiled at Dante. "My son, you broke the hold that entangled me for so long. You believed it could be done, and you did it, despite everything. You did what you came to do."

"You were to come back with me, Father." Tears covered his face. "This is not the ending I wished. This is not what I meant to do."

"It does not always come out as we envisioned." Ethan reached up and put a hand on his son's shoulder. "I know this is not how you thought to spend your last day with me, but it was a good day with you, my son. I missed so much of your world in these years. Yet, I saw so much of who you are, who you have become today, and how you faced it. I knew your skill with the sunspear, so that was no mystery. The struggles today required a different part of you than the sunspear. You faced it, and I saw you—your spirit, your heart in every moment. You are gentle, strong, unwavering, faithful, loyal, hopeful, and so much more. And you are my son. I'm glad I got to see all of you today. There is no greater gift."

"You and mother were the first to teach me all those things. I will miss you so much when you're gone."

"It will be okay. My son, there are those around you who care for you and will continue to teach you. Listen to their words. There is Seth and this other Elder who helps you. Then your cousin Lana, and Caleb and your friends. The Ancient One gives all those around you to help you and for you to help them. And you do, my son. No one that meets you can do anything but grow fond of you. You have your mother as well, Dante. She will be there to guide you." Ethan hesitated and saw the sad look in Dante's eyes. "Dante, she will awaken. She is strong as you are. The two spear-bearers rescued her against impossible odds, it sounds like, and we watched her life spared again today. I feel in my heart the Ancient One would not do all that if she is not to awaken. Do not give up hope, my son."

"I know you're right, Father. It's hard to see her in such a state for so long."

"But it's not long when you consider the length of time she was a prisoner. When she awakens, tell her I love her, my son, and I never stopped doing so."

"I will, Father."

"She is very beautiful."

Dante smiled at his father. He thought, at first, that his father spoke only of his Abigail and then realized the double meaning in the reference. Dante's smile spread to his eyes. "Yes, she is Father."

Ethan continued smiling at this son. "She possesses a gentle spirit and heart as well. The Ancient One walks beside her, my son."

"Those are what drew me to her. Today was the first time she appeared to me."

Ethan laughed softly. "I realized that from your reaction, my son." He paused. "To find both in one is seldom done. I found it in my precious Abigail. A beauty whose outside is only matched by the strength of her heart and spirit. Once found, a treasure, my son."

"I see that, Father. I believe I found mine as well."

Ethan and Dante smiled at each other as they turned for a moment and gazed over at the girl. She stood there waiting quietly until the Ancient One told her otherwise. She smiled back at them when she saw them turn and smile at her.

Ethan smiled back at his son, yet he could feel it. "My son, the time is almost here. Take care of your mother. I enjoyed my day with you. I meant so earlier. The son you became, I could not imagine. You have blessed me. The Ancient One will always be with you. You will never be beyond His reach." Ethan whispered to his son. "I love you so much, my son, Dante." He reached over and hugged his son.

Dante whispered, "I love you too, Father." as he embraced his father. He started to say something else, but he realized it. His father was gone. Dante held him and wept.

The girl didn't need to look. She felt Dante's grief wash over her the moment he knew his father breathed his last. The girl slowly dropped to her knees and bowed her head, feeling the tears pour down her face. Ethan was gone, and Dante's grief cried out to her. She could do nothing to comfort Dante right now.

The others did not say a word as they realized Ethan must be gone now. They knew the girl could not be comforted with how the Ancient One chose for her to be the messenger. They stood there helpless to comfort her in her grief, as she felt helpless to comfort Dante in his grief.

Dante and the girl heard it at the same time, and their tears slowed.

"My child, come, there are many to see you, but there is one most eager to do so. Here he comes now."

The sound of a child's laughter could be heard in the distance getting closer, and there was no mistaking to whom it belonged. The child said, "Father, you must see this."

"Collin, my child, come to me. I have not seen you for so long," Ethan said joyfully.

"What a strange thing to say, Father. We saw each other a moment ago." Collin laughed merrily as he hugged him. "Where are Brother and Mother? Are they coming as well?"

"Let me answer that one for your father, Collin. They will join the two of you, but they tarry for a while. What do you show your father?" asked the Ancient One.

"The fish, of course. They are so bright and colorful." Collin laughed merrily again.

"You do love those. Come, we will all go together and see them."

"Hurry, Father. You must see them."

"I'm coming, my son." Ethan laughed. Then he spoke to the Ancient One. "Time is ...?"

"Not measured here as you once did." The Ancient One paused and laughed lightly. "You will get used to it, my child, as all my children do."

The girl got up as she listened to the exchange, smiling.

Dante listened and smiled as the exchange ended as well. He regarded his father's body and sighed. He could not leave it here, but the strength needed to carry it felt beyond him.

"My child, when you are ready, you will not feel the weight. I will carry him for you. You will find no resistance to your ship. The fleet and soldiers retreated. They don't even realize their leaders did not go with them," said the Ancient One's gentle voice.

"Thank you, Ancient One." Dante glanced around to see if anything further remained. He walked over to the Dark Lord's body, threw a firestone on it, and walked away from it.

Returning to his father's body, Dante picked up his father's sunspear and his father's locket, putting them on his person. He did not want them lost in transport. Dante sighed. There was one last part of this day, one he did not wish to see end. He gazed up into the girl's eyes. He wondered where she was while she did all this today, how close she could be found from him now. "I suppose I must watch you leave me as well now."

The girl smiled at him, staring back into his soft brown eyes, and spoke gently to him, "Dante, since you have known me, tell me when did I ever leave you?"

From visions to messages relayed, to her presence felt, to her words taking hold of his heart and spirit in his brokenness, she was there. He knew the tears he cried, they were cried again by her. "You never left me. You have been with me in every tear, in every broken moment since I have known you."

"And Dante, I would not start now to leave you."

Dante continued to hold her eyes and said softly, "Between us a bond."

The girl finished it softly, "That cannot be broken." Her eyes were held by Dante's. She knew he held sway over this interaction.

Dante smiled at her as he searched her blue eyes, his voice soft. "This is only goodbye for a moment."

"Yes, only goodbye for a moment." The girl felt her heart race as he held her gaze.

"Try to make the moment brief because I long to see you."

She whispered to him, "It cannot be brief enough, but I will try for you, I promise, my Dante."

His own heart skipped a beat again. My Dante. He did not mind being called hers at all. He searched her eyes for a moment more and finally released her gaze.

Dante knew it was time to leave and take his father. He reached down to lift his father and found it felt as if his father floated in his arms. The Ancient One truly bore all the weight for him. He walked down the aisle of the Elders Hall and to the door, pausing one last time to look back at the girl. He saw the window beginning to fade, but he saw the girl smile at him one last time. Smiling back at her, he walked out of the hall with his father's body.

CHAPTER SEVENTY-TWO

Lana watched from the command center. "It is secured?"

"Yes, it's secured. Your husband, Ryan, and their squadron transported it safely through the portal, and it is being placed in the containment field room. Commander Gabe remained behind with the rest of the commanders and their squadron. It sounds like that is being wrapped up as well," said Seth.

"That's a relief to hear and one less facility the Dark Lord can attack us from."

"Yes, they did well. Have you heard from Dante?"

"No word at all from my cousin. I fear the worst."

"We mustn't think like that. I'm sure Dante is all right." However, Seth's voice could not hide his worry.

"Of course, if, I mean when he calls, I will let you know." Lana sat back in her chair. She longed to find her husband and see him safely back with her own eyes. However, she knew he was safe. She had not heard a word from her cousin, and the comments from the Dark Lord's agent kept playing back in her head. She whispered, "Please, cousin, you must be safe. Where are you?"

"Sir, it appears they took the item from the room and transported it with them. They also are destroying the facility," said a Black Dragon soldier.

"How strange. Why would they take it, I wonder?" asked the one sitting at the command chair. He studied something earlier from the facility. "Oh, I believe I guessed. The readings probably showed them disabled or inactive or something of that sort, did it not?"

"Perhaps it did, sir."

"They are happy with themselves. It will be short-lived. They believed it to be that, I suppose. They will be more unhappy once they get into the thing they spent time transporting. Are all the fleets called back?"

"Yes, sir, as you ordered."

"Splendid. We did what we needed. The operation proved successful. We know it works. We can move to the next phase. They will begin having the commanders contact their regions, and when those couple of planets do not check-in, the discovery will be made of our activities today."

"Is there anything, for now, sir?"

"Yes, is there any communication from the Dark Lord or the Black Dragon Commander? I still can't reach them."

"No, sir."

"What about the soldiers that were on the planet with them?"

"They left the planet some time ago when the order was given to come back with the rest of the fleet."

"What about Duvessa? Has she checked in today?"

"It does not appear so. Is there anything else?"

"No, I don't believe so." He began to wonder. He should be able to reach one of them by now. And that Duvessa. He knew the Dark Lord sent her on the one task, a recovery or assassin mission. The Dark Lord also hinted he was unhappy with her of late. Who knows what she had done now? Maybe that's why she didn't check in. Personally, he always thought she was given too long a leash to roam by the Dark Lord. He knew the Dark Lord kept her around for more personal reasons at times, and the other tasks almost came second. He didn't care for her. Now, though, it would be useful to track her down. It would be easier to send her to the planet and find out why he could not communicate with the Black Dragon Commander or the Dark Lord. It appeared he would end up sending a few soldiers back there later today. No, that could wait until tomorrow. He would go with the soldiers if he still could not reach either one of them. Presently though, he must make sure to tie up everything according to the orders they left.

CHAPTER SEVENTY-THREE

"Lana," said the voice through her communications device.

Lana jumped up from her seat and turned her attention from the screen she studied. "Dante, are you okay?"

"Yes."

Lana said, "Seth, it's Dante." Lana knew Seth would head her way now. "Dante, where are you?"

"I'm headed home."

"Is your father with you, Dante?"

"I'm not sure how to answer your question, Lana." Dante's voice turned sad instantly. "My father is returning with me, but he did not survive the encounter. My father was dealt a fatal blow by the Dark Lord's sword, one that should have been my death. The Dark Lord lays dead now from my sunspear, but it's only because of my father's sacrifice."

"Oh Dante, I'm so sorry." Lana's voice broke. "None of us wanted this for you. We wanted you both to return safely."

There was silence as Dante composed himself again. "I did as well. I will grieve the loss of my father, but I'm at peace with it. Father felt at peace as well when he left to be with the Ancient One. My father, whom I knew of my childhood, returned to me in the end. Things do not always go as envisioned. He said that today. His bondage was broken, and he experienced freedom from the Darkness as he met the Ancient One. I will be comforted by that truth."

Seth walked up at that point, but he heard the entire conversation as he listened to the two talk through the communication system on his way up.

"You sound at peace, Dante, despite the day's events. Seth is here now."

"Good. There is something else from today. A figure appeared to Father and me. The Ancient One enabled her to come to us from another location to give comfort to Father."

"She ..." Lana didn't get any more out as Dante took it over.

"She is ... stunning." His voice sounded far away as one remembering a pleasant dream.

Lana glanced at Seth. She wasn't used to hearing such a tone from her cousin. Seth tried to hold back his smile and shrugged his shoulders. Lana asked, "Dante, can you be more descriptive about who you saw?"

"She has a slender form, about my age, I'm guessing. She has silky, soft long brown tresses." Dante hesitated as one trying to convey something but not finding the words he needed.

"Anything else, Dante?" Lana had a light teasing tone this time. She couldn't help it.

Dante was unfazed by it as he continued. "Her smile ... it goes to her eyes ... and yes, her eyes ... she possesses the most beautiful blue eyes I have ever encountered."

"That is quite a description, Dante." Lana still tried to grasp the tone she heard from her cousin. She turned to Seth again, but he was not surprised, and a smile began forming.

"No, it doesn't come close to her image, but it's what I have. I'll see her again. She made a promise to my father she would take care of me."

"It a strange thing to say. Dante, depending on what she meant by it."

"She meant it in a good way. Everything she said to Father brought peace to his spirit, which is why the Ancient One allowed her to be there. Father was the one who asked her to make the promise. He was comforted by it once she did so, as with everything she said. I wasn't clear on exactly what the promise meant, but her and Father understood. I could tell."

"So, you don't know who she was." Lana wondered who the girl could be. Seth remained quiet.

"I didn't say that, Lana. I said I didn't know *her name* still. I *know who* she is and for quite some time now, in fact."

Something about Dante's words struck a chord with Lana. "But Alika's young spear-bearer was a ..."

"No, Alika never said that. We assumed such and ran with it. The whole time with us, he never used he or she." Dante paused, and his smile could be heard through the speaker. "I'm guessing not everyone is surprised by any of this, huh, Seth?"

Lana turned to Seth and found him smiling. Seth laughed. "No, Dante, I'm not, including your reaction once you saw her."

"You're correct, Seth. She did leave quite the impression. I hope her lovely image does not fade anytime soon from me." Dante's voice sounded far away again as he spoke. "I always suspected you knew more than what you said after meeting with Alika." Dante laughed softly. "We'll talk more in the coming days, Seth. I'll approach the portal in a couple of minutes and be home with both of you soon."

"We'll see you then, Dante," said Lana. She turned to Seth. "My cousin has certainly had a girl catch his eye for a moment and vice versa. It was exactly that. Nothing was to come of it. But this is different. I've never heard my cousin sound like he did. It's so strange."

"Yes, it is. Yet there has been nothing ordinary about their relationship since this began. Before they met today, they were sharing a connection through the visions, and that's how they came to care for each other. Obviously, she had a better understanding of what that looked like than Dante all this time. We would both agree his view is much clearer after today, more aligned with hers." He and Lana started walking toward medical to pick up what Dante would need for his father's body, and then they would head outside to meet his ship when he arrived. "Apparently, Alika's comment about his young spear-bearer was also correct."

Lana's eyes twinkled. "And it was?"

"He made it clear Dante would not be disappointed when he discovered the appearance of the young spear-bearer. I gathered her outward appearance matched everything she showed by her spirit and heart so far."

"That is certainly true from my cousin's speech or attempt at words. At least one good thing happened for my cousin today. Seth, I thought the worst. Dante took so long to contact us."

"We both did, but he is fine. It was a long day for him. He cried many tears, I'm sure, as did the young spear-bearer. The battle is over. Now he must grieve, and we will, with him."

They got down to the hangar as Dante's ship landed. A tired but safe Dante came out of the ship. Lana and Seth came up to him and wrapped him in a hug. Moments later, Ryan and Caleb ran over to them. Lana wrapped her arms around her husband tightly as they shared a long kiss. Ryan gave Dante a hug. He looked at him, his eyes questioning.

Dante shook his head. "My father didn't survive. He was killed by the Dark Lord's sword."

"I'm so sorry, Dante. What can I do?"

"Can you help me get my father down, Ryan?"

"Sure, Dante. Whatever you need."

Caleb heard the conversation and went over to them. "Here, let me help, too."

They carefully removed Ethan's body from the ship and put it on the stretcher Seth and Lana brought. Dante stared down at his father's body. He took off most of the Black Dragon gear. He threw it all in a pile along with the Black Dragon helmet and tossed a firestone on all of it. His father no longer resembled Black Dragon anymore as he laid on the stretcher. "Now my father is ready to be taken inside."

CHAPTER SEVENTY-FOUR

The girl sighed and turned from the cockpit window. The others saw something they had not seen for a long time from her. Exhaustion. Her eyes reflected it. "That part is finally over." She walked over to the couch and sat, staring out.

The others sat with her.

"What do you need, Chris?" asked Christopher as he put a hand on her shoulder.

"I don't know. I'm so tired all at once. It feels like when I made it back after falling from the rooftop thing."

"I didn't know about that until today, so I must believe you on that one."

"We all would like to have not seen that, Christopher." Alika turned to the girl. "Yes, it is much like that. You battled hard and poured yourself out today. You are feeling it now. We said the battle today would not be won with a sunspear, and we were correct. It was the battlefield you were dealt."

"And you cried so many tears today with Dante and Ethan. You were truly poured out today, as was Dante. It's no wonder you feel empty now."

"You're right, Alena." She turned to them. "We must see it. You know that."

"Child, you know what we will find there. You saw it in the vision."

"I need to be sure, Alika. Maybe I was wrong somehow." The girl tried to fight the exhaustion.

"The shadows of evening are upon us, and you're exhausted."

The girl stared back at him. She would not be deterred.

Alika's eyes reflected sadness. "As you wish, child, but I see only more grief in doing this. We will not in the dark and not in your current state. We know the last place they went. Although the shadows of evening approach here, evening will not approach at that place for a few hours. I wish you to go to your quarters and get sleep for the next two hours. I will awaken you at the close of those hours. We will go to the planet as you insist. If the planet appears as I believe it will, we know the other two are the same. That is my condition to pursue this trip to the planet."

"You will ..."

Alika nodded before she could finish. "I promise to awaken you in two hours, even if you remain completely exhausted. We will continue to the planet if you persist in doing so."

"I'll change back into clothing fitting to travel to the planet before I lay down, and then I'll sleep. I'll see you back in the cockpit in a couple of hours." The girl walked to her quarters and shut the door.

"You tried, Alika. Is she always so ...?"

"Stubborn is the word you search for," said Alena supplying the word for Alika. "And yes, she is."

"I fear this time it holds only more grief for her day. I wish my efforts to convince her had been successful."

"It was a long day for us as well, but nothing like what she and Dante experienced."

Alena understood what Christopher suggested they do with the time. "True, I'm curious what happened with the others while everything occurred at the Elders Hall. Perhaps we would be able to tell by now with the transmissions. You know Chris will ask as well once she isn't exhausted out of her mind."

"Yes, it will pass the time, and I know we all wish to know. Let's see if we can figure it out while she sleeps."

CHAPTER SEVENTY-FIVE

The figure walked into the Elders Hall, her cloak swishing on the floor with each step. She had tried to contact the Dark Lord to no avail. Although she hadn't wanted to, she then tried unsuccessfully to call the Black Dragon Commander too. She did not care to try to call the other one that thought he could take the place of the commander at the moment, and she did not know why the Dark Lord put him in charge in the first place. Despite the Dark Lord being displeased with her recently, she still thought the Dark Lord would entrust her with the task of helping with the attack. She did not dare go back immediately to him after the failure with Abigail earlier today. However, she could not reach him, but she knew where he was to be. As she walked down the hall, she saw clear evidence of new disarray in the hall and indications of a struggle. She was puzzled as she continued down the hall. She saw a sword lying down with dried blood on it with a pool of dried blood beside it. The figure instantly recognized it as the sword of the Dark Lord. The tapestry had fallen. Near it and on it revealed more blood as well. Also, ashes laid as if ... The figure glanced from that spot back to where the Dark Lord sword lay. She stared back at the ashes. A firestone thrown. An excellent way to take care of something, like a body, when one did not have the time to take care of it properly. Two bodies, probably. One taken either to be saved before death or for the rites of death to be observed. The other tossed aside and allowed for the firestone to do its work. The figure knew the answer as she did not feel anything further from the Dark Lord.

Slowly the realization hit her. Her eyes turned to fire, and her screams of fury rang out in the Elders Hall. "You will pay for this! I will make you pay! All of you!" It seemed as if the walls of the hall shook.

She tried to control her fury as she picked up the Dark Lord's sword. Taking out a vial from her cloak, she went to where the dried blood lay near the tapestry and poured something on the dried pool of blood. Instantly it became liquid again. She took out another vial from her cloak and collected a vial full of the pool of blood, sealing the vial. She took her knife and cut off a piece of the blood-soaked tapestry, placing it in another container from her cloak. Then she saw a small ornate box on the floor from the Elders Hall. She picked it up and placed a pile of the ashes into the box as she secured it as well. Standing with all the items secured, she smiled cruelly. "Let us see what may rise from these ashes. Your victory is hollow. The sword remains at your heart. You fail to see the point still approaching." She walked out of the Elders Hall with fresh determination.

~ele~

Alika studied the screen and sat back, his face reflecting puzzlement. Alena and Christopher shared the same expression.

Alena asked, "Do you think there is any possibility?"

"No, I don't. I admit pieces of it point to a more hopeful outcome. However, there is more not adding up. Moreover, the vision was clear. There is no mistaking those images."

Christopher said, "As much as I hate to state it, the two hours are done."

"Yes, I'm getting up now. We will all hear about it if she is not awakened as I promised. I doubt the sleep brought her to senses." Alika rose and walked into the girl's quarters. He sat by her bedside and gently nudged her arm to awaken her. "Child, wake up. Come now. I'm doing as you requested. Two hours are passed."

The girl slowly opened her eyes and groaned slightly.

"You may go back to sleep. This is not my idea. For the record, I believe it is a bad idea. Would you like to reconsider this decision?"

"No, we need to do this. I'm getting up now." The girl forced herself to sit up. She still felt tired. She sat at the bedside. "I'll be there in a minute."

Alika shook his head. "All right, we will head that way and see you in the cockpit."

Alika came back out, and Alena and Christopher appeared relieved when he returned alone. They found it short-lived. "She will be out in a moment. Let's head for the planet."

The girl came out soon enough. Her eyes still reflected the exhaustion from the day. As expected, she asked, "What happened while everything went on at the Elders Hall with Dante and Ethan and the Dark Lord? Surely you three passed the time somehow while I got my beauty sleep." She tried to manage a smile, but it missed its mark.

"It proved more perplexing than enlightening," replied Alika.

"How?"

Alena spoke with hesitation and chose her words carefully, "Caleb and the others secured the device from the facility."

"That's great news. Did they get it before the substance could be dispersed?"

Christopher said, "That part is unclear, Chris."

The girl waited.

Alika said, "One of the control ports near the device read activated when they got here. Later they tried something to overload the system, and a control port in the room read disabled."

The girl's eyes instantly lost their exhaustion. "That could mean they stopped it. Why are you perplexed? You should be happy."

"You need to wait until we get to the planet before you get your hopes up. They are happy at the moment, but certain pieces did not seem right with Caleb and the others while there. They shook off those misgivings, but I don't know," said Alena.

"But the screen said disabled."

"But it said activated when they came in, and there was no indication of how long it showed that," reminded Christopher gently.

"Let us see, child," said Alika uneasily, "We are approaching the portal."

The girl watched and tried to tell herself to hope as they went through it.

Alika pointed. "Let's land on top of the hill. We can get a clear view from there of the planet's condition, but it will not be in the center of town. We all need masks and helmets on in case the Dark Lord did disperse a chemical. No one leaves the ship until it's done." Alika went and got one for each of them. He handed the ship's controls off as Christopher offered to finish landing the ship.

The girl continued to watch and began to get a sinking feeling. The hill resembled another hill, a familiar one to her. She wanted to ask Alika to land the ship somewhere else, but she knew inside it would make no difference if the planet met the fate she feared.

The ship touched the ground, and the girl raced out the door first. The girl gasped at the scene before her. She saw this before, but now it was real. The horror of it struck her to the core. Everything laid waste. Yet, it was not the things that broke her spirit, but the life gone, suffering, and in bondage. She turned to Alena and Alika and saw them shake their heads. Christopher would be coming out of the ship soon. Then she heard it—below the hill from them. The sound of one in pain, existing somewhere between life and death still. There would be more like the one. She could not endure the pain of the one she heard. The girl turned away. She felt the hopelessness of the scene before her overcome her senses, and she fell to the ground, sobbing.

⁓ele⁓

Dante stood with Seth in his mother's room. He came to check on her.

"That was close, Seth. You and Lana got to her just in time." Dante stopped. He got a strange look in his eyes.

Seth watched him. "Dante?"

"I'll sit for a minute." Dante didn't know what it was.

"What's going on, Dante?"

"It's like when she had the vision, and I felt it. That's it. Something very unpleasant is going on with her."

"You've not usually been on the receiving end of her feelings in such a strong sense, well, except for during the encounter today."

"I think that's it. With today, it's lingering." Dante hesitated. "With what happened today, what could compare?"

"I don't know, but it can't be good. Is it getting better?"

"No, it's not. And she made it clear she would initiate the next contact. I once felt silly doing this, but not anymore." Dante paused and spoke again, but this time he spoke to the girl. "Are you all right?" he waited and shook his head. "She's there, but she's not answering yet."

CHAPTER SEVENTY-SIX

The girl heard Dante, but she couldn't answer him. She sobbed as she stared out at the planet. Finally, in her head, she answered him back bitterly, *don't bother yourself with me. Your day has been long enough today, Dante, without me adding to it.* She got up, not knowing what to feel. She felt so hopeless, despondent, and then it came. It was anger, blazing forth, but then the others came crashing back on her, and then they were there all at once mixed up, unable to be contained.

"It said disabled. How is this possibly disabled?"

Alika understood, and his voice spoke gently to her. "I don't know, child. The pieces did not make sense we saw."

"It doesn't help them. You speak of pieces, Alika. Their whole planet is what is in pieces."

"Child, we did what we could. You know that. It would be worse if we did not." Alika kept his gentle tone. He knew her spirit was in turmoil.

"It wasn't enough. We should have done more. How is this enough? How can I see this, hear all this pain, and it is enough, Alika?" The girl's eyes blazed and streamed with tears at the same time.

"It had to be enough. We did what the Ancient One instructed us."

"We should have gone after the device, stopped it before they could use it. This is my fault. I advised us wrong."

"And sacrifice Dante and Ethan. Is that what you wanted?"

"No, of course not. We didn't have to. We could have stopped the device, freed Ethan, and kept Dante safe. There was a way. There should have been a way. We didn't see it." The words continued to tumble out as she put her head in her hands.

"No, there wasn't, child."

The girl screamed back, "I just wanted the vision to be wrong this one time, Alika." The girl fell to her knees again and cried, "Why is it so much to ask from Him? For once, can the horror of the vision not be true that I see? Just one time?"

Alika felt tears stream down his face as he spoke to her, "One time only? Is that what you would ask? If you could take away one, which would it be? Which is the worst vision you saw? Today? You believe this is the worst, but is it? What about Dante facing the Dark Lord? What if we could take that event away? Ethan would still be alive but in bondage. What about Abigail? What if she were never captured and tortured? Would she be awake now because she had never been captured? Perhaps not. Maybe she would be dead because they killed her, as we suspected. Then there is Collin. What if that never happened? None of that would happen to Dante's family, we guess. Dante would be spared all this grief. Or perhaps the Dark Lord would simply find another way to enter and entrap Dante's family. Maybe Dante would be the one slaughtered. Or maybe captured and raised to serve the Dark Lord. Then there is the vision dear to you. Would you take that vision away, wipe it away from ever happening? Really, only one time is all you ask, my child? Could you stop there? "

"No, that's not fair. That's not what I meant, Alika. How can you even ...? You don't know the outcomes." The girl got up, upset, and faced Alika.

"And you don't either. There is only One who does."

"You're not the one who has the visions, Alika. The one responsible for them!" The girl shouted in anguish.

Alika was gentle, but he cut her off. "You are not responsible either for what happens in the visions. You are the messenger. You must stop putting on yourself that which you are not meant to carry. Place it on the one responsible."

"Who is that, Alika? Tell me!" she yelled back at him, at the air. She didn't know where to direct her pain, her anger.

Alika came over and gently took her by the shoulders, then turned her back around to face the planet. "You tell me. Who dispersed this poison to make these people suffer?" He turned her around again and looked her straight in the eye. "Tell me who struck down Collin in his innocence? Who took Abigail prisoner and tortured her? Who held Ethan in bondage for years? Who ended Ethan's life today before his own son? Who tried to take Dante from you and twist his heart today? Who is responsible for taking everyone dear from you, child? I don't need to tell you. You tell me now. Come on. Tell me."

The girl screamed back, "The Darkness! The Darkness! It doesn't matter if it comes as the Dark Lord or the cloaked woman, it is the same! Always the same! I hate it! I hate it!" The girl felt like she couldn't catch her breath. She fell to her knees again. Her arms went across her waist as her body physically hurt from the sobs racking her body again today. She could not stop them, though.

Alika knelt with the girl. He reached over and wrapped his arms around her. "Oh, my child, my child, your spirit will stop breaking at some point today. It must." Alika's own tears fell into the girl's hair.

—ℓℓ—

"I got an answer. It's strange. I'm back to getting the essence of the message rather than word for word. It's like the night before I left, " said Dante.

"What did you get back?"

"She's very despondent. I can sense that. She basically said, stop worrying about her. She feels bad she bothered me after what I faced today," Dante's eyes were a mixture of concern and hurt. "Seth, I don't understand why she would say such a thing after today, with everything we went through together and the words we exchanged."

Seth felt worried as well, but he knew he needed to reassure Dante. "Dante, she speaks from her anguish. You know her heart. Do not take it as you are. At this moment, her spirit is hurting over something. Alika and the other student, I'm sure, are with her, trying to break through to her."

"I'm sure you're right. Let me try, though," Dante asked. "What is happening? What is hurting you so badly? Please tell me." Dante waited but shook his head. "She's not answering. I don't sense her spirit any calmer, rather the opposite. I don't like this. It worries me greatly."

Dante and Seth tried to go back to talking about something else for a bit as Dante's concern for the girl persisted. They came back to the subject of Dante's mother.

"I know you hoped she would be awake by now, but we must be patient." Seth stopped and peered at Dante. "Dante, what is the matter? Why are you crying?"

"I don't know, Seth. I feel the young spear-bearer is so broken again." He could not continue. Her pain washed over him. She was crying uncontrollably. He could feel it.

Seth reached over and embraced Dante. "It will be okay, Dante. At some point, the tears must stop for the two of you."

Dante hoped so. Inside his head, he said, "I'm so sorry. I have not left you though and will not, my young spear-bearer."

Alika held the girl for what seemed like forever as sobs racked her body, but at some point, her cries quieted. She and Alika got up. She stared out one last time at the planet, at the misery before her. "I'm sorry, Alika. You were right. This only brought more grief to my spirit. I should have listened to your counsel." She walked away and headed back inside the ship as tears continued to stream down her face. Christopher put his arm around her shoulder and guided her back inside the ship. Alika began walking back to the ship with Alena.

"The vision was bad enough. I fear the child will never sleep now after seeing the vision in its fullness."

Alena turned around and shook her head. "She may not be the only one, Alika."

CHAPTER SEVENTY-SEVEN

The girl, Alena, Alika, and Christopher went through the portal back to their previous location. Alika's and Christopher's ships were parked safely where they left them.

The girl sat on the couch and stared out into space. She turned to Christopher. "You're staying until tomorrow at least with us, right?"

"Yes, it's what we agreed. Is that still what you wish, Chris?"

"Yes, there are things to sort out. It certainly appears that way now. I don't have any more left in me today, though."

"I understand, Chris. Why don't you go ahead and get rest now?"

This time the girl gave no objections. "I will." She got up and hugged him. "Thank you for everything you did, Christopher. I'll see you in the morning."

The girl walked over to Alika and Alena and hugged them goodnight before retreating to her quarters for the night.

The three watched her go.

Christopher asked, "Do you think she'll be okay?"

"We will see," replied Alika.

The three sat and talked for longer as they delved further into the day's events. Twenty minutes later, they heard something coming from the girl's quarters. It sounded like murmuring at first, followed by a thrashing sound.

"I'll go check on her."

Alena got up and quietly opened the door to the girl's quarters. Slowly turning the light on in the room, she saw it was as suspected but worse than the previous time with the vision. She walked over to the girl's bedside and carefully sat. "Wake up, dear. It's the images. It's not happening anymore. You're safe."

The girl sprang up in bed and opened up her eyes. The girl's eyes flashed wild with terror, and she began crying again. She clung to Alena. "I can't stop them now, Alena. The images won't stop. How do I get them to stop?"

Alena gazed back at Alika and Christopher helplessly as she hugged the girl.

⁓ele⁓

Dante finally called it a day. He and Seth agreed to speak further tomorrow about the details of today's encounter between Dante, his father, and the Dark Lord. Understandably, Dante was tired from everything, and Seth knew it. Seth was just happy to see Dante back safe at this point. Dante got back to his quarters, took a well-deserved shower, and dressed for bed. He laid down and felt sleep coming to him at last. Immediately, he found himself wide awake again. He sat up in bed, trying to figure out what brought him back to awareness. Then he felt who, the young spear-bearer. Whatever pain struck her spirit, it kept her from sleeping. Not just that, it caused her pain again. By extension, after everything today, he could not go to sleep tonight since she could not. At the moment, he wasn't concerned about himself, only what could be causing her such anguish.

⁓ele⁓

The girl stopped sobbing. "How about I try tea? I must get some sleep."

Alena said, "We'll get it now."

Alika already stood to get it for her. He brought it over to her, and she drank it before laying back down again. This time Alena waited until the girl fell asleep before leaving her quarters.

The three sat for almost the same length of time when they heard it again. "How long can it continue for her?" asked Alena, her eyes troubled. "I'll go again." Alena got up and went to the girl's quarters. It was the same. Alena awakened her and held her as she cried. Alika and Christopher came in, their troubled looks mirroring Alena's face.

"What am I to do? They won't allow me to sleep." The girl's eyes were overcome with exhaustion.

Dante started to drift off to sleep again, but he found himself awakened again. He knew again why. He thought about tea, but he knew it would not work. Anyway, it felt wrong to sleep somehow if she remained in such a state. He wanted to help her, but he did not know how. He sighed and reached out again. "I'm still here and listening whenever you're ready."

The girl said to Alika, "When I got this vision, you gave me something to help me sleep. Can we try it again? My body is begging for sleep and for the images to stop, Alika."

"We will try as it did work the last time. I will be back with it." Alika left and returned a minute later. He gave her the medicine. She took it, and it dissolved in her mouth. "This one is for longer as you need to sleep for the night. We will see. Goodnight, child."

The girl laid down as Alena pulled the covers up to her. Her eyes closed, and a couple of minutes later, the sound of her regular breathing could be heard. The three walked out of her quarters and sat back down on the couch.

"Do you think she will finally sleep?"

"I do hope so, Christopher." sighed Alika.

Almost twenty-five minutes later, and without warning, a scream rang out from the girl's room. Alika was the first to jump up this time and run to the girl's room. He reached her bedside and spoke to her, "Child, you're safe. Awaken. I'm here. They cannot hurt you."

The girl sat up in bed, her eyes wild as another scream started to come from her. She struggled to catch her breath. "I should have listened to you. How am I to get rest again?"

ell

Dante finally drifted off to sleep again. Suddenly, he found himself awakened again. This time it was far worse than the other times. He felt his body shaking violently as he woke up, and he struggled to catch his breath. Enough of this, he thought. He sat up in bed and realized it was a lost cause to sleep. She was stubborn, but he would be as well. He told her he was listening. He would wait her out. Either they both slept or neither did.

ell

They all wanted to come up with the answer, but nothing surfaced to help her at first. Alika gazed at the girl. "Yes, you are to get rest again. It must be." He smiled for the first time in a while today. "Perhaps you simply did not ask, my child."

"We tried everything, the tea, the medicine you gave me. The medicine worked last time."

"Perhaps you did not ask for the answer from The One who has it. You spun your wheels with your own solutions. Is it not worth a try?"

The girl stared at Alika and smiled. For the first time in the evening, her smile looked again as in the past despite her exhaustion. "It does seem rather simple when put that way, doesn't it? It's what I normally do. If I had followed that guidance earlier, I wouldn't be searching for this answer. I'm quite sure your counsel was His as well as far as the planet."

"I believe you're right, but it's no matter now. It is done and time to move on."

"I suppose." said the girl softly, and she met Alika's eyes, "Alika, I'm sorry for earlier on the planet, the way I spoke to you. The anger... I'm so sorry. I didn't mean ..." The girl could not finish.

"No more tears. You cried enough of them today. I knew and understood. You spoke in pain, and none of it was directed at me."

"So, you forgive me?"

"There is nothing to forgive, but if it eases your mind, yes, I forgive you."

Christopher and Alena drifted back to the cockpit area.

"I'm glad." Yet, the girl's eyes reflected sadness.

"Your eyes do not appear as such."

"You're not the only one I now regret my words to." The girl sighed. "Dante."

"All your words to Dante were nothing short of inspired. I believe I'm missing something."

"He felt everything today from me, including this evening. Something to do with what we experienced together today. It's lingering, only for today this strongly, I suspect. He felt the whole encounter on the planet, my pain. He reached out to me, and I answered him back." The girl closed her eyes and shook her head, hating her words now.

"And you answered him back in the same spirit you answered me at the moment."

"Yes, and I hurt him. I felt it."

"I'm sure he knew you did not mean it after what the two of you shared together. You can sense his mood. Surely, he is not still upset with you?"

"No, he's not upset with me, just concerned and confused. He is, as Dante always is, kind and caring. He continues to ask me what is hurting me and telling me he's there for me," the girl said softly.

"That does sound like young Dante. He cares for you deeply, and after today he has a new understanding of his affection."

"Yes, his words echo their sweetness from earlier to me. There are few with a spirit as gentle as Dante. I know he understands I didn't mean my words this evening, but even so, I wish I could take them back. Dante is also still awake. He senses all this turmoil from me this evening. Each time I awaken because of the images, he is awakened. So, now I am hurting both of us because neither one of us can sleep."

"Both of you not able to sleep, and after today, you both desperately need to sleep. I suspect there is another time recently, you both had trouble sleeping."

"Yes, it occurred the evening before Dante went to face the Dark Lord and get his father back."

"You tried tea. It did not work. We left you staring in the cockpit window, but eventually, you found sleep." Alika watched the girl's face.

The girl smiled as one who received a gift. "Yes, I talked to Dante. He could hear my thoughts that night for the first time. Then I was able to sleep." The girl smiled more and peered up at Alika.

Alika smiled back at her and got up from her bedside. "It sounds like you need to speak to him this evening to sort things out from earlier. He anxiously wishes to hear from you, and I feel sure your message will come through to him clearly this night." He hugged her. "Goodnight, my child. I will see you in the morning."

"Goodnight, Alika." She hugged him back.

Alika shut the door behind him and sat on the couch with Christopher and Alena.

"How many more times do you think she'll awaken tonight?" asked Christopher, concerned.

"Not anymore tonight once her eyes close in sleep this time."

"How can you be sure, Alika?" asked Alena.

"Because she found the answer she sought, the remedy."

CHAPTER SEVENTY-EIGHT

The girl lay in her bed. "Dante."

Dante heard the voice clearly as he did earlier in the day when she appeared and spoke to him in the Elders Hall. He smiled as he answered back. "I'm here. Are you all right?"

"Yes, I'm sorry about earlier this evening, Dante."

"It's okay. I was just worried about you."

"I know. The words I spoke to you and the spirit I spoke them, I know I hurt you. I'm sorry for that, Dante."

"Enough of that. You spoke them in your hurt. I know you're okay now. That's what's important to me."

"I don't ever want to be the reason you're hurting, Dante."

"You're not." Dante hesitated. "What pierced your spirit so much tonight?"

"It's too much to convey like this. I'm better now that I speak with you." There was a teasing tone to her voice. "Were you truly going to wait me out all night before you tried to sleep again?"

Dante laughed softly. "I was. So, I'm glad you decided to go ahead and talk with me."

"Me too." She felt a little sleepy, but she remained awake. "Strange how my heart is calmed, but I feel it race at the same time with you."

Dante smiled as he remembered his own heart skipping a beat several times earlier today in their encounter. Knowing he had a similar effect on her only added to his happiness. "You're able to do the same to my heart. So, I'm your Dante?"

"I feel it's the case, Dante. I know you spoke of me as yours. It took on a new meaning after today, I would hope. I gave you my heart for some time now."

He already knew, saw it as he searched her blue eyes today, but hearing her say it ... his heart skipped a beat now. He could see her image again, her gentle blue eyes looking at him, smiling at him. "Yes, I was pleasantly surprised today. You have my heart as well."

"I saw it when I looked in your eyes today, Dante. I could have kept staring in them." She finally sounded sleepy as one remembering a wonderful dream.

"What else did you read in them?" He felt sleepy too.

"Much, more than can be told tonight. For another time."

"Soon, then." He felt the girl becoming lulled to sleep.

"Soon, as I promised." She could see an image enter her mind of Dante smiling, with his soft brown eyes looking at her.

"Goodnight, my sweet young spear-bearer," whispered Dante.

"Goodnight, my Dante," she whispered back.

Dante smiled. He knew there would be nothing further from her tonight. It was okay, though, because he knew she finally slept for the night. Dante felt himself finally give in to sleep as well, with her image still there.

ABOUT THE AUTHOR

Elizabeth Lavender is the author of the Sunspear series. Originally from the Alabama coast, she currently lives in the Dallas area with her husband, Jeff, and her two children. She has a Master's degree in counseling from Dallas Baptist University and has studied psychology and English.

She enjoys science fiction and fantasy and hopes to bring some of that same enjoyment to others. She also enjoys suspense novels. However, as long as the storyline is intriguing, she will give it a try. Her reading spans from Les Miserables to Shakespeare to the Percy Jackson series to anything written by Ted Dekker or Frank Perretti.

She works full-time and has been at the same company for over twenty years happily. She is a huge football fan and has a decent throwing arm, despite what her oldest son says when he practices with her.

Although she enjoys Texas, she does love going home to Alabama to visit. Besides visiting family and friends, it is nice to be back near the water again, where the seafood is the best.

Find more books by Elizabeth at:
https://elizabethlavender.net